W9-AYS-913

The twenty-year Earth-Mars war was finally over. What was left of Earth—its crumbled cities, its ruined farmlands—was firmly and completely under the rule of the Martian Archon. And this powerful ruler had no intentions of allowing Earth any chance of regaining its lost glory.

But David Arnfeld, the former Earth Base Commander, was concerned with something more important than the fate of a defeated Earth. There was something about the whole chain of events that didn't add up. Why had both sides ignored countless chances to end that awful war in its first year or two? And why had the two planets gone to war in the first place?

After a little investigation and some lucky breaks, David began to get some answers—information that was vitally important to both Earth and Mars. But he would have to act fast. Too much was at stake and too many were involved in the WAR OF TWO WORLDS to let one man upset such carefully calculated plans.

— THE WAR OF TWO WORLDS is only one of the exciting interplanetary adventures in this collection by POUL ANDERSON.

POUL ANDERSON was born in Bristol, Pennsylvania, and was graduated as a physics major from the University of Minnesota. Writing was a hobby of his, and he sold a few stories while in college. With jobs hard to find after graduation, he continued to write and found to his surprise that he was not a scientist at all, but a born writer. Today he is considered one of the greatest writers in the field of science-fiction. He has also written mysteries, non-fiction and historical novels.

Poul Anderson presently resides in California with his wife and daughter.

Ace Books also publishes WAR OF THE WING-MEN (#872010, 95¢) by Poul Anderson

# THE
# WORLDS OF
# POUL
# ANDERSON

ace books

A Division of Charter Communications Inc.
1120 Avenue of the Americas
New York, N.Y. 10036

THE WORLDS OF POUL ANDERSON

Copyright ©, 1974 Ace Books

All Rights Reserved

An Ace Book

A magazine version of *Planet of No Return* was published serially in *Astounding Science-Fiction* and copyright 1954 by Street & Smith Publications, Inc.

*World Without Stars* was serialized in *Analog*, 1966 under the title *The Ancient Gods* and copyright 1966 by The Conde Nast Publications.

Printed in U.S.A.

# CONTENTS

"Wisdom is better than strength; nevertheless the poor man's wisdom is despised, and his words are not heard. The words of wise men are heard in quiet more than the cry of him that ruleth among fools. Wisdom is better than weapons of war: but one sinner destroyeth much good."

—Ecclesiastes, ix, 16-18

# *Planet of No Return*

## POUL ANDERSON

# CAST OF CHARACTERS

**Crew of the Spaceship *Henry Hudson*:**

| | |
|---|---|
| KEMAL GUMMUS-LUGIL | Turkish rocket engineer |
| JOHN LORENZEN | Lunarian astronomer |
| ED AVERY | North American psychomed |
| JOAB THORNTON | Martian physicist |
| TETSUO HIDEKI | Manchurian organic chemist |
| FRIEDRICH VON OSTEN | German mercenary soldier |
| MIGUEL FERNANDEZ | Uruguayan geologist |

**The "Rorvan" strangers:**

SILISH

YANVUSARRAN

ALASVU

DJUGAZ

# CHAPTER I

SOMEWHERE a relay clicked, and somewhere else a robot muttered to itself. Alarm lights shot through the spectrum to a hot and angry red, flashing and flashing, and a siren began its idiotic hoot.

"Get *out* of here!"

Three of the techs dropped what they were doing and shoved for a purchase against the nearest wall. The control panel was a yammer of crimson. Their weightless bodies slammed through the siren-raddled air toward the door.

"Come back here, you—!" They were gone before Kemal Gummus-lugil's roar was finished. He spat after them and grabbed a hand ring and pushed himself toward the panel.

*Radiation, radiation, radiation,* screamed the siren. Radiation enough to blaze through all shielding and come out with a fury that ionized the engine-room air and turned the alarm system crazy. But the effects were cumulative— Gummus-lugil got close enough to the meters to read them. The intensity was mounting, but he could stand half an hour of it without danger.

Why had they saddled him with a bunch of thumb-fingered morons so superstitious about gamma rays that they fled when the converter gave them a hard look?

He extended his arms before him, stopping his free-fall speed with fingertips and triceps. Reaching out for the manual cut-off, he slapped it down with a clank. Somehow the automatic safeties had failed to operate, and the nuclear fires in the converter were turning it into a small sun—but hell dammit, a man could still stop the thing!

Other relays went to work. Baffle plates shot home, cutting off the fuel supply. The converter's power output was

5

shunted to the generators, building up the damper fields which should stop the reaction—

And didn't!

It took seconds for Gummus-lugil to realize that fact. Around him, within him, the air was full of death; to an eye sensitive in the hard frequencies, his lungs must have glowed; but now the intensity should be dropping, the nuclei slowed in fighting the damper field till their speed dropped below resonance, and he could stop to find out what was wrong. He pulled his way along the giant panel toward the meters for the automatic safeties, and felt sweat prickling under his arms.

He and his crew had been testing the newly installed converter, nothing more. Something could have been wrong with one or another of the parts; but the immense complex of interlocking controls which was the engine's governor should have been self-regulating, foolproof, and—

The siren began hooting still louder.

Gummus-lugil felt his whole body grow wet. The fuel supply had been cut off, yes, but the reaction hadn't been stopped. No damper fields! Behind the casing, all the fires of hell were burning themselves out. It would take hours before that was done, and everybody who stayed on the ship would be a dead man.

For an instant he hung there, aware of the endless falling sensation of weightlessness, aware of the noise and the vicious red lights. If they abandoned the ship in her orbit, she would be hot for days to come and the converter would be ruined. He had to flush the thing—now!

Behind him, the shielded bulkheads closed, and the ventilation system stopped its steady whirr. The ship's robo-monitors would not let poison spread to swiftly through her entire body. They, at least, were still functioning. But they didn't care about him, and radiation was eating at his flesh.

He bit his teeth together and got to work. The emergency manuals still seemed okay. He spoke into his throat mike:

"Gummus-lugil to bridge. I'm going to flush this damned thing. That means the outside hull will be hot for a few hours. Anybody out there?"

"No." The supervisor's voice sounded small and scared. "We're all standing by the lifeboat locks. Don't you think we should just abandon ship and let her burn herself out?"

"And ruin a billion solars' worth of engine? No, thanks! Just stay where you are, you'll be okay." Even in this moment, the engineer snorted. He began turning the main flushing wheel, bracing his feet against his body's tendency to rotate the other way.

The auxiliaries were purely mechanical and hydraulic—for which praises be to the designers, now when all electronic equipment seemed to have gone mad. Gummus-lugil grunted, feeling the effort in his muscles. A series of ports opened. The rage of more-than-incandescent gases spilled out into space, a brief flame against darkness and then nothing the human eye could see.

Slowly, the red lights dulled to yellow and the siren moderated its voice. The radioactivity in the engine room was falling off already. Gummus-lugil decided that he'd not had a harmful dose, though the doctors would probably order him a couple of months off the job.

He went through the special safety exit; in the chamber beyond, he shucked his clothes and gave them to the robot. Beyond that, there were three successive decontamination rooms; it took half an hour before a Geiger proclaimed him fit for human society. He slipped on the coverall whch another robot handed him and made his way to the bridge.

The supervisor shrank from him, just a trifle, as he entered. "All right," said Gummus-lugil sarcastically. "I know I'm a little radioactive yet. I know I should go ringing a bell and crying, 'Unclean! Unclean!' But right now I want to make a call to Earth."

"Huh . . . oh, yes, yes. Of course." The supervisor scurried through the air toward the com-desk. "Where to?"

"Lagrange Institute head office."

"What . . . went wrong? Do you know?"

"Everything. More than could possibly happen by chance. If I hadn't been the only man aboard with the brains of an oyster, the ship would've been abandoned and the converter ruined."

"You don't mean—"

Gummus-lugil raised his fingers and ticked them off one by one: "S, A, B, O, T, A, G, E spells 'sabotage.' And I want to get the bastard that did it and hang him with his own guts."


## CHAPTER II


JOHN LORENZEN was looking out of his hotel window when the call came. He was on the 58th floor, and the sheer drop down made him feel a little dizzy. They didn't build that high on Luna.

Below him, above him, around him, the city was like a jungle, airy flex-bridges looping from one slim tower to the next; and it glowed and burned with light, further out than he could see, over the curve of the world. The white and gold and red and royal blue illumination wasn't continuous; here and there a wide patch of black showed a park, with a fountain of fire or glowing water in the middle of its night; but the lights reached for many kilometers. Quito never slept.

It was near midnight, when a lot of rockets would be taking off. Lorenzen wanted to see the sight; it was famous in the Solar System. He had paid double price for a room facing the wall of the spaceport, not without twinges of conscience, for the Lagrange Institute was footing the bills, but he'd done it. A boyhood on a remote Alaskan farm, a long grind

through college—the poor student going through on scholar-
ships and assistantships—and then the years at Luna Observatory, hadn't held anything like this. He wasn't complaining about his life, but it hadn't been anything very spec-
tacular either, and if now he was to go into the great darkness beyond the sun, he ought to see Quito Spaceport at
midnight first. He might not have another chance.

The 'phone chimed gently. He started, swearing at his
own nervousness. There wasn't anything to be scared of.
They wouldn't bite him. But the palms of his hands were
wet.

He stepped over and thumbed the switch. "Hello," he said.

A face grew in the screen. It wasn't a particularly me-
morable face—smooth, plump, snub-nosed, thin gray hair
—and the body seemed short and stout. The voice was rather
high but not unpleasant, speaking in North American English:
"Dr. Lorenzen?"

"Yes. Who . . . is this, please?" In Lunopolis, everybody
knew everybody else, and trips to Leyport and Ciudad
Libre had been rare. Lorenzen wasn't used to this welter
of strangers.

And he wasn't used to Earth gravity or changeable weather
or the thin cool air of Ecuador. He felt lost.

"Avery. Edward Avery. I'm with the government, but also
with the Lagrange Institute—sort of liaison man between
the two, and I'll be going along on the expedition as psy-
chomed. Hope I didn't get you out of bed?"

"No . . . no, not at all. I'm used to irregular hours. You
get that way on Luna."

"And in Quito too—believe me." Avery grinned. "Look,
could you come over and see me?"

"I . . . well . . . now?"

"As good a time as any, if you aren't busy. We can have
a few drinks, maybe, and talk a little. I was supposed to
approach you anyway, while you were in town."

"Well . . . well, yes, sure, I suppose so." Lorenzen felt

rushed off his feet. After the leisurely years on the Moon, he couldn't adapt to this pace they had on Earth. He wanted to spit in somebody's eye and tell him they'd go at his, Lorenzen's, speed for a change; but he knew he never would.

"Good, fine. Thanks a lot." Avery gave him the address and switched off.

A low rumble murmured through the room. The rockets! Lorenzen hurried back to the window and saw the shielding wall like the edge of the world, black against their light. One, two, three, a dozen metal spears rushing upward on flame and thunder, and the Moon a cool shield high above the city—yes, it was worth seeing.

He dialed for an aircab and slipped a cloak over his thin lounging pajamas. The 'copter appeared in minutes, hovering just beyond his balcony and extending a gangway. He walked in, feeling his cloak grow warm as it sucked power from the 'cast system, and sat down and punched out the address he wanted.

*"Dos solarios y cincuenta centos, por favor."*

The mechanical voice made him feel embarrassed; he barely stopped himself from apologizing as he put a tenner in the slot. The autopilot gave him his change as the cab swung into the sky.

He was set off at another hotel—apparently Avery didn't live permanently in Quito either—and made his way down the hall to the suite named. "Lorenzen," he said to the door, and it opened for him. He walked into an anteroom, giving his cloak to the robot, and was met by Avery himself.

Yes, the psychman was pretty short. Lorenzen looked down from his own gaunt height as he shook hands. He was only about half Avery's age, he guessed—a tall skinny young man who didn't quite know where to put his feet, unkempt brown hair, gray eyes, blunt homely features with the smooth even tan of Lunar sun-type fluoros.

"Very glad you could come, Dr. Lorenzen." Avery looked guilty and lowered his voice to a whisper. "Afraid I can't offer you that drink right now. We've got another expedition man here—came over on business . . . a Martian, you know—"

"Huh?" Lorenzen caught himself just in time. He didn't know if he'd like having a Martian for crewmate, but it was too late now.

They entered the living room. The third man was already seated, and did not rise for them. He was also tall and lean, but with a harshness to his outlines that the tight black clothes of a Noachian Dissenter did not help; his face was all angles; jutting nose and chin, hard black eyes under the close-cropped dark hair.

"Joab Thornton—John Lorenzen—please sit down." Avery lowered himself into a chair. Thornton sat stiffly on the edge of his, obviously disliking the idea of furniture which molded itself to his contours.

"Dr. Thornton is a physicist—radiation and optics—at the University of New Zion," explained Avery. "Dr. Lorenzen is with the observatory at Lunopolis. Both you gentlemen will be going to Lagrange with us, of course. You might as well get acquainted now." He tried to smile.

"Thornton—haven't I heard your name in connection with x-ray photography?" asked Lorenzen. "We've used some of your results to examine the hard spectra of stars, I believe. Very valuable."

"Thank you." The Martian's lips creased upward. "The credit is not to me but to the Lord." There didn't seem to be any answer for that.

"Excuse me." He turned to Avery. "I want to get this over with, and they said you were the expedition's official wailing wall. I've just been looking over the personnel list and checking up on the records. You have one engineer down by the name of Reuben Young. His religion—if you can call it that—is New Christian."

"Ummm . . . yes—" Avery dropped his eyes. "I know your sect doesn't get along with his, but—"

"Doesn't get along!" A vein pulsed in Thornton's temple. "The New Christians forced us to migrate to Mars when they were in power. It was they who perverted doctrine till all Reformism was a stink in the nostrils of the people. It was they who engineered our war with Venus." (Not so, thought Lorenzen: part of it had been power rivalry, part of it the work of Terrestrial psychmen who wanted their masters to play Kilkenny cat.) "It is still they who slander us to the rest of the Solar System. It is their fanatics who make it necessary for me to carry a gun here on Earth." He gulped and clenched his fists. When he spoke again, it was quietly:

"I am not an intolerant man. Only the Almighty knows the just from the unjust. You can have as many Jews, Catholics, Moslems, unbelievers, collectivists, Sebastianists, and I know not what else along as you choose. But by joining the expedition I take on myself an obligation: to work with, and perhaps to fight with and save the life of, everyone else aboard. I cannot assume this obligation toward a New Christian.

"If Young goes along, I don't. That's all."

"Well—well—". Avery ran a hand through his hair, an oddly helpless gesture. "Well, I'm sorry you feel that way—"

"Those idiots in the government supposedly running our personnel office for us should have known it from the start."

"You wouldn't consider—"

"I wouldn't. You have two days to inform me that Young has been discharged; thereafter I book passage back to Mars."

Thornton got up. "I'm sorry to be so rude about it," he finished, "but that's the way it is. Speak to the office for me. I'd better be going now." He shook Lorenzen's hand. "Glad to have met you, sir. I hope the next time will be under better conditions. I'd like to ask you about some of that x-ray work."

When he was gone, Avery sighed gustily. "How about that drink? I need one bad myself. What an off-orbit!"

"From the realistic point of view," said Lorenzen cautiously, "he was right. There'd have been murder if those two were on the same ship."

"I suppose so." Avery picked up the chair mike and spoke to the RoomServ. Turning back to his guest: "How that slip-up occurred, I don't know. But it doesn't surprise me. There seems to be a curse on the whole project. Everything's gone wrong. We're a year behind our original schedule, and it's cost almost twice the estimate."

The RoomServ discharged a tray with two whiskies and soda; it landed on the roller table, which came over to the men. Avery picked up his glass and drank thirstily. "Young will have to go," he said. "He's just an engineer, plenty more where he came from; we need a physicist of Thornton's caliber."

"It's strange," said Lorenzen, "that a man so brilliant in his line—he's a top-flight mathematician too, you know—should be a . . . Dissenter."

"Not strange." Avery sipped moodily. "The human mind is a weird and tortuous thing. It's perfectly possible to believe in a dozen mutually contradictory things at once. Few people ever really learn how to think at all; those who do, think only with the surface of their minds. The rest is still conditioned reflex and rationalization of a thousand subconscious fears and hates and longings. We're finally getting a science of man—a *real* science; we're finally learning how a child must be brought up if he is to be truly sane. But it'll take a long time before the results show on any large scale. There is so much insanity left over from all our history, so much built into the very structure of human society."

"Well—" Lorenzen shifted uneasily. "I daresay you're right. But, uh, about the business at hand—you wanted to see me—"

"Just for a drink and a talk," said Avery. "It's my business to get to know every man on the ship better than he knows himself. But that'll also take time."

"You have my psych-tests from when I volunteered for the expedition," said Lorenzen. His face felt hot. "Isn't that enough?"

"No. So far, you're only a set of scores, multi-dimensional profiles, empirical formulas and numbers. I'd like to know you as a human being, John. I'm not trying to pry. I just want to be friends."

"All right." Lorenzen took a long drink. "Fire away."

"No questions. This isn't an analysis. Just a conversation." Avery sighed again. "Lord, I'll be glad when we get into space! You've no idea what a rat race the whole business has been, right from the first. If our friend Thornton knew all the details, he'd probably conclude it wasn't God's will that man should go to Troas. He might be right, at that. Sometimes I wonder."

"The first expedition got back—"

"That wasn't the Lagrange expedition. That was a shipful of astronomers, simply investigating the stars of the Hercules cluster. They found the Troas-Ilium system in the course of studying the Lagrange suns, and took some data from space—enough to make a planetographic survey seem worthwhile—but they didn't land."

"The first *real* Lagrange expedition never came back."

There was silence in the room. Outside the broad windows, the night city burned against darkness.

"And we," said Lorenzen finally, "are the second."

"Yes. And everything has been going wrong, I tell you. First the Institute had to spend three years raising the money. Then there were the most fantastic mix-ups in their administration. Then they started building the ship—they couldn't just buy one, everything was committed elsewhere—and there were delays all along the line. This part wasn't available, that part had to be made special. It ran the time of building, and the cost, way over estimate. Then—this is confidential, but you might as well know it—there was sabotage. The main converter went wild on its first test.

Only the fact that one man stuck by his post saved it from being a total loss. Even as it was, the repairs and the delay exhausted the Institute's treasury, and there was another pause while they raised more money. It wasn't easy; public apathy toward the whole idea of colonization is growing with each failure.

"They're almost ready now. There are still hitches—this business tonight was just a small sample—but the job is almost done." Avery shook his head. "It's fortunate that the director of the Institute, and Captain Hamilton, and a few others, have been so stubborn about it. Ordinary men would have given up years ago."

"Years . . . yes, it's about seven years since the first expedition disappeared, isn't it?" asked Lorenzen.

"Uh-huh. Five years since the Institute started planning this one."

"Who . . . who were the saboteurs?"

"Nobody knows. Maybe some fanatic group with its own distorted motives. There are a lot of them, you know. Or maybe . . . no, that's too fantastic. I'd rather assume that Lagrange Expedition II has had a run of bad luck, and hope that the run is about over."

"And Expedition I?" asked Lorenzen softly.

"I don't know. Who does? It's one of the things we're supposed to find out."

They were quiet then for a long time. The unspoken thought ran between them: *It looks as if somebody or something doesn't want men on Troas. But who, and why, and how?*

*We're supposed to find the answer. But we're also supposed to bring the answer back. And the first expedition, as well equipped and as well manned as ours, did not return.*

# CHAPTER III

"—Interstellar distances have become almost meaningless with the invention of the warp drive—within an enormous range. It does not take appreciably more time and energy to go 100,000 light-years than to go one. As a natural result, once the nearer stars had been visited, explorers from Sol started investigating the most interesting ones in the Galaxy, even though many of these lie very far indeed from home, and temporarily ignoring the millions of intervening but quite ordinary suns. In the 22 years since the first Alpha Centauri expedition, hundreds of stars have been reached; and if the hope of finding Earth-like planets for colonization has so far been blasted, the reward in terms of scientific knowledge has been considerable.

"The first expedition to the Hercules cluster was purely astronomical, the personnel being interested only in the astrophysics of the cluster: a dense group composed of millions of stars belonging to Population II, with a surrounding space singularly clear of dust and gases. But while circling the double star Lagrange, the observers detected a planet and investigated. It turned out to be a double planet, the larger remarkably terrestroid. From its Trojan position, it was named Troas, the smaller companion named Ilium. Lacking facilities for planetfall, the expedition necessarily contented itself with studies from space . . ."

Lorenzen put down the pamphlet with a sigh. Almost, he knew it by heart. Spectrographic data on the atmosphere, yes, and the vegetation observed seemed to hold chlorophyl. Calculations of mass and surface gravity. Thermocouples confirming what the maps showed: a world still in the clutch of glaciers, but the equatorial regions cool and bracing, a

climate which knew snow and storm but also the flowering
of summer. A world where men could perhaps walk un-
armored, and build homes and farms and cities, a world
where men could possibly grow roots and belong. The seven
billion humans jammed into the Solar System were crying
for a place to go. And during his lifetime he had seen the
slow withering of the dream.

It had been foreseen, of course, but no one had believed
it till one ship after another had come trailing home, the
dust of stars on her battered hull, to bring the word. In all
the Galaxy's swarming myriads of planets, there might be
none where men could strike roots.

Life on Earth is such a delicate balance of chemical, physical, and ecological factors, many of them due to sheer geo-
logical and evolutionary accident, that the probability of a
world where men could live without elaborate artificial aids
is lower than one dares think. First you have to find an
oxygen atmosphere, the proper range of radiation and temperature, a gravity not too small to let the air escape and
not so great as to throw the human body fluid adjustment
out of kilter. That alone winnows the worlds like some
great machine; you have less than one percent left. And then
you have to start on the biology of it. Vegetation nourishing
to man, and the domestic animals which can eat it, cannot
grow without a gigantic web of other life, most of it microscopic: nitrogen-fixing bacteria, saprophytes, earthworms
—and these cannot simply be seeded on a new world, for
they in turn are dependent on other life-forms. You have
to give them an ecology into which they can fit. A billion
years of separate evolution will most likely produce native
life which is inedible or sheer poison; what, for instance,
are the odds against the duplication of all the vitamins?

Mars and Venus and the Jovian moons had been colonized,
yes, but it had been at enormous expense and for special
reasons—mining, penal colonies, refugees during two centuries of war and tyranny. But their system of domes and

tank food could never support many, however hard you tried. Now when the stars were open, nobody wanted another hell-planet. In money terms—which, ultimately, means in terms of value received for effort expended—it wouldn't pay.

A few worlds might have been colonizable. But they held diseases to which man had no racial immunity whatsoever, which would surely wipe out ninety percent of any colony before serums and vaccines could be developed. (The dying crew of the *Magellan*, returning from Sirius to radio their tragic message before they plunged their ship into the sun.) Or there were natives, unhuman beings as bright as man, often with their own technologies not too far behind his. They would resist invasion, and the logistics of interstellar conquest were merely ridiculous. Balancing the cost of sending colonists and their equipment (lives, too-scarce material resources, blood, sweat, and tears) and the cost of sending soldiers, against the probable gain (a few million humans given land, and the economics of space travel such that they could ship little of value back to Sol), yielded a figure too far in the red. Conquest was theoretically possible, but a war-exhausted humanity, most of it still living near the starvation level, wasn't that interested in empire.

Wanted: terrestroid planets, habitable but uninhabited, clean of major sicknesses, rich enough to support colonists without help from Sol.

Found: In almost a generation, nothing.

Lorenzen remembered the wave of excitement which had followed the return of the Hercules expedition. He had still been a boy then—that was the year before he got the scholarship to Rio Polytechnic—but he, too, had looked up through a wintry Alaskan night to the cold arrogance of the stars; he had also flung his head back with a laugh.

And the *Da Gama* had set out and had left Sol behind her. And after two years, men shrugged with a weariness that was dying hope. Murdered by natives or by microbes,

gulped down when the earth opened under them, frozen by
a sudden blast from the glacial north—who knew? Who
cared? You heard little talk nowadays about New Earth;
no utopian schemes for the fresh start man was going to
make were being published; more and more, men put their
shoulders to the tired old wheel of Earth, resigned to this
being their only home and their only hope through all time
forever.

"Two swallows do not make a summer . . . Statistically
inadequate sample . . . Statistical certainty that *somewhere*
there must be . . ." But funds for more investigations were
whittled down in every session of Parliament. More and
more of the great star ships swung darkly about Earth while
their captains begged for finances. And when the Lagrange
Institute dug into its own treasury to buy one of them,
it could not be done, there was always a reason. "Sorry, but
we want to keep her; as soon as we can raise the money,
we want to try an idea of our own . . . Sorry, but she's
already committed; leaving in two months for an xenological
expedition to Tau Ceti . . . Sorry, but we're converting her
to an interplanetary freighter, that's where the money is
. . . Sorry." The *Henry Hudson* had to be built from
scratch.

The Egyptians sailed to Punt, and could easily have gone
further; with a little development, their ships could have
reached the Indies. The Alexandrians built an aeolipile, but
there was enough slave labor around so that they had no
reason to go on from there and make a steam turbine. The
Romans printed their maps, but didn't apply the idea to
books. The Arabs developed algebra and then got more
interested in theological hairsplitting. Something has always
lain within the grasp of man which he just didn't care to
take hold of. Society must want something enough for the
wish to become an actual need before it gets the thing.

The starward wish was dying.

# CHAPTER IV

SOL WAS two billion kilometers behind them, little more than the brightest star in a frosty swarm, when they went into warp. The engines roared, building up toward the potentials beyond which the omega effect set in. There was a wrenching dizziness as the ship and her crew leaped out of normal energy levels; night and confusion while the atoms readjusted in their non-Dirac matrices. Then quiet, and utter blind blackness outside the viewports.

It was like an endless falling through nullity. The ship could not accelerate, could not spin, for there was nothing which she could move in relation to; for the duration of the trip, she was *irrelevant* to the four-dimensional universe. Weight came back as the inner hull started rotating with respect to the outer, though Lorenzen had already been sick—he never could stand free fall. Then there was nothing to do but settle down for the month or so it would take to reach Lagrange.

And the days passed, swept out by clocks, unmarked by any change—they were only waiting now, doubly held in timelessness. Fifty men, spacers and scientists, fretted out the emptiness of hours and wondered what lay on the other end of the warp.

It was on the fifth day when Lorenzen and Tetsuo Hideki wandered down toward the main lounge. The Manchurian was one of the organic chemists: a small, frail-looking, soft-spoken fellow in loose robes, timed with people and highly competent in his work. Lorenzen thought that Hideki made a barrier against the world out of his test tubes and analyzers, but he rather liked the Asian. *I've done pretty much the same myself, haven't I? I get along all right with people, yes, but down underneath I'm afraid of them.*

20

"—but why can't you say that it takes us a month to go to Lagrange? That is the time we measure aboard ship, is it not? It is also the time a Lagrangian or Solarian observer would measure between the moment we entered the warp and the moment we came out."

"Not quite," said Lorenzen. "The math shows that it's meaningless to equate time measured inside the warp with time measured outside. It's not even similar to the time-shift in classical relativity. In the omega-effect equations, the $t$ and $t'$ are two distinct expressions, two different dimensions; they have about the same numerical value, but the conversion factor is not a pure number. The fact that time spent in the warp is about the same no matter how far you go—within a terrifically big radius, up to the point where space curvature become significant—indicates that we don't have a true velocity at all." He shrugged. "I don't pretend to understand the whole theory. Not a dozen men can."

"This is your first interstellar trip, is it not, John?"

"Uh-huh. I've never been further than the Moon before."

"I have never even been off Earth. I believe Captain Hamilton and a couple of engineers are the only men aboard who have flown the star ways before now. It is strange." Hideki's eyes looked scared. "There is much which is strange about this trip. I have never heard of so ill-assorted a crew."

"N-n-no." Lorenzen thought over those he knew anything about. There had already been clashes, which Avery had not succeeded very well in smoothing over. "But the Institute had to take what it could get, I suppose, and there are all too many lunatic opinions left over from the wars and the Interregnum. Political fanatics, racial fanatics, religious fanatics—" His voice trailed off.

"I take it you support the Solar government?"

"Sure. I may not like everything it does, but it's got to compromise with many elements if it's to be democratic, and

stamp out many others if it's to survive. It's all that stands
between us and a return of anarchy and tyranny."

"You are right," said Hideki. "War is a monster; my people
know that." There was a darkness in his eyes. Lorenzen wondered if he was thinking of the Mongku Empire which Mars
had shattered, or if his thoughts went still further back, to the
lovely lost islands of Japan and the Fourth World War
which had sunk them under the sea.

They came to the entrance of the lounge and paused, looking in to see who was there. It was a big, low room, its
furniture and drapes and gentle illumination a rest from the
impersonal metallic harshness which was most of the ship;
but it seemed rather bare. The Institute had not had time
or money to decorate it properly. They should have taken
time, thought Lorenzen. Men's nerves were worn thin out
here between the stars, and they needed murals and a bar
and a fireplace full of crackling logs. They needed home.

Avery and Gummus-lugil, the ship's chess fiends, were
hunched over a board. Miguel Fernandez of Uruguay, geologist, a small dark lively young man, sat thrumming a guitar;
near him was Joab Thornton, reading his Bible—no, it was
Milton this time, and there was a curious lost ecstasy on the
ascetic features. Lorenzen, who dabbled with art, thought
that the Martian had a fascinating set of angles and planes
in his face; he'd like to do his portrait sometime.

Gummus-lugil looked up and saw the newcomers. He was
a dark, stocky man, his face broad and hook-nosed, his shirt
open over a wiry pelt. "Hello, there," he said cheerfully.

"Hello," said Lorenzen. He rather liked the Turk. Gummus-
lugil had come up the hard way. It had marked him: he
was rude and dogmatic and had no use for literature; but
his mind was good. He and Lorenzen had already sat through
several watches arguing politics and analytical philosophy
and the chances of the Academy team getting the meteor
polo pennant next year. "Who's ahead?"

"This bastard, I'm afraid."

Avery reached out and advanced a bishop. "Guard queen," he said. His voice remained almost apologetic.

"Huh? Oh, yes . . . yes . . . Let's see—" Gummus-lugil swore. "This is going to cost me a knight. Okay, okay." He moved.

Avery avoided the knight, but took a pawn with his rook. "Mate in . . . five moves," he said. "Care to resign?"

"Whuzzat?" Feverishly, Gummus-lugil studied the board. Fernandez' fingers rippled down a chord.

"You see, here . . . and here . . . and then—"

"Goddammit, stop that racket!" snarled Gummus-lugil. "How d'you expect me to concentrate?"

Fernandez flushed angrily. "I have as much right—"

Gummus-lugil showed his teeth. "If you could play, it'd be all right," he snapped. "But go do your caterwauling somewhere else, sonny boy."

"Hey, there, Kemal, take it easy." Avery looked alarmed.

Surprisingly, Thornton joined in on the engineer's side. "This should be a place for peace and quiet," he clipped. "Why don't you go play in your bunkroom, Señor Fernandez?"

"There are men off watch there who have to sleep," answered the Uruguayan. He stood up, knotting his fists together. "And if you think you can dictate to the rest of us—"

Lorenzen stood back, feeling the helpless embarrassment which quarrels always gave him. He tried to say something, but his tongue seemed thick in his mouth.

Friedrich von Osten chose that moment to enter. He stood in the farther doorway, swaying a little. It was well known he'd smuggled a case of whisky aboard. He wasn't an alcoholic, but there were no women along and he couldn't be polishing his beloved guns forever. A mercenary soldier in the ruins of Europe—even if he does get picked up for the Solar Academy, and makes good in the Partol, and is named chief gunner for a star ship—doesn't develop other interests.

"Vot iss?" he asked thickly.

"None of your damn business!" flared Gummus-lugil. Their two jobs had already required them to work together a lot, and they just didn't get along. Two such arrogant souls couldn't.

"I make it my damn business, den." Von Osten stepped forward, hunching his great shoulders; the yellow beard bristled, and the wide battered face was red. "So you are picking on Miguel again?"

"I can handle my own affairs," stated Fernandez flatly. "You and this Puritan crank can stay out of them."

Thornton bit his lip. "I wouldn't talk about cranks," he said, rising to his own feet.

Fernandez got a wild look about him. Everybody knew that his family on the mother's side had spearheaded the Sebastianist Rebellion a century ago; Avery had quietly passed the word along with a warning not to mention it.

"Now, Joab—" The government man hastened toward the Martian, waving his hands in the air. "Now take it easy, gentlemen, please—"

"If all you fuse-blown gruntbrains would mind your own business—" began Gummus-lugil.

"Iss no such t'ing as own business here!" shouted von Osten. "Ve iss all *zusammen*—togedder, and I vould vish to put you under Patrol discipline—vun day only!"

*Trust him to say exactly the wrong thing at the wrong moment,* thought Lorenzen sickly. *His being essentially right only makes it the more insufferable.*

"Look—" He opened his mouth, and the stutter that always grabbed him when he was excited made him wordless again.

Gummus-lugil took a stiff-legged step toward the German. "If you want to step outside a minute, we'll settle that," he said.

"*Gentlemen!*" wailed Avery.

"Are they, now?" asked Thornton.

*"Und du kannst auch herausgehen!"* bellowed von Osten, turning on him.

"Nobody insults me," snarled Fernandez. His small wiry body gathered itself as if to attack.

"Keep out of this, sonny," said Gummus-lugil. "It's bad enough your starting it."

Fernandez made a noise that was half a sob and jumped for him. The Turk sprang back in surprise. When a fist grazed his cheek, his own leaped out and Fernandez lurched back.

Von Osten yelled and swung at Gummus-lugil. "Give me a hand," gasped Avery. "Get them apart!" He almost dragged Thornton along with him. The Martian got a grip on von Osten's waist and pulled. The German kicked at his ankles. Thornton snapped his lips together over a cry of pain and tried to trip his opponent. Gummus-lugil stood where he was, panting.

"What the devil is going on here?"

They all turned at that shout. Captain Hamilton stood in the doorway.

He was a tall man, solidly built, heavy-featured, thick gray hair above the deep-lined face. He wore the blue undress uniform of the Union Patrol, in which he was a reservist, with mathematical correctness. His normally low voice became a quarterdeck roar, and the gray eyes were like chill iron as they swept the group.

"I thought I heard a quarrel in here—but a brawl!"

They moved away from each other, sullenly, looking at him but not meeting his gaze.

He stood for a very long while, regarding them with a raking contempt. Lorenzen tried to make himself small. But down somewhere inside himself, he wondered how much of that expression was a good job of acting. Hamilton was a bit of a martinet, yes, and he'd had himself psyched as thoroughly as he could be, to rid of all fears and compulsions irrelevant to his work—but he couldn't be that much of a machine. He had children and grandchildren in Canada; he liked gardening; he was not unsympathetic when—

"All of you here have university degrees." The captain was speaking very quietly now. "You're educated men, scientists and technicians. You're the cream of Sol's intellect, I'm told. Well, if you are, God help us all!"

There was no answer.

"I suppose you know expeditions like this are dangerous enough at best," went on Hamilton. "I also believe you were told that the first expedition to Troas never got back. To me, it seems reasonable that if we're to survive at all, we have to make a team and work together against whatever it was that killed the first ship. Apparently it does not seem so to you."

He grinned with careful nastiness. "Presumably you scientists also think I'm just the pilot. I'm just a conductor whose only business is to get you to Troas and back. If you believe that, I advise you to read the articles again—assuming you can read. I'm responsible for the safety of the whole ship, including your lives, God help me. That means I'm the boss, too. From the moment you entered the airlock at Earth to the moment you leave it again back at Earth, I'm the boss.

"I don't give one spitball in hell who started this or who did what in which manner to whom. It's enough that there was a fight where there shouldn't have been one. You're all going in the brig for a day—without food. Maybe that'll teach you some manners."

"But I didn't—" whispered Hideki.

"Exactly," snapped Hamilton. "I want every man aboard to have a vested interest in preventing this sort of thing. If your lives, and the lives of everybody else, don't matter to you, maybe your fat-gutted bellies will."

"But I *tried*—" wailed Avery.

"And failed. A rust-eaten failure if I ever saw one. You get brigged for incompetence, Mr. Avery. It's your job to see that tensions don't build up this way. All right, now—march!"

They marched. Not a word was said.

Somewhat later, Hideki murmured in the darkness of the brig: "It isn't fair. Who does he think he is, God Almighty?"

Lorenzen shrugged, his own easy-going temperament asserting itself, "A captain has to be, I guess."

"But if he keeps this up, everyone will hate him!"

"I imagine he's a pretty good rule-of-thumb psychman himself. Quite probably that's what he wants."

Later, lying in blindness on a hard narrow bunk, Lorenzen wondered what had gone wrong. Avery talked to all the men privately, counseled them, tried to ease their fears and hatreds so that they wouldn't turn on others. At least, he was supposed to. But he hadn't. Incompetent ass! Maybe there was a curse on Lagrange after all.

## CHAPTER V

THE SKY was incredible.

Here in the center of the great cluster, the double star was a double blaze. Lagrange I seemed as bright as Sol, though only half the apparent size, a blue-green flame ringed with eerie halos of corona and zodiacal light. When the glare was filtered out, you could see monstrous prominences on its rim. Lagrange II, a third of Sol's angular diameter but almost as luminous, was a rich orange-red, like a huge coal flung into heaven. When both their lights streamed through the viewports into a darkened room, men's faces had an unearthly color; they seemed themselves transfigured.

The stars were so brilliant that some of them could be seen even through that haze of radiance. When you looked out from the shadow side of the ship, the sky was a hard crystal black spattered with stars—great unwinking diamonds, flashing and flashing, confused myriads, a throng of them glittering in a glory such as Earth's dwellers had never seen. It was lonely to think that their light, which Earth now saw, had left when man was still huddled in caves; that the light now streaming from them would be seen in an unthinkable future when there might be no more men on Earth.

The *Hudson* had taken an orbit about Troas, some 4,000 kilometers out. The companion, Ilium, looked almost four times as big as Luna seen from Earth; the limb was blurred by the thin atmosphere, and the harsh glare of dead sea-bottoms mottled the bluish face. A small world, old before its time, no place to colonize; but it would be a rich near-by source of minerals for men on Troas.

That planet hung enormous in the viewports, filling nearly half the sky. You could see the air about it, clouds and storms, day and night. The ice-caps covering a third of its face were blinding white, the restless wind-whipped oceans were a blueness which focused the light of one sun to a cruel point. There were islands and one major continent, its north and south ends buried under the ice, spreading easterly and westerly halfway round the planet. It was green about the equator, hazing into darker green and brown toward the poles. Lakes and rivers were like silver threads across it. A high mountain range, rugged sweep of light and shadow, ran down either coast.

The half-dozen men in the ship's observatory hung in weightless silence. The mingled light of the suns gleamed off the metal of their instruments. They were supposed to compare notes on their several observations, but for a while they didn't want to speak; this was too awesome.

"Well?" Hamilton barked it out at last. "What have you found?"

"Essentially—" Lorenzen gulped. The anti-space sickness pills helped some, but he still felt weak, he longed for weight and clean air. "Essentially, we've confirmed what the Hercules expedition noted. Mass of the planets, distance, atmosphere, temperature—and yes, the green down there definitely has the absorption spectrum of chlorophyl."

"Any sign of life?"

"Oh, yes, quite a bit of it. Not only the plants, but animals, huge herds of them. I've got plenty of photographs." Lorenzen shook his head. "Not a trace of the *Da Gama,* though. We've looked for two of the planet's days, and we could surely have spotted their boats or an abandoned camp. But nothing."

"Could they have landed on Sister and come to grief there?" Christopher Umfanduma, the African biologist, gestured at the stark face of Ilium.

"No," said Hamilton. "Doctrine for these survey trips is that the expedition goes first to the planet it was announced it will go to. If for any reason they then go elsewhere, they leave a cairn big enough to be seen from space. We can check Sister, but my conviction is that the trouble happened on Junior. Sister is too typical, it's like Mars; nothing much *can* happen to well-trained spacemen on a place like that."

"Other planets in this system?" asked Hideki. "Maybe they—"

"No, there aren't any. Just a stinking little group of asteroids in the other Trojan position. Planetary formation theory and considerations of stability just about prohibit anything else. You know, don't you, that Junior doesn't have true Trojan stability? No planet of a double star can have it; the mass ratio of the suns is always too small. Junior is only metastable because of Sister's effect. Not that it makes any difference on the time scale of human history. No, there are no other planets here."

"Of course," ventured Avery, very softly, "the expedition could perhaps have left Troas in good form and perished on the way home."

Hamilton snorted. "Nothing can happen to a ship in the

warp. No, it's down—" his deep-set eyes went to the planet and rested there, darkly—"it's down on Junior that whatever happened to them, happened. But why no trace of them? The *Da Gama* herself ought still to be in orbit up here. The boats ought to be visible down there. Were they sunk into the ocean?"

"By whom?" Avery said it into a sudden enormous quiet. "Or by what?"

"There's no trace of intelligent life, I tell you," said Lorenzen wearily. "At this distance, our telescopes could spot anything from a city or an aircraft to the thatch hut of some savage."

"Maybe they don't build huts," said Avery. His face looked abstracted.

"Shut up," snapped Hamilton. "You've got no business here anyway. This is a mapping room."

Hideki shivered. "It looks cold down there," he said. "Bleak."

"It isn't," said Fernandez. "Around the equator, the climate ought to be rather like, say, Norway or Maine. And you will note that the trees and grasses go right up to the swamps at the foot of the glaciers. Glacial periods aren't anywhere near as barren as people think; Earth was full of animal life in the Pleistocene, and it wasn't till hunting got worse when the glaciers receded that man was forced to develop agriculture and become civilized. Anyway, those glaciers are on the way out; I've seen distinct moraines in the photographs. When we settle here and jack up the carbon dioxide content of the air, you will be surprised how fast Junior will develop its own tropics. A few hundred years, perhaps. Geologically, nothing!" He snapped his fingers and grinned.

"*If* we settle it," grunted Hamilton. "Now, how long before you can have reliable maps, Lorenzen?"

"Uummm—well—a week, maybe. But do we have to wait that long?"

"We do. I want one overall map on a scale of one to a million, and enough others to cover the central valley region where we'll land—say from five degrees on either side of the equator—on one to 10,000. Print up about fifty copies of each. Run your prime meridian through the north magnetic pole; you can send down a roboflyer to locate it."

Lorenzen groaned inwardly. He had the cartographic machines to help him, but it wasn't going to be fun.

"I'll take a boat and a few men and run over for a closer look at Sister," went on Hamilton. "Not that I expect to find anything much, but—" Suddenly he grinned. "You can name the conspicuous features down there anything you like, but for God's sake don't be like that Chilean map-man at Epsilon Eridani III! His maps had been official for ten years before they found out every one of his names was an Araucanian obscenity!"

He clapped the astronomer's shoulder and pulled himself out of the room. *Not a bad sort,* thought Lorenzen. *He's a better psychman than Avery; though Ed isn't such a slouch either. He just lacks personality.*

He decided to stick by the classical nomenclature of the Hercules expedition. Mount Olympus, Mount Ida, the huge river down there would be the Scamander—and, of course, it wouldn't last. When the colonists came, it would be Old Baldy, Conchinjangua, Novaya Neva—

*If* the colonists came.

"Let's, uh, let's get organized," he said aloud, awkwardly. "How many here know anything about cartography?"

"I do," said Avery unexpectedly. "I'll help out if you wish."

"Where in cosmos did you pick that up?" asked Fernandez.

"Part of my education. A lot of applied psychodynamics consists of conformal mapping, though we generally have to use spaces of several dimensions and non-Cartesian coordinates. I can handle a mapping machine as well as you can."

Lorenzen blinked. After a moment, he nodded. The modern science of human behavior was out of his line, but he'd seen some of the texts: they used more paramathematical symbols than his own.

He crooked an arm around a hand rung and let his legs stream out behind him. Avery had said his tendency to space sickness was mostly psychological. It might help him to take his mind off the work and the coldly shining planet out there, just for a few minutes.

"How precise is your science, anyway?" he asked. "The popular articles on it are always so vague."

"Well—" Avery rubbed his chin. He hung cross-legged in the air like a small Buddha, his eyes remote. "Well, we don't claim the precision of the physical sciences," he said finally. "In fact, it's been shown rigorously that we can never achieve it: a kind of uncertainty principle of our own, due to coupling between observer and system observed. But a lot has been learned."

"Such as what?" inquired Umfanduma. "I know about the advances in neurology; that's in my own line. But how about man as—as man, instead of as a biophysical mechanism?"

"The amount of knowledge depends on the particular field of study," said Avery. "Already before World War III, they were using games theory in military work, and later the big computers made it possible to analyze even complex phenomena like business from a theoretical viewpoint; that in turn led to some understanding of economics. Communications theory turned out to be widely applicable: man is, after all, essentially a symbolizing animal. The least effort axiom was useful. Gradually a mathematical and paramathematical system has been built up, in which the elements—potentials, gradients, and so on—can be equated with observable phenomena; thus it becomes possible to derive theorems. It's still hard to check the validity of many of these theorems because conditions at home are too confused even today and, of course, you can't very well run a controlled experiment with human beings; but insofar as we have data, they confirm the present theories. Quite often it's possible to predict large-scale things like economic cycles with high precision."

"Didn't the dictators know most of that?" asked Lorenzen. "They certainly had effective propaganda techniques. I was more interested in modern developments."

"Most of it is modern," snorted Avery. "Very little that went before was of scientific value. To consider only the history of my own region, North America: The propagandists of capital and labor, the advertising men, worked on such a primitive level, with such a primitive appeal, that quite often they produced a reaction against themselves. They were only part of the mass-psychological debacle that led to military defeat. The commissars were mentally blinkered by their own outworn ideology; they never dared investigate beyond its dogma. The self-styled liberators were only interested in getting that power for themselves; it wasn't their propaganda which won the people to them, but the commissars' tyranny, and they were soon just as unpopular. The warlords during the Interregnum did have psychomilitary analysts, yes, but the only original work then was done in Brazil. Later, in the theocratic period, research was pushed because the Mongku Empire presented a challenge, and the first politicomathematical analyses were performed. But it wasn't till after Venus had taken over and Earth was temporarily at peace and the theocrats tossed out of America, that really thorough research was done. Then, of course, we finally got the formulated psychodynamics, the field and tensor approach, and it was used to bring on the Mars-Venus war and unify the Solar System—but the completed science had been worked out by peaceful professors interested only in the problem itself; their type is still doing all the major new work."

"Whew!" laughed Umfanduma.

"Completed science, did you say?" inquired Lorenzen. "I thought—"

"Oh, yes, work is still going on, all the time. But the results are already far enough along to be of inestimable value. Control of the economic cycle, for instance; the most efficient distribution of cities; currency stabilization; the gradual weaning of man away from barbarism toward the first really mature civilization—a civilization where *everyone* is sane." Something glowed behind the pudgy face and the blinking pale eyes. "It's a heartbreakingly big job, it'll take centuries and there'll be many setbacks and failures and mistakes—but at least, for the first time in history, we have not only good intentions, but some idea of how to implement them."

"Yes, I suppose so," murmured Lorenzen. His mind continued: *You can't elect a psychocrat, any more than you can elect an engineer. I don't want an elite of any kind, the world has seen too many of them; with all its maddening drawbacks, parliamentary government is still the only way; the psychocrats must still remain only advisors.*

*But one gets into the habit of letting the advisors lead—* He sighed and shoved away from the wall. "Come on," he said. "Work to do."


CHAPTER VI


LORENZEN KNEW that an unknown planet was approached cautiously, but the knowledge had only been in the top of his head. This was the first time he lived through that care, and it nearly drove him crazy.

When the maps were ready, four boats descended—forty men, with a skeleton crew remaining on the *Hudson* in her orbit. Fernandez sweated on the way down; it was he who had picked the landing site, and his fault if it turned out to be a morass or an earthquake region. But nothing happened.

That was exactly the trouble—nothing happened. They landed some kilometers from the Scamander, on a wide green plain dotted with clumps of trees and hazing into blue distance. Silence fell when the rockets were cut off; the grass fire they had started burned itself out; and men stared wistfully through the viewports at the sunlit world outside.

The chemists and biologists were busy. There was detailed analysis to do—of air, of soil and vegetation samples brought in by robots. Thornton checked radiation and reported nothing harmful. A cageful of rhesus monkeys was set outside and left for a week. During that week, nobody stirred from the boats. The robots which came and went were sterilized with savage thoroughness in the airlocks. There was nothing for the rest of the men to do.

Lorenzen buried himself in his microbooks, but even Shakespeare and Jensen and *The Song of the Jovian Men* got wearisome. Others puttered about, quibbled with each other, yawned and slept and woke blearily to another day of nothing. There were no open quarrels on this boat because Hamilton was aboard it; but the captain often had to snap furiously over the telescreen at men in the other craft.

Fernandez came close to losing his temper once. He protested to Hamilton: "You can't be that frightened of sickness!"

"I sure as hell can," grunted the captain. "If evolution on this planet is as close to Earth's as it seems to be, you can bet your degree there are some microbes which can live off us. And I want to go home on my feet. The least I can do is make reasonably sure we won't catch anything airborne."

Hideki and his team reported on such plants as they had analyzed: essentially terrestroid, though denser and tougher. Some were poisonous because of heavy-metal content or the like, but most could be eaten quite safely. A man could live well on the wild vegetation alone. It would take more study, though, to determine just how many sorts you had to eat for a balanced diet.

It was quite an event when they had their first meal of Troan food. The flavors were indescribable. Lorenzen grew aware of how impoverished most human languages are with respect to taste and smell sensations—but there were hints of ginger and cinnamon and garlic. He grinned and suggested: "Perhaps the soul of Escoffier isn't in Paradise at all; maybe he was given special permission to fly around the Galaxy and see what he could whomp up."

Thornton frowned, and Lorenzen flushed—but how do you apologize for a joke? He said nothing, but winced when he remembered the incident.

Hamilton only permitted half the men to eat that meal, and observed them closely during the day that followed.

Now and then animals were seen, most of them small fleeting shapes that scuttled through the long grasses on the edge of the burned area; but once a herd of bigger quadrupeds, the size of ponies, wandered past: grayish-green, scaled, with long hoofed legs and earless reptilian heads. Umfanduma cursed with his impatience to get a closer look.

"If the reptiles have developed that far," he said, "I'll give odds there are no mammals."

"Reptiles in a glacial period?" asked Fernandez skeptically. "Not that big, my friend."

"Oh, not reptiles strictly speaking, but closer to that stage than terrestrial mammals. There are cold and warm seasons here, I'm told, so they must have warm blood and well-developed hearts; but they certainly don't look placental."

"That's another argument in favor of there being no intelligent life here," said Lorenzen. "It looks as if this planet is wide open, just waiting for man."

"Yes . . . just waiting." Avery spoke with a sudden surprising bitterness. "Waiting for mines and cities and roads, for the hills to be leveled and the plains filled up with people. For our dogs and cats and cows and pigs to wipe out the infinite variety of native life. For noise and dust and crowding."

"Don't you like the human race, Ed?" asked Gummus-lugil sardonically. "I thought your job required you to."

"I like the human race in its proper place . . . which is Earth," said Avery. "Oh, well," He shrugged and smiled. "Never mind."

"We've got a piece of work to do," said Hamilton. "It's not our department to worry about the consequences."

"A lot of men have said that throughout history," replied the psychman. "Soldiers, executioners, scientists building atomic bombs. Well—" He turned away, sighing.

Lorenzen grimaced. He remembered the green rustling stillness of the Alaskan woods, the stark wild glory of the Lunar peaks. There was little enough of that left in the Solar System, few enough places where you could be alone. It did seem a pity that Troas—

After a week, the monkeys were brought in. Umfanduma checked them carefully, killed and dissected them, ran analyses with the help of Hideki. "All normal," he reported. "I found some types of native bacteria in their bloodstream, living harmlessly and completely sterile; apparently they can't reproduce in the chemical conditions of the terrestrial body. You wouldn't even get a fever from them."

Hamilton's lean gray head nodded. "All right," he said at last, slowly. "I guess we can go out."

He led the way. There was a brief ceremony of planting the flag of the Solar Union. Lorenzen stood bareheaded with the rest, the wind ruffling his hair under an alien sky, and thought that in this big lonely landscape the whole affair was a little ridiculous.

For a couple of days the site boiled with activity as camp was set up, men and robots working around the clock. There was always light, from the green or red sun or both, or from the great shield of Sister, high in a sky that burned with an unbelievable glory of stars. The work was hampered by friction between men, though it seemed strange that they should quarrel when they were as isolated as men had ever been. But it went on. A neat circle of collapsible shelters grew up around the clustered boats; the main generator began to throb and there was electric light; a well was tapped, a sterilizing unit built, and there was running water; a ring of detectors and alarms and guns was drawn about the camp. The shelters became sleeping quarters, a mess hall, a sick bay, several laboratories, a machine shop. Their metal half-cylinders looked harsh and out of place in the soft landscape.

After that, Lorenzen found himself rather a fifth wheel. There wasn't much for an astronomer to do. He set up a telescope, but between the suns and the satellite there was always too much light for effective study. In the scurrying busyness of the camp, he began to feel homesick.

He went in their one aircar with some others to the Scamander, to take a closer look and gather specimens. The river was enormous, a slowly rolling brown sheet; when you stood on one reedy bank, you couldn't see the other. The fish, insects, and plants didn't interest him much; as a zoological layman, he was more for the larger animals, paraphylon and astymax and tetrapterus. Hunting was easy; none of them seemed to have known anything like man and a rifle bowled them over as they approached curiously closer. Everybody wore a sidearm, for there were carnivores, you could hear them howling at night—but there was really nothing to fear from them.

There were no tall trees; the low scrubby growths which dotted the plains were incredibly tough; an ax would hardly dent them and you needed an AH torch to cut them down. The biological team reported them—on the basis of dendrochronology—to be some centuries old. They wouldn't be of much use to man; he'd have to bring his own seedlings and use forced-growth techniques if he wanted lumber. But the catalogue of edible plants and animals grew apace. A man could be set down here naked and alone, and if he knew anything at all about flint-working he could soon be comfortable.

Then what had happened to the men of the *Da Gama*?

It could not have been Junior's own environment. It wasn't that alien; as far as wild beasts and disease went, it looked safer than some parts of Earth even today. Now in the warm season, the days were bright and the rains were merely cool; there would be snow in winter, but nothing that fire and furs couldn't stave off. The low carbon dioxide content of the air required a slight change in breathing habits, but it was easily, almost unconsciously made. The lighting was weird—sometimes greenish, sometimes reddish, sometimes a blend of both, with double shadows and the colors of the landscape shifting with the suns—but it was not unpleasing, surely nothing to cause madness. There were poisonous plants, a couple of men got a bad rash from merely brushing one herb, but anyone with half a brain could soon learn to avoid those types. The land was quiet, speaking only with a sough of wind and rush of rain and thunder, remote cry of animals and beat of wings in the sky—but that too was only a relief after the clangor of civilization.

Well—

Lorenzen puttered with his instruments, measuring the exact periods of revolution and rotation for the planet and the heavenly bodies. The rest of the time he helped out, awkwardly, where he could, or talked to men off duty, or played games, or sat around and read. It wasn't his fault, this idleness, but he felt obscurely guilty about it. Maybe he should consult Avery. The psychman seemed rather a lost soul himself.

Twelve of Junior's thirty-six-hour days slipped past. And then the aliens came.

# CHAPTER VII

A TELESCOPE swinging on its clockwork mounting. Sudden shapes moving in its field. A photocell reacts, and the feedback circuit holds the 'scope leveled on the approaching objects. As they come nearer, an alarm is tripped and a siren skirls into the quiet air.

Friedrich von Osten jumped from the cot on which he had been dozing. *"Lieber Gott!"* He grabbed a rifle, and loosened the magnum pistol at his waist as he ran from the tent. Other men were sticking their heads out of the shelters, looking up from their work, hurrying to their posts at the machine gun emplacements.

Von Osten reached the command post and poised on the edge of its trench, raising his field glasses. There were . . . yes . . . eight of them, walking steadily toward the camp. It was too far yet to see details, but sunlight flashed hard off metal.

He picked up the intercom mike and said harshly: "Stand by all defense stations. Iss Captain Hamilton dere?"

"Speaking. I'm up in the bow of Boat One. They look like . . . intelligence . . . don't they?"

*"Ja,* I t'ink dey are."

"All right. Stand by. Keep them covered, but don't shoot till I say so. That's an order. No matter what happens, don't shoot till I tell you to."

"Efen if dey open up on us?"

"Yes."

The siren rose to a new note. Alarm stations! General alert!

Lorenzen ran for the shack assigned to him. The camp was a scurrying confusion, shouts and thud of feet, dust

40

swirling up to dull the drawn guns. The aircar shot overhead, rising for a bird's-eye look. *Or tetrapterus eye?* thought
Lorenzen wildly. *There are no birds here. This isn't our
world.*

He entered the shelter. It was crowded with a dozen men,
untrained in militechnics and assigned here mostly to keep
them out of the way. Avery's round face gaped at him;
the light of Lagrange I, streaming in the window, looked
ghastly on his skin. "Natives?" he asked.

"I . . . suppose so." Lorenzen bit his lip. "Seems to be
half a dozen or so, coming on foot. What the hell are we
s-s-scared of?"

Thornton's long gaunt face thrust out of a shadowed corner.
"There is no point in taking chances," he said. "No telling
what those . . . things . . . intend, or what powers they
command. 'Be ye therefore wise as serpents—' "

" '—and harmless as doves,' " finished Avery. "But are
we?" He shook his head. "Man is still adolescent. And this
reaction is . . . childish. Fear of the unknown. With all the
energies we have to use, we're still afraid. It's wrong."

"The *Da Gama*," said Thornton tightly, "did not come
back."

"I don't think . . . simple planet-bound natives, without
so much as a city, could have been . . . responsible," said
Avery.

"*Something* was," said Lorenzen. He felt cold. "They
might have weapons—b-b-bacteriological—"

"It's childish, I tell you, this fear." Avery's voice wobbled.
"We've all got to die sometime. We should greet them
openly and—"

"And talk to them, I suppose?" Thornton grinned. "How
good is your Lagrangian, Avery?"

There was silence. The noise outside had died away, now
the whole camp lay waiting.

Lorenzen looked at the chronom on his wrist. It swept out
the minutes, one, two, three, ten, thirty, and time was hid-

eously stretched. It was hot in the cabin, hot and dusty. He felt sweat trickle down under his clothes.

Forever went by in an hour. And then the siren blew. *All clear . . . come out . . . but stay alert.*

Lorenzen almost bolted from the shelter. He was close enough to the point where the aliens were to get there ahead of the crowd.

A semicircle of men, rifles in the crook of their arms, faced the strangers and held back the approaching humans. Hamilton stood in front of the guard, stiff and massive, watching the newcomers out of expressionless eyes. They looked back at him, and there was no reading their faces.

Lorenzen took them in at one gulping glance, and then went back for details. He had seen films of extraterrestrials before, and these were not as unearthly as some that had already been found—but still, it was a shock to see them here in the flesh. It was the first time he truly, fully realized that man was not unique, not anything special in the immensity of creation.

They stood on their hind legs like men, though with a forward slant which reduced their potential one and three-fourths meter height by a good ten centimeters; a heavy kangaroo-like tail balanced the body, and was probably a wicked weapon for infighting. The arms were rather skinny, otherwise humanoid, but the hands had three fingers and two opposed thumbs; each finger had an extra joint, and ended in sharp blue nails. The heads were round, with tufted ears, flat black noses, pointed chins, whiskers above the wide black-lipped mouths and the long golden eyes. They seemed to be mammals—at least, they were covered with smooth gray fur, barred in darker color that formed a mask about the eyes. Their sex was probably male, though Lorenzen couldn't be sure because they were clothed: loose blouses and baggy pants apparently woven of vegetable fiber, and a kind of mukluk on the feet. They all had leather belts supporting a couple of pouches, a knife or hatchet, and what was presumably a powder horn; on their backs were small pack-sacks, in their hands long-barreled affairs which he took to be muzzle-loading smoothbores.

In the first moment, they all looked alike to him; then he forced himself to locate individual differences of size, build, face: they varied as much as humans.

One of them spoke, a throaty purr. When his mouth was open, you could see the long blue canine teeth, though otherwise they seemed dentally as unspecialized as man's.

Hamilton turned around. "They don't act like a war party," he said. His voice and the low murmur of wind were the only sounds. "But you can't ever tell—Avery, you're a linguist. Can you make anything out of their talk?"

"Not . . . yet." The psychman's face was shiny with sweat, and his voice jittered. Lorenzen wondered why he should be that excited. "They do have distinct words."

"Hell," grunted Gummus-lugil, "I can't even hear that. It all sounds alike to me."

Another of the strangers spoke. Straining, Lorenzen could make out the pauses between phoneme groups. He'd taken a course in comparative linguistics at college, but it was vague in his mind now.

"They act like—well, I don't know what," said Hamilton. "Except that we're obviously not great gods from the sky to them."

"Wouldn't expect that." Avery shook his head. "If they've progressed as far as gunpowder hand weapons, I imagine their society is pretty sophisticated. Those muskets look better than what they had on Earth in Newton's time."

"But where are they *from?*" cried Fernandez. "There are no cities, no roads, not even so much as a village—I doubt if there is a house in this planet!"

Hamilton shrugged. "That's what I hope we can find out." His voice grew crisp: "Avery, you work on their language, that's your line. Von Osten, maintain guards at the defense posts, and detail a man to accompany each of these creatures wherever he goes within the bounds of the camp. But no rough stuff unless they try something extremely suspicious, and no holding them here if they want to leave. The rest of you carry on as before, but keep your arms ready all the time and don't leave camp without checking with me first."

It was sensible, thought Lorenzen. The strangers didn't look formidable, but you never knew, you never knew.

Slowly, the group broke up. The aliens followed Avery docilely enough, and one by one the others quit staring after them. Lorenzen heard Fernandez' murmur: "Natives after all! And pretty highly developed, too."

"Yeh." There was an odd sag to Gummis-lugil's heavy shoulders. "It looks like this pretty well kills the idea of colonizing."

*Which may be the death-blow to all man's dreams about the stars.*

Lorenzen tagged along after Avery. "Can I help you, Ed?" he asked. "I'm at loose ends, you know."

"You're not a linguist, John," said the psychman. "I'm afraid you'd only be in the way."

Lorenzen felt a stinging sense of rebuff. He gulped and persisted: "You'll need help. Somebody to act out the verbs, and—"

Avery considered for what seemed a curiously long time. "All right," he said at last. "To start with, anyway."

## CHAPTER VIII

THE ALIENS were offered a bunkhouse and moved into it with alacrity; another was set up for the displaced humans. They were shown through the camp and the boats, but there was no telling what they thought about it. Men noticed that they always had somebody on watch while they slept. They didn't seem to like messing with the humans, and used their own utensils to cook native food given them. But they stayed around for days, and worked hard with Avery and Lorenzen.

It seemed they called themselves Rorvan, as nearly as a human throat could form the word. Individual names emerged for them: Silish, Yanvusarran, Alasvu. Pointing to objects and acting out verbs began to give an elementary vocabulary and the whole stock of phonemes: it was a flexible tongue, they had almost fifty. Tonal qualities seemed to be important, but in analyzing his data Avery said the language was not analogous to Chinese. "I'm pretty sure it's inflected," he declared, "but I can't make head or tail out of the grammar. Possibly the tones form the inflections, but—" He sighed.

"Why not teach them English or Spanish?" inquired Lorenzen.

"I don't want to scare them off by the prospect of so much hard work. They may be just a group of wanderers who chanced on us and will decide any moment to take off again. Don't forget, they could be anything from official ambassadors to hobos or bandits, or something for which we have no word. We know nothing about the structure of their society or about them personally." Avery ran a hand through his thin hair and looked at the notes he had. "Damn it, their language just doesn't make sense!"

"Let me study your data for a while," offered Lorenzen. "I know a little something about glossanalysis."

"Not just yet, John. I want to go over it myself a few more times. I'll run off a copy for you soon."

The next day Lorenzen was asked to go in the aircar to help in a specimen-collecting expedition. He could not very well refuse, though he fumed at the delay. When he came back, Avery gave him a sheaf of papers and a wry grin.

"Here you are," he said. "I got a lot of information yesterday while you were off, but it leaves me in a worse mess than before. A lot of it contradicts what I thought I knew."

Lorenzen spent hours over the copy and had to confess himself beaten. The word for too many important things, or the meaning of a given sound, varied without discoverable rhyme or reason. Sister, for instance, was referred to as Ortu, Omanyi, Valakesh, Arbvu-djangiz, Zulei, and a whistling noise answering to nothing in any human tongue; and it looked as if each of these words took on an entirely different meaning in other sentences. It didn't seem merely a question of synonymy: you wouldn't expect the Rorvan to be so stupid as to confuse the issue thus. The name seemed to depend on the context in some obscure manner. The whole mass of conversation held nothing identifiable as a statement.

He gave up, realizing with discouragement that he was doubtless only underfoot. Avery continued working doggedly, sitting up late to ponder each day's material. But he was the only one who didn't feel a darkness of futility.

"What the devil are we staying here for, anyway?" demanded Gummus-lugil. "There are natives. They seem to be in a position to make colonization impossible. Why not just go home and get drunk and forget the whole mucking place?"

"We're supposed to complete the survey," said Lorenzen mildly.

Gummus-lugil took out a foul old pipe and began to stuff it. His heavy dark face twisted into a scowl. "Survey my rear end! You know as well as I do this is a practical expedition. We're wasting time we ought to be using to find a planet we can have."

Lorenzen sighed. "I wonder if we ever will. It was tough enough to finance this trip. D'you think anybody can raise the cash for another? There's too much to do right at home for Parliament to spend more of the public funds on what's beginning to look like a wild goose chase, and individuals with money to donate are getting few and far between."

"Don't you care?" asked the Turk.

"Oh . . . yes. I suppose so. But I never intended to leave Sol permanently." With sudden understanding: "This means a lot to you, though, doesn't it, Kemal?"

The engineer nodded. "It does. It did. I'm getting to an age where I want to settle down somewhere and raise a family. Only what can a man do in the System? Work for somebody else, all his life. I want to be my own boss. I thought—oh, hell." His voice trailed off and he stared emptily across the plain.

"There is a bit of hope yet," said Lorenzen. "It may be that the natives live underground or some such thing. That they won't care if we colonize the surface. They'd stand to benefit, even, if that's the case—trade and so on."

"It could be." There was a brief flicker in Gummus-lugil's eyes, and then a hardness grew in him. One hairy hand doubled into a fist. "But *something* happened to the first expedition! I suspect the natives murdered them and buried the traces—"

"I doubt it," said Lorenzen, though a thin little fear rose in his breast. "How'd they have gotten at the ship in her orbit? How'd the personnel get so careless as to let it happen at all? No, I still think space got them somehow. A chance meteor, just at the wrong moment, or—"

"Things like that don't happen to spaceships any more."

"They could, if all the improbabilities worked out just right. Or look—you say there was an attempt to sabotage the *Hudson?*"

"Yeh. Wait a minute—d'you mean—"

"I don't mean anything, Kemal. But there are groups at home which are opposed to the whole colony idea. The Resurrectionists think it's against the will of God. The Monarchists, the Collectivists, and the Eugenicists are all fanatics and all know that even their infinitesimal chance of getting into power will be gone if men start moving out of the System. Then there's Hilton's group, with its vague fear of the whole notion, pseudoscientific ideas about ex-

traterrestrial diseases or invasion or the colonists mutating
into something different and hostile—you see?"

"A bomb planted in the *Da Gama*." Gummus-lugil rubbed
his chin. "It wouldn't have been too hard; she wasn't built
from the keel up like ours . . . Of course, it's hard to see
how our converter could have been monkeyed with. All
our workers, right down to the last electrician, were screened
by the government with just that sabotage idea in mind.
But it could be. It could be."

"In that case—" A small exultance rose in Lorenzen. "In
that case, we have nothing to fear."

"But those bastards have plenty to fear from me!" The
Turk's hand dropped to his gun.

Another day went by. The blue-green sun rose, mists
swirled and dew flashed and then the grasses lay with a
metallic sheen. Six hours later the red sun followed, and full
day blazed. Clouds were tinted red or green, the double
shadows had their color, the vegetation shimmered in shifting
hues as wind ruffled it. The first sunset was not so spectacu-
lar, with Lagrange II still high in the sky, but the late afternoon had an eerie quality when the only light was its fiery
glow. Paradox: it grew cool, even a little chilly, when only
the smaller sun was up, but the unearthly red radiance suggested a furnace. The second sunset was usually a gorgeous
bursting of crimson and orange and gold. Then it was night,
with a glittering glory of stars. Sister came up, red on one
limb and blue-green on the other, the center a dimness of
shadow vaguely lit by reflection from Junior. On the horizon,
she looked enormous, seeming to fill half the sky; when well
up, she was still so big that men used to Luna could not
get rid of an uneasy notion that she was falling on them. Her
light was a weird white rush of argence, glimmering off dew
and hoarfrost. The night was big and still and strange to
man.

It caught at Lorenzen. He walked alone in the chill quiet,
thinking his own thoughts, and felt the challenge of the sky

and the world about him. Maybe he would want to come here after all. A new planet would be wide open for any man; he could have his own observatory on a space station, try out his own ideas, look at his own land and realize it was his and his children's.

But the natives—His spirits sagged again.

Another day and another.

Lorenzen was sitting under his usual tree with his usual book when he heard his name called. He looked up, and the camp's loudspeaker rolled and boomed with Hamilton's voice: "—report to the captain's office." He got up, wondering, and made his way back inside the circle of guns.

Hamilton sat at a desk in one of the huts. Avery stood beside him, looking nervous. Thornton, Fernandez, Gummuslugil, and von Osten were already there, waiting.

"All here," said the captain quietly. "You may pass on your report, Mr. Avery."

The psychman cleared his throat. "I've made a little headway with the Rorvan language," he said. He spoke so low that it was hard to hear him. "Not much—I still don't understand the grammar or whatever it is they have, and any ideas above an elementary level just don't get across. But we can talk about very simple things. Today they said they want to go home. I couldn't follow their reason, though I imagine they want to report their findings."

"All of them going?" asked Thornton.

"Yes. I offered to have them flown home, but they refused. Why, I don't know. They couldn't have misunderstood me, I *think*. I took them to the aircar and made gestures. But maybe they don't trust us that much. They insist on going on foot."

"Where is their home?" inquired Lorenzen.

"Somewhere to the west, in the mountains. That's all I was able to gather. About a four-week hike, I'd say."

"Vell?" snapped von Osten. "Vot iss vit' us to do?"

"The Rorvan," said Avery slowly, "were quite unhappy

at the thought of our following them by air. I don't know why—it could be a taboo of some sort, or more probably they just don't trust us not to throw bombs down on their home. We're as much an unknown quantity to them as they to us, remember. If we tried to follow, I rather imagine they'd just disappear in the mountains and we might never re-establish contact. However—" he leaned forward—"there didn't seem to be any objection to some of us accompanying them on foot. In fact, they seemed anxious that we do so."

"Valking right into a trap? *Ich danke!*" Von Osten shook his head till the blond beard swirled.

"Don't be more of an ass than you can help," said Gummus-lugil. "They'd know the rest of our party could take revenge."

"Could dey, now?" Von Osten flushed and held himself in check with an effort. "How vould de oders know vere ve vere?"

"Radio, of course," said Hamilton impatiently. "You'd take a portable transceiver along—"

"But do de aliens know ve haff radio?"

"That's a good point," admitted the captain. "The chances are they've never heard of the phenomenon. And I don't think they should be told about it either—not till we can trust them more."

He made a bridge of his fingers. "Mr. Avery wants to go along with them, and I agree that we should send some men. It may well be our only chance to get in touch with the native government, or whatever it is they have. To say nothing of getting a closer look at their technology and all the rest of it. After all, they may not object to humans coming here to settle. We just don't know yet, and it's our job to find out.

"You gentlemen here aren't needed for the studies we're making, your essential work has been done and you seem logical choices for the contact party. You'll keep in touch with the camp by radio and, of course, make observations as you go along. I won't hide the possible dangers from you. There may be diseases, poisonous snakes, or anything else you can imagine. The Rorvan, not knowing that I'll know exactly where you are, may indeed murder you. But all in all, I think it's fairly safe for you to go. It's strictly volunteer, of course, and no shame to the man who doesn't wish to stick his neck out—but are you willing?"

Lorenzen wasn't sure. He admitted to himself he was frightened, just a little, and would rather stay in camp. But what the hell—everybody else was agreeing. "Sure," he said.

Afterward it occurred to him that the fear of being the only hold-back might have prompted all the others too. Man was a funny animal.

## CHAPTER IX

THE FIRST three or four days were pure anguish. Then muscles got used to it, and they were logging off some forty kilometers a day without undue strain. It got monotonous, just walking over a prairie that always receded into far distances. Rain didn't stop them, the humans slipped on their waterproof coveralls and the Rorvan didn't seem to mind. There were broad rivers, but all of them shallow enough to ford, and canteens could be filled there. The long-range terrestrial rifles knocked down the plentiful game at distances of a kilometer or two, and on days when no animals appeared there was always plenty of wild vegetation, stems and leaves and beans which were nourishing if tough. Gummuslugil, who carried the transceiver, signalled back to camp every evening—a dot-dash system, to keep the Rorvan from suspecting what the radio was. Hamilton had established three triangulation robostations which kept him informed of the party's whereabouts. His own reports held nothing exciting, merely further details on what they already knew.

The Rorvan used compasses and maps to guide them, the latter in a symbology easy enough to translate once you knew what the various features were; they were hand-drawn, though that didn't mean the aliens didn't know about printing, and had a delicate touch—almost Chinese. The Mercator projection with its grid of lines and what was probably the prime meridian going straight through the south magnetic pole, suggested that they knew the true shape of the planet.

Lorenzen grew aware of the personality differences between them. Alasvu was quick-moving, impetuous, given to chattering away; Silish was the slow and stodgy type; Yanvu-sarran gave an impression of short temper; Djugaz seemed the most intellectual, and worked hardest with Avery. Lorenzen tried to follow the language lessons, without much success; they had progressed beyond the elementary level where he could have caught on, though Avery said communication was still a baffling problem.

"You should teach me what you already know, Ed," urged the astronomer. "Suppose something happened to you—where'd the rest of us be?"

"At worst, you could signal the aircar to come pick you up," said Avery.

"But dammit, I'm interested!"

"Okay, okay, I'll make up a vocabulary of the words I'm fairly certain of—but it won't help you much."

It didn't. All right, so you knew the names for grass, tree, star, run, walk, shoot. Where did you go from there? Avery used to sit by the campfire at night, talking and talking with Djugaz; the ruddy light burned off his face and gleamed in the unhuman eyes of the alien, their voices rose and fell in a purr and a rumble and a whistle, their hands moved in gestures—none of it made sense to Lorenzen.

Fernandez had brought his guitar along—inevitably,

groaned Gummus-lugil—and liked to play and sing in the evenings. Alasvu produced a small four-stringed harp with a resonating board that gave its notes a shivery effect, and joined him. It was comical to hear them together, Alasvu butchering *La Cucaracha* or Fernandez trying to chord on the Rorvan scale. Gummus-lugil had a chessboard, and before long Silish had caught on and was giving him some competition. It was a peaceful, friendly sort of trip.

But the dark sense of its futility dogged Lorenzen. Sometimes he wished he had never come with the *Hudson*, wished he were back on Luna puttering with his instruments and photographic plates—all right, here was a new race, a different civilization, but what did it mean to man?

"We don't need more xenological data," he said to Thornton. "We need a planet."

The Martian raised his eyebrows. "Do you really think emigration will solve the population problem?" he asked. "You can't get rid of more than a few million people that way. Say a hundred million in the course of fifty years of continuous shuttle service—which somebody will have to finance, remember. New births will fill up the vacuum faster than that."

"I know," said Lorenzen. "I've been through all the arguments before. It's something more—something psychological. Just the knowledge that there is a frontier, that a man with his back to the wall can still go make a fresh start, that any commoner has the chance to become his own boss —that'll make an enormous difference to Sol, too. It'll relieve a lot of unhealthy social pressures—change the whole attitude of man, turn it outward."

"I wonder. Don't forget, some of the most ferocious wars in history were fought while the Americas were being opened and again when the planets were being settled."

"Then isn't now. Mankind is sick of war. But he needs to find something new, something bigger than himself."

"He needs to find God," said Thornton with a certain

stiffness. "The last two centuries show how the Lord chastises a people who forget him. They won't escape by going to the stars."

Lorenzen's face felt warm.

"I don't see why your kind is always embarrassed when I speak of religion," said Thornton. "I'm perfectly willing to discuss it on a reasonable basis, like any other subject."

"We'd never agree," mumbled Lorenzen. "Waste of time."

"You mean you would never listen. Well—" Thornton shrugged. "I've no great faith in all these colonization schemes, but it will be interesting to see what happens."

"I suppose . . . I suppose whatever comes, y-y-your Martian homes will be spared!" blurted Lorenzen.

"No. Not necessarily. The Lord may see fit to punish us too. But we'll live. We're a survivor type."

Lorenzen had to admit he was right there. Whether you agreed with the Dissenters or not, it was undeniable that they had worked and fought like heroes for their particular dream. It was they who seized control of the gaunt, barren, worn-out planet to which they had fled and made it blossom; it was their psalm-chanting armored batallions which had broken the Mongku Empire and fought Venus to a standstill. There was a vitality to the believer type—whether he called himself Christian, Zionist, Communist, or any of a hundred other faiths which had shaken history. It was too bad that the reasonable man didn't share that devotion. But then, he wouldn't be reasonable if he did.

He looked at the loping gray forms of the Rorvan. What dreams lay in those unhuman skulls? For what would they be willing to slave and kill and cheat and die?

Their planet?

# CHAPTER X

MIGUEL FERNANDEZ was born in that province of Latin America known as Uruguay. His family was old and wealthy, and he had been one of the few who always got enough to eat. And there had been books, music, theaters, boats, horses; he had played polo for his continent in the world matches and sailed a yawl across the Atlantic. He had done good stratigraphical work on Luna and Venus, had laughed with many friends, loved many women, and gone out to the stars with a song.

He died on Troas.

It came with cruel swiftness. After two weeks of open prairie, they reached ground which rolled slowly upward, toward the dim blue forms of mountains peering over the horizon. It was a land of long coarse grasses, thick clumps of trees, coldly rushing rivers; always the wind blew, and there were many wings in the sky. Progress slowed down a bit as the Rorvan circled to find the easiest slopes, but you could still count on thirty kilometers a day or so. Avery said he'd asked how much longer the journey would take, but had not understood the answer, which seemed to be highly qualified.

The party was strung out in a long line, scrambling over tumbled boulders. There was much life around here, tetrapteri broke cover with a flurry of all four wings, smaller animals bounded off in alarm, a distant herd of horned reptiles stopped and looked at the travelers with unblinking eyes. Lorenzen was walking near the front of the line, beside Alasvu, trying to improve his Rorvanian vocabulary by pointing to new objects. He saw a small bright-colored beast lying on a rock, sunning itself—rather like an oversized lizard —and indicated it.

"*Volanzu*," said the Rorvan. With practice, Lorenzen was getting so he could distinguish individual phonemes; formerly, all of them had sounded much alike to him.

"No—" It seemed odd to the astronomer that Avery still didn't know the words for "yes" and "no"; maybe the language didn't include them. But—"No," he said in English, "I know that word, it means 'stone.' I mean the lizard there." He stepped up close to the animal and pointed. It arched its back and hissed at him. The double sun made a jewel-play of its iridescent scales.

Alasvu hesitated, "*Shinarran*," he said at last, after peering closer. Lorenzen jotted it down in his notebook as he walked further.

A minute later, he heard Fernandez scream.

He whirled around. The geologist was already falling, and he saw the lizard clinging to the trouser leg. "*What the devil*—" He ran back, slipped on a rock, and got up in time to see Thornton grab the lizard by its neck and throw it to the ground and crush its head underfoot.

Then they were all crowing around Fernandez. He looked up at them out of tortured eyes. "*Hace frio*—" Thornton had slit his pants leg and they could see the fang marks and the purpling color around them.

"Poison—get that first-aid kit!" The Martian almost snarled it.

"Here—" Gently, Avery pushed him aside and knelt by Fernandez. As a psychman, he necessarily knew a good deal about medicine. His knife flashed, laying open the flesh.

Fernandez gasped. "I cannot breathe . . . *Madre de Dios*, I cannot breathe."

Avery bent to put his mouth to the wound, but straightened. "No use sucking it out, if it's already got to his chest." His voice was dull.

The Rorvan crowded helplessly about, looking as if they

wanted to do something but not knowing what. Fernandez'
eyes rolled up and they saw the breast lie suddenly quiet.

"It's paralyzed his breathing—artificial respiration—" Gummus-lugil's big hands reached out to roll the small man over.

"No." Avery was holding his pulse. "No use. His heart's
stopped too."

Lorenzen stood very still. He had never seen a man die
before. There was no dignity to it. Fernandez lay grotesquely
sprawled, his face mottled bluish, a little drool still coming
from his mouth. The wind slipped between the crowding
men and ruffled his hair. Death was an unclean sight.

"Call the camp." Gummus-lugil fumbled for the radio on
his back. "Call the camp, for God's sake. They've got means
of reviving."

"Not with this stuff in him," said Avery. "Smells like
prussic acid. The speed of it—! Good God, it must be all
through his bloodstream by now."

They stood quiet then, for a long time.

Gummus-lugil called Hamilton and reported. The captain
groaned. "The poor little devil! No, it's no use, we couldn't
bring him back if he's been poisoned that thoroughly." It
came out of the radio as a chatter of clicks. The Rorvan
watched, and there was no reading their faces. Did they
think it was some kind of ritual—that the humans thought a
god was speaking to them?

"Ask him what to do," said Avery. "Tell him the Rorvan
will still be going on and I, for one, am willing to follow
them."

Decision came out of the machine "Bury him where he
is and put up a marker. I don't think his religion would frown
on that, under the circumstances. Is anyone ready to give up
and come back here? The car can pick them up . . . No?
Good. Carry on, then—and for the love of man, be more
careful next time!"

It took a while to dig the grave with the few tools they
had. The Rorvan helped, and afterward brought rocks to

make the cairn. Avery looked at Thornton. "Would you like to say a few words?" he asked, very softly.

"If you wish," said the Martian. "But he wasn't of my faith, you know, and we haven't anyone of his along. I will only say that he was a good man."

Was it hypocrisy? wondered Lorenzen. Thornton, to whom Fernandez had been a papist; Gummus-lugil, who had cursed him for his noisiness; von Osten, who had called him a weakling and a fool; Avery, to whom Fernandez had only been one more factor to stabilize; he himself, who had never been particularly close to the man; even the Rorvan —here they stood around the grave, unspeaking save to voice a sense of loss. Was it only a meaningless form, or was it some recognition of the awesome stillness and the common destiny of all life? There was nothing more they could do for the dead flesh down under those rocks; did they wish they had done more while it lived?

By the time they were through, it was too late to travel further. They gathered dead branches, cut the sere grasses and bushes for a campfire, ate their evening meal and sat very quietly.

Djugaz and Avery went on with their language studies; von Osten rolled over and went grumpily to sleep; Thornton read his Bible by the dim red flicker of light; the other Rorvan murmured to each other, no more than a whisper. The fire crackled loudly; outside its wavering circle of light, you could see the moonlit world, and hear the wind talking in the trees. Now and then an animal howled, far off in the darkness, a long and lonely sound. It was not the night of Earth, not any night such as man had known—not with that double crescent huge in a cold starry heaven, not with those noises out there. A long way home, a long way for the soul of Miguel Fernandez to wander before it found the green dales of Earth.

Lorenzen murmured to himself, almost unconsciously, the ancient words of a Lyke Wake Dirge, and looked to the

vague red-lit mound of the grave. Light and shadow wove
across it, almost it seemed to stir, as if the one within had
loved life too much to lie quiet now.

"This  ae nighte, this ae nighte,
    *Every nighte and alle,*
Fire, and sleet, and candle-lighte,
    *And Christe receive thye saule.*"

(And in the north lay eternal winter, and moon like icy
rain on its glintering snows, the stars high and chill above the
blinking glaciers, between the weird pale glimmers of aurora.)

"When thou from hence away art paste,
    *Every nighte and alle,*
To Whinny-Muir thou comest at laste;
    *And Christe receive thye saule.*

"If ever thou gavest hosen and shoon,
    *Every nighte and alle,*
Sit thee down and put them on;
    *And Christe receive thye saule.*

"If hosen and shoon thou ne'er gavest nane,
    *Every nighte and alle,*
The whinnes sall pricke thee to the bare bane;
    *And Christe receive thye saule.*"

(What have we ever given each other, of kindness and help
and love, in all the long nights of man? What can we ever
give each other?)

Gummus-lugil moved over and sat heavily down beside
him. "One down," he murmured. The weaving light etched
the strong thrust of his face against darkness. "How many
more?"

"It was the little things Hamilton was afraid of," said
Lorenzen. "Not earthquakes and monsters and big-brained

octopi, but the snakes and germs and poison plants. And he was right."

"A thing with cyanide in its fangs—what kind of metabolism is that? Can't have blood like we do." The engineer shivered. "It's cold tonight."

"It can be licked," said Lorenzen. "If that's all we have to fear, it isn't much."

"Oh, sure, sure. I've seen worse than this. It was just so goddammed—sudden. Why, you almost touched that thing yourself. I saw you."

"Yes—" Lorenzen felt sweat at the thought.

It struck him then. Alasvu had not warned him.

He held himself quiet, admitting the realization piece by piece into his mind, not daring to let it burst in all at once. Alasvu the Rorvan had not pulled him back from the lizard.

He looked across the fire to the small group of the aliens. They were in shadow, only their eyes glowing out of darkness. What were they thinking? What had they planned for these strangers from beyond the stars?

He wanted to tell Avery . . . no, let it ride for now. It could have been an accident. Maybe the lizards were rare, maybe this group of Rorvan had never seen one before either. Alasvu himself had been within centimeters of the fangs. The aliens couldn't be so stupid as to think they could murder every one of the humans and make it look like an accident!

But the *Da Gama* had never come home!

He forced down a shudder. He was tired, overwrought, his suspicions were childish and he knew Avery would label them as such. And if he told von Osten, the German would probably want to shoot all the Rorvan on the spot. Gummuslugil and Thornton—well, not just yet, let him think and gather evidence before making a fool of himself.

He looked out into the western darkness. That was the way they were heading, into the mountains, into canyons and gorges and up thin slippery trails where anything could hap-

pen. And they couldn't turn back, not now, though they
had no dimmest idea of what might be waiting for them.

"From Whinny-Muir when thou mayst passe,
  *Every nighte and alle,*
To Brigg o' Dread thou comest at laste,
  *And Christe receive thye saule.*"


## CHAPTER XI

THE LAND climbed rapidly, until they were scrambling
through a wilderness of harsh rocky hills, between gaunt
patches of shrub, and across brawling rivers whose cold was
like teeth in their feet. It was hard to follow the Rorvan;
their light graceful forms wove and bounded over the tumbled country; Lorenzen's breath was often dry in his throat
as he gasped after them.

One evening, about a week after Fernandez' death, Hamilton's question clicked over the radio: "What the devil is
wrong with your guides, anyway? You're arcing north again.
Why haven't they led you straight to their home?"

Gummus-lugil looked surprised, but shouted the question
to Avery. "Ask one of those hairy brutes why, will you? I'm
sick of walking, myself."

"I have," said the psychman. "Didn't I tell you? But the
answer seems to be another of those untranslatable things.
I got an impression of dangerous territory which we have
to skirt."

Gummus-lugil passed the reply on to Hamilton, who closed
his sending with a click that might almost have been a grunt.
The Turk sighed. "Not much we can do about it," he said.

Thornton chuckled. "Perhaps they mean to run us bow-
legged and thus have us helpless," he suggested.

Von Osten clapped a hand to his rifle. "Dey lead us
straight or—"

"No, take it easy, will you?" Avery spread his hands.

"There isn't much we can do about it, I'm afraid. They *are* the guides."

Lorenzen scowled. It didn't ring true. More and more, the whole business was looking questionable.

He pulled out an aerial map of the territory and studied it for a long while. As far as he could see, there was nothing to distinguish the area which they were avoiding. Of course, there might be hostile tribes or something, but—

For every question he could raise, there was an answer. But all the answers were too *ad hoc*, they didn't fit into a consistent picture. All right, the poison lizard had been a species unfamiliar to the Rorvan, that much was pretty obvious; but why was it new to them? Any animal that formidable ought to have a pretty wide distribution—nor had the Rorvan come so terribly far from what seemed to be their own stamping grounds . . . Yes, the native language might be extremely difficult, but blast it!—a society, to be capable of the technology the Rorvan seemed to have, *had* to think and speak in terms which fitted the necessary concepts. When Western science was introduced to the Orient, the Chinese had generally talked and written about it in English or French because their own tongue wasn't suitable. So the Rorvan speech ought to have some structural similarity to the Indo-European group, enough so that Avery shouldn't be having all the trouble he claimed to be having . . .

For that matter, he was holding long conversations with Djugaz every night. He *said* they were language lessons, but—

Suppose they weren't?

Lorenzen sat quietly, letting the thought seep into his consciousness. He wanted to reject it. He liked Avery; and there was so little they could trust on this new world that if they couldn't even rely on each other—He must be getting paranoid.

Then there was still the *Da Gama*, a giant question mark floating somewhere out in space—

He lay in his sleeping bag, feeling the hardness of the ground beneath it, listening to the wind and the rushing river and the hooting of some unknown animal. His body was tired, but there were too many questions boiling up in his head for him to sleep. What had happened to the first expedition? Who had tried to sabotage the second? Why had it had such a heartbreaking series of minor difficulties before getting started? Why had Avery failed to mold its personnel into a unified team? Ill-assorted as they were (why?), it should still have been easy for a skilled psychman. Why were the Rorvan the only mammalian species encountered so far? Why didn't any of their artifacts show from the air? Why did they have such an incomprehensible language? Or did they? If not, why was Avery lying? Why had the Rorvan failed to recognize a danger which should be as well-known as a cobra on Earth? Their metabolism was enough like man's so that it should be a menace to them too. Why were they doubling the length of the journey to their home? Why, why, why?

For every question there was an answer, either given direct by Avery or advanceable as a plausible hypothesis. But taken *in toto*, the answers violated Occam's principle; each explanation required a new entity, a new set of postulated circumstances. Wasn't there any unifying fact which would account for it all? Or was the whole thing really a jumbled mess of coincidences?

Silish was on guard, prowling around and around the dying fire. He was a noiseless flitting shadow, only the faint gleam of light on his eyes and his musket to give him away. Now and then he would look over the sleepers—and what was he thinking? What was he planning? He might hunt and sing and play chess with the humans, but they were more alien to him than the bacteria in his bloodstream. Did he really feel any sense of kinship, or was he party to some monstrous scheme which had already swallowed one ship and killed a man of the second?

Avery might not be lying, at that. He was a trustful, friendly little cuss. A psychman should know better, but then, he wasn't dealing with humans. Maybe the Rorvan had blinkered his eyes for some purpose of their own. Or had he been bribed somehow? But what could they buy him with?

Lorenzen turned, hungering for sleep. It wouldn't come. He had too much to think about, too much to be afraid of.

Resolution came at last. He couldn't tell anyone else what he suspected, not yet. There wasn't enough privacy in the group. No telling—maybe the Rorvan had picked up some English. Anyway, he had no proof, nothing but a hunch. *Take it easy, take it very slow and easy.*

But he had the beginnings of a Rorvan vocabulary. Suppose, without telling anyone, he tried to learn more. Mathematical analyses of data were out—he'd be seen performing those, except for what he could do in his head. But if you assumed that the language was basically inflected, its structure not too unlike the Aryan, by listening in on conversations, he could recognize words he knew and get some of the conjugations and declensions, new words would come from context. It wouldn't be easy, it would take time, but maybe he could do it. A lot of words could be learned by just asking, if they didn't suspect he was on the trail.

Eventually he was able to doze off.

## CHAPTER XII

"It iss murder, I say!"

The wind whined about von Osten's words, blowing them raggedly from his beard. He stamped cold feet, and the ringing rock gave the noise back.

Around him and Thornton, mountains climbed steeply

toward an ice-blue sky, their peaks sharp and white against it, their lower slopes tumbling in a dark cruelty of rock down into a gorge and a remote hurrying river. The land had climbed terrifically in the last few days, a great block of stone thrust up between the plains and the sea. Waking in the mornings, the travelers would find a thin layer of snow on the barren ground, and their breath smoked white from their nostrils. Hunting was poor, and some days there was little enough to eat; progress was a slow scramble over cliffs and crags, down and up knife-like ravines. It had been agreed to make camp for a couple of days and devote the time to foraging—getting enough food for the last push over the pass that lay white before them.

Thornton hefted his rifle and met the German's angry gaze with steady eyes. "The Rorvan could hardly have known that lizard would be right in our path," he said.

"No, but it vas a chance for dem to get rid of vun of us." Von Osten hunched his shoulders under the inadequate jacket. "Iss too many t'ings vat don't fit togedder. Dere iss somet'ing fake about dese aliens, and I say ve should down all but vun and beat de trut' out of him."

"Matter of language difficulty there," said Thornton dryly.

"Lengvitch, hah! Dey just don't vant us able to talk vit' dem. No lengvitch can be so hard like dey make out. Ven dey don't vant to answer a qvestion, dey just tell soft-head Avery, 'Versteh nicht,' or dey jabber nonsense at him and he t'inks it iss some new trick of deir lengvitch. No, dey talk to him eassy enough if ve make dem vant to."

Von Osten reached out and tapped the Martian's bony chest. "And vy are dey leading us like dey do? I haff looked at our own maps. Vould be much qvicker and eassier to cross furt'er sout' and den follow de coastal lowlands nort'. I t'ink dis talk about skirting dangerous land is so much bull roar. I t'ink dey are giffing us a royal runaround."

Thornton shrugged. "Frankly, I suspect the same. But why approach me about it?"

"You iss de only vun I can trust. Avery iss a fool, Lorenzen iss a veakling, Gummus-lugil vould refuse to help just because it iss my idea. You and I can maybe do somet'ing."

"Hm—" Thornton rubbed his chin; the unshaven bristles felt scratchy. "Perhaps I can. But I don't want to rush into anything. Quite possibly the Rorvan intend to murder all of us. It is the easiest way to keep man off their planet. If the *Hudson* also fails to return, there will probably be no third expedition, and maybe the aliens suspect as much. But don't forget, they have to get rid of base camp too, which would be doubly alert if all of us disappeared. And the spaceship—how about it? How did they dispose of the *Da Gama?* It should have been in its orbit to this day, even if they lured the skeleton crew down somehow—"

Von Osten scowled. "I t'ink dey haff powers dey are not showing us. Maybe spaceships of deir own."

"While their warriors are armed with flintlocks? Don't be a fool!"

The German's sun-darkened face turned red. After a moment, he said quietly: "Please vatch your tongue. I vish to vork togedder vit' you, but not if you haff no manners . . . Haff you neffer t'ought maybe dose muskets are part of de game? If ve t'ought dey had not'ing better, it vould put us off our guard."

Thornton whistled. "In the name of the great Jehovah—!" Suddenly he turned. "Come on, we're supposed to be hunting."

"But my idea?"

"I want to think about it. I'll let you know."

They felt their way cautiously along the ledge that wound up the mountain face. Now and then they stopped to scan the harsh scene with field glasses. Dry snow scudded along the crags, but there was no sign of life. Thornton felt hunger gnawing in his belly, and suppressed the awareness. He had no business now complaining about the flesh.

If the Rorvan were *not* so primitive as they claimed to

be, it opened up a whirl of nasty possibilities. If they were anywhere near the interplanetary level of technology, they would have been able to detect the *Hudson* as she approached; and in her equatorial orbit, she would make such frequent transits of Sister and the suns that the smallest telescope could spot her. Even if the Rorvan were only at the gunpowder stage, it was probable that they had telescopes. But if they were further along yet—then they could live underground, synthesizing their food; the custom might have grown up during a period of atomic wars. They could wipe out the camp and the ship with a couple of long-range guided missiles . . . Why hadn't they done so before? Maybe they wished to learn all they could first, and appearing in the guise of primitives was certainly a good way to disarm suspicion.

Thornton shook his head. It still didn't quite make sense, there were too many loose ends and unanswerable questions. But he had to assume von Osten was essentially right. He dared not do otherwise. And if so—what to do? A quick blast with an automatic rifle, to wipe out the Rorvan in camp; maybe saving one for questioning. The commissars had taught humanity how to get truth out of any creature which could feel pain. A call to the camp, a quick return of all personnel to the *Hudson*, retreat into outer space—And then what? Troas would still be a mystery. He couldn't see the Solar Patrol making up a punitive force—but it would have to. It couldn't refrain, lest someday the Rorvan strike out of the sky at Earth.

Avery would scream to high heaven, pointing out that this was sheer unprovoked murder; he would doubtless lodge criminal charges when they got back to Sol. Lorenzen would, somewhat reluctantly, back him. Gummus-lugil was an uncertain quantity . . . How about Hamilton? The captain might put Thornton and von Osten in irons and stay here regardless; his caution never stood in the way of his duty as he saw it.

*I have a duty too. A hard road to walk, O Lord.*

It might be best to stage a mutiny, to gun down all those humans who would not string along. And that would certainly mean a trial when they got back to Sol, prison, psychiatrists turning his mind inside out . . . Thornton's wife and children would weep, alone in their home on Mars, and bear themselves with bitter pride in the face of their neighbors.

But the Rorvan were not human; the Noachian dominies doubted that any aliens even had souls, and in all events they were surely heathen . . .

Thornton knew what an anguished wrestling with himself he must have before decision came. But already he thought he knew what the decision would be.

"Dere! Ofer dere!"

He lifted the field glasses at von Osten's whisper. High above them, peering over a massive jut of rock, was a horned head—game!

The two rifles cracked almost as one. The beast screamed and was gone. Furiously, Thornton began to run, leaping over stones and splits in the ledge. His breathing was fire in his lungs, but he had to catch that animal before it got away, he had to!

The upper ridge bulked in front of him. He scrambled, clawing himself fast to the rock. Von Osten grunted at his side, grabbing for handholds. It was like going over a fence. They reached the top.

And went over!

The moment was too swift for understanding. Thornton had a brief wild knowledge of falling, something smote him on the back and ripped his flesh open, he heard the angry whiz of a loose rock going past his ear, and then thunder and darkness came.

He awoke slowly, for a long time he was only aware of pain. Then vision cleared and he sat up, holding a head that seemed ready to split. "Von Osten," he groaned.

The German was already on his feet, looking dismayedly about him. "You iss all right?" he asked. His tone was perfunctory, he had checked the unconscious Martian and found nothing serious.

Thornton felt himself. There was a long shallow cut in his back, his head was painful and bleeding from the nose, and there were more bruises than he cared to count. But— "Yes, I think so."

Von Osten helped him to his feet. "Iss a curse on dis planet," he snarled. "It iss here only to murder men. I t'ink ve are caught in here."

Thornton looked around. The bluff they had climbed was the outer wall of a sort of pothole, about six meters deep and four wide; the animal they had shot had been on the further side of it, and by sheer ill luck they had gone over the bluff at exactly the wrong spot. The walls of the pit were nearly vertical, worn smooth by centuries of wind and frost and melting snow; a small hole in the bottom must lead to a channel that drained off the water.

He walked unsteadily about, examining the edges of the trap. Von Osten, who had suffered less, made several increasingly frantic attempts to climb out, but finally gave up. There was no way to do it without equipment they didn't have.

"Two more for de Rorvan," he said hoarsely.

"They couldn't have known—"

"Dey haff led us t'rough dangerous country. Chance has done for dem vat dey oddervise vould haff done for demselves. *Gott in Himmel!*" Von Osten shook his fists at the sky.

"Don't take the name of the Lord in vain." Thornton went to his knees and prayed. He didn't ask for help; whether he lived or died, that was God's will. He felt more composed when he was through.

"The others will come looking for us when we don't return tonight," he said. "They know approximately the route we followed."

"*Ja*, but iss a hell of a big territory to search, and ve vill not last very long in dis cold." Von Osten hugged himself and shivered.

"We'll have to fire shots at intervals, and take our chances of starting an avalanche. But we may as well wait a while with that, nobody will be coming this way for hours yet. Here, break out the first-aid kit and bandage me a little, will you?"

After that there was nothing to do but wait.

It grew colder when the blue sun set. Shadows began to fill the pit, and the air was like liquid. There was no breeze down here, but the men could hear the thin cold harrying of the wind up around the edge of the hole. They tried to exercise to keep warm, but there was no strength in them.

After the second sunset, they huddled together in an abysm of darkness, under the keen merciless blink of stars. Now and then they dozed, and woke with a shudder. They were only half conscious, time stretched horribly for them and the night was full of fleeting visions. Once Thornton thought he heard someone calling him, and started nearly awake; the voice rang hollowly down the long bare slopes, crying that he had sinned, and he knew it was not one of the searchers.

The long night wore on. When the first stealthy gray slipped across their little patch of heaven, they felt a dim surprise that they were still alive.

Now and then they curled stiff fingers around their guns and fired into the air. The echoes howled around them, and Thornton recalled the topography of this region with an effort. It was hard to think, but he suspected the surrounding cliffs would prevent sound from carrying very far. They might never be found, their bones might lie here till the double star was ashen.

The first sun climbed higher. They couldn't see it yet, but it melted the night's frost and a dozen bitter trickles of water ran down into the pit. Von Osten rubbed a frozen toe, trying to bring life back to it. Thornton sought to pray, but words wouldn't come, it was as if God had cursed and forgotten him.

Full sunlight was blazing into the pit when the Rorvan came. Thornton saw them peering over the edge and didn't recognize them at first, his mind was vague and stupid. Then knowledge came and he snapped to wakefulness with a jerk.

Von Osten spat an oath and hefted his rifle. "*Morderische Hund!*" Thornton knocked the weapon down just in time.

"You idiot! They're here to rescue us!"

"Are dey, now? Dey're here to see ve die!"

"And what good will it do us to shoot them? Give me that gun, you devil!" They scuffled feebly. Three Rorvan stood on the pit's edge and watched them. Wind ruffled their fur, but the masked faces were utterly impassive and they said nothing.

Thornton got the rifle away from von Osten and looked up again. There was no sign of the aliens. It was like a cold hand around his heart. So simple, so easy. If the Rorvan meant them all to die, here were two men murdered for them already. They need only report that they had found no trace of the missing ones.

So easy, so easy—Thornton felt his mind buckling. "Lord God of Hosts," he whispered between his teeth, "smite them! Stay not Thy vengeance!" And some sick corner of himself laughed and said that maybe the Almighty was tired of man, maybe these were his new chosen people who would scourge a sinful humanity out of creation and down into hell.

He felt death within himself, he was doomed to freeze and die here, thirty thousand light years from his home, and God had turned his face from Joab Thornton. He bowed his head, feeling tears harsh in his eyes. "Thy will be done."

And then the Rorvan were in sight again. They had a rope, and one of them took a turn around his body and the other was climbing down it into the pit. Down to rescue the humans.


## CHAPTER XIII


BEYOND THE PASS, there was another steep drop, cliffs falling terrifically into a remote glimmering sea. It reminded Lorenzen of parts of the California coast—the savage splendor of mountains, the grass and shrubs and low dark-leaved trees along their slopes, the broad white beach far below; but this range was bigger and sharper. Newer—he remembered Fernandez pointing out that the glacial era on Troas was due to a recent period of tectonic activity. The huge satellite probably made diastrophism here a more rapid process than on Earth. Lorenzen thought of the little geologist and his grave. He missed Miguel.

A good thing that Thornton and von Osten had been saved. He remembered a long talk he had had with the Martian afterward; Thornton had told of his plans, in short harsh sentences wrenched out by an inner need to confess to someone, and admitted he had been wrong. For if the Rorvan intended murder, why should they have rescued him? Lorenzen said nothing to anyone else about the conversation, but added the question to his own list.

Von Osten was still sullen and hostile to the aliens, but had obviously shelved his own schemes. Thornton, shaken by his experience, had swung the other way, to a trust of the Rorvan almost as great as Avery's seemed to be. The Martian was now brooding over the theological problem of whether or not they had souls; he felt they did, but how to prove it?

Gummus-lugil slogged cheerfully and profanely along the interminable trail. Lorenzen felt very lonely these days.

He was making progress with the language. He could almost follow the talk of Avery and Djugaz, nearly enough to be sure that it was not just a lesson. The psychman remained blandly smiling, turning all questions with a deftness that left Lorenzen stuttering and incoherent. Yes, of course he was getting along with Djugaz, and the Rorvan was telling him some interesting things about his own race. No, he didn't want to take time out and teach Lorenzen what he knew; later, John, later, when we can all relax.

Almost, Lorenzen was ready to lay down the burden. Give it up, take Avery's word at face value, stop thinking and worrying and being afraid. There would be an answer to all questions in due time. It was no concern of his.

He stiffened himself and bent bleakly to the job. It did not occur to him how much he was changing himself, how little stubborn and aggressive he had been before this. Apart from his research, he had been like most men, content to let others do his thinking and deciding for him; he could never quite go back to that.

The climb down to the sea was grueling, but took only a couple of days. Once they were on the flat coastline, it was like a vacation. Avery said Djugaz had told him it was only a few more days to their goal.

At this point of the shoreline, the coastal plain hardly deserved that title: it narrowed to a kilometer-wide beach, a thin strip of grass and trees, and then the high rocky bluffs at the sheer foot of the mountain. The strand was also Californian, a great stretch of fine sand piled into tall dunes and scudding before the salt wind. But Earth had never seen a surf as furious as that which foamed and roared at its edge, nor a tide so swift and deep as the one which marched up almost the whole width of the beach twice a day. There didn't seem to be any game here, but the party could live off herbs and wild beans for a while.

Lorenzen felt a tautness rising within him as the kilometers fell behind. A few more days, and then—the answer? Or more questions?

Death guested them again before they reached an end of wandering.

The tide was coming in near the first sunset that day, when they came to a point where the hills fell directly into the sea. Bluffs and wind-gnawed boulders lay half-buried in the sand, making a low wall across their path; beyond, the beach curved inward, a long narrow loop at the foot of a ten-meter cliff, forming a bay. The water here was scored with the teeth of rocks thrusting out of its surface; a kilometer from the beach, the mouth of the bay was white violence where the sea thundered against a line of skerries.

Lorenzen paused on the top of the wall, looking uneasily ahead at the thin strip of sand. "That stuff is under water at high tide," he said. "And the tide's coming in."

"Not that fast," said Gummus-lugil. "It'll take less than half an hour to get across, and we won't even get our feet wet. Come on!" He jumped back down to the sand, and Lorenzen shrugged and followed. The Rorvan were already ahead of them, moving with the light rippling grace which had grown familiar in these weeks.

They were halfway across, hugging the foot of the cliff, when the sea broke in.

Lorenzen saw it as a sudden white curtain rising over the barrier. The roll of surf became a rising cannonade, ringing and screaming between the stones. He sprang back as the water level rose and rushed in across the beach.

A wave toppled over the outer skerries and came in with a blinding speed. Lorenzen yelled as its teeth closed around his knees. Another was on its back, green and white fury, spray exploded in his face and the sea got him around the hips. He fell, the water sheeted over his head, he rose with a howl and a fist seemed to batter him down again.

Rising, striking out wildly, he was whirled outward by the

undertow. His boots dragged at him, yanking him beneath. The waters bellowed and tossed him back, against the white rush of surf at the cliff's edge.

Clawing for a hold in the churning water, he looked about him through half-blinded eyes. There, up ahead in the fury, a rock rising—He twisted, fighting to stay above water. Briefly, a Rorvan was whipped by him, he heard a dying scream and then the sea snarled up to shake the world and he went under again.

Up . . . over . . . strike, kick, reach—The slippery stone would not take his hands. A wave grabbed him and dashed him away—then back, over the rock, he closed his arms around something and hung on.

The water whooshed about him, he couldn't see or feel or think, he clung where he was and lay blind, deaf, dumb, half dead, only a barnacle will to survive kept him there.

And then it was over, the wrathful waters sucked back with a huge hollow roar. He fell waist-deep and scrambled for the wall cutting off the bay. Before he got there, the sea was coming in again, but he made it. A wave sloshed after him as he climbed the wall. Almost hysterically, he fled from it, collapsing on the grass above high-water mark. He lay there for a long time.

Presently strength and sanity returned. He got up and looked around him. The wind tossed smoking spindrift into his face, and the noise of the sea drowned his voice. But there were others, a group gathered, they stood mutely together and looked with wildness at each other. Human and Rorvan eyes met in a common horror.

Slowly, then, they took stock. Three missing—Gummus-lugil, Alasvu, Yanvusarran. Silish groaned, and it sounded like the anguish of a man. Lorenzen felt sick.

"Let's look around." Avery had to speak loud, but it came to their ears as a whisper under the anger of the sea. "They may be . . . alive . . . somewhere."

The tidal bore was receding, and von Osten climbed the

wall and peered over the bay. Two forms stood on the opposite side and waved feebly at him. The German whooped. "Gummus-lugil and vun oder iss still alife! Dey lived!"

Silish narrowed his eyes, squinting across the sunset blaze that shone off the waters. "*Yu Yanvusarran.*" His head drooped.

"What did it?" breathed Avery. "What was it that hit us?"

"The p-p-place here is a goddammed trap," stuttered Lorenzen. "The c-conformation of the bay, a s-s-steep slope of the bottom . . . it makes th-th-the tide come in like all the legions of hell. We've got s-similar things on Earth . . . and here the t-t-tide is so much stronger—i-i-i-if we'd only known!"

"De Rorvan!" Von Osten's lips were white. "Dey knew! It vas a plan to kill us all."

"D-don't be more of a fool than y-y-you can help," said Lorenzen. "It got one of them and nearly got the rest. It was an accident."

Von Osten looked at him in surprise, but shut up.

The tide dropped swiftly. They crossed the bay by twilight, to join Gummus-lugil and Alasvu. The Rorvan was collecting driftwood for a campfire, and the Turk was reporting the affair on his miraculously undamaged radio. There was no sign of Yanvusarran; he must have been swept out to sea, or maybe his corpse rolled at the foot of the barrier reef and waited for the fish.

The Rorvan set up a low keening. They stood in a line, holding their hands out to the water. Lorenzen listened to the funeral chant, and was able to translate most of it. "*He is gone, he is faded, he walks no more, no longer for him the winds and the light, but his* (memory?) *shall live within us . . .*" Their grief was genuine enough, thought the astronomer.

Darkness came, walling in the little circle of firelight.

Most of the party slept, exhausted; one Rorvan guard prowled up and down, and Avery and Djugaz were sitting up talking as usual. Lorenzen stretched himself out near them and feigned sleep. Maybe tonight, he thought, he would get a clue. He hadn't been able to make much sense out of their talk before, but sometime soon he must catch on to the knack, and then his vocabulary would be large enough—

He had it!

Avery spoke, slowly and heavily: "I (unknown) not make-think others. Some not (unknown) laughing (?) with what I-say."

The trick was to cast what was heard into normal English, filling in the meanings of unfamiliar words from context, and to make the translation fast enough so that he didn't lose the reply. "I hope this does not make the others think (or: suspicious). Some are already not very happy with what I tell them."

Djugaz answered gravely: "Swiftly (unknown) theirs you, (unknown) time (?) to *Zurla* we-get see past shadow (?) they." Lorenzen's mind raced, unnaturally clear: "You must swiftly disarm their suspicions, lest when we get to the *Zurla* they see past the shadow (or: deception)."

"I do not think they will. How could they? And after all, I have the weight of authority (?), they will listen to me. At worst (?), that can be done to them which was done to the first expedition (?), but I hope (?) that will not be necessary. It is not a pleasant (?) thing to do."

A harsh flare of fanaticism: "If we must, then we must. There are larger issues (?) at stake than a few lives."

Avery sighed and rubbed his eyes like a man driven to immense weariness. "I know, There is no turning back. Even you do not realize how much is involved (?)." He looked up at the high cold radiance of the stars. "Perhaps (?) all of that—the entire universe (?) —all time and all space." There was a croak of pain in his voice. "It is too much for one man!"

"You must."

"Sometimes I am afraid—"

"I too. But it is more than our lives (?)."

Avery laughed without humor. "*You* think this is an enormous issue! I tell you, Djugaz, you do not begin to understand how much—"

"Perhaps not." Coldly: "But you depend (?) on me as much as I on you—possibly more. You will follow my lead (?) in this."

"Yes. Yes, I will."

Lorenzen could not follow the rest of the talk; it went into generalities, abstract concepts for which he had no words. But he'd heard enough! He lay in the sleeping bag and felt cold.

## CHAPTER XIV

THE MOUNTAIN range swung suddenly inland, at the same time growing lower and gaining an easier slope. Here there were rolling grasslands, trees and meadows and running streams between the hills. The Rorvan hastened their steps.

Another of their race, armed and dressed much like themselves, met them. There were whistling cries of recognition; Djugaz and Silish ran up to him and conferred swiftly, then the newcomer nodded and ran off.

"He's going to spread the news," said Avery after a talk with Djugaz. "The village will want to welcome us. They're a pretty friendly people, these Rorvan."

"Hm." Gummus-lugil gave him a close look. "You seem to be kind of familiar with their language after all."

"Yes. In the last few days, I finally got the key to it, and everything fell together all at once. Fascinating semantics it's got. I'm still not an expert by any means, but I can understand ordinary conversation."

"So? Who are these boys with us, then?"

"They were a delegation to another town, returning home after a . . . business conference of some sort; I can't quite get the exact meaning there. They happened on us and realized pretty quickly what we must be. Their knowledge of astronomy is good, about like our eighteenth century, and Djugaz quickly grasped what I told him about the true structure of the universe—its size and so on."

Lorenzen couldn't refrain from asking: "Where are their observatories? How did they detect the finite speed of light? They could hardly use Römer's method in this system and—"

"I don't know yet." Avery looked annoyed. "Don't be so dogmatic, John. Does every science have to develop the same way ours did?"

Lorenzen shut up. No sense giving himself away—God, no! It could mean a knife between his ribs.

"Underground towns, as we suspected earlier," went on Avery. "That custom seems to have grown up in the past couple of thousand years, when the climate was colder than it is now. Originally, I suppose, it was merely because a dugout requires less building material and is easier to heat, but now it's become almost a matter of morality, like our taboo on public nudity."

"And dey haff farms underground, too?" Von Osten frowned, trying to understand.

"No, they never developed agriculture—so much of the wild vegetation is edible the year around. Then too, they have herds of grazing animals for meat, induced to remain in the vicinity by some means I don't yet comprehend. Djugaz gave me the word for it, but I can't find a corresponding concept in any human language."

Alasvu was listening to the talk, his head cocked on one side, as if he knew what was being said. Doubtless he had the drift of it, thought Lorenzen. There was a wicked mirth in the amber eyes.

"It's wonderful that they were still able to become civilized," said Ashley. "A gifted race . . . perhaps without original sin . . . Do you know how many of them there are?"

"Quite a large population, I gather—at least a hundred million, though none of our party knew the exact figure. This is just a small village, a hamlet, we're going to; but then, they don't have any really big cities like us, they spread out more uniformly."

Lorenzen looked at the psychman. The weeks of wandering had leaned him down and burned his skin dark, but still there was nothing impressive to look it, still he was a small round man approaching middle age, soft-spoken, genial, everything about him said he was dull but steady, mildly benevolent, a little timid—And he was party to a scheme which juggled with the destiny of stars! There was some goal which made him so ruthless that the fate of two ships and the will of seven billion human beings was nothing. Lorenzen shrank a little closer to the stolid, comforting bulk of Gummus-lugil. He'd just about have to let the Turk know, if no one else—

One of the mountains hemming in the eastern horizon thrust long roots out toward the sea. As the party approached one of these, it appeared as a low escarpment fronting a giant hill. The surrounding land was bare, tracked and trampled by many feet. Trees grew thickly before the cliff, some of them ancients almost three meters tall, and out of this grove the Rorvan began coming.

They moved quietly, saying little, none of the babbling excitement a human crowd would have shown. There must be some fifty or sixty of them, estimated Lorenzen, about equally divided between male and female. The latter were dressed in kilts and sandals; the four breasts were not very human-looking, but gave the final proof that this race was mammalian. Some of the males carried muskets, the rest were unarmed. They closed in on the humans, in a friendly enough way. A purr of talk rose from them.

"How come no young?" asked Thornton.

Avery put the question to Djugaz, and replied after a moment: "The children all go into special . . . crèches, I guess you'd call them. I gather the family here has a radically different structure and function from ours."

Pushing through the grove, the throng came to an entrance in the hill—a great artificial doorway, ten meters wide and three high. Lorenzen forced down a shudder as he walked through it—would he ever see sunlight again?

Thick columns of rammed earth supported a broad corridor running into the hill with many branches leading off to the sides. The air was cool and fresh, Lorenzen saw ventilator grilles in the walls. "Good pumps, then," commented Gummus-lugil. "And they use electricity." He nodded at the fluorescent tubes which lined walls and ceiling and gave a steady bluish light. "Their technology can't be entirely on an eighteenth-century level."

"You wouldn't expect it to be," said Avery. "A lot of engineering advance in our own history has been sheer accident. If the early researchers had investigated the Crookes tube more thoroughly, we might have had radio and radar before 1900."

The corridor was quiet, save for the murmur of the air blowers and the shuffle of many feet. It sloped gently downward for a good half kilometer. Glancing in the side tunnels, Lorenzen saw doorways presumably leading into rooms or suites.

The main passage opened on a great cubical cavern. This was lined with entrances screened off by tapestries that seemed to be of woven fiber. "Downtown," said Avery with a wry smile.

"They don't seem to have much artistic sense," said Lorenzen dubiously. The whole place had a depressingly barren air to it, neat and clean but without sign of decoration.

Djugaz said something and Avery translated: "This is quite a new settlement. They haven't had time to fix it up yet. It's partly a colony, partly a military post; I gather that the females fight as well as the males."

"So dey are not united here?" rumbled von Osten.

"No, not quite. I've already learned that the continent is divided among several nations. Currently they're at peace and cooperating, but it wasn't so long ago that they had a terrific series of wars and the armies are still maintained at strength."

The German's eyes gleamed. "Dey could maybe be played off against each oder."

"I doubt it . . . even if we would be morally justified in such a course," said Avery. "I rather imagine they know as much about the *divide et impera* game as we do."

One of the Rorvan made gestures at a pair of doorways, talking fast. "We're honored guests," said the psychman. "We're invited to make ourselves at home here."

Inside, the apartments had the same bleak military look: each had two rooms and bath, furnished with a few low concrete couches and stools; that was obviously an easier material to work with than the native wood. But there was hot and cold running water, a flush system, a kind of soap. Apparently the village had a communal kitchen.

Avery disappeared for a while, talking with Djugaz and the villagers who seemed to be local leaders. Von Osten looked around the suite in which the other humans waited, and sighed gustily. 'Iss dis all ve haff come so far to see?"

"I'd like more of a look," said Thornton. "Their apparatus, the general lay-out of the town, their daily lives—it should be interesting."

The German grunted and sat down. "To you, maybe. For me, I haff come t'irty t'ousand light-years and seen not'ing vort' de trip. Not efen a good fight at its end."

Gummus-lugil took out his pipe and got it going. His face was moody. "Yeah. I have to agree. Unless these Rorvan will actually let us settle here, the trip has been for nothing. We can't take over a planet from a hundred million well-armed natives with a high grasp of military principles. They could raise merry hell with us, just using what they have, and I'll bet they could soon be copying our own weapons too. Unless we could bluff them . . . but no, the bluff wouldn't last, they'd catch on fast enough and massacre the colonists."

"Dey could be conquered!"

"At what expense? Spending how many lives? And all for the benefit of the few million people who could be shipped here. They don't command that many votes! Parliament would never agree."

"Well . . . the Rorvan may still be persuaded—" Thornton said it as if he didn't believe it himself. Nobody did. A race capable of building electric generators wasn't so stupid that it would allow several million aggressive aliens to settle on its home world. It could easily foresee the consequences.

Avery came back after an hour or so. He was wearing a poker face, but his voice sounded tired: "I've been talking with the local bosses, and gotten messages sent to the government of this nation—they have a few telegraph lines, its something new for them. That government will doubtless communicate with the others. We're asked to stick around for a while till they can send their scientists and so on to interview us."

"What's the chance of their letting people settle here?" asked Gummus-lugil.

Avery shrugged, "What do you think? It'll have to be officially decided, of course, but you already know the answer as well as I."

"Yeah. I guess I do." The engineer turned away. His shoulders slumped.

# CHAPTER XV

THE REST of the day was spent in a guided tour of the village. There was quite a bit to see. Gummus-lugil was especially interested in the power station, which he was told drew its energy from a hydroelectric plant in the mountains, and in the small but well-equipped chemical laboratory; von Osten took a good look at the arsenal, which included some large-sized mobile cannon firing explosive shells, a set of flame throwers, grenades, and a half-built experimental glider which ought to work when it was finished. Thornton leafed through some printed books and inquired, through Avery, about the state of Rorvan physics—which had apparently gotten as far as Maxwell's equations and was working on radio. Lorenzen tried hard to keep up a show of interest, and hoped he was succeeding. But every now and then one of the aliens gave him a sidelong look which might mean nothing or might mean death.

In the evening there was a banquet; the whole village gathered in a decorated mess hall for a series of excellently prepared dishes and the entertainment of musicians. The town commander made a mercifully short speech on the "hands-across-space" theme, and Avery replied in kind. Lorenzen faked boredom as well as he could, as if he didn't understand a word of it. Underneath, he was churning with worry. All that day the farce had been kept up. The Rorvan had asked the expected questions of Avery—about his race, its history, science, beliefs, intentions—well, that would fit in with the astronomer's deductions of the truth; the aliens would still have a normal curiosity about man. But why this solemn rigmarole of talks which presumably only Avery would understand? Was it for his, Lorenzen's, benefit—had

84

Avery warned them that he might know more than he let
on? And if so, how much of what he knew did Avery know
he knew?

This was getting worse every minute; questions within questions. And what to do, what to do? Lorenzen glanced down
the long bright table. The Rorvan were there in their Sun-
day best, barbaric splashes of color against the drab, soiled
gray of the humans' hiking clothes—rank upon rank of them,
face after face, each one mobile and smiling and completely unreadable to him. What did lie behind those golden
eyes? Was he sitting at the table with the real masters of the
universe? Self-appointed gods playing at humble peasant
and soldier? When the Rorvan smiled, you could see the
long fangs in their mouths.

It ended, finally, after a polite nightmare of hours. Lorenzen was sweating when he got up, and he couldn't keep
his hands from trembling. Avery gave him a look which
showed only sympathy—but what was *he* thinking? God in
Heaven, was he even human? Surgical disguise, synthetic
thing—what lay under the round bland mask of Avery's face?

"You don't look well, John," said the psychman.

"I feel . . . rather tired," mumbled Lorenzen. "I'll be all
right after a good night's sleep." He yawned elaborately.

"Yes, of course. It has been rather a long day, hasn't it?
Let's toddle bedwards."

The party broke up in murmuring, soft-footed knots of
aliens. A guard of honor—or was it just a plain guard?—
shouldered arms and marched behind the humans on the
way to their apartments. They had two adjoining ones, and
Avery himself had suggested that Lorenzen and Gummus-
lugil should take one, the other three the remaining one.
If they were to be here several days, that was a tactful
measure to avoid a clash between the Turk and von Osten,
but—

"Goodnight, boys . . . See you in the morning . . .
'Night . . ."

Lorenzen drew the curtain that shut his place off from the street. Inside, it was a barren cave, coldly lit by the fluoros in the ceiling. There was a great sudden quiet, this was not a human town with its restless life. Gummus-lugil spied a bottle on the table and reached for it with a delighted grin. "Some of their wine—nice of them, and I could sure use a nightcap." He pulled out the stopper with a faint pop.

"Gimme that. I need it bad." Lorenzen almost had the bottle to his lips when he remembered. "No!"

"Huh?" Gummus-lugil's narrow black eyes blinked at him. "All right, then, hand it over here."

"God, no!" Lorenzen set the bottle down with a thud. "It might be drugged."

"Huh?" repeated the engineer. "You feel okay, John?"

"Yes." Lorenzen heard his own teeth clapping in his head. He stopped and drew a long shuddering breath. "Listen, Kemal. I've been hoping to get you alone. I want to . . . tell you something."

Gummus-lugil ran a hand through his coarse dark hair. His face grew wooden, but the eyes remained watchful. "Sure. Fire away."

"While I'm talking," said Lorenzen, "you better check your pistol and rifle. Make sure they're loaded."

"They are. But what—" Gummus-lugil started as Lorenzen flipped the curtain aside and looked out into the street. It was empty, utterly dead and silent in the chill electric radiance. Nothing stirred, no sound, no movement, it was as if the village slept. But somewhere there must be wakeful brains, thinking and thinking.

"Look here, John, we'd better let Ed have a look at you."

"I'm *not* sick!" Lorenzen whirled about and put his hands on the Turk's shoulders and shoved him to the bed with a strength he hadn't known was in him. "Goddammit, all I want you to do is listen to me. Then when you've heard

me out, decide if I'm crazy or if we really are in a trap—
the same trap that got the *Da Gama*."

Gummus-lugil hardly moved, but his mouth grew suddenly tight. "Talk all you want," he said, very quietly.

"All right. Hasn't anything struck you about these—Rorvan? Hasn't there been something strange about them, this
whole time we've known them?"

"Well . . . well, yes, but you can't expect nonhumans to
act like—"

"Sure. Sure, there's always been an answer, for every
question we raised." Lorenzen was pacing up and down, his
fists clenching and unclenching. Oddly, in this moment his
stutter had left him. "But just think over the questions again.
Consider the weirdness of it all.

"The Rorvan group, traveling on foot across a huge empty
plain, just *happens* to find us. Improbable, isn't it? They
are the dominant race, the intelligent ones, they are mammals, and there are no other mammals on this planet. An
evolutionary biologist would wonder about that. They live
underground and have no agriculture, seem to make no
use of the surface at all except for hunting and herb-gather-
ing. A moral code, we're told—but damn it, no morality
lasts that doesn't make *some* sense, and this one is ridiculous. Our guides fail to recognize a type of venomous lizard
which is probably widely distributed and certainly a menace
to them; even if they personally never saw one before, they
should surely have heard about, just as any American knows
what a cobra is. Then, even worse, they get trapped by a
tidal bore and lose one of their number—*within sixty kilometers of their own home!* They didn't know about the
damned thing!

"I tell you, the Rorvan are fakes! They're playing a game!
They're no more natives of this planet than we are!"

Silence. It was so complete a silence that Lorenzen could
hear the remote humming of the village power station. Then

his own heart began to beat so furiously that it drowned out all but Gummus-lugil's: "Judas priest! If you're right—"

"Keep your voice down! Of course I'm right! It's the only picture which fits all the facts. It explains, too, why we were taken the long way around to this place. They had to build it first! And when the 'scientists' and 'government representatives' arrive to greet us—they'll be from the Rorvan spaceship!"

Gummus-lugil shook his head, slowly and amazedly. "I never thought—"

"No. We were rushed along, with smooth, pat explanations every time we did pause to wonder. That phony language barrier helped a lot too; we naturally shelved our questions—in our own minds as well—till they could be answered directly. It's not a difficult language at all. I've learned the basics of it myself, once I decided that it was *not* hard. When I first tried to study it, I was given a lot of confusing data—faked! There's no more variation in the name of an object, for instance, than there is in English or Turkish. Once I'd thrown out the false information—"

"But why? Why are they doing this? What do they hope to gain?"

"The planet, of course. If we go home and report that there are highly civilized natives, Earth will lose interest in Troas and their own people can come here in droves. Then it'll be too late for us, they'll *have* the planet and we won't be able to get them off it."

Gummus-lugil stood up. There was a grimness in his face; he had changed his mind about a lot of things in a few minutes. "Good work, John! I'm pretty damn sure you're right. But . . . d'you think they intend to murder us?"

"No. They rescued Joab and Friedrich, remember, whom they could just as easily have left to die. I don't think they'll kill us unless they suspect we know the truth. Our negative report at home will be of more value to them than our disappearance."

"Why—" Gummus-lugil grinned, a savage white flash of teeth in the broad swarthy face. "Then it's simple. We just string along with them till we get back to our camp and then tell—"

"But it's *not* that easy, Kemal! Avery is in cahoots with them!"

## CHAPTER XVI

THIS TIME the engineer said nothing, but his hand dropped to the gun at his belt as he waited.

"Avery . . . little old Ed Avery," said Lorenzen. There was a sick laughter in him. "*He* faked those language data. He supplied most of those answers to our questions. He learned Rorvan and sat up late at night talking with them—" He sketched out the conversation on which he had eavesdropped.

"You mean the *Da Gama* case is . . . related to ours?" Gummus-lugil's voice was thick.

"It fits in, doesn't it? The first expedition disappears. The second endures a string of troubles which would have made anyone but a bunch of near-fanatics like the Institute's directors quit. The government helps recruit personnel for the trip, and we get the most badly selected, conflicting, inefficient crew which ever took a ship into space. Avery is along as psychman and does nothing to mitigate those conflicts. Avery is also in an official position, one of the advisors on whom Parliament and the people are coming to lean more and more . . . And when we bull through in spite of everything, the Rorvan show up. And if we come home and don't make a negative report on Troas—well, the *Da Gama* vanished!"

Sweat gleamed on their faces as they stood confronting

each other. They were breathing hard, and Lorenzen was beginning to shake again.

"But the *government*—" It was almost a groan from Gummus-lugil.

"Not the official government. Parliament operates in a goldfish bowl. But the psychocrats, the advisors, the quiet unassuming power behind the throne—they have men everywhere. One Patrol ship, manned entirely by men sworn to their service, would have been enough to take care of the *Da Gama*. Will be enough for us."

"But why? In God's name, why?"

"I don't know. Maybe I'll never live to know. But you could imagine an older civilization than ours—maybe the Rorvan are the real bosses of the Galaxy, maybe the psychocrats on Earth are their tools, or maybe both are cat's-paws for some other planet. They don't want man in interstellar space."

There was another silence while they thought of a billion suns and the great cold darknesses between.

"All right," said Gummus-lugil. "What can we do? Now?"

"I don't know," said Lorenzen desolately. "Maybe we should wait, play for time, till we can get Captain Hamilton alone and talk to him. But on the other hand, we may not be allowed time."

"Yeah. Anything could happen, couldn't it? If somebody—something—learned what we know . . . Or maybe the Rorvan won't give us a chance, maybe they'll decide not to risk our figuring things out on the way home and will blow up the works while Hamilton is still unsuspicious." Gummus-lugil looked at the radio set where it stood in a corner. "I doubt if we could call from here. There's enough metal in these caves to shield us off, probably. We'll have to go outside."

"All right." Lorenzen went over and picked up his rifle. "Now is as good a time as any, I guess." There were robo-monitors at the camp set to ring an alarm and start recording when a call came from the portable set.

The astronomer peered out into the street again. Nothing moved—silence, graveyard stillness. Under the violent thudding of his heart, he wondered if they could go out and make their call and come back undetected.

But if not—that had to be risked. That, and a bullet in the belly, however frightened he was. His own sweat stank in his nostrils, it was hard to keep from shaking, but some jobs had to be done. It was more than the possession of Troas. The Solar System, all humankind, had to know who its secret masters were, or there could be no peace for John Lorenzen in all his remaining days.

Gummus-lugil thrust his arms through the shoulders straps of the transceiver and stood up, grunting. He had a rifle in one hand, and a knife stuck in his belt. The preliminaries were over, now they were playing for keeps.

They stepped out into the street. Their eyes wandered to the curtained entrance of the adjoining apartment—Avery was in there. It would have been good to have Thornton and von Osten along, but they couldn't risk waking the man or creature or thing who called himself Edward Avery.

Down the long row of doorways, their hushed footfalls seeming thunder-loud; out of the central cave, slowly upward through the silent empty tunnel to the open sky.

A Rorvan stepped out of a side tunnel. He had a musket, and it swung to cover them. The yellow eyes blazed with sudden alarm, and he rapped out the question: "Where are you going?"

Lorenzen checked himself just before answering; he wasn't supposed to know the language. He smiled, spreading his hands, and walked closer. The Rorvan's gun wavered. If they were unsuspecting guests— Then decision came, and he waved them back.

"Of course," whispered Gummus-lugil bitterly. "And tomorrow we'll be told it was for our own good, there are dangerous animals out there . . . Go on up to him, John. Don't act threatening, but give him an argument."

Lorenzen nodded. He approached till the musket was almost in his stomach. "Look," he said patiently, "we just want to take a walk. Anything wrong with that? All we want to do is take a stroll, and you're a flea-bitten son of an illegitimate alley cat."

The guard snarled, "No!" and tried to thrust him back.

Then Gummus-lugil was behind Lorenzen. He reached out and grabbed the musket and twisted the barrel aside. Lorenzen's own hand followed, jerking the weapon loose and stepping aside. The Turk leaped forward, his fist going before him. There was a dull crack, and the Rorvan lurched back and fell. Gummus-lugil tumbled on top of him, getting hands on his throat.

After a moment: "All right. Cut some pieces from his shirt—tie him up, gag him. Might be simpler to kill the bastard, but—"

In a minute they were again moving up the tunnel, fast. There had been little sound, no alarm. But at any moment, the whole cave might wake with a scream.

The end of the passage loomed before them, blue-black darkness and the pitiless brilliance of the Hercules stars. They burst out of it, and the trees were around them and the sky overhead and they heard the remote squall of a hunting animal.

"Over here—away from the cave—that damned sentry! Now the grease is in the fire, whatever we do." Gummus-lugil squatted under the low, massive bole of a tree and slipped off his radio set. His fingers were deft in the gloom, feeling for the controls. "Got to warm it up—what'll we do when we've sent the call?"

"I don't know. Try to hide out somewhere—or maybe surrender." Lorenzen drew a shuddering breath. He wondered if the pounding of his heart could be heard.

The dial face of the transceiver glowed, a round eye in

the shadows. Gummus-lugil slipped on his earphones and tapped the sender key a few times, experimentally. "Not quite hot yet."

An alarm went off, a high screaming note which went through Lorenzen like a sword. He sprang back, jerking his rifle up and sucking in a gasp of air. "My God, they've found that sentry."

"Or they have a hidden detector somewhere, set to whistle when we try calling base." Gummus-lugil cursed luridly.

Slim leaping forms were boiling up in the tunnel entrance, black against its light. A Rorvan voice howled above the yell of the siren: "Stop that! Stop that radio (?) or we will kill you!"

Gummus-lugil began tapping out his message.

Lorenzen ran away from him, zigzagging between the trees till he was several meters off. The wiry underbrush snagged at his ankles, he stumbled and cursed and crashed an elbow numbingly against a hidden branch. But the enemy's attention had to be drawn from the radio, Gummus-lugil had to live long enough to send the word. Lorenzen yelled defiantly. There was no time now to be frightened.

A dozen muskets cracked. He couldn't hear the hungry buzz of lead around his ears, but several slugs thudded into the tree behind which he stood. It was a heavy trunk forking into two main branches at one and a half meters' height; he rested his rifle in the crotch, squinting between the blur of leaves, and thumbed the weapon to automatic fire. The Rorvan sprang for him.

His gun spoke, a soft chatter, no betraying streaks of light. The indistinct mass of running shadows broke up. He heard them screaming raggedly, saw them topple, and even then felt the sorrow of it. *Djugaz, Alasvu, Silish, Menusha, Sinarru, you were good comrades. You were my friends once.*

The Rorvan drew back, out of the grove and away from the silhouetting cave entrance. They'd circle around and close in; but *dit-dit-dah-dit, dah-dit-dah,* every second they lost betrayed them.

Something like a tommy gun began to stutter, throwing a sleet of white-hot tracers into the darkness under the trees. So now they were pulling out their real armory! Lorenzen shot back, blindly, and waited for death.

More of them came from underground. Lorenzen fired, forcing them back; but some must be getting past his curtain of lead. The gunstock was cool and hard against his cheek. He was dimly aware of dew wet and heavy underfoot. A glow in the sky said that Sister was rising above the eastern mountains.

Something blazed in the cave mouth. Lorenzen saw a knot of Rorvan explode, falling and fleeing. Two figures loomed huge against the light—Thornton, von Osten, they'd heard the racket and come out to fight!

The German fired in the direction of the tracer stream. Suddenly it went out. Von Osten roared and moved away from the tunnel entrance. He wasn't quite fast enough. Lorenzen heard another metallic rattle. Von Osten spun on his heels, lifted his arms, and tumbled like a rag doll. Thornton flopped to the ground and wormed for the shadows.

The night was full of eyes and flying metal. The Rorvan had surrounded the grove and were shooting wildly into it, even as they crawled and zigzagged their own way under its trees.

"John! Where are you?" The urgent whisper ran like a snake under the low gnarled branches.

"Over here, Kemal."

The Turk belly-crawled to Lorenzen's tree and stood up with his rifle poised. The first pale streaks of moonlight fell between the leaves and dappled his face. There was no sound of victory in his tones, no time for that, but he muttered quickly: "I got a message off. Not time for much of one, just that we were in trouble with the natives and they weren't really natives at all. Now what?"

"Now," said Lorenzen, "I guess we just stand them off as long as we can."

"Yeah. It'll take the boys at base a while to play back my message, and triangulate our exact position, and send some armed boats here. We won't last that long."

Gunfire crackled to their right. A heavy form rose and burst into the grove, running fast. "Over here!" cried Lorenzen. "Over here, Joab!" He and Gummus-lugil fell to their stomachs as lead snapped after his voice.

The Martian, almost invisible in his black pajamas, eeled up to them. He was breathing hard, and a stray moonbeam turned his face chalky. "Heard the noise . . . got up, saw you gone . . . Avery said stay there, but . . . Rorvan tried to stop us, we fought through them . . . Just a guess you were being attacked, but a right one . . . What's going on?"

Lorenzen didn't answer. He was leading a crawl away from their position, toward a spot of deeper shadow. Here several trees grew almost in a circle, forming a high barricade. They slipped between the trunks and stood up, leveling their rifles in three directions through the boughs.

Then the Rorvan charged, and for a moment it was all blaze and thunder, yelling and shooting, golden-eyed shadows rushing out of shadow and falling again. A couple of grenades were lobbed but exploded on the outside of the natural stockade. The Solarian rifles hammered, hosing explosive shells. Rorvan bullets wailed and thudded, other tommy guns were waking up, a storm of killing.

The charge broke and drew back, snarling in the moon-spattered darkness. A few wounded aliens crawled out of sight, a few dead lay emptily where they had fallen. There was a sharp reek of smoke in the chill windless air.

Stillness, for what seemed like many minutes. Then a human voice called out of the dark: "Will you parley?"

Avery's voice.

# CHAPTER XVII

"ALL RIGHT," said Gummus-lugil. "Come alone."

The moon rose higher, and a long slant of light caught the psychman as he stepped from behind a tree. There was no sight of the Rorvan, no sound from them where they lay ringing in the place of siege. After the racket of battle, it was as if an immense hush had fallen over the world.

Avery walked up to the ring of trees and looked into the mouth of a rifle. "May I come inside?" he asked gently.

"Mmmm—yes, I guess so," said Gummus-lugil.

The psychman forced his body between two boles. Lorenzen's eyes were getting used to the darkness now, he could see Avery's face vaguely, and there was no mistaking the horror that wobbled in his voice. "What do you want?" asked the astronomer harshly.

"To find out if you've gone crazy, all of you—why you turned on your hosts, friendly natives—"

Gummus-lugil laughed sardonically. Thornton shrugged and murmured: "They didn't seem very friendly when they killed Friedrich von Osten." Lorenzen made the full answer: "They aren't natives, and you know that as well as I do. You ought to! Or are you really one of them in disguise?"

"What do you mean?" cried Avery. "Are you all gone lunatic?"

"Stow it," said Lorenzen wearily. In a few cold words, he explained his conclusions. "And what has happened since certainly bears me out," he finished. "They detected our radio. They produced submachine guns as good as any at Sol. And they tried to kill us before we could call base."

Thornton whistled, and then clamped his lips thinly to-

96

gether. Avery nodded, with a great weariness. "All right," he said tonelessly. "What did you tell the camp?"

"What I've told you."

"There wouldn't have been time. Not in Morse code."

Lorenzen felt admiration for the brain behind that pudgy face. "You win," he said. "But we did get across that we were in trouble and that the Rorvan are not natives. With that much of a clue, Hamilton can put two and two together as well as I."

"You might tell the Rorvan that," said Thornton. "If they kill us, the boats from camp should be prepared to—punish them."

Suddenly Avery was raging. He shook his fist, standing there in the middle of them, and spat at the shadowy ground. "You fools! You utter blind blundering idiots! Don't you realize—the Rorvan run the Galaxy! You've set yourselves up against the Galactic Empire!"

"I wondered about that," whispered Gummus-lugil.

"Call the camp again. Tell them to stay away from here. They wouldn't have a chance. The Rorvan science is ten thousand years ahead of ours." Avery's voice dropped, becoming calmer, but he spoke fast. "It may not be too late to repair the damage. If you'll help me flange up a story that will satisfy Hamilton, things can still be patched up. But Sol must never know her true status. I'll explain why later, to you three only. But move, now! But those boats!"

Almost, he had them. The whip-crack in his voice brought Gummus-lugil's rifle down and the Turk half turned, as if to go back to his radio. Thornton's long jaw sagged.

Then Lorenzen laughed. "A nice try, Ed," he said. "Damn nice. But it won't go over, you know."

"What are you talking about? I tell you, if those boats come here they'll be disintegrated, the Rorvan will have to wipe out the whole camp and the ship."

Lorenzen's mind felt unnaturally cold and clear, it was like the high chill heaven above him. His words came hard and fast: "If the Rorvan are that good, why didn't they just annihilate us with a distintegrator beam? Or jam our radio? Why did they go through all this clumsy deception in the first place? No, Ed, you're bluffing again." With an angry snap: "And now, before God, you can tell us the truth or get out of here!"

Something broke in Avery. It was indecent, watching the sudden sag in him, how he slumped over and dropped his eyes. Lorenzen was obscurely glad the light was so dim.

"The boats ought to be loading," said Thornton. "It won't take them many minutes to fly here."

Sister was well above the mountains now, her strange face turned to a blue-green crescent ringed in by a thousand frosty stars. A low little wind sighed through the grove and rustled the leaves. Out in the shadows, two Rorvan spoke together, a dull mutter of unhuman voices; and far off, the sea pulsed on a wide beach.

"All right," whispered Avery.

"It's some plan of your clique in the government at home, isn't it?" Lorenzen thrust relentlessly against the man's buckling resistance. "You were the boys responsible for the *Da Gama* and for all our troubles, weren't you? Tell me, did you hire the Rorvan for this job?"

"No. No, they just happened to be here when the *Hudson* came." Avery spoke so soft that it was hard to make him out. "Their home lies, oh, I guess ten thousand light-years from Sol; it's an Earthlike planet, and their civilization is at about the same stage as ours, technologically. They were also hunting worlds to colonize. This expedition found Troas and was investigating it when we showed up. They saw our ship transitting the moon as we went into orbit.

"They got alarmed, of course. They couldn't know who we were, or what we intended, or . . . anything. They moved their own big ship into an orbit normal to ours and further out; naturally, not looking for any such thing, none of us have spotted it. They camouflaged their spaceboats and their camp, that job was done before we'd gotten around to photographing this particular area. For a while they watched us from space as we set up our camp and began working. It wasn't hard to guess that our intentions were the same as theirs, but of course they wanted to be sure, they wanted to know all about us while betraying as little as possible about themselves. So they decided to pose as natives . . . The party which guided us here was set down a few kilometers from our camp, after its artifacts had been manufactured, in their machine shop. It went in on foot."

"Nice idea," murmured Thornton. "The strategy is even brilliant. Naturally, we would show and tell much more to primitive natives than to alien spacemen who might be potential enemies or competitors."

"Meanwhile," resumed Avery, almost as if he hadn't heard, "the rest of them were making this fake village. A heroic labor, even with their machinery and atomic power to help. They figured the presence of civilized natives—if we could be fooled into believing that—might scare us off for good. You guessed rightly, John. So did I, as I studied their language back in camp. Little discrepancies kept popping up, things for which a psychman gets a kind of feel . . . I finally confronted Djugaz with the evidence and told him I wanted to help. Since then I've been working with the Rorvan."

"Why?" Gummus-lugil's tones roughened. "Goddam you, why?"

"I wanted to spare the *Hudson* the fate of the *Da Gama.*"

Silence again. Then: "Murdered, you mean?" growled Thornton.

"No. No, let me explain." The flat, beaten voice ran on, under the shadows and the distorted moon. "You know doctrine for a returning interstellar ship, one that's landed men on a new planet. It calls the Patrol base on Ceres, Triton, Ganymede, or Iapetus, whichever is closest, makes a preliminary report, and gets clearance for Earth. We knew the *Da Gama* would report to Ceres, and we suspected it would report Troas colonizable. So we took care to have Ceres Base staffed with men loyal to us. When the ship returned and called, it was boarded and taken over. But no one was hurt. You remember New Eden? The very beautiful planet of Tau Ceti which has civilized natives? We've made an arrangement with them. The men of the *Da Gama* are there. It isn't prison, they're free to live as they wish, we've even provided women. But we don't want them back at Sol!"

"A lot of them had families," said Gummus-lugil.

"Somebody has to suffer a little in great causes. The families have been pensioned . . . But I still wanted to spare all of you even that much. I wanted to—well, I have my own wife and kids. I was chosen by lot to be psychman for this expedition, and was ready never to see my people again. Then this looked like a chance—we could have come home in the normal way, reported failure, Troas would have been forgotten."

"All right," said Lorenzen. "So the psychocrats want to keep man from colonizing. Before long, the economic failure of interstellar travel is going to keep him from the stars completely. Now tell us why."

Avery looked up. His face was tortured, but a dim hope stirred in his tones. "It's for the best," he said eagerly. "I want you to work with me, fool Hamilton and the others when they arrive—we can talk about an unfortunate misunderstanding, a riot, some such thing—I tell you, the whole future of our race depends on it!"

"How?"

Avery looked higher, up to the cold glitter of the stars. "Man isn't ready for such a step," he said quietly. "Our race's knowledge has outstripped its wisdom before now, and we got the two-century hell from which we've just emerged. The psychodynamic men in government were opposed to the whole idea of interstellar travel. It's too late to stop that now, but we hope to choke it off by discouragement.

In a thousand years, man may be ready for it. He isn't yet.
He's not grown up enough."

"That's your theory!" snapped Gummus-lugil. "Your brain-
sick theory!"

"It is history, and the equations which interpret and explain and predict history. Science has finally gotten to a
stage where man can control his own future, his own society; war, poverty, unrest, all the things which have merely happened, uncontrollably, like natural catastrophes, can be
stopped. But first man, the entire race of man, has to mature; *every* individual must be sane, trained in critical thinking, in self-restraint. You can't change society overnight.
It will take a thousand years of slow, subtle, secret direction
—propaganda here, education there, the hidden interplay
of economics and religion and technology—to evolve the culture we want. It won't look like anything which has gone
before. Men won't be blind, greedy, pushing, ruthless animals; there will be restraint, and dignity, and contentment—
there will be thought, everyone will think as naturally as he
now breathes. *Then* we can go into the Galaxy!"

"Long time to wait," muttered Gummus-lugil.

"It is necessary, I tell you! Or do you want your race to
stay forever animal? We've expanded far enough physically;
it's past time for us to start evolving mentally—spiritually,
if you like. We . . . psychocrats . . . have a pretty good
idea of the path to be followed, the slow directed evolution
of society. We have the data, and we've set up a lot of the
initial conditions out of which Utopia will evolve. Little
things—but a university has been founded in England, and
in another two centuries Europe will again be a full member
of civilization; the balance of economic power is gradually
shifting into Asia, India will become a leading part of the
Union, the contemplative Hindu philosophy will tend to
leaven the aggressiveness of Western man . . . We have it
planned, I tell you. Not in detail, but we know where we're
going."

"I think I see," murmured Lorenzen. The wind wove around his voice, and a moonbeam flitted across his eyes. "Interstellar travel would upset this."

"Yes, yes!" Avery was speaking easily now, his tones played on them, vibrating through the grove like prophecy. "Suppose men learn that Troas is habitable. The Rorvan can't compete, they haven't our talent for military organization—that's why they were bluffing, and if the bluff fails they'll bow out and go look for another planet. It'll change the whole attitude of man. Suddenly the psychic atmosphere will become another one.

"If desultory search turned up one useable planet in twenty years, then a fleet of hunters would almost guarantee one every four or five years—more territory then we will ever need. Men will realize they *can* emigrate after all. The orientation of society will change, outward instead of inward; there will be no halting that process.

"Our psychodynamic data won't be valid any longer, we'll be as much in the dark as anyone else. The rush of emigration will produce a turmoil which we couldn't possibly control, our created conditions will vanish and we won't be able to set up new ones. The colonists will tend to be elements which were malcontent at home, and many of them will be rather unfriendly to Sol's government for a long time to come—more trouble, more unpredictability, no way to direct it at all! Before long, the scale of human society will become so big as to be forever beyond control. The idea of a unified Galaxy is nonsense, if you stop to think about it; there isn't that much trade or intercourse of any sort. A million eccentric little civilizations will spring up and go their own ways.

"Interstellar exploration will be given a tremendous boost. Absolutely unpredictable new factors will be forever entering, to prohibit stability—alien planets, alien civilizations, new knowledge about the physical universe, mutations—

"And man will again be the victim of chance. There will

be chaos and suffering, the rise and fall of whole cultures, war and oppression, from now till the end of time!"

He stopped for a little while, his words rolling away into silence. The four of them stood unmoving, huddled together inside a ring of alien guns. It was as if they waited.

"All right," said Avery at last. "You have my answer. Now I ask for yours. Will you help me explain all this away; will you go back home and keep your mouths shut for the rest of your lives? It's asking a lot of you, I know—but can you face the future you have betrayed if you don't?"

## CHAPTER XVIII

THEY STARED at each other. "You'll have to decide quickly," said the psychman. There was a sudden calm over him, he met their gaze and smiled a little in the wan half-light. "The boats will be here any minute now."

Gummus-lugil scuffed the ground with his boots. Misery twisted his face. Thornton sighed. It was Lorenzen who felt decision hard and sharp within himself, and who spoke.

"Ed," he asked, "do you *know* all this is true?"

"I've worked with it all my life, John."

"That isn't an answer. In fact, you've used more than your share of semantically loaded words tonight. I asked how certain your conclusions were about what will happen if man stays in the Solar System, and what if he doesn't."

"The first is a virtual certainty. We *know* how history can be made to go. Of course, you could always say what if a dark star crashes into our sun—but be reasonable!"

"Yet you say with one mouth that if man goes to the stars, his future is unpredictable and his future will be black."

Gummus-lugil and Thornton jerked their heads up to stare at Lorenzen.

"Unpredictable in detail," said Avery, with a ragged edge in his tone. "In general outlines, I can foresee—"

"Can you, now? I doubt it. In fact, I deny it altogether. Reality, the physical universe and all its possibilities, it's just too big to be included in any human theory. And if things go wrong somewhere in the Galaxy, there may well be other places where they go right, more right than you or anyone else could predict."

"I didn't say we should stay out of space forever, John. Only till we've learned restraint, and kindliness, and the difficult process of thinking."

"Till we've all become molded into the same pattern— *your* pattern!" said Lorenzen harshly. "I claim that man crawling into his own little shell to think pure thoughts and contemplate his navel is no longer man. I claim that with all our failures and all our sins, we've still done damn well for an animal that was running around in the jungle only two hundred lifetimes ago. I like man as he is, not man as a bunch of theorists thinks he ought to be. And one reason we've come as far as we have, is that nobody has ever forced the whole race into a copy of himself—we've always had variety, always had the rebel and the heretic. We need them!"

"Now you're getting emotional, John," said Avery.

"A neat, loaded answer, Ed, which dodges the fact that this is an emotional issue. A matter of preference and belief. Personally, I believe that no small group has the right to impose its own will on everybody else. And that's what you were doing, you psychocrats—oh, very nice and gentlemanly, sure—but I wonder how lonesome the wives of the *Da Gama* men are!"

Lorenzen turned to the others. "I vote for telling the truth, going out to the stars, and taking the consequences," he said. "Good, bad, or most likely indifferent, I want to see what the consequences are, and I think most men do."

Avery's eyes pleaded with the remaining two.

"I . . . I am with you, John," said Thornton. "Men ought to be free."

"I want that little farm," said Gummus-lugil. "And if my great-great-great-grandson can't go find his own, then the race will've gone to hell and it's too damn bad for him."

Avery turned from them, and they saw his tears.

"I'm sorry, Ed," whispered Lorenzen.

Now it was only to tell Hamilton and the rest of the crew. The *Hudson* would go home; she would not call the Patrol, but head for Earth and tell her story directly to its radios. Then it would be too late for suppression. The government would fall, there would be a new election, the psychocrats would be booted out of office. Lorenzen hoped some of them could return later; they were good men in their way and would be needed in the days to come. But it didn't matter much, one way or another, not when men were looking up again to the stars.

"I should ask the Rorvan to kill you," said Avery. His voice came thin and shaking as he wept. "I won't, but I should. You've sabotaged the real future of man, maybe the future of the entire universe. I hope you're pleased with yourselves!"

He stumbled from them, back into the forests. Lorenzen saw flitting shadows out in the night; the Rorvan were retreating. Back to their own spaceboats, he guessed. Maybe they'd take Avery with them, to hide till the anger of men had faded.

From afar he heard the nearing thunder of Hamilton's rockets.

Two men and how many aliens, as much thinking, feeling creature as they, had died, and a government and a dream would follow them, so that all men might own the sky. Had Avery been right after all?

Lorenzen knew bleakly that his last question would not be answered for a thousand years. There might never be an answer.

# The War of Two Worlds

by

POUL ANDERSON

# CAST OF CHARACTERS

## David Arnfeld

If he were such a loyal Earthman, why couldn't he hate the Martians?

## Catherine Hawthorne

She had her own code of honor, and it didn't keep her from looking behind locked doors.

## Sevni Regelin dzu Coruthan

The antennae on his forehead marked him as a Martian, but his deeds marked him as a friend of Earth.

## Fred Gellert

Was he really two people—or just a lightning-fast quick-change artist?

## Alice Hawthorne

Only three years old, she was an important pawn in an even more important war.

## Doctor Hansen

He would have been better off if he spent more time tending his patients and less time listening to newscasts.

SUNDOWN was brief, night came swiftly out of the Atlantic and flowed across the world. A few lamps blinked on in the city, but most of it lay in darkness; there was more light overhead, as the stars came forth. Intelligence Prime, lord of the Solar System, opened the window and leaned out to watch the constellations and breathe the warm air that sighed in from the endless Brazilian lands. A lovely world, he thought, a broad fair planet, this Earth—one to fight for, to seize and hold like a beloved mate.

It was not risky for him to appear at the window. His secret office was so high above darkened Sao Paulo that the very noises were lost.

Up here there was only the slow sad wind, quiet and loneliness everywhere.

He sighed, turning away as the lights strengthened automatically in the room. Weariness lay like a weight on his shoulders.

The hunt was over, yes, this last episode was finished—but was it? And what would come after? So much to do, so terribly few to do it; he himself, chosen ruler of his people, was a slave to their own conquest. What would strike at them next, and how soon? When could they ever know peace under friendly stars?

He sat down at his desk, shoving the vague despair out of his mind with an effort. Overwork, nervous strain, it was no more than that, he thought irritably. And there was no place for it in this enormous age. He took up some papers, reports from Mars, and began studying them.

A chime sounded, jarring him in the great quiet. When would they ever let him get his work done? "Come in," he

5

said. The annunciator carried his voice to the ante-chamber, and the door opened.

Intelligence Prime looked up as the sub-officer entered. "What do you want?" he asked. "I'm busy."

The sub-officer halted, and one arm rose in a rubbery motion, a salute. "It's more on the Arnfeld case, lord," he said. "Some new material, just brought to me."

"Well, let's see it, then. Don't just stand there. Death and corruption, this business was the tightest spot we've been in since the Exodus."

The sub-officer moved slowly across the floor and laid the book on the desk. "They found it while taking that cabin apart, lord," he said. "Apparently Arnfeld was making a last attempt to tell the story to his people—he'd hidden it under the floorboards."

"Pathetic, in a way," said Intelligence Prime. "I can admire that creature and his friends. They were a brave group. Even the woman who betrayed them at the last did so for a selfless reason."

The cold light of the flouros gleamed off his great crested head as he bent over the relic. It was a school notebook, torn and dirty, and the first few pages held a child's scrawl, a few arithmetic sums, a clumsy drawing. Then the adult hand began, and the rest of the book was filled with it—a firm masculine writing, small and close together, obviously done in haste.

"Rather long," he said. "Must have taken Arnfeld several days to finish this, at least."

"They had several days in the cabin, didn't they, lord?" asked the sub-officer.

"Yes, I suppose so." The bleak eyes studied the first sentences: *This is being written by David Mark Arnfeld, a citizen of the United States of America, planet Earth, on 21 August 2043. I am of sound mind and body, and investigation of my service psychiatric record will show that I can hardly have gone insane as has been claimed. I wish only to tell the whole truth in a matter that concerns all of my race and all of Mars.*

"Hm." Intelligence Prime looked thoughtfully up. "We'll have to see about altering his record, just in case somebody does think to check it." He grinned. "I have Mr. Arnfeld to thank for reminding me of that!"

"It seems to be an account of—"

"I can see that for myself. Bring me the woman, I want to question her about this."

"Yes, lord. At once." The sub-officer glided from the room.

Intelligence Prime continued his perusal. *In order to overlook no detail which will give verisimilitude and which can be checked to confirm my story, I will tell everything that has happened, down to minute details of conversation and subjective impressions as nearly as I can remember or reconstruct them. If this lends my work the appearance of fiction, I regret it, but implore anyone who reads this to take it secretly—I cannot overemphasize the need for secrecy —to Rafael Torreos, formerly colonel of the U. N. Inspection Service, in Sao Paulo, Brazil, and give it directly into his hands.*

*And I must be allowed a little latitude anyway. I once wanted to be a writer, and have whiled away many hours by scribbling. Since this is probably the last writing I shall ever do, you must let me tell the story in my own way.*

"Torreos," mused Intelligence Prime. "The woman did not mention his name . . . Oh, yes. He's been working with the Martians . . . Hm, yes, we'd better take care of him pretty soon, just in case."

The chime sounded again. The door opened, silently, and two guards accompanied the sub-officer into the room. Between them was a woman. She could have been a goodlooking creature in happier circumstances, thought Intelligence Prime; even now, her hair was a tangled web of gold that caught the light in a thousand shimmers. But her face was thin and white, her eyes were reddened, and she trembled unceasingly.

"Christine Hawthorne," he asked without preliminary, "have you seen this book before?" His voice was quiet, toneless, and he shaped his vocal cords to speak unaccented English.

"Where is my child?" she answered harshly. "What have you done with her?"

"The child is being well cared for," he said. "It will be restored to you in due course, if you cooperate with me."

"Haven't I done enough?" she asked dully. "Wasn't it enough that I sold out Dave and Reggy and my whole race?"

"What you cannot seem to understand," said Intelligence Prime with a chill in his words, "is the finality of our victory. David Arnfeld and Regelin dzu Coruthan are dead. The bodies are in our possession, what is left of them. Why—you killed them yourself!"

"I know," she said.

"Their story, such little of it as ever came out, has been totally refuted, buried, forgotten. You, the last survivor, are our prisoner—officially dead yourself, and we will never let you go. It behooves you to act accordingly. Now, have you seen this book before?"

She came closer and looked down at it. "Yes," she said at last. "It was lying in the cabin when we got there. Dave wrote in it, day after day, and finally he hid it, just before the end. He didn't tell me or Reggy where he was going to hide it, so we couldn't tell you if we should be captured alive."

"He might have known we would make a *thorough* search. Still, he had nothing to lose." Intelligence Prime jerked his thumb. "Take her away." As the group reached the door, he added with an impulse of kindliness: "You might as well give her the child, too."

"Thank you," she whispered.

The door closed behind them. Intelligence Prime sighed and leaned back, the tiredness flowing into him again. It had been a long hunt.

Well—he'd better read this thing himself. The full account

of the episode, told from the enemy's side, might contain some useful hints.

He skimmed briefly over the autobiographical paragraph. Those details he knew. David Arnfeld had been born in 2017 in upstate New York, of an old and wealthy family. He had been only five years old when the war broke out; at twelve he had been selected for Lunar Academy, at sixteen he had graduated directly into spatial service, and since then most of his time had been spent as officer on various spaceships and interplanetary bases. At twenty-five he had been exec of Pallas Base, and then the war had ended and he had come home.

Intelligence Prime squinted, cursing the close handwriting, and began to read with more interest.

I

WE GOT the news from a courier boat, several weeks after the event, because the radio had been out for quite a while. We'd been expecting to hear of Earth's defeat, the end had been in sight when the Martians took Luna, but nevertheless the word left a hollowness in us. Many men wept. I couldn't cry, somehow, but I went through my duties in a mechanical fashion, and my inward self seemed to have withdrawn. It was worst during sleep-period, lying there in the dark and loneliness, and staring at nothing.

There was plenty to do, and I was glad of that, it kept me from thinking. I was virtual commander of the asteroid, the Old Man had gone into an unspeaking numbness and we hardly ever saw him. I had to wind up the paper work, of course, and there was a lot; I had to oversee the engineers and make sure they didn't sabotage the installations. Once I caught a man at that, he was deliberately wrecking the safety controls on our main power pile so it would blow out sooner or later. When I put him on the carpet, he was truculent. "Are we going to turn this over to the Marshies?" he demanded. "Are we just going to give it to them, and kiss their skinny bums into the bargain?"

"The proper form of address for a superior officer is 'sir,' " I answered wearily. "We have orders from HQ, which is acting under the armistice agreement, to yield this base in good condition, and I'm going to see that those orders are carried out." Loosening up a bit, I added: "Mars has us by the throat. If we don't do as they say, it'll go hard with Earth. You have a family there, don't you?"

"Maybe," he said. "And maybe they were killed in the bombardment."

"We gave them a good fight," I said. "Twenty years of it. Maybe we can get our revenge later, but that won't be for a long time yet. Meanwhile, yes, we will kiss the Martians if it's necessary to keep our people alive."

I let him off with ten days in hack, but posted a warning that the next offense meant a summary court-martial. By and large, the men knew I was right. Something had gone out of them, they were beaten, and it was not a pleasant thing to see. I invented jobs for them, games, exercises, anything to jerk them back toward life, but it went slowly.

We had a four months' wait without a sign from HQ. I began to worry, we'd been on short rations for a long while and now our supplies were terribly low. I wondered if I shouldn't violate orders myself, commandeer a rocket, and go after help. Hilton's Planetoid wasn't far away now, as astronomical distances go, and they had hydroponics and yeast vats there.

The asteroid spun swiftly through a great cold dark, between a million frosty stars and the glittering belt of the Milky Way. The sun was remote, a tiny heatless disc whose light was pale on the cruel jagged rocks. Outside the base proper, it was always silent, your breathing felt thick inside the helmet.

The relief came at last, without warning: four great troop-ships orbiting up with a vivid splash of rocket flame, and the lean black form of a Martian cruiser for convoy. We lined up as smartly as we could and received the officers with all due ceremony. For we were Pallas Base and the fighting men of Earth's United Nations, we had beaten off three murderous attacks in a year and we had lasted out the long grinding wait between them. I think the Martian commander was pleased at our appearance. He didn't offer to shake hands, which was tactful of him, but he bowed his seven-foot body stiffly from the waist in the best manner of their military aristocracy.

"Are you in charge, Commander?" he asked. He spoke in Portuguese, and did it better than I. The Brazilian dialect may be the dominant tongue of Earth, but we were mostly Britons and *Norteamericanos* here and had used English.

"At the moment, Sevni," I answered as formally. "Captain Roberts is—indisposed." As a matter of fact, I knew the Old Man was in bed with a bottle, probably crying as he often did these days, but there was no reason to admit it.

"I am sorry for the delay in relieving you," said the Martian. "But there has been much work to do, as you will understand. The ships here will discharge our men, and then take yours back to Earth. We will set you all down at Quito, and provide you with tickets to whatever major cities are nearest your homes."

"You are very kind," I said.

"Thank you." The Martian waved one lean hand. I was struck anew by the odd fact that it isn't the six fingers or their extra joint or the smooth, leathery-brown skin which makes a Martian hand look unhuman to me, it's the peculiarly squared nails. "There has been too much strife. It is time for friendship between our peoples."

*Friendship?* I thought. *After what you did to Earth?*

We were embarked and settled down for the long run

homeward. Most of the time, of course, we orbited, and I forced the men to exercise regularly. After the long time of low asteroid gravity, and now the many weeks in free fall, we wouldn't be used to Earth-weight. I think I got all of us into pretty good shape—underfed, naturally, but hard and supple, darkened by the harsh spatial sunlight.

The officers and crew aboard were Martian, but they kept to themselves, we hardly ever saw them, and the trip went without incident. Toward the end of it, I noticed the apathy breaking in our men and in myself. Defeated or not, we were going *home!* The old worn photographs came out again, the torn and smudged letter flimsies, voices were heard in argument and reminiscence and even song. There were plans made for an annual reunion, and out of my bitterness I began to see that there had been some good times, now and then, in all these lost years.

We took orbits around Earth, and I spent a long while at the viewport, staring at her as she turned, blue and beautiful, against the stars. There was no sign of the war on her serene face—man and Martian were small things, after all, and space and time were very big.

Ferries took us down to Quito in relays. It had been heavily blitzed, it was still one vast ruin, full of broken rocks and dead men's bones, but the radioactivity was gone by now and the mountains were as lovely as I remembered them. A new spacefield had been built, with a huddle of shacks around it that might eventually become a reborn city. I didn't kneel to kiss Earth, as many did, but I stretched my muscles against the glorious massive feel of her pull and I drew the clean sharp air deeply into my lungs, and my eyes blurred for a while.

Terrestrial liaison officers met me and I spent a couple of days in the routine of disbanding my unit. The men got their tickets and back pay, with a bit extra to make up for the inflation that was putting the knife into our dying economy; they got ration books appropriate to the areas where they lived, and a printed pamphlet describing the new laws and enjoining obedience to the occupation authorities. They got their discharge papers too, but what with the clothing shortage we were allowed to wear our uniforms sans insignia. I looked at the Winged Star for a long time after it was off my tunic, before wrapping it up and slipping it into my pocket.

The human district commander, Gonzales, saw me off. "Won't you stay for a while?" he invited. "I would not advise going to New York. It was badly hit. Conditions are hard."

"Things are bad everywhere, senor," I answered.

"Aye, so. We are thrown back to a primitive economy which cannot support our population." He grimaced. "You are fortunate to have arrived almost a year late. Last winter and spring—ugh!"

"Famine?"

"And plague. The Martians could do little to help us, though I must admit they tried. But millions are dead already, and still it goes on." He looked grayly across the field. Our Globe and Olive Branch still flew, but Mars' Double Crescent banner was on a higher staff. "It is the end of human independence," he said. "From now on, we are cattle."

"We'll come back," I said. "Give us twenty years to recover, and we'll rearm and—"

He winced. "I think I would almost rather have Martian rule than the kind of fascism that would entail, Commander," he said. "However, they do not intend to let us try. We are to be de-industrialized and made a province. They will keep us that way forever—you know the Martian nature. They are not vindictive, but they are careful, farseeing, and very patient."

I thought it was a Draconian measure. Our population would likely have to be halved before we could return to an agricultural economy—and then there would be unending centuries of humans turned into peasants, handicraftsmen, fishers and loggers and miners; at best we could only become lesser bureaucrats in the Martian imperium. We would stay here, shackled by ignorance, while science and industry and the soaring starward adventure went to Mars.

Still—in their place, I'd have done the same! We had so many natural advantages, we'd come so close to annihilating them—oh, if there'd been some brains on the General Staff, we could have taken Mars in five years! Instead, we made one ghastly blunder after another, and only the fact that the Martians made almost as many had kept us going. Of course, this was the first space war in history, one couldn't expect to foresee everything, but it was weird how both sides had fumbled it and turned what might have been a sharp, clean blow into twenty ruinous years of attrition.

Well—too late now. Too late forever.

"Farewell, Commander," said Gonzales. "And good luck to you."

"And to you," I said, shaking his hand. "To all of us."

"We'll all need it, Commander," he said.

The rocket flight to New York was uneventful. My fellow passengers, all human, all shabbily clad and grim about the mouth, plied me with questions about the space war, and I was as eager to learn about what had happened at home. I hadn't been on Earth for five years. Well, the last several months had been rugged—atomic bombardment from space, capitulation, famine and plague. Our transportation and manufacturing centers had been so thoroughly wrecked that it hadn't been possible to feed the huge urban majority, or take care of them in any way. Crime and anarchy had risen out of the ruins and still snarled around the world, though the Martian occupation forces were now cooperating with U. N. and local police to smash that violence.

"And it'll get worse," said an American gloomily. "There's years of hunger in front of us, before the population is down far enough. We can't do anything to recover. The Marshies are systematically dismantling whatever important industry we have left. There won't be any in five or six years. We'll be traveling by sailboat and horseback. This rocket line here is scheduled to be confiscated in another few months, when its most urgent freight-hauling duties are over."

"We gotta fight," said another man. "There ain't many of them. Mebbe five million Marshie troops, spread thin in, uh, garrisons all over this planet. They got the gravity against 'em, too. We got to get together and throw 'em out."

"With what?" I asked wearily. "Hunting rifles and kitchen knives? Against artillery, machine-guns, flame throwers, armor, aircraft? And don't forget their bases on the moon, either. Any time we act up, they can shoot some more rockets at us."

"You've surrendered, spaceman?" A young, prematurely hard-looking woman gave me a contemptuous glance.

"I guess so," I said. "If you want to call it that."

## II

WE LANDED near evening, and I went up in the control tower of the clumsily rebuilt airport and spent a very long and quiet while looking over the city. They'd told me New York had had it bad, but I'd never realized it would be like this.

The haughty skyline of Manhattan was a jumble of steel skeletons, stripped, snapped off, and stark against the sky. Some of the buildings had caught a freakish heat-gust and melted where they stood, so that they were brittle crags of lumpy, twisted, fire-blackened steel.

Outside the great bowl of the main crater, it was all rubble, a dead wilderness of heaped rock, and I saw dust and ash scudding over it in the wind. Brooklyn was another tumbled ruin, though a few empty shells still tottered erect. Haze and gathering dusk hid the remainder of the city from me, but I saw no lights anywhere, no lights at all.

The human airport chief, who had let me climb up to see, nodded wearily at me when I came down. "I warned you against going, Commander Arnfeld," he said. His voice was flat, gray as his face. The eyes were sunken and feverish. "It's—ugly."

"How many live here now?" I asked.

He shrugged. "Who knows? A million, perhaps. Those who could, fled out into the country when the famine and diseases got under way; there were plenty of battles between farmers and the mobs. Now we truck in some food, and we can offer jobs at rubble clearing and so on, so conditions are a little better. Not much, but a little."

"How'll I get upstate?" I asked. "My home is there."

"Shank's mare, Commander, unless you can hitch a ride on one of the farm wagons. But they don't like city people since last winter."

"Well—" I looked out the window. Airport lights were feeble against the darkness that flowed in from the sea. "I'd better stay here overnight, then. Can you recommend a place?"

"How much money you got?"

I grinned without humor. "Back pay, fifty thousand U. N. dollars. Inflation allowance, one million."

"That allowance was decided on four months ago. Now it'll just about buy three meals and two nights' lodging. The city has to pay its workers in food, clothes, and what little medical care we can offer." He tugged nervously at his ear lobe, avoiding my eyes. "I wish I could put you up for the night, Commander, but there are seven of us in one room as it is, and—"

"I know. Thanks, but I'll find something."

"Try the Benedictine Hostel. Little group of monks got together, built a shack, and put up anyone who'll help with the work. If there's any room left at all, they'll give you a doss and let you help with the chores."

"Suits me. I'll even contribute something—say half a million dollars."

"They'd appreciate it. They have a lot of cripples to look after, who can't work." He gave me directions; it was about three miles off. "But be careful," he warned. "Plenty of gangsters around. They'd as soon kill you as look at you. The last few months made people pretty desperate."

I slapped my holstered Magnum repeater. As an officer, I'd been allowed to keep my sidearm. And my spaceman's gray ought to get me some respect too—unless somebody decided to kill me for the suit.

It wasn't entirely dark yet, but the dusk was thick as I walked from the airport. I wasn't sorry; it blurred the gaunt buildings on either side of the street, empty windows and gaping doorways, now and then a burnt wreck. There weren't many others abroad, and they shuffled unspeakingly past, without aim, without hope. The silence was complete—utter blank quiet, dense and heavy, making the noise of my boots and the whimper of raw wind unnaturally loud. I walked faster, hoping to find light and kindliness.

The hand on my arm sent me leaping away, whirling around and yanking the pistol out with a snarl. When I saw that it was a woman, I knew how tensed I had been. My heartbeat was a fury in my ears.

"Hello, spaceman," she said.

I lowered the gun and took a step toward her. "What do you want?" Trying to hold my voice steady, I made it a harsh snap.

"I—well—" She looked away from me, cringing back into the doorway where she had stood. Approaching closer, I saw her draw a shuddering breath and square her thin shoulders and turn back to face me.

"Want shelter tonight?" she asked.

I looked at her for a long while, not saying anything.

"You're just in from space, aren't you?" Her voice was very low, and it wavered. But it wasn't a slum voice; she had been well educated.

"Yes," I said.

"Well, do you want to stay with me tonight?" She had to gulp before she could get it out. "I have a place."

I went up and stood before her, peering into the gloom to make her out. She was medium tall, and her figure must have been good once, but the legs under the tattered dress were pathetically thin. Young, too—early twenties. Her face was pale, the cheekbones stark under enormous eyes, but her nose had a pert tilt to it and her mouth was soft and gentle. She was trembling and breathing hard, not able to meet my gaze.

"Who are you?" I asked.

Her voice lifted raggedly, "Look, don't be this way. If you —want me, then say so. Otherwise, get on—please!"

I had been almost ten years in space, rarely seeing Earth or a human colony, so I knew a prostitute when I met one. "This is your first try, isn't it, sis?" I asked.

She nodded mutely.

"The city offers jobs," I said. "You don't have to do this."

"All the jobs left open are too heavy for me." Her tone was a mumble now. "I can't haul bricks—I tried it and collapsed. I can't get out into the country. No room left there, even if the farmers would take in another stray. And I've got a little girl to look after."

I shook my head, smiling with an effort. "Sorry, sis. I can't take advantage of you that way."

"If it isn't you, it'll be someone else," she said hopelessly. "I'd rather it was you. My husband was a spaceman."

I came to a decision. "How much do you—charge?"

"I—" A dry whisper. "Half a million. Is that too much?"

"Well," I said, "I'm looking for shelter, and you seem to have a place. I'll pay half a million for bed and breakfast—and nothing else."

That's when she started to cry. I held her close till it was over, stroking the long gold hair that was still beautiful. Her dress, I noticed, had been fairly good once, and it was almost painfully clean; how she'd managed that, without soap, I didn't know. Sand and water, maybe.

We walked hand in hand toward her dwelling. She guided me deftly through heaps of rubble, smashed stone, broken girders, sharded glass, now and then a human bone. It was altogether dark, and I often stumbled.

A big hotel had collapsed freakishly, leaving a cave in its mountain of ruin. She had camouflaged the entrance with a couple of splintered doors and one of the bushes which had begun growing here and there in the city.

We crawled through a narrow tunnel to a hole roughly seven feet square and four feet high. It was as clean as her dress, and almost as drab: a few salvaged utensils, a mattress, a dim oil lamp, and some books. There was a girl playing on the floor, a pretty little three-year-old with her mother's shining hair and huge green eyes. She ran to the woman, who took her up and murmured to her.

"You weren't lonely, Alice, were you?"

"Oh, no, mom-muh, I finked up Hoppy an' Hoppy came sat down on a lamp an' he got big eyes an' wings an' you brought'a daddy home wif you an' Hoppy says—"

I sat down in the corner. "You'd have let your daughter watch?" I sneered. There was an emptiness in my breast.

She turned on me with a flare of rage. "If you don't like it," she yelled, "get out! You've been taken care of, you had food and work and order around you, if you died it would've been quick and decent. You didn't have any gangs to hide from, anyone else to keep alive—go on, get out of here!"

"I'm sorry," I said, "I wasn't trying to be holier than thou. A man who helped bombard Zuneth can't look down on anyone."

"You were there?" Her anger ebbed from her, and she smiled. "That was our greatest victory. We must have killed a million Marshies then."

"Yeah," I said. "Hit 'em from space, just as they hit Earth later on. A million living, feeling creatures blown to bloody shreds. I'm not proud of it."

"I'd like to kill every one of them," she murmured. "Every last damned one."

"Forget it," I said. I thumbed through the books, which, from their markings, she had dug out of the library. Shakespeare, the Greek tragedies, Goethe's *Faust* in German, Whitman, Benet, and—sentimentally—Brooke. Yes, she was of good family. I thought of her huddled in here, reading *The Trojan Women,* and shook my head.

"What's your name?" I asked.

"Christine Hawthorne," she said. "My friends called me Kit." I saw a flush go up her cheeks after that impulse; she thought she'd inadvertently given me a come-on after all.

"No fears, Kit," I said, "I'm what they call normal, and haven't seen a woman in a long time, but—No fears. I'm Dave Arnfeld."

We talked for a long time. She had, like me, grown up in war, but until last year the strife had been far from Earth and she'd enjoyed a fairly decent existence. Her people had been well-to-do, cultured and cosmopolitan, she'd traveled and gone to college and known something of our heritage. Four years ago she'd met Lieutenant James Hawthorne— she showed me the faded picture of his boyish, pleasant face—and married him; but he was dead in the Battle of Juno when she bore his child. A linguist in Comcenter, she'd been at home when New York was destroyed, only a miraculous improbability had saved her and the girl, Alice. After that it had been the usual tigerish struggle to keep alive, until her will finally broke. It was coming back now, though, I could see resolution rising in her.

Only what good was that when there was nothing she could do to live?

"Where are you going?" she asked me.

"Upstate," I said. "I own a place near Albany, inherited it from my parents, and no one else is alive but me. It'll have gone pretty much to pot, but I can start it up again, I hope. Turn farmer—there isn't much else for a man to do, these days."

I knew what she was thinking, but pride made her try to

change the subject. "I didn't think there were many Germans up that way."

"Swedish, if you please," I laughed. "Though most of the stock is Dutch and English from colonial days."

*We fought the nation's battles since the French and Indian War. Now we've gone down to defeat with her.*

"Look," I said, "I'll need a housekeeper and general assistant. You seem to be tough. Why not come along?"

She held the child close. "It's a dangerous trek," she said.

"All right," I snapped, out of weariness and hunger. "Stay here then."

We quarreled for a while, made it up, and went to sleep. She agreed, of course. And I saved half a million dollars.

Breakfast was a quarter can of corned beef, with water lugged from the river. After that we took the kitchenware and started out. Most of the time I carried Alice, who was a gentle, quiet kid. She didn't seem too scarred by what she had been through, though Kit said she often screamed at night.

"When she gets older," I said, "you'd better get a psychiatrist to work on that trauma." Then I remembered that there probably wouldn't be any psychiatrists for Earth. Half-trained doctors would be the best we could hope for, because skilled men might do something with bacteria against the Martians.

It took us most of that day to get out of the city, and hunger was sharp within us. My uniform got me permission to buy food and a night's rest in a hayloft from one farmer, but he warned me that he was an exception.

"I thought we were all Earthmen together," I said.

"So did I, once," he answered. "Then the mobs and gangs came out o' town. I was lucky, so I ain't bitter about it, but men who seen their houses burned and their kids killed and their women attacked and their grain and livestock stole— they ain't gonna be so friendly. It's all the city can do to make 'em sell anything."

"I see," I said.

"Your being a spacer might be dangerous, too," he said. "A lot o' people are mad about the whole war. There's stories that Earth started it—mebbe the Marshies planted that rumor, I dunno, but it's a fact you spacers bungled it so they could grab the moon and blitz us."

"I wasn't in charge," I said. "But then, I imagine people in your situation can't be expected to be very logical."

Thereafter I turned bandit. Military training and good physical condition helped. I stole a horse and wagon so we could ride, a cow to give us milk, chickens and vegetables for food—just marched in and took them at gun point, with a promise to return them with rent money as soon as possible.

The law was slack, we had no trouble with the overburdened police; but a couple of times we were shot at. Kit bore it bravely, death was a little thing to her who had seen so much of it. She was already beginning to fill out and get some color, she'd soon be striking.

We rolled and bumped through the green countryside, and memories came like drawn knives. This village, that monument, the river shining between long hills, I knew them all, I remembered. I was often silent, and Kit would smile and touch my hand.

The day came, nearly two weeks later, when we turned off the main highway and went along a rutted gravel road. My heart was loud in my breast, and I rose in the wagon and swept my arm around the horizon. "Ours," I said.

Kit's green eyes widened. "All of it?"

"Four hundred acres," I told her, and there was a high pride in my voice. I hadn't known till now just what a rootless shadow life mine had been, flitting between the worlds like a hunted ghost.

The fields were well cared for, full of young grain. I assumed the neighbors had worked them. Well, good, I'd settle for shares and have something to start on next spring. If they didn't want to share—my hand dropped to my gun.

But no, that wouldn't arise, the Smiths and Rackhams and Challengers were old friends. I was home again.

The grove of trees about the gate was still there, and I saw the long double line of beeches flanking the drive up to the big white Colonial house. That was all I saw before an oath ripped from me and my gun clanked free. Kit shrieked and snatched her daughter to her.

The Martian at the gate slanted his rifle up to cover me. "Halt!"

## III

THERE WAS no help for it. The enemy had decided to quarter an officer here, and I was cruelly impotent to change the fact.

We were conducted up the drive under guard, and the officer himself came out on the wide, colonnaded porch. Sunlight streamed through the trees of Earth to dapple his alien face. I stood for a silent moment, studying that countenance.

There are those who call the Martians ugly, but that isn't true, not even by human standards. Consider the long straight legs, the lean waist and arms, the tremendous breadth of chest and shoulder—it isn't a caricature of man, in some ways it is a refinement. The head, with its hairless brown skin, high cheekbones, domed forehead, narrow chin, and long pointed ears, might have been sculptured by Brancusi; the small flat nose does not break that symmetry, the mobile mouth could be human, and the big, slant, golden eyes, under the graceful little antennae, are certainly things of luminous beauty.

Nevertheless, as he stood there in his flawless black uniform, with silvered collar and the Double Crescent on his breast, I hated him.

He waited impassively for us to speak, meanwhile considering my dusty grays. The transparent third lids were drawn across his eyes against the glare of the westering sun; it gave him a blind, remote look.

I gathered all my military dignity and said flatly: "I am David Mark Arnfeld, former commander in the United Nations Interplanetary Forces, and owner of this property. May I ask the meaning of your presence, Sevni?"

He looked at me for a while longer. My medium height, stocky build, and blunt, lined face hardly fitted in with his notion of an aristocrat. But finally he bowed. "I am honored, sir," he said. "There is a likeness of you in the living room, and I have wondered if you would be returning." His English was fluent, though too crisp to be native. Vannzaru is a harsh language, half of it up in the supersonic range where humans can't talk or hear. "Permit me to introduce myself. I am Sevni Regelin dzu Coruthan, representing the Archate of Mars in this district." His face remained wooden, but his eyes flickered an inquiry toward Kit, where she stood looking defiantly at him.

"This young lady is a guest of mine," I said coldly. I wanted to add: "And you are not," but he understood my implication well enough.

"Please come in," he said. With the curiously tender Martian smile: "Or perhaps I should wait for you to invite me." Then he dismissed the guards with a curt order.

We entered the cool dimness of the house. It was as I had known it, polished hardwood floors, golden oak wainscoting, burnished glass and silver, the old books and pictures and furniture, all here. I wanted to cry. But I turned to Regelin instead and asked for an explanation; I made it so chill as to be insolent.

He explained courteously. Most of the occupation forces on Earth were in garrisons, but individual officers were spotted over the planet as observers and local administrators.

He was in charge of the whole New England area. It had been decided to quarter him and his guards and assistants— ten in all—in this unoccupied house, since that would be inconveniencing nobody. "I am afraid it is too late to change now," he said. "But we will try to keep out of your way, and of course you will be paid a fair rent."

"Very nice of you, isn't it?" exploded Kit. Her hair swirled about her shoulders as she turned on him, where he stood looming a foot and a half above her. "After you've burned our homes and killed our people and ruined our planet, it's easy to be polite, isn't it? I suppose you think you're being generous!"

"Kit," I said. "Kit, please."

"I fear the lady is overwrought," said Regelin. He faced around to me. "I have to warn you, Mr. Arnfeld, that while it is not the Archon's intention to interfere unduly with the private lives of Terrestrials, any attempt at sabotage or obstruction of his purposes will be severely punished."

"All right," I said. "You've got us by the damper rods."

Wistfulness flitted across the dark face. "I would like to be friends," he said. "We are both spacemen. I was at Juno and the Second Orbit, among other battles, and lost comrades, even as you did. Can we not forget old grudges now that the war is over?"

"No," I said.

"As you wish, Mr. Arnfeld." He bowed and left me, his tall form erect.

The Martians were considerate guests. They moved out of the quarters they had held and took over the north wing of the house, where there were several rooms they converted into offices and a dormitory; they left the rest of the house strictly alone, except at mealtimes. A sentry was always at the gate and one at the north door, pacing slowly back and forth. You saw the staff whiz in and out on their scooterbugs, reporting to Regelin where he worked, but they weren't noisy. They often sat in the garden or strolled through the woods, but if you chanced to meet one he would jump up and bow. We never returned the greeting.

In many ways, they were actually an asset. They had made arrangements with the neighbors about my land, so that was taken care of. They had installed their own power plant, so we had all the electricity we wanted. They had found domestic help, an elderly couple named Hoose who lived in the servant cottage behind the mansion. Their rent payment was generous, and helped my finances a lot. All in all, I had nothing against them except that they were Martians. The conquerors.

Meals were awkward affairs to begin with. Military etiquette insisted that Regelin use the dining room, while his men ate in the big kitchen. After a few dreary meals together, with silence on both sides, we made a tacit agreement: Regelin ate an hour ahead of Kit, Alice, and myself. Then we hardly ever saw him.

I couldn't help feeling sorry for the Martians. They were a long way from home, and Earth's conditions were barely tolerable for them. The dragging weight, the air pressure, heat, humidity, sun-glare, even the blatant, swarming greenness, were hard to endure.

"Though at that," I remarked once to Kit, "they're luckier than we would have been occupying Mars."

She frowned, the tiny crease between arched brows which I found so endearing. "Why?" she asked.

"Well, they can live here without special equipment, if they must," I said. "But put a man on Mars, without an airsuit or a dome around him, and he'd choke to death immediately. At that, he'd freeze almost as fast, after dark anyway."

"They don't breathe at all, do they?" she asked.

"Oh, yes," I said, "but it isn't our kind of breathing. A Martian's lungs are very different from ours—huge spongy masses that not only draw oxygen from the air but get it out of food—symbiosis with anaerobic bacteria. Their metabolism is pretty strange all around, though I suppose ours looks as odd to them." I sat back, longing for a cigarette. Sunlight streamed in the window and caressed Kit's hair. "They're a lot tougher than we, they can stand more punishment. Though physically we did have a whale of a big advantage in the war, in that we could endure twice the acceleration they could." I scowled. "If Admiral Swayne had had the sense to use that fact, we wouldn't have lost at the Trojans. And that was a critical battle, some say it was the turning point of the war."

"Too late now, Dave," she sighed.

She was giving most of her time to Alice, the rest went to helping with the housekeeping, working in the garden, reading, or listening to our extensive music library. It was a quiet life, but mother and daughter were blooming under it. As for me, I found the hours rather heavy on my hands. I couldn't assist the neighbors much, having no farm experience at all, and though they were teaching me what they could they didn't have a lot of time to spare for that. I took long walks, rode horseback, puttered around the house, visited old friends, went down to the village or to Albany for an occasional spree. I tried to write, but that didn't come to much. What was there to write about, these days?

It was frank boredom which finally drove me to talk to Regelin. I had wandered from the house into the woods, following a dim old trail. It was quiet here, a rustle of leaves, a twitter of birds, a squirrel running like red fire up a mossy trunk. I had some heavy thinking to do.

*Let's face it, boy,* I told myself, *Kit is beginning to mean a lot to you. Call it propinquity if you like, the fact remains she's a brave and loyal and intelligent girl and it's about time you settled down anyway. Only—damn it!—she owes me too much! She's given no sign of anything but friendship for me, I think Jim Hawthorne is still very much with her. Or is he? How should I know? I've seen too little of women, I've been too nearly a monk, to tell what they're thinking. . . . If I asked her to marry me, she'd probably say yes out of gratitude and to give her daughter a home—but I don't want that. Gentlemanly instincts again? Hell, no, just masculine ego. But I can't get rid of it.*

I was getting nowhere. It was almost a relief to come around a thicket and see Regelin. He was alone, tall and stiff and black-uniformed, but his face was buried in a cluster of wild roses.

He turned, though I tried to retreat softly. Martians have preternaturally keen ears in our dense atmosphere. I couldn't read his face, but he laughed harshly, embarrassed.

"How do you do, Mr. Arnfeld," he said. "You seem to have caught me in a strategically bad position."

I grinned, enjoying his discomfiture. "Aren't officers allowed to smell flowers?" I asked.

"Oh, we have a different etiquette on Mars," he said eagerly. "Our officer corps is recruited from the old aristocracy, you know, and its members are expected to have an esthetic sense." He touched the frail blossoms. "Exquisite," he whispered. Then: "However, you of Earth seem to feel that manliness includes—ah—a certain blindness to such matters."

I leaned against a tree bole and shoved my hands in my pockets. "Your civilization is older than ours," I said, rather cruelly. "Some have called it decadent."

He bowed, with ice in his eyes, and turned to go.

"No, wait." Impulsively, I went after him, even took his arm. "I'm sorry. There was nothing decadent about the way you whipped us at Juno."

"I understand your grace," he said. It was the old Martian formula for accepting an apology.

"Sit down, if you're not in a hurry." I lowered myself to a fallen trunk, and after a moment he joined me. We sat quietly under the sun-spattered shadows till he said, slowly and without looking at me:

"Yes, forty thousand years of recorded history is a long time. But it never got off its planet, we weren't technically minded, and it had fallen into feudalism when you came. You taught us to build machines, draw energy from the atom; your challenge and example drew us together into the Tarketh dzu Zanthevu—Archate of Mars, as you call it. We had, of a sudden, new hope and new strength, and our eyes turned starward. The younger taught the older. Mars owes much to Earth."

"But you destroyed us," I said. I felt no bitterness just then, in that oddly suspended moment; it was as if we were old comrades talking of something that had happened centuries past.

"In self-defense," he said, equally low. "You declared war on us."

"After your fleet seized Hera."

"We had to. You claimed the asteroid group from which we got most of our thorium, and were about to grab it. We needed a defensive base."

"Let's not hash it over," I said. "It's a long, ugly story of growing commercial and military rivalry, clashing imperialisms, rising tensions. It finally blew up in our faces."

Regelin shook his head. The light turned to molten gold in his eyes. "I cannot understand it," he said. "I am a military man, not an Assembly politician or a Cabinet noble, so perhaps I do not grasp some essential fact. But *why* should that rivalry have built up? Why should one incident after another have strained relations between our planets? There was enough in space for both of us."

"I don't know," I said. "It often puzzled me, too. Of course, we were told it was a matter of Martian aggressiveness, and you were no doubt told the same thing about us. Now the propaganda blanket is so thick we'll never get at the facts."

"Even so," he said, "it should have been a short war—a limited war for limited goals, such as you Earthlings used to have in your fifteenth or eighteenth centuries." I blinked, surprised that he'd studied so much of our history, and realized how blankly ignorant I was of his. "It shouldn't have become that long-drawn, hideous doom-of-gods it was."

"Well," I said, "space is big. In the beginning, as I recall, there might only be one engagement a year."

"One engagement might have settled it, if either side had had truly competent commanders. It is not for me to criticize my superiors, Mr. Arnfeld, but you must know yourself how often the chance for a decisive victory was lost—by both sides. For instance, if we had pushed on after Juno, instead of going home—" His fists clenched and his voice grew thin. "Skyblast! I was in Intelligence then. We *knew* we could catch your Task Force Three beyond Venus and annihilate it in detail. After that, the war would have been virtually over. But no, we went back to Mars."

"Well, you haven't a monopoly on such blunders," I said. "There was a near mutiny when we let your ships escape after Second Orbit. And if the chief admiral hadn't panicked at Mars and taken us back, if we could have kept on bombarding you—"

"The destruction of Zuneth was your most terrible mistake," he said gravely. "Before then, we would have settled for very moderate terms, even after an absolute victory. But when you laid waste our greatest and oldest city, the pride of all Mars, well, that atrocity made us howl for blood. After that the Archon and the Assembly all voted to end Earth as a power in space."

"We shouldn't have done it," I mumbled, wondering if he knew I had been there. "If we bombarded at all, we should have been thorough—but it was wrong to do it in the first place, yes."

"Still," said Regelin, "we would not have been vindictive. We would have settled for your disarmament and an indemnity, I think. But your politicians and admirals were too reckless. When we finally broke through and took the moon, they must have seen the game was up. They should have surrendered then and there. But no, they managed to keep the very fact secret from a people who would otherwise have revolted. They called for their remaining fleet to come home and give battle. After that, we had no choice. We took over the U. N. rocket bases and wiped you out. And now the temper of Mars is such that you will never be given another chance."

"I understand," I said.

"A fourth of our small population dead," he said heavily. "Our economy shaken, groaning under taxes, the folk impoverished, the whole history of our race thrown back. It will take us a hundred years to recover. Oh, a cold victory!"

We sat without talking for a long while then. I think the same thought was in both of us: *It's as if Earth and Mars together had an evil genius, as if something has driven our two unhappy races, against reason and desire and decency, to this war that wasn't needed, that only brought ruin. But forget that. It's our own stupidity. Any other assumption is paranoia.—But was the war less mad?*

"How long will you be here, Sevni?" I asked finally.

"On Earth? I don't know. Several years, I'm afraid. Reorganizing your planet will be a long and difficult task." Regelin smiled wryly. "You, the defeated, are home, comfortable, safe, you can pick up your life again and be free. We, the conquerors, are chained here on a world we cannot love. Strange war, strange victory!"

"They might bring your family here," I suggested.

"Oh, no, I would never wish that for them. Let them stay in the old castle on the edge of the Purple Gulf, let them breathe air that is clean and cool, and gather thorn-blossoms, and hear the crystal bells across the redsand plains at sunset."

I couldn't see anything attractive about his grim and barren world, but I nodded.

He felt eagerly in his tunic. "Here, let me show you," he said. "I have a portrait, my wife and three children—"

Martian females look less human than the males, but I pretended a degree of admiration.

"That is a most attractive young woman you have," he said shyly.

"She's not mine," I said, and got up. "I'm going back to the house."

We walked slowly along the trail talking. Regelin was fond of our classical music, but hadn't felt free to attend the concerts in Albany or, since I came, to use my tapes. "Go a-head," I offered. "Borrow as many as you like."

"You are most gracious, Commander," he said. I knew enough of the curiously knightly Martian code to realize that his addressing me—illegally—by my old rank was a consid-erable honor. "It is a shame you cannot hear the total range of my people's music. But I have been amusing myself by transposing some of it to your range, when I find time, and it might interest you—"

"Sure," I said. "We have a good piano, and I used to be pretty fair on the violin, too. Let's try it sometime."

The conversation shifted, as such do. I was astonished by the range of his reading in our literature. Much of it puzzled him, but he tried hard to put himself into the hu-man personality. I suggested some books to him, and he told me which were the best English and Portuguese translations of Martian classics.

We came out on the lawn, side by side. Kit was playing with Alice on the grass, and I saw how the light and shadow touched the curves of her.

She looked up and saw us. Regelin bowed, but she turned to me, and her eyes were the bleakest sight I have ever seen. "What were you doing?" she asked. There was a thickness in her tone.

"Why," I stumbled, "just talking. Talking with Senvi Regelin. He—"

"I see." She bit off the words, one by one. "I see. Well, Mr. Arnfeld, I will be leaving tomorrow. Thank you for your hospitality."

"Hey, now!" I grabbed for her arm. She shook me off with an angry gesture. "Kit! Kit, you can't—"

Her lip quivered, and I saw the tears begin. "Let me alone," she said.

Regelin stood like a black steel pillar, his long shadow falling across us. Looking up into his face, I saw that it had gone blank. His voice snapped like a clicking trigger. "Mr. Arnfeld, I am sorry to have bothered you, but my business forced me to do so. As for the records we discussed, you need not concern yourself. I do not require them after all. I trust I shall not have to disturb you again."

He bowed and strode off, past his saluting sentry and into his office. I didn't see him at all for several days.

Kit wiped her eyes after a while, apologized, and followed me into the house. That night I went down to the village and got drunk.

## IV

THERE IS NOT always a sign on the events that change your life, to tell you what they are. The chain of destruction which was ended here where I sit helplessly waiting, began with Regelin's announcement to me, a few weeks after our talk, that we would have visitors. He spoke with the court formality that had become habitual, and the third lids veiled his eyes from me.

"We will have two guests tomorrow, who will stay for three or four days. They are Dzuga ay Zamudring, inspector for the Commandant of North America, and a terrestrial liaison officer. Since the Martian quarters in this house are filled, and you have an extra bedroom in your section, I must request that you offer them accomodations."

"That was not in the bargain," I said as stiffly as he.

"A fair rental will be paid you. I would prefer to keep this on the basis of a request, Mr. Arnfeld."

Well, there was nothing I could do. My refusal would simply have made him order me to house the strangers, and that would have strained the thin relations between us close to breaking. I agreed with as good a' grace as possible, and went to find Kit. There were three bedrooms in a row on the second floor of our wing: mine, hers, and the empty one, which lay at the end of the hall. She made a wry face. "Next to me?" she asked. "I could stand the Martians, maybe, but a human traitor—"

"Some of us have to cooperate, if Earth is to keep any vestige of self-government," I said tiredly. "I'll trade rooms with you, if you want."

"Hmmm—well." She stroked her chin with one slender hand, and I saw thoughtfulness in her eyes. "Who are these creatures, anyway?"

"An inspection team, checking up on the various districts for the continental commandant. Important officers."

"I can stand it." Her voice was remote. "We needn't swap." Suddenly she came to some kind of decision. Her laugh was brittle. "Do me a favor, Dave?"

"Sure," I said. *Anything at all, Kit.*

We had a little museum of family relics, and it turned out that she wanted to borrow the ear trumpet of a nineteenth-century ancestor, to amuse Alice. I agreed, of course, and she laughed with real merriment and kissed me. It was all I could do to keep my response—brotherly.

That evening I noticed that the bath hose was missing. I swore, because it would be impossible to replace, and called Mrs. Hoose to task for it. She denied any knowledge of its whereabouts, and started a grumbling search, without luck. The trivial thing soon faded from my mind.

The inspector came the following afternoon, roaring up the drive in a long ground-car, accompanied by a squad of scooterbug-riding guards. Those wore light body armor and carried guns at the ready; there must be a good deal of sniping at Martians. The guards set up camp in the back yard while the inspector, a tall wrinkled Martian who seemed to creak with age, and the only human in his party, a plump, balding, middle-aged man introduced as Hale, were received by Regelin in the living room. Kit and I were asked to join them, and she surprised me by turning on all her charm, smiling and laughing and ringing for drinks. *What's she up to?* I wondered.

Hale offered cigarettes, which I hadn't seen for months, and lifted his glass. "I'm happy to see you people so hospitable and—considerate," he said with a politician's geniality. His voice was loud, it didn't fit in this long quiet room. There was a tradition that Thomas Jefferson had once been entertained here. I nodded, keeping my face chill, but Kit responded gaily to him.

"It has been a cruel war," said Hale, "but now, thank God, it is over, and we must start rebuilding." He looked at me. "Perhaps, Mr. Arnfeld, you would consider taking a job similar to mine. We're badly in need of human go-betweens at occupation headquarters." My manner froze him off, and he turned to Kit. "Miss—ah—Mrs. Hawthorne, possibly you—"

"I'm afraid not," she said. "I have a daughter to look after. But it must be interesting work."

Hale boomed on. He told a couple of off-color stories which obviously embarrassed the Martians, though they smiled mechanically. Dzuga was almost wholly silent, and Regelin said little more than I. Hale and Kit more or less took over the conversation, then and at the evening meal which we all attended. I gathered that he and Dzuga would use this house as a base for the next few days, while they surveyed the district. I was glad when bedtime came and they were shown to their room. I let Kit do that; the room had been my parents'.

She met me in the hall afterward, and I saw her flushed and angry. "He pinched me," she whispered furiously.

"Well," I said, "you invited it, my dear."

She gave me an odd look. "They've locked their door," she said, "but you can hear them talking."

I paused outside the room, listening. There was a low mumble from it, but I could not make out any words.

A couple of hours later I was sitting in my own room, try-ing to read. Except for the lamp, I was in darkness. Warm summer air blew through the open window, stirring the cur-tains. I was so absorbed in Housman—a strangely right poet for today—that I didn't notice the door open. She was at my side before I knew she was there.

"Dave," she said.

I looked up, startled. The lamplight threw her against night, all shadow and shimmering glows. She wore a robe over her pajamas, sheath-like around her slim form. My heart began to thump.

"Yes?" I asked.

"Come along, Dave." There was a queer, strained note in her voice, and her eyes were frightened. "I want you to—hear something."

"Hm?" I got up, thinking more of the way her long loose hair tumbled over her shoulders than of anything else. "What's up? Are your neighbors telling dirty jokes?"

"No, this isn't funny." She caught my arm with tensed fingers. "I've been—listening in on them. Using that ear trumpet. I meant to do that all along, just as a gesture. I didn't think it would mean anything."

I scowled. "That could be a dangerous hobby, Kit."

"*Listen*, won't you?" She stamped her foot, and her voice was a sudden fierceness. "They're talking in there, and it isn't in any language I ever heard. Not English or Por-tuguese or —anything!"

"So they talk Martian," I shrugged. "What of it?"

"Damn it, Dave," she cried, "I was in Comcenter!" Lower-ing her voice again: "I had to get a working knowledge of linguistics. I can follow half a dozen human languages, and Vannzaru and three other Martian dialects, and rec-ognize most of the others. This isn't *any* of them. It doesn't even sound like them!"

She grabbed my hand and pulled me toward the door. I followed, suddenly unsure and wondering. "Some special, ar-tificial language?" I muttered.

We entered her room. Alice was sleeping in a crib, whimpering a little. Briefly, I wondered what the child's dreams were like. Kit took the ear trumpet off her bed. She had tied it to a broomstick, and slipped my bath hose over the narrow end. "Here," she whispered. Sweat glistened on her forehead. "Here, use it for yourself."

Decision. I went to the window, and my right hand edged the stick along the wall until the trumpet was just under the guest-room window. My left hand brought the hose up to my ear. I listened.

*"Tahowwa shab-hu gameel weijhak."*

*"Shakheer! Kesshub umshash woteeha."*

I felt coldness along my spine, and muttered a curse. It was not only that the grunting and sibilant noises were strange to me. It was the rhythm of them, the low rise and fall, the whistling overtones and the rattle and gurgle beneath. I wondered if any human or Martian throat could form those syllables.

In any case—those were not the voices of Robert Hale and Dzuga ay Zamudring!

Slowly, I withdrew the trumpet. My hands were shaking. Kit and I looked at each other for a long and silent time.

"Who are they?" she gasped after a moment. "*What* are they?"

Alice moaned in her sleep. The old grandfather clock ticked noisily in the night stillness.

"I don't know," I whispered.

She came close to me, and I drew her against my breast. She was trembling so hard that her teeth rattled in her head. "We've got to find out," she forced through stiff lips.

"How?" I stood holding her, thinking with a brain that seemed frozen. "We can't go to Regelin, you know how he'd react, and there isn't anyone else."

"We can get proof." Her tones were wild. "We can convince the Martians—"

"How do you know this isn't some secret gadget of theirs?" I demanded. "It's got to be that."

"We have to *know*," she mumbled. "Alice here, and those —creatures—in the next room—"

I kissed her, blindly and harshly, and she clung to me in the same search for comfort. "We can't do anything," I said. "Not a thing. We're helpless. But I'll stay here tonight."

"Dave—"

I went back into my own room, got my automatic, and returned to hers. We locked the door, and I sat by her bedside, holding her hand, till she dropped off into a restless sleep. Those voices had been too unnerving for me to think of anything but defense—now. I sat all night in the chair, sometimes dozing and coming to with a jerk. About midnight, the yellow square of luminance on the lawn snapped out; the strangers had turned off their light. I wondered if they slept.

Dawn was cold and gray over the wide, empty fields. I waited till I heard Dzuga and Hale go downstairs before venturing out myself. Kit stirred, opening shadowed eyes to mine, and I bent over and kissed her cheek. "They're gone now, darling," I said. "Go back to sleep."

She smiled drowsily and turned over.

I washed, shaved, and went downstairs myself. Hale and Dzuga were still at breakfast. The—human—greeted me with a sly wink. "Good morning, Mr. Arnfeld," he said cheerily. "You seem tired."

I gulped the scalding chicory which Mrs. Hoose gave me.

"I couldn't help noticing that your bedroom door was open and your bed hadn't been slept in," went on Hale. He winked at me. "Ah, some people are lucky."

"Mr. Hale, if you please," said Dzuga with affronted rigidity.

I looked at them. They were so perfect, the gross well-fed man and the gaunt, almost prudish Martian. Every last detail, every curve of cheek and glitter of eye, the dress, the voice, the manner. I wondered if I had dreamed those mutterings in the night.

No—I hadn't done that. My head still felt hollow from

weariness, the stolen ear trumpet still lay up in Kit's room, and Hale *had* noticed I'd not slept in my own bed.

"We will be gone all day, I imagine, Mr. Arnfeld," said Dzuga. "We must lock our room and ask that under no circumstances be it opened, under penalty of the espionage statute. There are important documents in it."

"Of course," I said dully.

I was out on the lawn, soaking in the bright early sunlight, when Kit joined me. She sat down and laid a hand in mine.

"Dave," she said, "we've got to break in there."

"And get shot as spies?" I asked. "Don't be silly. This is some Martian secret. Forget it. We'll trade rooms tonight."

She smiled and rumpled my hair. "You're such an old-fashioned gentleman, Dave," she said. "You're almost a Martian yourself."

"That room," I said, "is to be left strictly alone. Savvy?"

She lowered her eyes. "Yes, master," she said demurely.

I worried about her for a while. We were both fighters of a kind, I supposed, but my spirit was the careful, slogging sort, war had been a trade to me, based on calculated odds; hers was buoyant, almost gay, often reckless. She had sloughed off her terror of the night like a cast skin. But she behaved herself 'til well after lunch. Then my own tiredness caught up with me and I went to take a nap.

I was shaken back to consciousness and sat blearily up. The sunlight had a late-afternoon quality, I must have slept for hours. A look at Kit's whitened face brought me out of bed with a violent surge.

"You haven't!" I groaned.

She nodded. "I had to. Nobody else is around. Come on, come quickly, you have to see this."

I slipped on a robe and followed her. My mouth was dry, and sweat prickled my body. But it was too late now. I could only try to repair the damage.

A skeleton key from the museum had easily turned the ancient lock. Inside, the room looked utterly normal, the beds neatly made, nothing disturbed. But a Martian-type trunk was on the floor, and Kit opened it. I saw a few changes of clothes, it looked harmless enough.

"There's no shaving kit," she told me in a flat voice.

I thought of Hale's blue jowls. "Maybe he lost his razor," I said. "Or maybe he just carries it with him, or—"

She opened the upper compartment, below the lid. It was filled with papers. I took the sheaf out and went through it, careful to keep the items in order. Lists, notes, maps—but the uncial writing was not one that Earth or Mars had ever known. Shakily, I restored the bundle and lifted the folded clothes.

On the bottom of the trunk lay two—pistols? I didn't know. They were massive, stubby things of blued steel, stamped with a strange symbol, and they didn't fit my hand very well. They wouldn't fit a Martian's, either.

"What are they?" she breathed.

"These? Weapons, I suppose." I laid them back.

"No—*they*. The strangers."

"I don't know." I shook my head, slowly. "Do the Martians have allies from—outside?"

"Allies who look and act exactly like our two races?" She hissed it with a note of anger.

"Let's get out of here," I said.

We replaced everything, closed the trunk, and locked the door behind us. I put on some clothes, and then we went downstairs and into the living room to return the skeleton key.

Regelin was there, waiting. One of his guards stood behind him with a cradled carbine. "Where have you been?" he asked, very softly.

I held face and voice steady with an effort that seemed to drain me. "Upstairs," I said. "Having a nap."

"I wondered—" He looked at my hand. "That is the skeleton key from your museum, isn't it?" He spoke like a snapping whip.

"I—"

"We couldn't unlock my door," said Kit.

"You have been in the guestroom." It was not a question but a statement. "You have been spying."

Something collapsed within me. I'd had no training for this work, I'd bungled the job disastrously, and now I read death in his eyes. I stood there, saying nothing.

"Yes, we have!" cried Kit. "And I'll tell you what we found, too."

"I am not interested in gossip." Regelin's tone was ice and darkness. "You are under arrest."

"Listen!" she screamed. "It concerns Mars, too. Those things aren't Martian, aren't human!" She babbled the story in a shaking rush of words.

I couldn't read his face. He said thinly: "My oath obliges me to obey my superiors. I shall have to report this affair in detail." With a flicker of gentleness: "I shall request clemency."

"You fool!" she raged. "You idiot!"

Regelin turned to his guard. "*Zurdeth agri.*" Take them away.

We were locked into Kit's bedroom. She burst into weeping and held Alice close to her. I sat looking out at the dying day.

"I'm sorry," she gasped at last. "I got you into this."

"Never mind," I said. "I'm glad you did." Which was a lie, but worth it to see the comfort it gave her.

There was a sentry under our window and one outside the door—no chance to escape. We sat holding hands while darkness thickened. It was about ten o'clock when the door opened and Regelin's aide motioned us curtly to come. We went downstairs between the guards.

Hale and Dzuga were seated in the living room, Regelin stood by the window, the four other Martians snapped to attention against the wall. Warm lamplight filled the place but it was very quiet.

Dzuga finally turned to me. His face was impassive, and

his voice was old and tired. "Sevni Regelin has told me an unpleasant story," he said.

"You shouldn't'a done it." Hale shook his head, and light glistened on his scalp. "You're in bad."

"Under the occupation law, you are subject to death without trial," said Dzuga. "We will take you to headquarters tomorrow. Possibly clemency can be arranged, but I doubt it."

"No." Kit's tone was small and dry. "We'll never get there alive. You can't let us tell the authorities. We'll be found dead in a ditch."

"Mrs. Hawthorne, please—" said Regelin.

"You too," she told him. "We told you what we know. You're coming along, aren't you?"

"I have been ordered to accompany you and give testimony," he said.

"You'll never give it," she answered.

"Your conclusions are altogether fantastic," said Dzuga. "Because we find it necessary to use codes, and have also some experimental models of weapons, you assume that—" He waved a hand and snapped an order in Vannzaru. *Take them back upstairs. Lock them in till tomorrow.*

I swayed a little on my feet, and out of terror and despair I managed a jeering note. "Your character is slipping, Inspector," I said. "No Martian aristocrat would send a prisoner hungry to bed if he could avoid it."

"We forgot," said Hale. "We'll send you some food."

A great steadiness came over me. All right, I had leaped to conclusions, built up a crazy structure of hypothesis, but—

What did we have to lose?

I measured distances with a fleeting, unnaturally clear glance. Four armed Martians standing against the farther wall, but ignorant of English, not knowing what was being said and not expecting trouble; a single floor lamp three feet away, with Dzuga sitting four feet beyond that; French windows, six feet to my left, opening on the front lawn and darkness. And a spaceman develops fast reactions.

I took a stride toward Dzuga. I whined, and was curiously aware, at the edge of my mind, of Regelin's sudden contempt. "Sir," I begged, "we were wrong. We're nervous, had delusions—"

"That will do," he snapped.

My hands closed on the floor lamp and I rammed it forward like a spear, into his face. Light exploded before us, and then darkness thundered over us. "The windows, Kit!" I bawled. "The windows!"

Plunging forward, I hit a solid form in the gloom. Regelin! My fist smashed into his belly, and I heard him grunt. He twisted his arms about me, dragging me down.

*"Get out, Kit!"* I yelled. *"Get out!"*

Two flashlights snapped in the hands of guards leaping forward. They shone on horror. Dzuga wasn't a Martian.

Wasn't anything!

## V

HE WAS slumped half-conscious across his chair, and his moaning was not that of human or Martian throat. In the flying glimpse I had, I saw that the black uniform was drawn tight over a suddenly thickened and shortened body, a pale soft skin. The head was muzzled, chinless, a fleshy crest rising on the skull—animal. The exploding lamp had burned that face, and the great colorless eyes looked out of a seared ruin.

Then the light caught me, where I still struggled with Regelin, and a Martian voice barked an order I knew from the war. It was too late. I couldn't get away. Slowly, Regelin and I released each other, and I raised my hands.

Someone clicked on the ceiling lamp. My eyes went to Kit, who had been grabbed by a Martian and had just now given up her kicking, biting, clawing fight. Her face was wild under the disheveled gold hair, and her breasts rose and fell in a swift gulping. It had been hopeless, that attempt of ours. But—

We turned to look at the thing which writhed and whimpered in the chair. A soldier whispered a curse, another signed himself with the Double Crescent. Otherwise there was only our heavy breathing and the night outside.

Hale stood forth, a little, baldish, pot-bellied man with a sudden iron calm on him. "This is unfortunate," he said. "You have stumbled on a top state secret."

The door to the Martian wing began to open. They'd heard the racket in here and come to investigate. Hale snapped a command in Vannzaru, and the door closed again before they saw.

"And you're one of them too," I said.

He nodded. "Obviously." With a smile that was drawn steel: "We are an—experimental model. Something from the Martian laboratories."

Regelin's gaunt hand rested on his sidearm. "Don't," said Hale. "I am your superior officer."

The sevni snapped to attention.

My mind was moving more swiftly than I had thought possible, cold and clear as lightning in the sky. "It won't wash, Hale," I said, and was dimly amazed at the evenness of my tone. "You're no more Martian than I am."

His eyes narrowed, exactly as a man's would. "You will go back to your room immediately," he said.

I turned to Regelin. "They talk between themselves in no language of this planetary system," I said. "They keep notes in an unknown writing and weapons not of Martian make. If there really were such beings developed on Mars, they'd be a military secret of the first rank. They wouldn't be allowed to gallivant over this planet where any accident might betray them."

"That will do!" snapped Hale. "Sevni, send these Earthlings back to confinement."

"If you do," I told Regelin, "you're selling out your own planet; and they'll kill you into the bargain."

The guards stood with guns covering us, eyes flickering from one to another, waiting for orders.

"Sevni," said Hale, "remember your oath."

"Which was to be loyal to the Archate," I said. "Not to aliens who have infiltrated it."

Regelin stood there, unmoving, for a century of minutes. His face was withdrawn, expressionless, but the golden eyes blazed. No one spoke. I looked at the thing called Dzuga ay Zamudring. It—no, he, the uniform had split and I could see he was male—was recovering himself, sat almost upright, breathing hard. He was hairless, his skin white, his eyes flat in the round theriomorphic face. There was a big braincase—though the head had changed shape too. Teeth and nails were almost gone, and he had seven stubby fingers on each hand, and the whole body gave an effect of rubbery bonelessness. He stood about as tall as I, but was broader, a square build.

Finally Regelin sighed. His pistol came out, and he barked an order to the guards. They looked almost happy as their carbines swung to cover Hale and Dzuga.

"You will regret this, Sevni," said Hale.

"I am going to contact headquarters," said Regelin. "You and—your friend—are under arrest. So are you humans, though I'll give you the run of the house and grounds till further notice. I am duty bound to report this."

"I tell you, it's top secret!" cried Hale.

"I shall report directly to the continental commandant," said Regelin. "Meanwhile, no others shall see you."

The prisoners were led upstairs, locked into their room with the four guards told off to watch them. Regelin gave Dzuga some ointment for his burns, but had me carry the trunk downstairs. We went through it item by item.

"Quite possibly Hale is right and we shall all be shot for this," said Regelin evenly. "However—" He turned to Kit and me, formally. "I apologize for the earlier misunderstanding. You were right and I was wrong."

Impulsively, Kit took his hand. He sighed, wheeled about and went into the Martian wing.

We moved Alice in with the Hooses, just in case. Neither of us could sleep. We went back to the house, threw together some kind of meal, and afterward sat in the living room. We didn't say much.

Regelin came back about midnight. He sat down across from us, and his eyes were dull. "I finally got through on a closed circuit to the Commandant," he reported. "Ruanyi dzu Varek himself. He ordered me to absolute secrecy and said he was sending a squad at once."

"Didn't he say anything about whether this is a Martian project or not?" I asked.

"No. Nothing. It is very strange."

Kit looked at him. "If he were roused out of bed and given such a story," she said, "he might not be able to think fast enough. He might slip out of character, just a little bit."

Regelin closed his fists. "What do you mean?" he asked.

"You know it as well as I do." Her voice was ferocious. "If these aliens can make themselves look like anybody, and if they have infiltrated, they'll be in the highest governmental posts."

"This inspection team wasn't too high-ranking," he said.

"They'd want to check up for themselves," said Kit. "See just how their war has succeeded."

"*Their* war—"

"It fits, doesn't it?" I asked. "The unnecessary war. Two peaceable worlds, lashed to battle by one provoked incident after another. The bungling on both sides that made the thing such a long and bloody mess, that nearly wrecked both planets. Yes, I think they've controlled both our governments for decades."

"But if they can simply come in, disguised as us—if they

can take over all our riches—why *should* they destroy us—make us destroy ourselves?"

"I don't know. Softening us up for invasion, perhaps. Maybe the armada from Alpha Centauri is already on its way."

"No! That doesn't make sense! The logistics of it are simply ridiculous." Regelin got up and began pacing, back and forth, back and forth. "And a race capable of mounting an interstellar invasion would be so far advanced technologically that it wouldn't need to conquer anybody."

I leaned back in my chair, suddenly exhausted. "Be that as it may," I told him, "I predict this: The squad will come with orders for you to release those two things. By then, Dzuga will again be Dzuga. You and we and your four guards will be hustled off and never heard from again."

The iron in him broke. "I can't mutiny," he groaned.

"No," said Kit viciously. "You can only die."

"Give us a chance, at least," I begged. "Let us take a car and get out of here."

"I have to think," he said hoarsely. "I don't know what to do."

He paced up and down for a long time. His boots fell dully on the carpet.

I leaned over to whisper to Kit—I'd attack Regelin, we could overpower him and get away—I had forgotten how well Martians hear. He looked at me with a haggard smile and said: "Don't."

Then, after another moment, he threw back his shoulders, suddenly calm, his decision made. "I am with you in this."

Kit leaped up and kissed him. I could only clasp his hand.

"Don't make assumptions," he said quickly. "I am a Martian before all. If Hale was telling the truth, I shall be shot for mutiny; and doubtless lives will be lost before that happens. But I cannot take the chance—those few lives are nothing against the possibility that Mars is being conquered from within."

We laid swift plans, but they got us no further than escape; beyond that we couldn't think. Kit went back outside
to get Alice while I packed a few necessities and as much
food as I could. Regelin ordered his private car made ready,
and gave me a huge roll of greenbacks to take. We went upstairs together, then, and down the hall to the guestroom
door.

Regelin dismissed the guards. It was, perhaps, cruel to
abandon them, but they couldn't be trusted not to turn on
us. Then he opened the door and we went into the room. I
switched on the lights.

Hale still wore his human form, and Dzuga had reassumed
Martian shape. They got out of bed and stood looking down
the muzzle of our guns.

"You are going to tell us the truth," said Regelin. "The
whole truth."

Anger flushed Hale's face. "I have already done so," he
said.

"I know something of biological science," declared Regelin,
"and I also know that revolutionary weapons are not developed overnight. I do not believe any Martian laboratory
could have created your kind. You are from outer space—
*aren't you?*"

Hale shook his head. I gathered myself, ready to beat the
truth out of them. Whether I could have brought myself to
torture or not, I don't know. We were already too late.

Regelin lifted his hand as I moved toward them. "Listen!"

We heard it soon after, the steady thunderclap of a rocket
drilling the sky, and it was coming nearer. The squad from
Headquarters!

No—they couldn't have gotten here that soon. Ruanyi must
have called up a nearby garrison and had them send that
vessel. Which meant it was really urgent to him—

We shot the aliens in the head, feeling no remorse for
executing the murderers of our planets. I had half expected
them to change shape in death, but they remained the

same as they sprawled on the floor. *They died like men,* I thought with a grisly humor.

"Hurry!" gasped Kit.

Regelin tossed a sheet of paper to the floor, on which he had typed an account of our findings. If the squad was of hostile aliens, it would be useless; they'd burn it. But if Hale had told the truth, it was some small justification for our mutiny, and perhaps the authorities would try to take us alive. Perhaps.

We clattered down the stairs and out to the driveway. The car stood there, idling—a long black ovoid, Diesel-powered. Kit tumbled into the back seat, Regelin and I into the front; he let me drive, and we slid away from the house.

"Now where?" he asked.

"Try Albany," I said. "We can hole up there for the night, maybe."

The engine roared behind me. By the vague dashlight glow, I saw our speedometer creeping over the 200 mark. The wind of our passage bellowed, but I could hear Alice crying in the back seat and Kit soothing her.

Regelin leaned toward me. "The hunt will be on by morning," he said. "They will have the number of this car."

I nodded. "We'll ditch it in Albany."

It was only minutes to the town at our speed. We slowed and purred down empty streets. The moon was hidden by the buildings, and lamps were turned off to conserve Earth's thin remaining trickle of power.

I parked in an alley and we walked out into the night. Our feet sounded loud on the pavement, we were the only ones abroad. This was a run-down district, hangout of what crooks and bums the city had. I knew a disreputable hotel, and halted before its dim blue light. Leaving the others outside, I walked in, my nose in a handkerchief that managed to cover most of my face. A sleepy clerk looked up. "Yeah?"

"Single for tonight," I muttered. "Hurry up, please—I gotta bad nosebleed." I had cut myself to draw blood and stain the handkerchief.

The clerk demanded a quarter million in advance, and I peeled it off and carried my own trunk—with all our possessions—up a dark stairway to the shabby No. 18 he had given me. I let myself in, locked the door, and climbed down the fire escape. We four went back up it. Kit and Alice were quickly asleep on the bed, while Regelin and I tossed for the chair. I lost, and stretched myself on the dirty floor. Oddly, I wasn't long about falling asleep either.

In the early morning, we opened a can of beans for breakfast, and conferred over it. "The alarm will be out by now," said Regelin. "And what can we do?"

"Go to someone we can trust," I said. "We can't talk to just any local sheriff or Martian officer or whatnot. Even if he believed us, which is unlikely, he'd have to go through channels, which means the enemy would soon be able to stop him." I scratched a bristly chin. "The man I'd like to see right now is Rafael Torreos. He's an old friend of mine, I *know* he's all right. And he is, or was, a colonel in our Intelligence, and has some connection with Martian higher-ups. He's be able to do something," I chuckled drearily. "But unfortunately. Torreos is in Brazil."

"Could you send him a letter?" asked Kit.

"With the postal service shot? No. Unless we can find someone going to Brazil who'll deliver it."

Regelin scowled. "I think I could vouch for Sevni Yueth dzu Talazan, in our own Intelligence," he said. "And he would have much more influence than your Torreos. However, he will not believe so fantastic a story without proof. I would not believe it myself."

"And if Yueth's in your C.I.A., as you say, he's way to hellangone in North America GHQ," I grumbled. "He might almost as well be in Brazil. It's fifteen hundred miles."

"Nevertheless—"

"I'm s'ill hungry, mom-muh," said Alice. It reminded me joltingly of how awkward a party we were.

Proof. The best proof, perhaps the only one, would be an alien. If dead, the corpse would have to be in alien form,

unless disection would reveal its otherness. I wondered
how many of them there were. *Anyone you meet, the coffee
shop proprietor, the aid station attendant, the cop on the
corner, the boy on a bicycle, any one of them may be a
monster.*

No, probably not. They might assume humble disguises
for special purposes, but generally they would be the rulers
—officers, nobles, politicians, big businessmen, key bureaucrats. Society is a great machine, and they had to be in the
vital positions to control it.

I didn't think their numbers were enormous; but the fact
that they gave the orders would turn every man's and Martian's hand against us.

So—the aliens would be concentrated in the big headquarters, in important offices. We'd have to go clear to the
stronghold of Ruanyi dzu Varek himself, and *he* was almost
certainly of the enemy. Clear to Minneapolis, with all the
nation hunting us.

But at least it would be an unexpected direction. Logically,
we ought to head north for the woods. And Regelin's friend
Yueth would be in Minneapolis too.

I got up off the floor. "Let's go," I said.

## VI

IT WAS UP to me to get transportation; Kit and Regelin were
too conspicuous. I left them talking, he soothing her with an
account of his family and their home on Mars, and went
downstairs. The ordinary slack suit, such as I was wearing,
offers no way to mask a face; and the weather outside was
damnably bright, which gave me no excuse to wear a hood-

ed raincape. I would just have to rely on the fact that most people are unobservant. I crossed the lobby with my skin prickling.

I passed the desk. Different clerk now, why did it have to be that alert-looking boy? "Back after breakfast," I flung at him over my shoulder. So nobody would blunder into the room—

Having occasionally ridden here for a spree, a few hours to forget I was beaten and broken, I knew the district fairly well. There was a small garage with a used-car business on the side, not far from the hotel. I'd never talked to the owner, but he was a young man with a missing hand, the prosthetic was a service issue—a former spaceman. He was tinkering with a car when I walked into his shop. Nobody else was there, and my breath shuddered out of me.

He straightened and regarded me with spaceman's eyes, the long steady squint against actinic glare. "Yes?" It was a voice full of bitterness and protest.

"I want to buy a small truck," I said.

He looked surprised, then, and gratified; his business must be almost zero these days. "I got a couple good ones," he said. "Come on out and look at 'em."

When the sunlight was full on my face, his eyes hardened. I could almost read his mind, remembering: *Five feet eleven, stocky build, brown hair, gray eyes, snub nose, cleft chin . . . Reward . . .*

"What was your outfit?" I asked. In the effort to hold itself steady my tone was flat. "I was with the Sixth myself."

"Fireballs," he answered, very slowly.

"The Ninth—yeah. A good fleet. You were with us at Second Orbit."

"That's where I lost my flipper," he said. "You were—lucky."

"Not so far. In fact, my luck's been so bad I've decided to leave town. There are better places. Something might still be done to help Earth get on her feet again."

"Maybe," he said doubtfully. "I'd like to see that happen, but I got a wife and kids. I know better'n to buck the Marshies."

"Some people don't," I said. "But a wise man who'd like to see better days might keep his mouth shut instead of getting poor damned fools into trouble. Even for a reward. My name's Robinson."

He grinned then. "Okay, Mr. Robinson. Maybe I could let you have a truck cheap. Only it won't get you very far, you know. Even charcoal's hard to come by."

"Oh, I'll make out. I'm just an average guy trying to get along in the world. So damned average that people often fail to recognize me."

"Yeah, your face is easy to forget. Okay, now here I got—"

We finished the deal quickly: a battered old pickup with a canvas-covered box was mine for a price which cut deeply into our funds but was nevertheless a bargain. I shook hands with the dealer as I left, the plastic claw was hard and cool in my palm. "Good luck, Mr. Robinson," he said.

I clattered back to the hotel and into the alley behind it. No one in sight, no one watching, but any minute a face might show at a window, someone might walk in on us. I whistled softly, and my companions scrambled down the fire escape and crouched in the box while I went in and got my trunk and checked out of the hotel.

Coming out of Albany and onto the road to Rochester was like being born again. I looked at green fields and old trees and the homes of men, sunlit under the tall blue sky of Earth, and laughed aloud.

The wheezy old wreck could hardly make Rochester before dark, but that suited me well enough. It was clearly hopeless to try to get to Minneapolis on the highways. Lack of fuel, mechanical breakdowns, and the occupation police like hounds on our trail—impossible! We had to take another route.

I stopped after a while and let the others into the cab with me. Regelin wore a hat and one of my shirts, he would seem human enough to a casual glance, and Alice was hidden on her mother's lap between him and me. We could pass for any local farm family—I hoped.

"Where we goin', mom-muh?" asked the girl. A breeze through the cab ruffled her fine light hair, and the big eyes looked out on a world which at that age is all fable.

"On a long trip, dear," said Kit gently.

"Can I bring Hoppy too?"

"Of course," said Kit. "We wouldn't do without Hoppy."

Regelin smiled. "Who is this Hoppy?" he asked. "Your doll?"

"Oh, no," said Alice. "Hoppy's a mons'er. He got wings an' come sit onna bed inna mornin' an' talk to me. I fink up Hoppy when I get lonesome. You know any mons'ers, Mista Marsman?"

"A few," said Regelin gravely. "Here and there."

Kit shook her head. "It's like a nightmare," she murmured. "So slowly, with them chasing us, and we're going right toward the heart of the danger."

"It might be well if we left you and the child to hide with someone," said Regelin.

"Won't work," I said bitterly. "Who can we trust? If anybody took them in, he might get scared later and betray them for the reward or just to save his own skin. And with the breakdown of travel and communications, everybody is naturally becoming more interested in what his neighbor's doing. Strangers arriving to stay with someone would stick out like the good old sore thumb."

My garageman had, with elaborate casualness, told me the public announcement, which had gone on the air about dawn and been rebroadcast periodically. We three wanted dead or alive for mutiny, murder, and conspiracy. We were believed to be insane, with systematic delusions to which no one should pay attention. The reward was considerable—a hundred million U. N. dollars, convertible into Mars' hard currency if desired. Handbills and posters with the same information and our pictures would be issued soon.

Kit whistled at what I said. "They want us *bad!*" With a forlorn little smile: "Never thought I'd be worth that much to anybody."

"You are to me, Kit." I reached down and squeezed her hand. She gave me a strange look.

Regelin's face was haggard. "When my family hears of this—" He shook his head, letting blankness slide over him.

It was mid-afternoon when we heard the siren. We had just gone through a village, and I saw the pursuing car streak from it. My heart gave a leap and then settled down into a steady, furious drumming. "Down!" I yelled. "Out of sight!"

Kit had already pulled Alice to the floor. Regelin dropped over her. I threw a blanket across the two and laid my gun beside me. The siren howled and the blue ovoid edged alongside us, forcing us off the road.

I stopped and turned to face the man who was climbing out. There was another with him, holding a tommy gun. State troopers—young, both of them, ordinary decent lads from the green dales of Earth. My voice sounded blurred in my ears: "What is it, officer? What'd I do wrong?"

"We're checking all vehicles. Orders." He leaned in the window, his revolver level at my temples. "Let's see both your hands on that wheel, mister."

"Look here—"

He did, and I saw the tautening of his face. "Come out of there," he said slowly. "With hands up."

"I haven't—"

"We'll have to hold you for investigation. Come on, now, out!"

Something slumped within me. "Officer," I asked dully, "are you collaborating with the Martians too?"

"So it *is* you—"

I'd given them their chance. Now I moved fast. My left hand chopped down on the barrel of his gun, sweeping it aside and grabbing the wrist, while my right pulled up my own weapon. I fired, and his head exploded before me.

Regelin was up in the same movement with me, throwing

himself across my lap and pumping shots at the man in the police car. The tommy gun stammered once, and then he collapsed in the seat and fell slowly to the floor. Magnum bullets do not leave a pretty corpse.

We got out. The fields were empty around us, two neat white houses peeked through a screen of trees, the sunlight was bright and warm on the road and the blood and brains. Somewhere a thrush was singing.

"I'm sorry," I whispered to the dead men. "I'm sorry, boys."

Kit was weeping, not hysterical but quietly, hopelessly, shielding her daughter from the sight. Regelin and I put the bodies in the car and drove it off on the shoulder. He mopped the spattered mess off me, as well as he could, and we took the car's armament and drove on.

After a while Kit looked up and touched my mouth. Her fingertips were cold. "You were hurt, Dave," she said. "You're bleeding."

"I bit my lip too hard, I guess," I said tonelessly.

"It wasn't murder, David," said Regelin. The first time he had ever called me by my name. "This is war."

"I wonder what the difference is," I said.

We turned off the highway and followed dusty country roads into the lowering sun. We didn't talk much between ourselves, but Kit prattled all the time to Alice, trying to keep her happy. After dark we stopped to eat, and then pushed on.

Lake Ontario lay quiet under the moon, its darkness broken by a ripple of cold light. You could hear waves lapping on the shore, and the stars were majesty overhead. "I know this region pretty well," I told them. "Lots of little resort towns hereabouts. Should be one with a yacht club not far away."

We chugged into it—a pretty little place, plastic cottages under trees, on lawns that were dew-glimmering in the moonlight. Few windows glowed, Earth had no time or money for resorts these days, but there were permanent residents. We pulled up on the dock and stretched ourselves gratefully after the long, cramped ride. My belly muscles were still drawn tense. Walking over hollow-sounding planks, I selected our boat, a sweet craft whose owner took obvious pride in it. I felt sorry for him.

While Kit and Regelin made it ready, I drove the truck back out of town, to a spot where the weed-grown lawn of an empty house sloped into the lake. I set the controls on automatic, pointed the truck at the water, and got out. If my garageman had done a competent job of repair on its water shielding, it should get quite deep before it stopped.

By the time anyone thought to hunt for our tracks—a boat thief wouldn't likely be identified with the mad killers —they should be gone. I walked back to the yacht club and jumped into the boat. We cast off and tacked against the landward breeze, out onto the lake.

"And where will this take us, did you say?" asked Regelin.

"Clear to Duluth," I said, "if the bombardment didn't wreck the St. Lawrence waterway. And there'll be little if any traffic on the lakes, and we needn't worry about fuel."

I took the first watch. Kit and Alice had the boat's one bunk, Regelin rolled in a blanket beside them and was asleep at once. Earth gravity must have worn him down more than he admitted. I sat alone by the tiller for an hour or so. Then the door of the little cabin opened and Kit came softly out to sit down beside me.

"I couldn't sleep," she said. "Will you talk to me, Dave? I feel so horribly alone."

"Sure," I said.

She looked up toward the sky, where the Great Bear wheeled and Andromeda's nebula was a tiny whorl of silver impossibly far away and the Galactic belt's clustered suns ran like a pale river between the constellations. "I wonder," she said. "I wonder which of those stars they came from."

"No telling," I said. "It's a big universe."

"Big and cold." She shivered. I laid an arm about her waist, drawing her close to me.

"I'm not afraid for myself," she said in a thin voice, a child's voice full of pain that is not understood. "I've seen too much in the last year to be afraid of what can happen to me. But Alice—she's all there is left to me."

"Well," I said, "I'm no hero either. We've been forced into this. We're not trying to save Earth, but our own necks. Reggy is the only true altruist, I'm afraid."

"He's—good," she said. "I never knew Martians could be so gentle." Fiercely: "And they turned us against each other! They made us kill each other."

"Maybe they're doing it for the wife and kids too." I said. "War is always an ugly business."

She looked at me a long time. "Can't you hate at all?" she asked finally, wonderingly.

I shrugged. "Sure. But I'd rather not. A man is thrown into himself, out in space. You do a lot of thinking, and things no longer look as simple as you might wish them to be."

"Dave—if by some miracle we should win out—if these aliens can somehow be exposed and overthrown—what then?"

"I don't know. I assume Mars will ease up the conditions of peace for us. She probably won't abandon control of us at once, but we'll be allowed to rebuild. In a few years, maybe, they'll get together on an interplanetary union, like the U. N. One is at least allowed to hope."

"And you—what will you do then?"

"Can't say. Go into business, maybe; there's a wide field for research and development in rocketry. Or settle down and really try to write. I'd like to hand on some of the thinking I did out there, and tell the whole story of space."

"Don't you ever want a family?"

"Sure." I forced a laugh. "Want to apply for the job?"

"I think—" She fell silent. Then, slowly and very softly: "I think perhaps I might."

The boom nearly crowned me when I let go of the tiller.

I needn't go into detail on that voyage. It was a strange and utterly happy interlude. Sun and rain and wind, glitter on the lakes, forests green on the shores, loneliness around us like a wall— We were on short rations, we huddled wet and cold against the rains, we cursed contrary winds, we felt a hand close on our hearts when one of the infrequent aircraft flashed overhead, we were cramped and comfortless, but we wished the trip might last forever.

Regelin was tactfully blind and deaf, he spent most of his time playing with Alice. Sometimes all three of us would talk together, otherwise it was Kit and me, all the years before us bright and insubstantial as sunlit, wind-driven clouds. Our little time was like a life, bounded on either end by darkness, but it was today, held in our hands, and today was forever.

We made landfall some two weeks after our departure, grounding the boat on a pebbled beach north of Duluth and splashing ashore to the forest. That night we slept on pine boughs with the wind talking in the trees overhead. Our interlude was ended, and we started out next day for the new capital of North America.

## VII

DULUTH had been a busy port, but with Chicago in ruins the upper midwest cities could be left without bombardment to die on the vine. We circled it and began hiking across country, traveling by night along empty roads, under heartlessly brilliant stars. By day we hid ourselves in copses, haystacks, grainfields. The farmers here had not suffered as much from city mobs as in the east, and I had little trouble begging enough food for my party—our own supplies had been consumed in the boat.

Minneapolis-St. Paul had been fairly important for a while

after World War III, as a terminal for the rapidly expanding air-freight lines; but technology made such pivots unnecessary within a decade, and the double city had been left to dignified obsolescence, a minor airport and manufacturing center, rather quaint and old-fashioned. Its undamaged buildings and central location made it a natural choice for Martian continental headquarters. Neither Kit nor I had ever been here, but Regelin knew the place well; there was a sad humor in our being guided by him.

A week's hiking from Lake Superior brought us to the outskirts. We stopped in a wooded tract to clean up, washing ourselves and our nylon clothes in the river until Kit and I looked like any civilian couple. Regelin's uniform came out of his bundle, to be scrubbed and dried; its plastic-fabric snapped to a crisp military neatness and the silver glistened on its black.

"And now," he said, "we break up the group temporarily. If either division fails to make the rendezvous, the other must go ahead as best it can." His words rang with decision, and his six-fingered handclasp was firm. I had to admire him; for myself, I felt only a dull hopeless dread, a slogging sort of courage which went on because there was nothing else to do.

Kit and I crouched in the long grass and watched him stride confidently out on the highway. It wasn't long before a Martian truck came from the north; he flagged it down and stepped coolly inside. He needn't even bother explaining himself unless there was another officer around. "Lucky devil," I muttered.

"Till someone recognizes him," said Kit.

We began trudging at sunset, a man and woman and child. By midnight we were well into the neat northern residential section, walking down the dark length of Lyndale Avenue. There was a stirring of life at the corner of Broadway: a few bars open, a thin flow of traffic. My heart sprang when I saw a Martian standing on the corner with a notebook.

Kit drew me back into the gloom and her hand was cold in mine. "Let's go around the block," she whispered.

"No," I said, forcing it out between my teeth. "We can't afford to act furtive. He's observing everything, but it must only be routine. Traffic analysis, maybe. Come on."

We went right past him. His incurious yellow eyes brushed us and wandered away again. To the untrained Martian, humans of a particular race look very much alike. We were leaning heavily on that fact.

Later on, we met others: a patrol walking down the streets, a party of drunken enlisted men singing one of their weird ballads, a young-looking soldier drifting past with loneliness on his face. Their cars and trucks purred by us, big steel beasts wearing guns like horns. Now and then an aircraft whooshed overhead, murmuring in for a landing. I saw Martians coming out of homes in which they had been quartered, more of them every minute as we got closer to the loop. It was a strange sight, those tall gaunt forms and unhuman helmeted heads against the shabby-genteel homeliness of a minor human city. It made the occupation wholly real to me.

We turned off on Seventh Street and went through a neat district of impersonal multi-family units—that meant there'd once been a slum here, I thought—toward the glow of the downtown section. The loop was concentrated within a small area, some ten blocks square, bounded sharply by warehouses, factories, and cheap hotels. The rendezvous was one of the latter, the Rocket Haven, only three blocks off the main drag. We entered the dingy lobby and went up to the deck. "Room for two," I said.

"Sorry, mister." The clerk's sleepy eyes hardly noticed me. "Place is full up. Martians, you know."

"Now there," whispered Kit with a wry grin, "is an unforeseen complication."

"Look," I said, "we just got in from Des Moines and we're ready to keel over. We've tried several other places in town, and none of them'll give us a thing. I got a wife and kid here—have a heart!"

"I said we're flat out," answered the clerk. "Can't even spare a bathtub."

I looked at the register where it lay open before me. A name, picked almost at random—Fred Gellert of Duluth— "Why, say you've got an old friend of mine here!" My voice came out dull with weariness, but I tried to smile. "Mr. Gellert, see? I meant to meet him anyway, knew he'd be in this place. He won't mind sharing."

"That's his business," shrugged the clerk. Indifference was like a mantle over him, he was one of Earth's broken men. "His key ain't here, so he's most likely up there now."

"We'll go see. And look—" I slipped one of our few remaining thousand-dollar bills onto the desk. "My name's Robinson. James Robinson. I'll just call you up from the room when we get it straightened out, and I'd like you to write my name in by Mr. Gellert's. I'm expecting a visitor, you see."

We climbed three flights of stairs, not daring to say anything when the halls were full of Martians. Enlisted men, I noticed; the top officers would naturally have the big hotels, the lesser ones be billeted in private homes. These were a quiet, almost stolid lot, the peasantry and hunters of the dry sea bottoms and the stony hills. We heard the wailing of their songs like sorrow in the air.

When I knocked on Fred Gellert's door, we were briefly alone. Kit hissed in my ear: "Are you crazy, Dave? He won't take us in. This is just drawing attention—"

"We've *got* to meet Reggy here," I said, with a bite in my tone. "There's no other way to do it. If he can scout around through town, right out in the open, we can—"

"Yeh, what is it?" A grumpy, half-awake sound, the door opening a crack. "Who the hell you think y' are?"

I opened the door and stepped inside, my pistol leveled on Fred Gellert's stomach. Kit closed the door behind us and sat down on the bed, watching us with large eyes. "Don't say anything," I told him. "I wouldn't hesitate to shoot you, though I'd rather not."

His eyes narrowed after the first amazement. An undistinguished-looking man, pudgy, his sandy hair tousled with sleep, his pajamas gaping over a pink expanse of belly—but he reacted fast, there was a quick hard brain in him. "You," he said. "Arnfeld."

"Uh-huh," I nodded. "We need this room tonight. Maybe we'll need it tomorrow too. You won't be harmed if you cooperate. If you have any needs of nature, attend to 'em now, because you're going to be tied and gagged for quite a while."

I did an efficient job of it, ripping up a sheet and lashing him fast; he hadn't a chance of working free. I laid him in a corner and turned to Kit. She had phoned the clerk and had then undressed Alice. The two of them were already in bed, asleep.

I couldn't bring darkness to my own eyes, not all at once. So I sat down and told Gellert the whole story, not expecting him to believe it, just hoping forlornly that if we spread the tale widely enough it might live on after we were dead. I wondered why he was in town—maybe he'd taken one of the fat jobs the Martians offered to humans—but felt too tired to question him or search his effects. Presently I dozed off.

A knock brought me awake, sleep draining out like spilled water. The gun was in my hand as I slipped the door open. Regelin stood there, tall and black against the dim hall light. I let him in and woke Kit, brushing my lips across her cheek. Reggy folded his long frame into the chair, sighing with weariness. He looked a query at Gellert's bound form, and I explained.

"Good work," he said with a brief crooked grin. "Now as for my adventures, things went quite well. There are so many of my people here that I needed only mingle with the crowds; I went right to the Foshay Tower itself, the heart of NAHQ, and studied the directory. Then I had a friendly conversation with a little human switchboard operator, who was very flattered at attention from a Martian officer. We went out and had coffee together, and I got quite a bit of information about administrative personnel."

Kit frowned. "That surprises me," she said.

"Oh, not all your race hates us," said Regelin. "Those who haven't suffered too much from the war and its after-math, and have received good treatment at our hands, and have decided they might as well learn how to get along with us—What is useful, of course, is that none of them is likely to tell one Martian from another."

He leaned forward, clasping his hands together. "What we have to find is a Martian officer who is actually an alien, and whom we can capture and expose. I believe I have located our victim. Yoakh Alandzu ay Cromtha is an aide to Commandant Ruanyi, and has charge of all reports and data filed by the inspection teams as well as the regular oc-cupation officers; in short, he gets all the information about this continent, and helps correlate it with that from the rest of the planet. It is a natural spot for an alien. When I learned further that Alandzu is a taciturn, unfriendly sort, who never unbends unless perhaps with his own staff, and whose antecedents are uncertain—well, that seemed to clinch it. My girl looked up his quarters for me: Suite 1847 in the New Dyckman Hotel. He'll have a bodyguard, who will doubtless be an alien too, but surely they won't be ex-pecting us to assault them."

"So we grab them quietly and call up your friend Yueth and have him come look at the evidence," I said slowly. "All well and good. Only how will we make Alandzu oblige us by changing his shape?"

"Well—" A ghostly smile hovered on Regelin's lips. "You might try breaking a lamp over his head."

I stood up, feeling the eerie tingle of readiness in me. There was no longer time to be afraid. Holding Kit against me, I kissed her for a long while. Then Regelin and I went out and into the street. I let him walk well in front of me.

It was about 3 a.m. then, darkness and silence like a muted

ocean over the city. A few lamps glowed one-eyed along Hennepin Avenue, a car purred down its empty length, a pair of Martian patrollers moved at the remote end of vision. I had a sense of enormousness around me, the city was like one vast organism sleeping, crouched to wake with a scream.

Half a block further along, the facade of the New Dyckman held a dim blue glimmer. It slid off the helmets of the two sentries who paced before the entrance, up and down, up and down. I saw Regelin turn past them, casually flipping an answer to their salute. Darkness masked his face as he disappeared inside. I slouched on down Hennepin till I came to the alley tunneling in toward the parking lot at the rear of the hotel. There would be guards here, too. I walked into the courtyard.

*"Halt!"* The command rapped out in an indescribable accent. Turning, I saw the two sentries approach me with rifles at the slant. They weren't very suspicious—what could one wanderer mean? I moved toward them until they stood almost against me, tall black shadows casqued in metal. I made my voice thick, and swayed on my feet.

"Yeh? Wha'ya wan'? I gotta zheneral's car. Zheneral tol' me get 'is car, 'e did—"

"Go," said the nearest. It must have been one of his few English words. He took my arm and tried to steer me back out of the alley. "Go."

I hit him, then, the edge of my hand full into his larynx. It is a brutal blow when you know how to deliver it. He went down with a sob, clattering to the hard ground. My foot was already behind the ankles of the other, I pushed him and he fell, and my boot crashed against the temples of both. I hope I didn't kill them.

Then I had to run. With Martian hearing what it is, there'd be somebody to investigate in seconds—but the two guards would be in no condition to say where I'd gone. It would be assumed a purposeless act of resentment—I hoped!

Weaving between the cars, I made a jump, caught the fire escape, and swung myself up. *I seem to be getting ad-*

*dicted to fire escapes,* I thought in a moment of fleeting gallows humor. But I couldn't run up it, that would have been a public announcement. I had to *flow.*

By the time I'd reached the seventh story, there was turmoil underneath me. I waited, fighting the need to gasp air into starved lungs. Soldiers were yelling and flashing lights around. One beam swept me where I lay, and for an instant I awaited the shock of bullets. But I was wearing dark clothes and not moving at all.

We couldn't time this. Regelin would almost certainly be in 1847 before I—and what then? I was to be the second wave of the attack, in case one was needed. I lay clawing myself fast to the iron, it was wet with dew under me, and thinking that this was nonsense. If Regelin could get to the door at all, we had succeeded. Alandzu would never suspect a Martian voice calling him, saying it was an urgent message; he'd open the door and find himself looking down a gun barrel—Of course, we might have to fight later on, if help didn't come in time. I'd be needed then.

It was forever before the commotion down there began to even out. I crawled up the stairway on hands and knees, hoping that what racket still went on would cover my noise. Eight, nine, ten—Was it ten? Had I lost count? Inside myself, I cursed.

Seventeen, eighteen. My knees were rubbed raw. I opened the door and stepped into the corridor's dim length. The room beside me was 1823. So I'd gotten it right after all.

I padded down the empty hall, letting the numbers slide by. This way, around this corner—yes, a thin sliver of light streaming under the threshold, that must be our door. Regelin was sure to be there now, covering the aliens, maybe wondering what was holding me up.

I paused. All right, my nerves were drawn nearly to snapping, I was plagued with nightmare fancies, there was no time to lose in melodramatics. Only—why take chances?

I went on past the door as quietly as I could, turned a couple of corners, and found a fire escape on the east side.

It fronted on another blank wall, just across an alley. And there was a ledge running around the hotel building, below the windows: for the washing machines, I supposed. Sticking the gun in my belt, I edged out on the strip, spread-eagling myself, and began working my way along. Oddly, the acrobatics soothed me, I was alone in clean darkness with nothing to fear but my own awkwardness. And a spaceman is necessarily a good tumbler.

Rounding the corner, I saw the window I was after, shining into night. I shuffled closer until I was against the edge of it; then, craning my neck, I peered briefly in.

I swear I had only thought Regelin might not have arrived yet. He had to be the one to enter first; they'd be too suspicious of a human voice. But I saw him standing with raised hands, disarmed, four guns aimed at his midriff.

*Four* Martians watched him.

No—four aliens. They must be!

Somehow they'd gotten the drop on him. Warned? How? I clung there with a thin breeze whimpering under my feet, digging my fingers into the wall. What to do, what to do?

If I burst in like the U. N. Marines to the rescue and yelled "Hands up!" they'd have time to shoot him and me both; I couldn't get all of them that fast. For a sick instant I thought of returning to Kit and running with her, running away forever.

No, the hunt would never stop till we were dead, and that wouldn't take long. I set my teeth. Drawing the gun, I clicked it to automatic fire. I leaned over, catching the window sill with my left hand, and shot through the pane.

The noise was like doomsday. I saw them fall, marionettes scythed down without warning, a spurting of ruined flesh and bone. Almost with the same movement, I went through the shattered window myself and sprawled on the floor.

"Good man!" said Regelin grimly. "They were expecting me when I came in. I never had a chance. Of all the incredibly bad luck—David, Gellert is an alien!"

There was no time to think of it then, no time to see Kit

and Alice alone in the room with a monster. We had to get away. Regelin must have planned this out while he stood guarded, schemed in the pale hope that I could save him. He flung open the door of the suite's adjoining room and pointed me to the bed. I dove under it. He himself stood rigid against my side of the door.

It was only moments before the main entrance was being smashed in. I lay there hearing boots crash on the floor and a howl of Martian voices.

It was a crowd that jammed inside, an excited crowd. Regelin took a long chance, but the only one. He stepped out again into the larger room, mingling with the swarm. "No one in there," I think he shouted. "The killer must have gone out the window." He began to give orders—you three go have all the fire escapes watched, you go call the military police, you pass the word to the main office. The rest of you get out, you're messing up the trail, I'll stand guard here.

Incredibly, it worked. Or maybe not so incredibly. Martians are not that different from us: a murder had been done, the crowd was too feverish to think, and he was a high-ranking officer who seemed to know what he was about. In a couple of minutes, we were alone.

I crawled from under the bed to find Regelin going through the pockets of Alandzu's batman. "Here," he said. "The keys to his car. It ought to be down there in the parking lot."

We went out the window and fumbled our way recklessly fast along the ledge until we came to the fire escape above the courtyard. Regelin clattered briskly down it, with me creeping well behind him. A pair of guards at its base challenged him. "No one on this stair," he must have said. "Here, help me down. . . . Now quick, which is Yoakh Alandzu's car? He wants me to follow a trail for him."

They didn't realize who had been killed. Time crept past, second by thundering second, while Regelin opened the car and got in and started it. He ordered the guards to watch in the alley mouth and they snapped to it, vanishing into the shadows. He slid the car near the staircase. I dropped down, landing on my toes, and bounced into the front seat and huddled on the floor. The car got smoothly into motion.

"And now for Kit," he said tightly. "If she is still in that room."

*If she is still alive.*

VIII

It was a wild and desperate chance to take, but we had little to lose. Our minds were reasoning mostly on the subconscious level now, throwing their conclusions into the taut-drawn awareness, and we couldn't stop to follow out that logic. We had to escape.

The car slid down the few blocks to the Rocket Haven, past it, around the corner. Its facade was dark, empty. No one in sight, no one had been summoned, unless they waited in ambush. Regelin rounded the block and stopped in front of the hotel. I got out and dashed inside. The lobby was deserted, only vaguely lit, even the clerk had gone to bed. Shadows flowed monstrously around me as I went up the stairs.

It made sense, I thought somewhere in the thrumming that was my mind. Suppose Gellert was an alien, one who in human form was doing some job for his race—perhaps spying on mankind, or worming his way into our councils, or merely observing. He wouldn't want to reveal his true nature to the Martians, either. He'd acted coolly and boldly—remaining a helpless prisoner till he learned our plans. Then he must have broken loose, overwhelmed Kit, and phoned Alandzu with a warning. But he'd stay alone with her and the child until members of his own race could arrive to hustle them off. He'd assume that Alandzu and the others, prepared for Regelin and me, could handle us. As they damn near had done!

I stopped in front of the door. Empty hall, empty house, silence thick around me; but there was light inside the room. The revolver was heavy in my right hand as my left slid the key into the lock. I turned it as softly as I could, threw the door open, and burst in.

The monster turned and met me with a whistling curse. I barely glimpsed the weapon which one hand swung around. My left closed on that wrist, while my right brought the heavy barrel of my own gun down on the animal snout. The blow shocked back into my muscles and I saw blood. Gellert grunted in pain, shaking that unhuman head, and tried to wrench the alien weapon loose. This time my gun barrel smashed down on the wrist, and at the same time I kneed the creature in the belly. I tore the weapon loose as Gellert lurched back, and brought up my boot, a football kick to the jaw. Gellert fell heavily, twitching and moaning.

Kit was in my arms, then, sobbing uncontrollably. "He grew *thin*," she gasped. "He made himself *thin*."

I looked at the strips with which our prisoner had been bound. Yes—that plastic flesh could almost ooze out of such lashings, hurl itself forward to overwhelm unarmed Kit— Alice was clinging to my legs, weeping. "Daddy, daddy!" I picked her up, kissing the wet terrified little face—what a sight it had been for a child!—and gave her back to her mother.

A glance at the door—No one stirred out there. Gellert and I had been equally anxious to keep the fight silent. Whatever Martians had heard it must have decided it was none of their business and gone back to sleep. And I—God, I *had* my alien!

I kicked the heaving flanks. "Get up," I said. "Get up or I'll shoot you here and now."

Gellert staggered erect. She—yes, *she*, in the torn and now ill-fitting pajamas—grabbed at the wall for support. I stuck her own—gun?—in my belt, and gestured with mine. "Let's go."

She moved slowly forward. She was as squat and powerfully built and rubbery-limbed as the male I'd once seen; the wig had fallen off the crested head, and the little pigment-spots which had given her jaws a man's blueness were absorbed again by the colorless skin, but brows and lashes and body hair, fastened on with infinite skill, still clung. She shambled before me, wiping her bloody muzzle with one seven-fingered hand.

"Reggy's got a car outside," I whispered to Kit. "We'll get this thing to Yueth like we planned, at his home. After that, he'll protect us till an inquiry can be made."

We went down the stairs again, and out onto the sidewalk—just as a police car drew near. Its probing searchlight dazzled my eyes, wobbled, and held firm. I heard the Martian oath loud in the night. *"Kevran yantsu!"*

"Into the car!" I gave Kit a shove that sent her spinning forward with Alice in her arms. Gellert chose that moment to fight, whirling on me and grabbing my gun hand and punching savagely for my face. I launched myself against her, throwing the whole weight of me at her solidity, dropping my gun so I could wrestle.

A pistol cracked, and another and another. A siren began to shriek. I slugged Gellert toward the car. Kit, in the front seat, opened the back door. I got my hands on Gellert's throat and lunged. Both of us toppled into the back seat. Regelin got going. I heard a tommy gun start its yammer.

We fought there in the car, kicking and punching and gouging, while Regelin shot up Seventh. The police beam held us like a long gleaming finger, they roared behind us and their gunner was shooting. I slugged Gellert, hard jolting blows into the rubbery face. A hand was on my throat, clamping shut. I got my teeth on its wrist and bit like a dog.

Kit knelt in the front seat, reaching over and fumbling at

us where we struggled in darkness. Her hands closed on the fleshy crest of the alien and she pulled. Gellert snarled in pain, her head yanked upward. My fist slammed into her throat. She had grown claws and begun raking me.

We turned the corner on a wheel and a half and roared up Lyndale. Houses were a blur, fleeing past at 200 miles an hour. The car lurched wildly to avoid a collision, jumped up on a lawn, and bounced down into the street again. The police held steady, fifty yards behind. The ether must be crackling with their calls for help.

One more blow, two, three. Gellert slumped, all at once. I lay there beside her, gasping, darkness whirling in my head.

Consciousness returned. I crawled into the back seat and sat with my feet on Gellert's body, my head in my hands. "I've got the thing covered," said Kit. She was holding Regelin's sidearm, pointing it at the monster.

The car shook to the bursting of machine-gun explosives on its armor. We couldn't hold out long, sooner or later one of them would find a vital part. Or a jet would come overhead and strafe us. I forced full awareness back into my spinning brain.

"If we surrender now—" Regelin's voice was dim under the roaring of cloven air. "We've got the alien here for proof."

I felt the writhing under my feet. The searchlight glare, probing in through our canopy, showed the face of Fred Gellert. The wig was gone, yes—but what Martian had ever paid attention to one little man, enough to remember his appearance?

Kit's voice was thin and savage. "Change back," she said. "Change back, damn you, or you get a bullet in the stomach."

A hoarse defiance: "Do you think that matters to me?"

The car drummed and rattled with the slugs.

I felt the strange gun hard against my belly. "We may have a chance," I said slowly. "I don't know what this thing

does, but we can try. We've got no other weapons that'll
stop that car."

Regelin nodded bleakly. "Get ready to shoot, then," he
said. "I'll let them pull alongside."

He slowed our hurtling pace. The police car drew up, long
and lean and black. I rolled down the window. The gun
was cold and heavy, awkward in my five-fingered hand,
but there seemed to be a firing stud. Gellert cursed, trying
to sit up. "Don't," said Kit.

They weren't shooting now, but tommy barrels must be
firm on us. I aimed the new gun and pushed the stud.

There was no noise, no recoil. But suddenly the other car
disintegrated. I saw a flash of smoke and steam and fire, the
air was full of flying steel. There was only a heap of fragments and burning fuel between the front and rear ends
as Regelin got into full speed again.

We heard the whistling overhead. Looking up, I saw the
jet diving. I leaned out the open window, into the ripping
wind, and shot again. The jet hailed down on us.

"Okay." Kit's tone was hard. "Let's go."

We had no chance to turn back and try to find Yueth.
There was a hornet's nest behind us by now.

We had to run. Already we were out in open country.
Regelin turned off on the first side road and sent us bullet-
like over dirt and gravel, bearing north.

"I'll cover our friend, Kit," I said wearily. Strength had
drained from me with our escape. It seemed a thousand years
since I had eaten or slept, a million since I had known unfrightened peace. "Give me the revolver."

We made Gellert crouch on the floor, in the far corner
from me. Kit crawled into the back seat and wiped my face
and slashed body, crying. I held her close with one arm
while we fled.

It was dawn by this time. Clouds had piled up, and sunrise was hidden by a veil of rain. That was helpful, and we
badly needed help just then. It was an hour or so later that
we spotted the abandoned farm.

There are a lot of them in this north country—weed-grown yards, fields where a thin growth of forest is creeping back, a decayed shack and outbuildings. This one had a fairly good barn, though. We drove in through the sagging doors, stopped, and got out. My legs wobbled under me.

"Kit, you and Alice may as well sleep in the car," said Regelin. His tones were dull with exhaustion. "We shall stay here till nightfall."

Alice whimpered and huddled against her mother. She was shivering, and Kit brought my hand over to feel her forehead. Hot, and the pulse was high. Kit's eyes looked at me out of caverns of shadow.

"Fever," she said. "What shall we do?"

"Wait," I told her. "There's nothing else for us."

"No food, no medicine, no—" She slumped and turned away, carrying the girl in her arms. My face twisted.

The barn was cold and damp, it smelled moldy. Outside, the rain fell strong and steady, veiling the spruce woods, turning the road into mud. Regelin coughed, more miserable even than I.

We sat down. Gellert squatted a few feet away, facing us with a blank expression. I held the revolver loose, ready to shoot if need be.

"Well," said Regelin, "what do we do now?"

"I don't know," I said. "I just don't know."

The rain drummed loud on the roof. Water dripped in through the holes and runneled along the dirt floor.

After a while Regelin smiled. "For a cup of zardak, I think I would trade my ancestry," he said. "If I were also allowed a dish of ruzan, they could have my right arm."

"Bacon and eggs, toast and coffee," I answered .

We were beginning to revive a little. Hunger was fading to a weariness within us, muscle aches becoming a throb instead of a pain, numbed minds clearing. I felt some return of decisiveness.

"We're not too badly off," I said. "We're still alive and free, more or less, and we've got the prisoner we wanted, even if we can't deliver her as yet. We'll think of something."

Regelin's eyes hardened, and he slanted his antennae toward Gellert. "Yes," he said bleakly, "I think we may as well hold an interrogation."

A smile crossed the pseudo-human face. "If you think I am afraid of you—" said Gellert.

"Look," I told her, "we're not sadists. We have no desire to use torture. Nevertheless, this seems to be an issue transcending such scruples."

"It is for me too," said Gellert quietly.

"Why don't you tell us your real name at least?" asked Regelin in an almost casual tone.

She shrugged. "If you wish. I am called Radeef l'al Kesshub." That is the nearest I can come to those thick syllables. I noticed the throat contracting as she said them; human vocal cords couldn't master those noises.

"Now look," I said, "we already know you must come from the stars, and that you've used your peculiar powers to infiltrate the governments of both planets. You've egged them on to a war in which you were the real victors. We can also safely assume that there are not too many of you; otherwise, with a weapon like this gun, you could have taken over openly. So you see, we already have the basic facts, and the rest is largely a matter of satisfying our own curiosity."

"Remain curious, then," said Radeef sullenly.

"This gun, now." I turned the squat thing over in my free hand. "How does it work?"

"You expect me to give away military secrets of my people?"

"They may not be so secret as you think." Odd how cold and clear my brain was. "I can make an informed guess about this weapon. Both Earth and Mars have been experimenting with sub-molar forces, with a view to designing frictionless machines. I've studied some of the declassified results. In theory, it should be possible to generate a dense force-field and project it from some such instrument as this. That would be noiseless and recoilless, too. When the field, sent out in a tight beam, encounters solid matter, it reacts with the intermolecular forces and yields its energy to the molecules themselves. They fly apart with fantastic violence—in all directions, to conserve momentum, but mostly, if the gun is well-designed, in a plane normal to the force beam. Theoretically, the object struck should be reduced to gas, single molecules and atoms; in practice, obviously, it disintegrates into small chunks. Molecular bonds being strong, the chunks don't get far apart, maybe only a few inches, and there isn't much noise. The object just falls apart."

Radeef remained silent.

"Why are you doing it?" asked Regelin, very softly. "What harm have we ever done to you?"

"You exist," said Redeef. But it was not a malevolent statement, somehow. I thought I heard vague regret in it.

"I don't think you are the vanguard of an interstellar invasion," I went on. "Even if logistics permitted such an operation, there is the question of motive. No reason why a highly advanced culture should have to conquer anyone else. It'd be much easier to make what they needed right at home. Or if you *had* to overrun somebody, it wouldn't be a powerful civilization nearly as far along as your own You'd pick on backward races, primitives, wouldn't you?

"In short, I doubt that this is an invasion or the preparation for one. I think you're a private group, acting on your own, a sort of filibustering expedition. And you had to tackle us because you had no choice; if you have any sense, you'd much rather deal with savages or barbarians. So—were you marooned here?"

No answer. I hated to use the third degree; it probably wouldn't accomplish anything, anyway.

"What puzzles me," said Regelin, "is why Dzuga should have changed to his natural form when you hit him. None of the others did, you know—blows, bullets, death itself, didn't make them revert. What was there peculiar about your assault on Dzuga?"

"Heat?" I wondered. "He got burned, you know."

"Possibly. Though it seems precarious. It is too easy, these days, for anyone to touch hot metal. And if you stop to think about it, David, a bullet in the body generates considerable heat."

"Then—"

Lightning glared outside, and thunder boomed after, trembling in the rickety old barn.

*"Electric shock!"*

Regelin nodded. "Yes," he said, "I think that must be the answer. We can try it out easily enough."

Radeef flinched, snarling. "Go ahead," she jeered. "Waste your time."

"We have nothing else to waste," said Regelin mildly.

He guarded our prisoner while I went to the car after supplies. There was a Martian flashlight with its powerful 12.3-volt battery. I took out the lens, bulb, and reflector, and used the car's complete repair kit to bolt the tube to a three-foot length of broomstick which some scratching around in the barn turned up. On either side of the stick I taped spare cables for the husky dieselectric engine, from the battery to the end of the stick, with the wires bared a few inches beyond the end. When I touched them and pressed the button, I felt a tingling jolt. It didn't seem like much, but—

"Come here," I said.

Radeef snarled and backed away. Regelin followed, covering her with his gun. I forced her into a corner and jabbed.

The shock rippled through her, body shrinking and thickening, face melting, crest rising out of the naked shape-changing skull. She cursed and fought for balance, flowing back toward human shape. I shocked her again, batting aside the hands that clawed for my rod. Radeef spat and gave up, assuming the alien form.

I turned with a high sense of victory to look at Regelin. "That's it," I said. "That's how we prove our story. It's also the simple test by which all of them can be flushed out."

"Hm. Yes." Regelin studied our enemy thoughtfully. "Though I rather imagine that the intricate details of histology, and even the internal organs, cannot change so readily as the outer shape. Is that true?"

Something seemed to collapse in Radeef. She sat down and buried her face in her hands. Her angry defiance had been long and brave, but she'd had a rough time of it too.

"Yes," she whispered. "We can adjust the oxygen system to a wide range of different atmospheres, but otherwise, if you dissected the abdominal cavity of one of us, or looked at the brain, or got some cells under a microscope, you would find it unalterable—not Earthling or Martian."

"X-rays, then," said Regelin. "Another test."

"But all the men in both our armed services got those," I protested.

"Yes, but the aliens have been high officers, remember. They could easily arrange for their physical checkups to be made by doctors who were of their own race. Then the only danger is that one of them might die in battle or accident and be, ah, looked into. But that isn't a great risk; who would look closely at an unpleasantly mangled heap of intestines?"

I stared at our captive where she huddled at my feet. "Where are you from, Radeef?" I asked softly.

She didn't look up, and her voice was a whisper. "Sirius."

"And why did you come here? What do you want of us?"

"It began long ago," she said. "Two hundred or more years ago. There are four intelligent races in the Sirian System. They had advanced about as far as you have now—ahead in some ways, behind in others, but on the whole your equals. There was a great war in that system. The people of Sha-eb were masters of biology, they have created things you do not yet dream of at Sol. They wanted spies and infiltrators. They developed us, as artificial mutations."

I shook my head, stricken quiet by the vastness of it. Not only the immense way to Sirius, almost nine light-years of utter black distance; not only the concept of other races, other civilizations, isolated in loneliness throughout that enormous dark; no, it was the achievement of Sha-eb. I knew enough biology to realize what was called for in such a protean being: pigmentation cells; flexible tissue; a fantastic calcium system which could grow bones and teeth to order, within seconds (probably depositing them around a cartilaginous base already there, I thought; the calcium-holding cells would be enbedded in the cartilage itself); a still stranger nervous system which could control that intricacy down to the minutest details—

No wonder an electric shock would upset the equilibrium. Nerve currents are themselves electrical. The unbelievable thing was that the duplicate was so stable to all other influences.

"How long did it take them to create your race?" I asked.

"I don't know," she said tonelessly. "A decade, perhaps. They used forced-growth techniques. They could manipulate individual genes. We don't know their science any more than you do."

She sighed. "With our help, as well as its other weapons, Sha-eb was victorious. Peace was firmly established in the Sirian System. And we, the changelings, we were not needed any more. We were feared, hated, discriminated against, forbidden to assume the shape of any—natural—race. As if all life were not born of the same forces! At last we were forbidden children, we must die out.

"We banded together, secretly, and tried to seize the government of Sha-eb, using our power of disguise. It failed. Most of us were killed. Some of us managed to seize a great spaceship which was to be used for exploring the outer planets. We fled the Sirian System altogether, such few of us as remained. Sol was our choice, because astronomers believed that single stars have more planets. We would have a better chance of finding a home. The voyage lasted almost a hundred years, with most of us spending the time in suspended animation to stretch out the meager supplies." She chuckled drearily. "Why do I say 'us'? I wasn't born yet. But we Tahowwa think of ourselves as a race. It has to be us few banded against a universe that has no room for us.

"Fifty years ago, we entered the Solar System. Secretly, we scouted it. We found only Earth and Mars fit habitations; everywhere else, we have to live penned in steel and plastic, sunless, windless, dead metal and no earth we could call our own. Carefully, assuming native forms, we studied your worlds. There was no place for us. We might be welcomed, yes, we might even be given a few small reservations to live on, but that was not enough. Always there would be the watchfulness and the unvoiced fear; who could ever wholly trust us? We wanted a planet to call *ours*. One where we could live openly, as masters, in our natural shapes, where we could bear children and raise them to be free. You cannot know that hunger, you who belong. We have always been the disinherited.

"Some wanted to push on, some wanted to reveal themselves openly, but the final vote was for remaining here and fighting—in our own peculiar fashion. There are heavy armaments in the great spaceship, where it circles beyond Pluto; if Earth and Mars could be pulled down far enough, we could finish the job ourselves.

"I need not describe the details of the past fifty years. You can guess them, I suppose. We few thousand worked long, laying the ground. One by one, after they were known in full, high officials of both planets were quietly assassinated with their families—by their guards, who were our people. Their places were taken by us. It has required every member of our race. Children are almost born into their work, raised in secret places and thrown into the task before they are fully mature. I have borne children myself, and not seen them since. It is not easy."

Her voice faded out. The rain roared down, and streamers of mist curled through the barn's gloom.

"And now," I said slowly, "you have broken Earth. Not quite, we could still recover fast if we had a chance, but Mars will soon reduce us to helplessness. Then what plans do you have for Mars?"

She didn't answer that.

Regelin's chuckle was harsh. "Conquered," he said. "Conquered by refugees!"

"It's a common enough process in history," I answered. "Look at Rome: the Goths were running from the Huns, who'd been kicked out by the Chinese. Only these—Tahowwa—are smarter about it. They let us do their fighting for them."

"So few of them," said Regelin between his teeth. "So few, so thinly scattered, so easily unmasked if you only knew what to look for. And still we are helpless against them. It is maddening."

"We'll have to keep trying," I said. "A long-distance call to Yueth? No, the lines are down. A letter? I imagine the mail of all non-aliens of rank is monitored. An attempt to sneak back into the city? Hopeless. But we'll think of something. We've got to find a way."

I turned and went over to the car at Alice's cry. Kit held the little girl close. She was crying herself. Alice babbled something I couldn't follow, but there was delirium in it.

IX

AFTER DARK we drove further, not very sure of just where we were and not feeling that it mattered a great deal. It was about ten when we came into a village, a few houses and a general store and a bank and a farm dealer. Regelin halted out of sight while I went to knock on the door of a lighted home. A man came out, and I stood with my face in shadow and asked the way to the doctor's. "Had a little accident," I said. "Got lost in the woods and fell and hurt my arm."

He squinted, trying to discern me. "Where you from?" he asked. I imagine news was very scarce here, with mail service irregular and only the official Martian telecasts.

"I'm on the road," I said. "Came through Duluth, but there weren't any jobs there, so I drifted further."

"You been drifting a long ways, then." I could almost read his mind: *This guy might turn thief. He might already have stolen.*

"I got an uncle in North Dakota who'll fix me up when I get there," I said. "Now where's the doctor, please?"

"Two houses down. His name's Hansen, Bill Hansen."

"Thanks." I turned away, wondering how much I'd betrayed myself. My accent was Eastern, though the years in space had blurred it.

There was darkness in the doctor's home. We parked across the road, under a gloom of trees, and I went and knocked again. I hoped he was in.

Alice whimpered in my arms. Her eyes were bright and blank, they no longer recognized me.

A window opened overhead. "Who's there?" An old man's voice, but still firm and resonant.

"A patient for you," I answered as quietly as possible. "Emergency."

"Okay, I'll be right down."

The town had electric light, which was unusual; I suppose they'd managed to build a wood-burning generator. The glow from the opened door was sharp in my eyes, and I stepped swiftly inside and closed the door behind me.

Hansen stood looking me over. He was a lean, somehow aristocratic man, white-haired, his face gaunt and seamed, his eyes blue and steady behind old-fashioned glasses. He'd pulled trousers over his pajamas but not stopped for anything else.

"The kid's sick," I said. "Been running a fever for a good twelve hours, and delirious by now."

"Hm." He took Alice gently in his arms and bore her into the living room. "Switch off the hall light, will you? We're only allowed one bulb at a time." He laid her on the couch and opened his bag. I stood in the doorway, watching him work, thinking of Kit sitting out there and holding Regelin's hand because there was nothing else for her to hold to, nothing in all the world.

Hansen finished his examination and turned to me. "How'd she get this way?" he asked.

"Does it matter?" I replied.

"It sure does. I have to know what she's been through."

"All right." I dropped one hand into my jacket pocket, where it closed on Regelin's gun. "She's been sketchily fed on whatever we could give her, for weeks. She hasn't gotten anything for the past two days, because we didn't have anything. She's been badly frightened, time and again. She's had inadequate sleep. She's been in a cold, damp place all this day. That enough?"

He regarded me for a long time. I must have looked rather unhealthy myself, thin and hollow about the eyes, dirty and unshaven. "It is, Mr. Arnfeld," he answered. "I understand."

"So you've heard those alarms too?"

"How could I avoid it? It was on the nationwide 'casts for days. Only this morning it came on again, with the information that you'd committed murder in the Twin Cities and were believed to have fled northward."

I shrugged. "All right. But what about the kid?"

"Bad case of flu, and it might be complicated by bronchial pneumonia. People who treat children this way ought to be shot." He said it evenly, without rancor, but there was no smile on his face.

"We hadn't any choice," I replied. "Those who're after us wouldn't have cared for her at all, except maybe dig her grave."

"Well," he said, "I think I can pull her out of this. We've

no penicillin here, but I do have a good supply of abiotin, and it'll take worse cases than hers. But she's going to need absolute rest, with care and good food, for quite a while."

"I'm afraid we're broke," I said. "Nor do I imagine we can stay here very long."

"Hardly." He picked up the girl again. "Why not bring your friends inside while I start tending to her?"

"And have you call the sheriff? We'd have to fight him too, and we've done enough harm."

"Don't be stupider than you can help, Arnfeld. Anyway—" this time he did grin— "I'd kind of like to hear your story."

I went out and fetched them while he carried Alice upstairs. As the door closed behind us, he emerged on the landing and stood there unmoving, his imperturbability shaken.

Surely we were a strange crew. I looked like any tramp, but there was Kit, with her lithe form and loose golden hair and pale, thin, lovely face; Regelin towering over us, dark, amber-eyed, somber in the Martian uniform that still held its hard neatness; and Radeef the monster, shuffling before us at gun point, snouted unhuman head bent so the light glistened off her crested skull. Against that quiet middle-class home, we were like invaders from somewhere outside all reality.

Hansen drew a long breath. "All right," he said. "Sit down and wait a while. Will you help me with the girl, ma'am?"

Kit ran up the stairs, almost falling in her urgency.

It seemed a long time before they came down again. Hansen was smiling and nodding. "I've given her the first injections," he said. "She's resting easy and should start mending pretty quick." His eyes swiveled around among us. "I daresay you could all use some supper. Come on into the kitchen and I'll fix it."

While he prepared the meal, we outlined the story for him. I don't imagine he, or any sane being, would have believed it without the sight of Radeef squatting on the floor.

As it was, he became very still, only asking a few questions to clear up some points. At the end, he compressed his lips and shook his head.

"It is a terrible thing to learn," he said.

"You needn't fear, doctor," said Radeef suddenly. "It happens not to be true. Actually—"

"Go ahead," I ordered her. "Change your form."

She grinned at me. "How can I? What you say is obviously impossible." Turning to Hansen: "Doctor, the truth is, briefly, this. I am from Sirius, yes, belonging to a crew of explorers who arrived only a few months ago. We contacted the Martian government, since that was the only effective one left, and—"

"She's lying!" Kit's voice was shrill and ragged. "She'll make us out to be crazy, when we—we—"

"Oh, no," said Radeef. "They are fairly sane. But the political situation is—peculiar. Normally we would invite Mars to join the interstellar union which already comprises a dozen stars, and the Archon is, indeed, anxious to do so. However, a powerful group is in strong opposition to the surrender of sovereignty this would entail, so the Archon's party has had to negotiate secretly, to present them with a *fait accompli*. Getting wind of this, the opposition tried to break it up and create ill will by murdering and kidnapping members of our crew. This is the only case in which they have succeeded."

Hansen looked steadily at all of us. "Why should Earthlings help them?" he asked.

An owl somewhere outside hooted loudly, very loudly in the stillness.

Radeef shrugged. "It is difficult to say, especially when one considers the benefits Earth would derive. You would not have to be kept subjugated, you know, since with the Solar System in our union Mars would have no reason to fear Earth. I imagine these people were bought by promises of rewards."

"Hansen," I said, "I fought for Earth since I was sixteen years old."

"So he claims," said Radeef. "And even if true, what of it? He was drafted, or would have been."

Nightmare. What to do, how to convince this old man, or force him, or—? We couldn't stay here, guarding him, without being discovered; we couldn't take him captive with us, for Alice's sake—what to *do*?

Regelin's harsh laugh broke the waiting. "*Aklan tubat!*" he exclaimed. "I can admire you for that attempt, Radeef. However—" He leaned forward, hard and chill. "You say it is impossible for you to change your form as we claim?"

"Of course," said Radeef. "Dr. Hansen, as a medical man you—"

Regelin lunged. One foot smacked her against the wall, holding her pinioned, while his left hand grabbed her arm and stretched it out. The right, in the same blurring motion, snatched a sizzling skillet off the stove and brought it savagely down against the captive arm.

It happened so fast that her reaction was sheer reflex. The arm stretched itself, grew thin and long, jerking back from the pan. Regelin laughed again and let her go, banging the skillet back into place. Radeef snarled and restored herself. "Doctor," she cried. "It's true we can—"

"Never mind," said Hansen. "It was a nice try you made."

Afterward we went into the living room and sighed, our tired bodies seeming to melt into the chairs. Hansen paced up and down, hands behind his back, trying to think of a plan for us.

"The ordinary police won't do," he said. "They'd almost certainly report the affair to Martian GHQ, like they're supposed to, and then the invaders need only murder them as well as you people. Even if the cops keep the secret, how can anyone be contacted who matters?

"If the Commandant himself is an invader, then the true Martian officer who believes your story will have to organize a coup—a mutiny. It'll have to be done so smoothly that no other headquarters, on Earth or Luna or Mars, knows about it before something can be done against them. All that will need time."

"Yueth dzu Talazan," said Regelin. "He is our main hope. I am quite sure he is a true Martian, for he is not high-ranking enough to call for a substitute; and at the same time he is a bold, able officer. If he could be convinced—"

"Well," said Hansen, "I can try and get a message to him. You write something that'll bring him to you alone, or with only a few trusted friends—and secretly, of course. Then you can show him this—Radeef. After that, he may be able to shelter you somewhere while he goes to work against the enemy."

"If you expect me to be fooled again," snapped Radeef, "I feel sorry for all of you!"

"Oh, there are other ways," said Hansen evenly. "Your metabolism is obviously much like ours, apart from the cell-control characteristics. I'm pretty sure scopolamine or some similar drug would work on you. Or a good husky insulin shock would probobly make you go into form-changing convulsions."

She didn't glare this time. There was a sudden forlornness about her. I wouldn't have liked to be a prisoner of desperate alien enemies.

"Well—" Regelin rubbed his forehead, above antennae that drooped with weariness. "Well, I can write Yueth a letter, telling him the story and begging him in the name of our old friendship to come see for himself. I think he would, even if he did not believe. He is that sort. But how to get the message to him, secretly—?"

"I'm needed here," said Hansen, "but I could arrange to have the letter delivered. There's a smart young kid here who sometimes works for me and would love a chance to go to the cities. I could tell him some story about having heard, from a Martian passing through town tonight in the search for you—that'd explain the car as well, if anyone's noticed it—I could tell him of having heard that this Yueth can ar-

range for penicillin distribution and that I'm appealing for
a little. God knows I could use it!"

An eagerness lifted within me, but I had to fight it
down: "The Martians will know that's ridiculous. Yueth
is in Intelligence."

"But they don't have to know. That's just the story I
tell the kid, and I'll ask him to keep mum. As far as the
Martians will know, it'll only be a personal message to Yueth.
I daresay their officers get quite a few from humans, begging
for this or that."

"*Unven!*" Regelin's eyes blazed. "I think you have the
answer, doctor. I think we can do it!"

"All right, then. There's my desk. Write your letter."

While Regelin's tall form folded itself awkwardly around
the human furniture, Hansen turned to me. "You can't stay
here, of course," he said. "I couldn't possibly conceal you,
and there are people in this village who'd cheerfully betray
you for the reward. Let's arrange a hiding place where you
can go. Yueth can come to me, and I can direct him further."

"Okay," I said. "Where?"

He smiled. "You look like you could use a little rest and
food yourself, son. Why not take a few days off and go fishing? I have a cabin about a hundred miles from here, up
in the Arrowhead country. I'll bet nobody else is closer than
twenty miles. Good place to hide."

"Alice—" began Kit.

"She'll have to stay here. It'll be safer for her anyway.
I can hide one child all right. She'll be taken care of and get
well, I promise you."

Kit nodded, slowly and mutely.

"And you'll need food, too," said Hansen. "I got a lot of
canned goods and vegetables and stuff down in the cellar.
Help me load it in your car."

"But you have to eat, too—" I said.

"I'll make out. Come on, now, hop to it."

We got several cases into the vehicle, moving with immense quiet not to wake the sleeping homes around us.

"That'll do for a couple of weeks," said Hansen finally. "You ought to catch enough fish to stretch it out, too. Never saw such a lake for northerns."

We returned to the house and he drew me a map. I folded it up and said: "Doctor, I've no good way of saying thanks."

"Then don't," he grunted.

Regelin finished his letter, sealed it in an envelope, and addressed it to Yueth at his private quarters. Kit rose and started up the stairs. "Come along, Dave, will you?" she asked.

We stood for a while over Alice. The girl was sleeping peacefully now, and I thought she looked less feverish. Kit stooped over and kissed her. "So long, brat," she whispered. "I love you very much."

We went back downstairs. Regelin was waiting. He bowed formally to Hansen, giving him the Martian salute of respect, and Kit and I shook his hand. Then we herded Radeef out into the car and started our journey again.

X

A COUPLE of times we lost our way, and there was a bad moment when a jet swooped low overhead—Regelin heard it from far away, and we pulled off the road under some trees and crouched there to wait; but it flashed on by. Still, we reached the cabin well before sunrise, with about two drops left in the fuel tank. "There can be no more running for us," said Regelin.

Kit stood under tall windy trees and drew a lungful of the air that blew in from the lake. "I'm not sorry," she answered.

There was a woodshed in which we could hide the car. The keys let us into a four-room cottage, neat and compact and gracefully furnished. Regelin and I stood watch over Radeef till dawn, while Kit slept like a tired child.

Sunrise came in a shout of light. The long grass outside was one glitter from dew, and the lake rippled and flashed beyond a screen of spruce and beech and sumac. It smelled of growth here, green leaves, needles and forest mould, water and sunlight.

After breakfast, I studied the woodshed again. It was as sturdy as the cottage against which it was built, a ram would be needed to break it down, and it had a concrete floor. I took the car out again, standing it by the house and chopping branches to conceal it; then I moved a cot and a few other necessities into the shed, and made Radeef enter.

She sat down on the cot and changed her face so it could smile. I suppose she meant it well, though it was frightening to watch. "If I must be imprisoned," she said, "it could be worse."

"We can't hold a gun on you all the time," I said. "We'll keep you in food and so on till Yueth gets here—that'll take a week or so, I guess, since Hansen's messenger will have to go on horseback. Want some books? There's a small library in the cabin."

"No," she said. "We Tahowwa don't mind just sitting and thinking. But thank you."

"I wish you hadn't been so—conquest-minded," I said awkwardly. "You probably aren't a bad race. If you'd come to us openly, we'd have provided something for you."

Bitterly: "Yes—a charity ward."

"Well," I said, "I imagine a few of you will survive anyway. Most of you, even, if you surrender once the game is up."

"Which it isn't, yet."

"No, I'm afraid it isn't. Want to tell me anything more about yourself and your people, Radeef?"

"No. Please go away."

I padlocked the door and returned to the cabin. I wanted to sleep, but my nerves were still drawn too thin. Regelin was more resilient, he was already stretched out with his legs reaching over the end of the bunk. Kit and I made the cabin shipshape and then went for a swim.

"I'll take this side of the point," I said, "and you can have the other."

She cocked her head at me. "Dave," she said, "you're an awful prude at heart, you know that?"

The water was cold, transparent as glass, sliding sensuously along the skin and tingling in the blood. We came out laughing, for the first time in a long while, and lay down on the grassy bank and let the sun have us. It felt strange not to be skulking about after dark.

"I wonder how Alice is," said Kit presently.

"She's okay," I answered. "She'll miss you, of course, but Hansen is a nice old codger. And with luck, you should see her again inside a couple of weeks."

"Or never—No!" She shook her head till the blonde hair flew. "I won't think about it."

I laid my hand on hers, and then I kissed her. She responded with a sudden wild hunger.

In the afternoon Regelin and I hunted up the boat, where it lay under a lean-to, and took the doctor's fishing tackle out on the lake. It was wide and empty there, ringed in with forest and roofed with sky, everywhere was quietness. We brought in a pike and some smaller fish, and Kit had found a blueberry patch, so that was a cheerful supper.

Kit said, next morning, that she'd slept poorly—nightmares plagued her, now that the pressure was off but the danger not over. I took her for a long walk, clear around the lake. We passed a few other cabins, but they were all deserted; this place was too far from civilization to be accessible nowadays. We talked of many things, there under the dappled shadows, and I need not repeat them, except that at the end Kit whispered to me: "Why wait, Dave? We may be dead tomorrow. Why should we wait?"

We came back toward sunset. Regelin sat on the porch reading a book. He regarded us gravely and shrewdly, as we approached hand in hand. Finally he smiled.

"Earth," he said, clearing his throat, "is now under Martian law, and there is one item in the code of which you may not have heard. A military officer is empowered to perform marriages. Does that interest you?"

"*Does it?*" I whooped, and Kit ran to kiss him.

None of us could remember just how the Christian ceremony went, but we stumbled through it as well as we could. Then Regelin said the Martian words, translating them for us afterward—strange to hear them under the sky and in the bowers of Earth, but they had an austere pagan beauty I cannot forget. Afterward we had a wedding supper, opening the bottle of cheap wine which Hansen had thrown into one of his boxes, and then Regelin said he'd always wanted to try moonlight fishing and this was his chance.

It was a strange honeymoon, but we didn't think much about that. Perhaps the fact of our having it on the edge of darkness made it sweeter for us, though that hardly seems possible. I am afraid that Regelin was rather neglected, though it was partly his own fault—he was so seldom around.

Kit, my dearest, if you should ever read this, remember those days and nights. Remember that I will always love you.

I found other things to do, now and then. For one, I investigated the Sirian weapon as much as I dared. It seemed to be what I had theorized, a super-powerful and compact version of the Colson resonator with a projector for the generated forcefield. Its charge was a coil of some wire which fed into the firing chamber an inch at a time and disappeared on my shooting the gun; I suspect it was an alloy in an abnormal energy state, though how produced and maintained in its metastable condition I cannot say. There was also an adjustment stud which could regulate the width of the force-beam—broad for a lesser effect over a wider area, to kill a man noiselessly by disrupting cell nuclei, without leaving much outward mark on him; narrow for a hard, cracking discharge which would blow a thin section almost to atoms at longer range, without disturbing anything beyond that circle of destruction. A lovely, versatile weapon! And the principle would have innumerable uses for peacetime industry, I thought with a stinging regret.

From time to time, also, we worried about Hansen's message. There was so much which could go wrong and bring death down on our heads. We arranged defenses for the house, to give a decent account of ourselves if it should come to that.

We took the heavy machine-gun off our stolen car and mounted it in the front door, behind a barricade of earth-filled sacks and boxes. The windows all had burglarproof shutters, closing from the inside, through which we drilled loopholes—except in the kitchen window. Our theory was that if we were attacked, one of us at the machine-gun could hold the lake entrance, and one in the rear of the house defend the two bedrooms; the third would be off duty in the kitchen, prepare food or sleep, and could give warning of any funny business in that sector.

I also dug up a permapen and this old notebook (did it belong to a child of Hansen's once? I do not know. Perhaps I will never know.), and spent a few hours each day recording everything which has led up to this moment. If we should, after all our striving, fail, I can perhaps hide the book; it might give a clue to someone in the future who chances across it, and he might resume our work. A silly thing to do, I suppose, but—

I have just added a foreword. It is my time off watch, and I should sleep, but I cannot. For us, now, the end is close, and I have written that fact in bitterness. Now let me go back and finish our story.

It was nine days after our arrival. I was sitting on the lakeshore, enjoying the afternoon sunlight, when Regelin's long shadow fell athwart me. "Hullo, old chap," he said. "Where's the wife?"

"You've been reading too many English novels," I answered. "As a matter of fact, she shooed me out of the house; said her hair was a mess and she wasn't ready yet to spring anything so unglamorous on me as whatever it is she does to it."

He stretched out on the grass beside me.

"I wonder what is delaying Yueth?" he asked.

"No telling. But he couldn't just up and leave, I imagine. If he's to come secretly, he has to arrange things so he can go away on some ostensible business." I scowled, not wanting to think about the realities.

"Even so—" Regelin sat up, cocking his ears toward the western sky. "What's that?"

"Hm?" I could only hear the wind in the leaves and the small wavelets lapping on the shore.

"It's a jet—quick! Under cover!"

We rolled over, scrambled to our feet, and ran. We were hardly on the cabin porch when I heard the noise above my suddenly racketing heart. The jet, a Martian scout, swooped low overhead, almost skimming the lake. In moments it was beyond the horizon.

Kit came out and held me close. "What is it?" she whispered. "What do they want?"

"Maybe nothing, honey," I said, but I exchanged a grim look with Regelin over her shoulder. There was no reason why the occupation forces should fly over the Arrowhead, and Yueth would not send an advance scout.

The Martian drew me aside. "I don't like this very much," he said. "I wonder if one or two of us shouldn't slip away now, in case—"

I shook my head. "Wouldn't do much good, Reggy. If Yueth himself is coming, it's pointless; and if it's the enemy, whoever escapes will only be hunted down as we were before." Clenching my fists: "I'm tired of running. Let's have it out now, once and for all."

He nodded, wordlessly, and I went back to Kit. We sat on the porch for a long time, holding hands and saying little.

The sun declined, shadows crept over the land. It was three hours later that Regelin came back to us from the woods. "I've heard a car approaching," he said.

"Well—" I got up, stretching to ease the tautness in me. "This is the end, then, one way or another." I ruffled Kit's hair with one hand, and we went into the cabin. Regelin stayed on the porch, a rifle from Alandzu's car at his side.

The new automobile drove out of screening brush and came to a halt. It was a fast, armed vehicle, a heavier version of the one we had stolen. Looking through a loophole in a shuttered window, I saw half a dozen Martian shapes in it. One of them got out, a tall being in uniform. "Regelin," he called. "Regelin dzu Coruthan?"

"It is Yueth," our friend said to us; but his voice was not lightened. Then he broke into Vannzaru, the message we had agreed on: "I am glad you came, old comrade, but we can only show this to you. Come forward alone, into the house."

There was a crisp answer which Regelin translated: "He refuses. He says he doubts our story even now, and cannot trust us not to kill him. We must come out to them."

"Nothing doing," snapped Kit.

They bargained for a while. Finally Regelin said to us: "I have agreed to let him bring two companions inside. Be prepared for—anything."

"Get into the bedroom, Kit," I whispered. "Leave the door ajar. Cover us." She nodded and disappeared. I stood waiting, the electric stick hidden behind my back.

Regelin preceded the three Martians inside. They looked about with wary eyes, their guns held alertly. When they saw that I was unarmed and that Regelin had stood his rifle against the wall, they relaxed a little. Regelin kept them moving, talking fast, herding them toward the kitchen and the shed behind it.

Yueth brushed me as he went by. I whirled the stick from its concealment and jabbed it against his hand and squeezed the button. Even as he yelled and his face dissolved toward otherness, I was plunging against him.

I hit him with my shoulder and we went down on the floor, cursing and struggling. Regelin sprang aside and Kit's gun barked. The two soldiers fell, clawing at their weapons. She stepped forth and fired again and again until they were still.

I rolled over, clutching for the neck of the false Yueth. His body was frozen in form, half Martian and half Tahowwan. I slugged hard, behind the ear. He spat blood as I hit him in the mouth. Dimly I heard an explosive crash: Regelin had fired out at the car with the Sirian gun, blowing it apart.

I got my knee on my opponent's stomach, my hands about his throat, and banged his head against the floor. After a moment he was still. I crouched over him, sobbing breath into my lungs. The guns were talking again, I heard bullets thud against the cabin.

"Dave, Dave, Dave!" Kit was bending over me, weeping. "Are you all right, Dave?"

"Yeah," I muttered, leaning on her as I climbed to my feet. "I'm okay."

Regelin turned a bleak face to me from the window. "I got one of the others with their car," he said, "there are two left, circling around the brush. Get to the defenses."

I dragged the pseudo-Yueth, who was beginning to stir and groan, into the kitchen; opening the shed door, I flung him in with Radeef, then I locked the door again and returned to pick up a gun.

The sun was very low now, and the lake a blaze of gold. I heard birdsong in the trees, unfrightened by our warring. There was no sign of the enemy.

Kit searched the bodies of the two she had killed, throwing their weapons onto those I had taken from "Yueth." There were three automatic pistols and two Sirian disin-

tegrators, all told, added to the guns we already had. They
would be useful.

"Let's take our defense positions," I said woodenly.

"We've failed." Kit shook her head, a sudden enormous
weariness seemed to have fallen on her. "After all our trying, we've failed. Now what do we do?"

"We keep fighting," said the Martian. "I am still of the
Regelin dzu clan."

"And something may turn up, if we hold out long enough,"
I mumbled.

We waited for a long while as darkness grew around us.
Once I left my post for Kit to hold and went into the kitchen
and opened the shed door. Two Tahowwan forms moved
through the shadows, toward me. This way was their only
escape, we'd fastened the outward door tightly. I gestured
them back with my automatic.

"What is your real name, stranger?" I asked. "We don't
want to use Yueth. He was Regelin's comrade."

"I am called Naseer." The answer was sullen, out of thick
gloom. "I advise you to give up now. Your position is hopeless."

"Not yet it isn't. But as a matter of curiosity, how did you
find us?"

"It was clear you would try to communicate with someone of rank, and Yueth was known to be an old friend of
Regelin's. We intercepted the message you sent to him.
Then we went to Hánsen and questioned him with the help
of drugs."

"I suppose Yueth and Hansen are both dead?"

Indifferently: "Of course. As you will be, unless you surrender quickly."

"The—child? The one who was with Hansen?"

"No, there was no reason to injure her. She knows nothing."

"Thanks for that much." I locked the door on them and
went back to the others and told them what I'd learned.

"Now we have to try to slip away, before they close the ring on us," said Regelin.

"I'll bet they've done so already," I answered. "This is too big for them to take chances. The only hope for us that I can see is to put up a hell of a good fight when they attack. Maybe we can break their lines enough to slip through in the confusion."

We waited.

Toward midnight, another car arrived, and a light tank trundled behind it. I saw the armor gleaming vaguely by starlight. Kit woke up from a troubled sleep, and we crouched at the loopholes, watching. A Tahowwa—none of them bothered to change shape now—climbed out of the automobile and through the long wet grass, holding a white flag. Regelin stepped out to parley.

"If you do not surrender," said the alien, "we will have to destroy you. A single shell from that tank can blow your cabin apart."

"Then why don't you start shelling at once?" asked Regelin coldly.

"For the sake of the prisoner, or prisoners, you hold. We are prepared to bargain. Your lives for theirs."

"Even if you kept the bargain," said Regelin, "I do not fancy prison life. Go away."

The Tahowwa removed himself. I took aim with a Sirian gun and fired. The vehicles were just out of effective range. Narrowing the beam to a needle point, I tried again. I cut a line up the armored side of the tank. Its engine roared as it started to back. I hit its big gun, and the long barrel slumped.

Triumph was savage in me. "So much for their shells!" I called.

"Take your posts!" Regelin's voice snapped out of darkness. "There are foot soldiers approaching!"

THEY came in a silent wave, rushing out of shadows toward the walls of the cabin. We used disintegrators at wide beam, firing again and again. I saw them blown apart, spattered, destroyed, heaped under our eaves, and still they came. Behind me, in the front entrance, Regelin sat at a raving machine-gun.

The bullets were a steady hail against our walls. Now and then flame throwers opened up, trying to burn us. But chemically hardened timber is like concrete. We stood them off, shooting, shooting, and in the end they withdrew. Then there was only silence and starlight, blood and dew.

I could not see Sirius among the constellations, but I thought of it like an ominous eye in heaven. *Why did you do it?* I raged within myself. *Why did you wish them on us?*

"I think it's over for now," said Kit. Her voice was small and trembling in the shadow that filled our house. "I think they've given up."

"Maybe so," I answered gently. "Get some sleep, darling."

"I wonder—" Regelin's tone was almost musing. I saw him etched black in the doorway against the star-clouds. "I wonder why they are doing it this way. We took a frightful toll. There must be a score dead out there. And there are not so many of them in the Solar System that they can be reckless with troops. Why don't they just annihilate us with a bomb or shell?"

"I think I can guess," I answered slowly. "A modern high explosive would leave this place in splinters. There'd be nothing identifiable remaining. And they don't know if we're all here. For all they know, we split up while we were waiting for Yueth, and one of us is still at large. . . . Nor can they be sure how many people we've told our story to. They want to be sure they have all of us, and pre-ferably at least one of us alive for questioning."

"That sounds reasonable. But they won't sacrifice every-thing to that purpose. Before long, they will take their chances on blowing us up."

"Yeah. We've got to get one or more of us away before then, to try and spread the word. We should have done that before, I suppose, but —well, too late now."

The long night wore on. We could hear them moving out there, crashing brush, grinding engines, now and then a voice lifted in thick gutturals. "It must be an armored squad at least," said Regelin. "A compliment!"

"That kind of compliments I can modestly do without," I said.

At dawn the jets came, two of them whistling from the sky to blast us with rockets.

We stood on the porch, firing our disintegrators as they rushed down. One of them broke open in midair and smash-ed into the earth and skidded across the clearing into the woods. The other wobbled out of sight, trailing smoke. Our walls were gouged by the rockets but still held firm.

Temporarily, it was impasse. They couldn't get close enough to break down our defenses with low-powered explo-sives, heavy armor, or disintegrators—our own Sirian guns forbade that. And they didn't want to destroy us utterly. But sooner or later they were bound to find a way out of the dilemma: near-miss precision bombing from high up, for instance. Or they could simply starve us out.

"There's no two ways about it," I said at breakfast. "We're going to have to try a break-through." My head felt gritty from sleeplessness, it was hard to think. "If we could pro-voke them into an all-out rush, and then perhaps one or two of us slip away in the melee—"

"That requires darkness," said Regelin grayly. "Do we have until nightfall?"

Kit gave me a long and serious look. "The prisoners, too

*Intelligence Prime scowled. A page had been torn from the book. Why?*

*It could be for some simple purpose. Maybe to wipe up blood, or light a fire, or—anything. But he didn't like a story with missing pieces.*

*David Arnfeld and Regelin dzu Coruthan were almost three weeks dead now, and Christine Hawthorne was a captive. She had blurted her answers with such hysterical readiness that there had seemed no reason to question her under drugs —always a tedious and time-consuming process. But perhaps it would be wise to do so after all.*

*Skimming ahead in the narrative. Intelligence Prime decided that the missing page probably related the killing of the two prisoners, Radeef and Naseer, as a precautionary measure, which Hawthorne had told about. Their bodies had never been found for certain; their ruined flesh was doubtless mingled with the shattered unidentifiable remnants found in the cabin after the last charge of the Tahowwa. Perhaps, thought Intelligence Prime, Arnfeld had not wanted to leave the account of an outright murder in his record.*

out of the woods again, spilling Tahowwan forms from their armored doors. Our guns flamed, cutting them down, reaping them, but they moved fast. In seconds they were thundering at the front entrance.

Regelin's machine-gun stopped as he rolled away from a hurled grenade. It exploded viciously, showering the cabin with steel splinters. I crouched behind a table, sweeping them with the disintegrator beam as they came in the front door. Behind me, in the bedrooms, Kit raked their sappers trying to blow down our rear wall. The cabin shook.

Then it was over. Suddenly it was over, they had retreated again. Our home was a wreck of tumbled, broken furniture, splashed and streaming with the fragments of living creatures. We had driven them back again, but now we must live with horror.

Regelin sat up, holding his left arm. I went over to him,

shakily, and bandaged his wound. The arm would be out of action, but he could still handle a gun. He smiled in a tired way and lay down on the kitchen cot to sleep.

"They almost made it that time," I said to Kit. "I'm sorry I got you into this, darling."

"No, it was I who involved you—remember?" She made a forlorn attempt at laughter. Her dear face was smudged and streaked with dirt, and she could not halt the incessant small trembling within her.

"Well," I said, "it'll soon be over. I'm beginning to think we ought to give up. This is useless."

"No," she said. "We're finished anyway. Death now, or life in one of their jails, what's the difference? But I hope they let Alice go. Someone could adopt her."

"Sure," I said. "They'll let the kid go, to some orphanage I suppose. Alice will be all right."

"I wish—" Her voice was so low I could hardly hear it. "I wish you and I could have had children, Dave."

I held her close. The afternoon sun shone brilliantly in through the shattered door. Then we had to leave each other for our posts.

It was toward evening that another Tahowwa appeared, holding a flag of truce. Regelin and I went out to talk to him, Kit stayed within to guard the rear; but she heard the dialogue.

He squatted on the ground in front of the stoop, weird against the serenity of Earth's forest. "Your stubbornness is ill-advised," he said matter-of-factly. "There will be no one coming to help you."

"Don't be too sure of that," said Regelin.

"If you imply that you have scattered the truth wider than we thought—" It was a slow, tight murmur.

Regelin shrugged. "Think whatever you like," he said.

"Look," I said, "we'll make a bargain with you. Give us a jet and a head start, and—"

"Please, let us not waste words." The Tahowwa laughed. "You know, Arnfeld, we admire you and your friends. We do not hate you, in fact it would be pleasant if you were on our side. But necessity drives us to make a harsh ultimatum."

"Which is—?"

"We have had the child, Alice Hawthorne, brought here. We insist that you surrender to us. Otherwise the child will be killed."

I heard Kit's gasp somewhere behind me. My own head swam a little.

The Tahowwa gestured. Another of his kind stepped briefly out of the woods. He was carrying Alice. I could see that she was crying.

"How long—" I forced it out through a stiffened throat. "How long do we have to decide?"

"Until dawn tomorrow," he said, not unkindly.

He turned and walked off. All of them were hidden from sight. There were only the corpses, and the blood, and buzzing flies.

I went back into the cabin and took Kit in my arms and held her very close.

It is late as I write these final lines. Outside, there is the cool northern night, and the shimmer on the lake and the whisper of trees. A dim light glows for me, a flashlight laid on the table. I am in the south bedroom, Regelin at the front entrance, Kit sleeping in the kitchen, if she can sleep.

None of us can see the others, the great loneliness is already on us.

There is really no need to mount guard. I think the Tahowwa will keep their word. Why shouldn't they? Final victory is theirs. But habit keeps us watchful, our brains feel empty and there is only habit left.

We talked of it in broken sentences, after the Tahowwa had gone. Kit wept, dry shuddering sobs, and when I tried again to comfort her she drew away from me.

"What's the use?" she asked us, over and over again. "We're beaten. We've got to give up anyway."

Regelin shook his head. "Not alive," he answered.

"But Alice! They'll *kill* her. They'll take her out where we can see and cut her throat."

"I am sorry," he said. "But they have already murdered two worlds. We cannot let one child—"

"It's not as if there were any hope." Her voice was raw. "It's not as if any chance at all remained."

The iron of his breed closed down on him. I thought of the unbending Martian code—no, Regelin, raised in it from birth, could never give up while he lived. He shook his head again.

"They know Reggy and I survive," I said. "But they may not be sure about you, Kit, even now. If we two surrender, you could perhaps escape, sneak into the woods tonight—"

A flicker of her old temper burned at me: "How do I know you two won't break your word and fight on?"

"I'd never do that to you, Kit," I whispered.

"And they'd find out anyway," she cried. "They'd know that one of us was still loose, when they questioned you—"

"They would not kill Alice on that account," said Regelin. "They are not fiends, in spite of all they have done."

"I can't," she croaked. "I can't go and leave her."

Regelin looked at me. "Then one of us can," he said. "You are the logical one, David. You are uninjured, and also would be less conspicuous on Earth. You could perhaps reach this Torreos."

"It seems to be the only way," I answered dully.

"Dave—no!" Kit's protest was wild.

"Yes," I said, not meeting her eyes. "I'm sorry, but there's no choice."

She looked at me for a very long while. Then she turned and went away from us, into the kitchen, and closed the door behind her. I have not seen her since.

—It is now, I think, almost midnight. Regelin will soon make a rush into the woods, firing, drawing attention to himself, and while he is cut down I will try to slip past the besiegers. It is so thin a hope that it is no hope at all, but we must try. Kit can wait here and surrender to them when they come. I hope they will not harm Alice on my account, and that Kit will not think too harshly of me.

I want to finish this record and leave it here. I have loosened a floorboard and will slip the book underneath and fasten the board again. Perhaps some man years hence will stumble across it. Perhaps—

The gods must be laughing now. But a man has to keep trying.

## Epilogue

INTELLIGENCE PRIME laid the stained, tattered book aside. It was late. There was silence all around him.

He got up and glided to the window. The high tower of Mars' Earth Headquarters looked dizzily down onto the nighted reaches of Sao Paulo. Here and there a dim light glittered, and the land curved darkly away over the rim of the world. His own secret office was a very tiny thing, perched above immensity.

*Yes*, he thought, *we shall have to nab Torreos. I will give the orders tomorrow morning.*

He sighed. War was a cruel and senseless business. Sometimes he wished his fathers had not decided on it. But now the feet of the Tahowwa race were set on that road and there was no turning back. He could only guide his people as best he was able.

*I would have liked to know Arnfeld and Regelin,* he thought briefly. *As friends. I wonder what was in their minds, there at the end?*

For that matter, what had been in the mind of Christine Hawthorne? She had loved both of them. And yet she had

taken a disintegrator and stolen out of the kitchen and destroyed them before they could leave her. Afterward she
had run weeping and shrieking out to the Tahowwa, raising a clamor which drew them from all around to look at
her with a creeping horror.

Well, there must have been horror enough in her own
heart—must still be. There had been little left of her husband
and her comrade: the shattered faces were just barely rec-
ognizable, the rest not pleasant to think about. But she had
saved her child.

*I imagine the kindest thing to do is to put the girl in an
orphanage, and then kill the mother some night when she is
asleep. I don't know. Maybe I should ask her.*

Well—victory. The book had done little except confirm
the woman's story. The fact of the Tahowwa's existence was
thoroughly stamped out now, the hunt was over, it was
time to resume work. First the Martians to reduce Earth,
and then the plan for wrecking Martian industry, and then
the open declaration, the Tahowwa riding in as overlords.
Intelligence Prime reflected sardonically that the future would
make him a great hero. How many other conquerors had
felt his doubts and fears and guilt, alone with their own
souls at night?

The soft chime brought him jerking to full awareness. He
cursed his overstrained nerves. *"Mu-afeen chelbakeesh!"*
Then, with a return of control: *"Houn."* Come in.

The door opened. He looked down the barrel of a gun.

Slowly he raised his eyes. The face behind the gun was
human—gaunt, burning-eyed, unkempt hair and savagely
twisted mouth. The heart of Intelligence Prime leaped
against his ribs. He backed against the farther wall, raising
his hands before his breast.

"Where is she?" said David Arnfeld. "Where is my wife?"

Others were behind him, uniformed Martians and armed
humans, a small force that peered into the office and then
flowed quietly on down the corridors. Arnfeld took a closer

step, jabbing his gun at the Tahowwa. "Where is Christine Hawthorne?"

"You'd better tell him," said Regelin dzu Coruthan. "He is not in a mood to play games."

"Cell—Cell 27," gasped Intelligence Prime out of nightmare. "She—the child—they have not been harmed."

"Come on," said Arnfeld curtly to a Martian staff officer. "You can guide me." They vanished down the hall.

Others entered, Yoakh Dzugeth ay Valkazan, undercommandant of Earth, who had always been considered safe, stalked over to the communicator. He began at once to call sections of the great building and give orders.

Intelligence Prime crouched in a corner, looking with blurred vision at Regelin. "How did you do it?" he whispered.

The Martian didn't answer immediately. One hand held a gun on the Tahowwa, the other, still bandaged, flipped through Arnfeld's book. "I see you found this," he said at last, idly. "Interesting souvenir. Hm—yes, it carries the story almost to the end. And, incidentally, it tells the truth. When David wrote those last lines, he was indeed desperate. So the book is true enough as far as it goes."

Dzugeth looked up with satisfaction. "I think we hold the entire building now," he said. "And the Commandant is on his way—I told him it was an emergency."

Mars' Supreme Commandant of Earth, Darheesh of the Tahowwa, on his way to an ambush! Intelligence Prime fought not to shriek.

"You, of course, will send messages for us to the continental HQ's," Regelin told him. "It should not take us many weeks to organize the overthrow of your rule on Earth and Luna, without any of your folk on Mars being aware of it. Then we can think about the next step."

"How did you do it?" The voice was dead.

"Oh, that!" Regelin chuckled. "A bit of complicated thinking. David told us his plan, in whispers, then he and I went back to our posts. Kit, who was hidden from either of us by the kitchen doors, opened the shed and talked to Radeef and—what was his name?—oh, yes, Naseer. She told them that she had to betray us, lest our recklessness bring the death of her child. She couldn't bring herself to shoot us, she said, but she released the aliens and gave them guns, warning them that we were alert and suspicious. Naturally, they assumed David's and my shapes and whatever appropriate clothes they had; then each of them went to his opposite number, my duplicate to David through the one bedroom, his to me through the kitchen door, so neither he nor I would suspect anything. However, we were prepared, you see. They were armed and ready to kill us, so when they came to us, we shot, with no special compunctions. The disintegrators left a mess!

"Kit went into her hysterical act, running out and screaming and drawing attention. David and I used the time to hide ourselves well in the dark shed. We waited while they came in and verified what she had told them; then, at the first chance, we slipped away.

"Being in possession of our 'bodies,' you, of course, called off the hunt, which made things fairly simple for us. David went to Duluth and hid, while I bluffed a ride to Sao Paulo on an official jet. Once here, I was soon in touch with Torreos and, through him, Dzugeth; we kidnapped an obscure Tahowwa officer for proof and interrogation, fetched David, and organized this mutiny."

Intelligence Prime, lord of the Solar System, raised his head, and his eyes pleaded for the life of his people.

# WORLD
# WITHOUT
# STARS

by

POUL ANDERSON

## SPACEWRECK BEYOND THE STARS

Stranded on a far-flung planet in the dark space between galaxies, the Earthmen had little hope for survival. The ship and its communications system were
wrecked, and now that the twilight planet's inhabitants
had discovered the Earthmen's blasphemous presence—
they were as good as doomed.

For the dread Ai Chun would not believe the Earthmen's story: that they came by starship from *another*
world countless light-years away.

This was not possible, the ancient Ai Chun insisted,
for their planet was the *only* world: the world created
by themselves, the omnipotent god race of the universe.
How could the Earthmen hope to challenge a race of
gods . . . ? Moreover, a race of gods who could and
would enslave them . . . and destroy their minds in the
process.

## I

G<small>OD WAS RISING</small> in the west, and this time the
sun was down—only lately, a few clouds were still red above
the eastern treetops, against purple dusk; but over the hours
that light had waned, until it was little more than an echo of
what now swung above Lake Silence—so that His pale glory
stood clear to be adored.

The Pack could not all make worship. They had met on a
ridge near the lairs and howled when the fingers of God's
foremost arm glimmered into view. But He would take long
to mount so high that His entire self was revealed. The hes
must hunt, the shes wreak, the youngs gather, lest God's
Coursers perish. Moreover and worse, the whole Pack unmoving here, so distant from their hills, could draw the notice of a downdevil out of the sea depths; and night or no, the
downdevil might then send a war fleet of the Herd . . . if,
indeed, that which had lately arrived in fire and thunder was
not enemy work itself. Ya-Kela, the One, had brought some
bold followers who would go with him to see about that. But
first he stood his watch of homage on behalf of the whole folk.

5

Slowly, slowly, God climbed into heaven. Ya-Kela crouched on the back of Crooked Rock and sang. He sang the Welcome, and the Praise, and the Strength. Then the last coals of sunset went out, and the sky was empty of everything save God, the angels, and three planets, and God cast a white glade from the world's edge, down the width of Lake Silence until it was lost among the reeds at this shore. The night was still and cool. A breeze gusted, smelling of damp; a fish leaped in a single clear spash, a wing cried its lonely note, reeds rustled and were answered by the inland brush; but otherwise ya-Kela and God had darkness to themselves.

He stopped a while to rest and eat. He was hoarse, the rock was harsh beneath his webs and tail, and weariness dragged at him. *Yes,* he thought, *I grow old. But I am yet the One of the Pack.* —A distant boom made him start. Drums? It was not impossible for the Herd to come raiding by night. But it was rare. The downdevils feared God and so their worshipers did too. . . . *Only a twyhorn, off in Umber Swamp,* he decided.

He looked west again, and was astonished to see God's body flame in sight. *Why, I must have dozed,* he thought in dismay. *Does that mean anything other than that I am in truth old?* Hastily he went through the invocations and gestures he had missed, until he was caught up. The legends haunted him about creatures that had long ago come from the sky and returned—to Herd day or Pack night, who knew save God and the downdevils? Were these unknown newcomers at Balefire Head, whom he must presently seek out, the same ones? More than ever, the world needed shielding against strangeness. "I call to Thee, we call to Thee, Thou Who casteth out the sun, arise, arise, arise . . . . "

## II

ON ANOTHER EVENING, very far away, I had heard another song. This was when I got back to City.

Like most who colonize a planet, the settlers of Landomar wanted nature and elbow room. There is no other good reason for planting yourself at the bottom of a gravity well. The reason is not quite logical—after all, most of us can satisfy our ape instincts with an occasional groundside visit somewhere, or just with a multisense tape—but I suppose that a gene complex still crops up occasionally which makes the owner want to belong to a specific patch of earth. So if you can find a habitable uninhabited world (statistically rare, but consider how many stars the universe holds) you go with a band of like-minded people to claim it. I don't know whether breeding then reinforces the instinct, or the original parents remain culturally dominant over the centuries. In all events, after a while you have a scattered population which doesn't want outsiders building a starport.

At the same time, starports are necessary. Theoretically they shouldn't be, when any point in space is as close as any other point. In practice, though, an expanding race needs them. First, you have to make up energy differentials between one system and the next in stages. That's obvious enough in the case of the really remote galaxies; we could get there, but we couldn't match a relative velocity which is a goodly fraction of $c$. However, just the variation between, say, the inner and outer part of a spiral arm is a bit too fuel-consuming to overcome in a single jump.

Then second, you need a base for observation, so you can

establish precisely where your next goal is and how fast it's moving. And third, of course, you want docks, yards, supply depots. Those could be built anywhere, but since the advanced bases are required for the first two reasons, they soon serve the third function also. And the fourth: rest, recreation, a place to roister and brag and ease off. For this purpose, even a spaceman born is happiest when the environment isn't entirely artificial.

They were more reasonable on Landomar than on some worlds I could name. They wouldn't let us build on the ground, but they made no objection to an orbital satellite. We could go down to their villages and farmsteads, hunt in their forests, sail on their oceans. They didn't mind our money in the least. Then, as City got bigger, with more and more to offer, their young folk started coming to us, to visit, eventually to work. The elders grumbled, until we brought in sociodynamicists to extrapolate the trend for them and prove that it would never really affect their own timeless oneness with the planet. At most, a cluster of small space-oriented service enterprises would develop groundside. Which is what happened.

I had spent several days there, arranging for stores, isotopes, and so forth. I also hoped to recruit a gunner. But in that I'd failed. Those few who applied had no aptitude. Well, there was a man, a hunter by trade; but the psychograph showed that he enjoyed killing too much. I felt a little tired and depressed. It didn't help, either, that Wenli was ill. Nothing serious, but the kid would doubtless be adult when I returned, and I like to remember my get as happy while they're small.

So I was eager to leave dust behind. My boat hit sky with a yell. Landomar became a giant cloud-banded shield, soft blue against the black. Before long City hove in view.

You can't add randomly to a satellite, or the spin properties would get ridiculous. But City had existed for a few centuries now, and grown in a way that the Landomar elders would not admit was organic. I remembered the original cheerless metal shell. Today I saw towers rocketing from parapets, domes and ports glowing brighter than stars, the Ramakan memorial rakish across the galactic clouds; I could see ships in dock and boats aswarm; and as nearly as any spaceman (except Hugh Valland) ever does, I felt I was home.

I cycled through the lockfield faster than was strictly safe and did no more than tell the mechmen to check out an irregularity which had registered in the boat-pilot's gamma rhythm. At once, wreck all formality, I was out of the dock area and its crowds, along the ramps and through the halls toward Lute's place.

She lives in high-weight, overlooking space itself. That's expensive, but her husbands can afford to pay their share. Not that she picks them on any such basis—not Lute—it's only that a handsome, intelligent woman attracts able men. She's probably my favorite portwife.

So I hurried down the last corridor. It was empty at the moment. My feet thudded on the floor, which gave me a springier response than Landomar's overrated lawns, and the ventilators seemed to purr louder than usual. The color patterns in the walls happened to be grays and greens, and that was right too; they fitted with the touch of sadness, homesickness-in-advance, which counterpointed my pleasure in getting back.

The music did likewise: so much so that I was almost on top of it before it registered on me. An omnisonor was being played, uncommonly well. The tune was archaic, paced like sea tides, but with ringing chords below; and then a man's voice joined in, quite softly:

*"Mary O'Meara, the stars and the dewfall have covered your hilltop with light.*

9

# WORLD WITHOUT STARS

*The wind in the lilies that blossom around you goes*
*bearin' your name from the height.*
*My girl, you are all of the night."*

I rounded the hall's curve about the satellite and saw him.
He lounged in a bay close to Lute's door. The broad port
framed him in darkness and a crescent moon. His fingers ran
casually over the keys of the instrument in his lap, his eyes
were half closed and he was singing to himself.

*"A ship out of shadow bears homeward by starlight, by*
*stars and the loom of your hill.*
*A hand at a brow is uplifted in peerin', salutin' and*
*shakin' with chill.*
*My dear, are you waitin' there still?"*

In a pause for breath, he noticed me. Something I did not
understand went out of his face, to be replaced by a friendly
grin. "Hello," he said. His accent had an odd lilt. "Sorry
about the racket."

"Enjoyable, sir," I answered formally.

"I was passin' the time," he said, "waitin' for Captain
Argens."

"Myself." I bowed.

He unsprawled his height, which was considerable, and
thrust out a muscular hand. Archaic for certain! But I made
the clasp, and took that moment to study him.

His dress was conventional: blue tunic, white breeks, flexible halfboots. The comets of a Master's rating glowed on his
wide shoulders. But the physical type was one that you don't
see often: fair skin over craggy features, close-cropped yellow
hair, fire-blue eyes. "Hugh Valland," he said, "off the *Lady
Lara*."

"Felipe Argens," I responded, mechanically in my startle-

10

ment. I'm old enough to recognize that anyone bearing a name like his must be a great deal older.

"Hear you're lookin' for a gunner," he said.

"Well . . . yes." That was no surprise. Gossip flies fast when more than one ship is in port. "You're interested?"

"Yes, sir, I am. The *Lady's* inbound again, so her skipper don't mind lettin' me off my contract. Understand you're goin' to Earth."

"Eventually," I nodded. "Might be some time, though."

"That's all right. Just so we get there."

I made a fast computation. If this man had served on the *Lady* he'd have a record and shipmates to consult: much better than a psychograph. Though he already looked good.

"Fine; let's talk," I said. "But, uh, why didn't you wait in the apartment? My wife would have been glad—"

"Hear tell she's got a sick kid. Didn't know if she'd want to play hostess." I liked him better and better.

The door dilated for me and Lute met us. "How's Wenli?" I asked after presentations.

"Fretful," she said. "Fever. I had her down to the clinic and they confirmed it's a neovirus."

Nothing to be alarmed about, oh, no, not with supportive treatment. But when a thing that was extraterrestrial to start with mutates, the biotechs in a frontier post like City don't have the equipment to tailor a quick-cure molecule. In twenty years or so, having reached optimum adulthood, Wenli would get her antithanatic; thereafter her cells would instantly reject any hostile nucleic acids. But for now my little girl must rely on what poor defenses nature had provided. Recovery would be slow.

She was asleep. I peeked in at the flushed round face, then went back to the others. Valland was jollying Lute with an anecdote from his latest voyage. They'd needed to gain prestige in a culture which rated poetics as the highest art, so he'd introduced the limerick. Watching her laugh, I felt a

11

twinge of jealousy. Not personal; Lute is so thoroughly decent that it isn't even awkward when two of her men happen to be in port at the same time. No, I only wished I had Valland's gift of blarney.

Yet when we invited him to dinner, he accepted with a courtliness you rarely see anymore.

He and I went onto the porch for cocktails while Lute programmed the food mechs. Space dropped dizzily from the viewport, thin starred black here on the rim. Huge and shapeless—we being still more or less within it—the galaxy streamed past and was lost to sight; we looked toward remoteness.

"I need a gunner in case of trouble," I told him. "We'll be dealing with a technologically advanced race, one that we know almost nothing about. But of course we don't really expect a fight, so we want a man who can double as second deck officer. If he has some xenological skill to boot, that's ideal."

"I think I can claim the whole lot," he answered. "No formal trainin'. By the time they got around to foundin' academies in those subjects, I'd already been in space for quite a spell. But you can check me out with the people aboard *Lady Lara*, and on a psychograph too if you want."

Luck seemed to have fluxed in my direction. Unless—"You may change your mind when you know where the *Meteor's* bound," I warned him. "Or do you?"

"No. Just that it's a pretty long hop, and you'll call at Earth afterward. Otherwise none of your gang has blabbed." He chuckled. "Reckon you'd rather not have competition in the early stages of contact, when the cream's at its most skimmable."

"I'll have to tell you, though, and trust you as a Guild brother. We're going to some Yonderfolk."

"Eh?" He started gratifyingly. "Beyond this galaxy? Like M 31?"

"No," I said. "Not that far. Though where we're bound, we'll be much lonelier. Intergalactic space."

Valland settled back, crossed his legs and twirled his glass between calloused fingers. I offered him a cigarillo, but he declined in favor of a pipe from his tunic: another archaism. Having lit up, I explained:

"There are stars between the galaxies, you know. Dim red dwarfs, so widely separated that this neighborhood looks crowded by comparison; nevertheless, stars. Hitherto no one's thought it worthwhile to investigate them in any detail. Not when we'll take millions of years learning about this one Milky Way of our own, let alone its sisters. But lately . . . some of the intergalactics have made contact with us. They might be worth trading with, goods or knowledge or both. We're going out to have a look. If anything develops, we'll stay for a few years to get the business established."

"I see." He blew a slow cloud. "Sounds interestin'. But after that, you'll head for Earth?"

"Yes. A universarium there is one of the *Meteor's* co-owners, and wants a direct report." I shrugged. "Science is still alive on Earth, if nothing else."

"More'n that," he murmured. "Earth'll always be Man-home."

"Look here," I asked bluntly, "if you're so anxious to go back, why not get a ticket?"

"No hurry." His affability was unruffled. "I'd've done so in time, if need be. I've done it before. But passage across an energy gap like that isn't cheap. Might's well get paid for makin' the trip."

I didn't press him. That's no way to get to know a man. And I had to know my crew, so that we wouldn't break under the years of otherness.

Lute had arranged a good dinner. We were enjoying it, talking the usual things—whatever became of old Jarud, did you hear what happened on Claw, now once I met the damnedest nonhuman society you ever, let me warn you from bitter experience against gambling with the Stonks, is it true they've made a machine that—when Wenli came in. She was trying not to cry.

"Daddy!" she begged of me. "I got bad dreams in my head."

"Better start the hypnopulser, Lute," I muttered as I picked up the slight form. Having operated out of City enough consecutive years to know as well as beget the child, I hurt at her pain.

My wife half rose. " 'Scuse me, mistress," Valland said. "Don't you think best we chase the dreams off for good before we put her to sleep?"

She looked doubtful. "I been around a while," Valland said apologetically. "Not a father myself, but you can't help pilin' up observations. C'mere, little lady." He held out his arms and I passed Wenli to him.

He set her on his lap and leaned back from the table, letting the plate keep his food warm. "All right, my friend," he said, "what kind of dreams?"

She was at a shy stage of life, but to him she explained about blobby monsters that wanted to sit on her. "Well, now," he said, "I know a person who can take care of that. Let's ask him to come give a hand."

"Who?" Her eyes got quite round.

"Fellow name of Thor. He has a red beard, and he drives in a wagon pulled by goats—goats are animals with horns and long *long* whiskers—and the wheels make thunder. You ever heard thunder? Sounds like a boat takin' off in a terrible hurry. And Thor has a hammer, too, which he throws at trolls. I don't think those blobby characters will stand a chance."

I started to open my mouth. This didn't look semantically right to me. Lute laid a warning hand on mine. Following her gaze, I saw that Wenli had stopped shivering.

"Will Thor come if we ask?" she breathed.

"Oh, yes," Valland said. "He owes me a favor. I helped him out once when he got into an argument with an electrostatic generator. Now let me tell you more about him."

Afterward I learned that the tall tale he went on to relate came from Earth, in days so old that even the books are forgetting. But Wenli crowed and clapped her hands when Thor caught the snake that girdles the world. Lute laughed. So did I.

Finally Valland carried Wenli back to bed, fetched his omnisonor, and sang to her. The ballad was likewise ancient—his translation—but it bounced right along, and before he had finished cataloguing the improbable things that should be done to the drunken sailor, my daughter was asleep with no machine needed.

We came back to the 'fresher room. "Sorry to poke in like that," Valland said. "Maybe you should've curbed me."

"No." Lute's eyes glowed. "I've never seen anyone do anything better."

"Thanks. I'm a childish type myself, so—Hoy, meant to tell you before, this is one gorgeous piece of steak."

We went on to brandy and soda. Valland's capacity was epical. I suppose Lute and I were rather drunk toward the end, though we wouldn't have regretted it next day if our idea had been workable. We exchanged a glance, she nodded, and we offered our guest our total hospitality.

He hadn't shown much effect of alcohol, beyond merriment. Yet now he actually blushed. "No," he said. "Thanks a million, but I got me a berth in dock country. Better get down there."

Lute wasn't quite pleased. She has her human share of vanity. He saw that too. Rising, he took her hand and bowed above it.

"You see," he explained with great gentleness, "I'm from way back. The antithanatic was developed in my lifetime—

15

yes, that long ago; I shipped on the first star craft. So I have medieval habits. What other people do, fine, that's their business. But I've only got one girl, and she's on Earth."

"Oh," Lute said. "Haven't you been gone from her for quite a time, then?"

He smiled. "Sure have. Why do you think I want to return?"

"I don't understand why you left in the first place."

Valland took no offense. "Earth's no place for a live man to live any more. Fine for Mary, not for me. It's not unfair to either of us. We get together often enough, considerin' that we'll never grow old. Between whiles, I can remember . . . . But goodnight now, and thanks again."

His attitude still seemed peculiar to me. I'd have to check most carefully with his present captain. You can't take an unbalanced man out between the galaxies.

On the other hand, we're each a bit eccentric, one way or another. That goes along with being immortal. Sometimes we're a bit crazy, even. We don't have the heart to edit certain things out of our memories, and so they grow in the psyche till we no longer have a sense of proportion about them. Like my own case—but no matter.

One thing we have all gained in our centuries is patience. Could be that Hugh Valland simply had a bit more than most.

# III

We were nine aboard the *Meteor*, specialists whose skills overlapped. That was not many, to rattle around in so huge a hull. But you need room and privacy on a long trip, and of course as a rule we hauled a lot of cargo.

"Probably not this time, however," I explained to Valland and Yo Rorn. They were the only ones who hadn't shipped with me before; I'd hastily recruited them at Landomar when two vacancies developed for reasons that aren't relevant here. To make up the delay, I hadn't briefed them in detail before we started. But now I must. They'd need days of study to master what little we knew about our goal.

We sat in my com chamber, we three, with coffee and smokes. A steady one gee of acceleration gave weight, and that soft engine-pulse which goes on and on until finally it enters your bones. A viewscreen showed us Landomar's sun, already dwindled, and the galaxy filling half the sky with clots and sprawls of glow. That was to starboard; the vector we wanted to build up ran almost parallel to the rim. Portward yawned emptiness, here and there the dim spindles of other stellar continents.

"Mmm, yeah, don't look like we could find a lot of useful stuff on a planet where they breathe hydrogen and drink liquid ammonia," Valland nodded. "I never did, anyway."

"Then why are we going?" Rorn asked. He was a lean, dark, saturnine man who kept to himself, hadn't so much as told us where in the cosmos he was born. His psychograph indicated a tightly checked instability. But the readings also

17

said he was a good electronician, and he had recommendations from past service. He stubbed out his cigaret and lit another. "Someone from a similar planet would be logical to deal with the—what did you say their name was?"

"I can't pronounce it either," I replied. "Let's just call them Yonderfolk."

Rorn scowled. "That could mean any extragalactic race."

"We know what we mean," said Valland mildly. "Ever meet the natives of Carstor's Planet?"

"Heard of them," I said. "Tall, thin, very ancient culture, unbearably dignified. Right?"

"Uh-huh. When I was there, we called 'em Squidgies."

"Business, please," Rorn barked.

"Very well," I said. "What we hope to get from our Yonderfolk is, mainly, knowledge. Insights, ideas, art forms, possibly something new in physics or chemistry or some other science. You never can tell. If nothing else, they know about the intergalactic stars, so maybe they can steer us onto planets that will be profitable for humans. In fact, judging from what they've revealed so far, there's one such planet right in their home system."

Valland looked for a while into the blackness to port. "They must be different from anybody we've met before," he murmured. "We can't imagine how different."

"Right," I said. "Consider what that could mean in terms of what they know."

I cleared my throat. "Brace yourself, Yo," said Valland. "The Old Man's shiftin' into lecture gear." Rorn looked blank, then resentful. I didn't mind.

"The galaxies were formed by the condensation of monstrous hydrogen clouds. But there wasn't an absolute vacuum between them. Especially not in the beginning, when the universe hadn't yet expanded very far. So between the proto-galaxies there must have been smaller condensations of gas, which became star clusters. Giant stars in those clusters

18

soon went supernova, enriching the interstellar medium. Some second and third generation suns got born.

"But then the clusters broke up. Gravitational effect of the galaxies, you see. The dispersal of matter became too great for star formation to go on. The bright ones burned themselves out. But the red dwarfs are still around. A type M, for instance, stays fifty billion years on the main sequence."

"Please," Rorn said, irritated. "Valland and I do know elementary astrophysics." To the gunner: "Don't you?"

"But I begin to see what it means," Valland said low. Excitement coursed over his face. He clenched his pipe in one fist. "Stars so far apart that you can't find one from another without a big telescope. Metal poor, because the supernova enrichment stopped early. And old—old."

"Right," I said. "Planets, too. Almost without iron or copper or uranium, anything that made it so easy for us to become industrialized. But the lighter elements exist. So does life. So does intelligence.

"I don't know how those Yonderfolk we're going to visit went beyond the Stone Age. That's one of the things we have to find out. I can guess. They could experiment with electrostatics, with voltaic piles, with ceramics. Finally they could get to the point of electrodynamics—oh, let's say by using ceramic tubes filled with electrolytic solution for conductors. And so, finally, they'd extract light metals like aluminum and magnesium from ores. But they may have needed millions of years of civilization to get that far, and beyond."

"What'd they learn along the way?" Valland wondered. "Yeah, I see why we've got to go there."

"Even after they developed the space jump, they steered clear of the galaxies," I said. "They can't take the radiation. Where they live, there are no natural radioactives worth mentioning, except perhaps a few things like K-40. Their sun doesn't spit out many charged particles. There's no galactic

19

magnetic field to accelerate cosmic rays. No supernovae either."

"Why, maybe they have natural immortality," Valland suggested.

"Mmm, I doubt that," I said. "True, we're saddled with more radiation. But ordinary quantum processes will mutate cells too. Or viruses, or chemicals, or Q factor, or—or whatever else they may have on Yonder."

"Have they developed an antithanatic, then?" Rorn asked.

"I don't know," I said. "If not, that's one valuable thing we have to offer. I hope."

I saw in the brief twist of Valland's mouth that he understood me. Spacemen don't talk about it much, but there are races, as intelligent and as able to suffer as we ourselves, for whom nobody has figured out an aging preventive. The job is hard enough in most cases: develop a synthetic virus which, rather than attacking normal cells, destroys any that do *not* quite conform to the host's genetic code. When the biochemistry is too different from what we know— Mostly, we leave such planets alone.

I said in haste: "But let's keep to facts. The Yonderfolk did at last venture to the galactic rim, with heavy radiation screening. It so happened that the first world they came on which was in contact with our civilization was Zara. Our own company had a factor there."

We didn't yet know how many suns they visited first. Our one galaxy holds more than a hundred billion, most of which have attendants. I doubt if we'll ever see them all. There could be any number of civilizations as great as ours, that close to home, unbeknownst to us. And yet we go hopping off to Andromeda!

(I made that remark to Hugh Valland, later in the voyage. "Sure," he said. "Always happens that way. The Spanish were settlin' the Philippines before they knew the coastal outline of America. People were on the moon before they'd got to the bottom of the Mindanao Deep." At the time I didn't quite follow him, but since then I've read a little about the history of Manhome.)

"Zara." Rorn frowned. "I don't quite place—"

"Why should you?" Valland replied. "More planets around than you could shake a stick at. Though I really can't see why anybody'd want to shake a stick at a planet that never did him any harm."

"It's the same type as the Yonderfolk's home," I said. "Zara, that is. Cold, hydrogen-helium atmosphere, et cetera. They made contact with our factor because he was sitting in the only obviously machine-culture complex on the surface. They went through the usual linguistic problems, and finally got to conversing. Here's a picture."

I activated my projector and rotated the image of a being. It was no more inhuman than many who had been my friends: squat, scaly, head like a complicated sponge; one of several hands carried something which sparkled.

"Actually," I said, "the language barrier was higher than ordinary. To be expected, no doubt, when they came from such an alien environment. So we don't have a lot of information, and a good deal of what we do have must be garbled. Still, we're reasonably sure they aren't foolish enough to be hostile, and do want to develop this new relationship. Within the galaxy, they're badly handicapped by having to stay behind their rad screens. So they asked us to come to them. Our factor notified the company, the company's interested . . . and that, sirs, is why we're here."

"Mmm. They gave location data for their home system?" Valland asked.

"Apparently so," I said. "Space coordinates, velocity vector, orbital elements and data for each planet of the star."

"Must've been a bitch, transforming from their math to ours."

"Probably. The factor's report gives few details, so I can't

21

be sure. He was in too big a hurry to notify headquarters and send the Yonderfolk back—before the competition heard about them. But he promised we'd soon dispatch an expedition. That's us."

"A private company, instead of an official delegation?" Rorn bridled.

"Oh, come off it," Valland said. "Exactly which government out of a million would you choose to act? This is too damn big a cosmos for anything but individuals to deal with it."

"There'll be others," I said fast. A certain amount of argument on a cruise is good, passes the time and keeps men alert; but you have to head off the kind which can fester. "We couldn't keep the secret for long, even if we wanted to. Meanwhile, we do represent the Universarium of Nordamerik, as well as a commercial interest.

"Now, here are the tapes and data sheets . . . . "

## IV

THE SHIP DROVE OUTWARD.

We had a large relative velocity to match. The days crawled past, and Landomar's sun shrank to a star, and still you couldn't see any change in the galaxy. Once we'd shaken down, we had little to do—the mechs operated everything for us. We talked, read, exercised, pursued our various hobbies, threw small parties. Most of us had lived a sufficient number of years in space that we didn't mind the monotony. It's only external, anyhow. After a century or three of life, you have plenty to think about, and a cruise is a good opportunity.

I fretted a little over Yo Rorn. He was always so glum, and apt to be a bit nasty when he spoke. Still, nothing serious developed.

Enver Smeth, our chemist, gave me some concern too. He was barely thirty years old, and had spent twenty-five of them under the warm wing of his parents on Arwy, which is a bucolic patriarchal settlement like Landomar. Then he broke free and went to the space academy on Iron—but that's another tight little existence. I was his first captain and this was his first really long trip. You have to start sometime, though, and he was shaping up well.

Very soon he became Hugh Valland's worshiper. I could see why. Here the boy encountered a big, gusty, tough but good-natured man who'd been everywhere and done everything—and was close to three thousand years old, could speak of nations on Manhome that are like myth to the rest

23

of us, had shipped with none less than Janosek—and to top
the deal off, was the kind of balladeer that Smeth only
dreamed of being. Valland took the situation well, refrained
from exploiting or patronizing, and managed to slip him bits
of sound advice.

Then came the Captain's Brawl. In twenty-four hours we
would be making the jump. You can't help feeling a certain
tension. The custom is good, that the crew have a final blast
where almost anything goes.

We ate a gourmet dinner, and made the traditional toasts,
and settled down to serious drinking. After a while the saloon
roared. Alen Galmer, Chu Bren, Galt Urduga, and, yes, Yo
Rorn crouched over a flying pair of dice in one corner. The
rest of us stamped out a hooraw dance on the deck, Valland
giving us the measure with ringing omnisonor and bawdy
words, until the sweat rivered across our skins and even that
mummy-ancient line, "Why the deuce aren't you a beautiful
woman?" became funny once more.

> "—So let's hope other ladies
> Are just as kind as Alixy,
> For, spaceman, it's your duty
> To populate the galaxy!"

"Yow-ee!" we shouted, grabbed for our glasses, drank deep
and breathed hard.

Smeth flung himself onto the same bench as Valland.
"Never heard that song before," he panted.

"You will," Valland drawled. "An oldtimer." He paused.
"To tell the truth, I made it up myself, 'bout five hundred
years back."

"I never knew that," I said. "I believe you, though."

"Sure." Smeth attempted a worldly grin. "With the experience you must've had in those lines by now. Eh, Hugh?"

"Uh . . . well—" The humor departed from Valland. He emptied his goblet with a sudden, almost violent gesture.

Smeth was in a lickerish mood. "Womanizing memories, that's the kind you never edit out," he said.

Valland got up and poured himself a refill.

I recalled that episode at Lute's, and decided I'd better divert the lad from my gunner. "As a matter of fact," I said, "those are among the most dispensable ones you'll have."

"You're joking!" Smeth protested.

"I am not," I said. "The really fine times, the girls you've really cared for, yes, of course you'll keep those. But after a thousand casual romps, the thousand and first is nothing special."

"How about that, Hugh?" Smeth called. "You're the oldest man aboard. Maybe the oldest man alive. What do you say?"

Valland shrugged and returned to us. "The skipper's right," he answered shortly. He sat down and stared at what we couldn't see.

I had to talk lest there be trouble, and wasn't able to think of anything but banalities. "Look, Enver," I told Smeth, "it isn't possible to carry around every experience you'll accumulate in, oh, just a century or two. You'd swamp in the mass of data. It'd be the kind of insanity that there's no cure for. So, every once in a while, you go under the machine, and concentrate on the blocs of memory you've decided you can do without, and those particular RNA molecules are neutralized. But if you aren't careful, you'll make big, personality-destroying gaps. You have to preserve the overall pattern of your past, and the important details. At the same time, you have to be ruthless with some things, or you can saddle yourself with the damnedest complexes. So you do *not* keep trivia. And you do not overemphasize any one type of experience, idea, or what have you. Understand?"

"Maybe," Smeth grumbled. "I think I'll go join the dice game."

Valland continued to sit by himself, drinking hard. I wondered about him. Being a little tired and muzzy, I stayed on the same bench. Abruptly he shook his big frame, leaned over toward me, and said, low under the racket:

"No, skipper, I'm neither impotent nor homosexual. Matter's very simple. I fell in love once for all, when I was young. And she loves me. We're enough for each other. We don't want more. You see?"

He hadn't shown it before, but he was plainly pretty drunk. "I suppose I see," I told him with care. "Wouldn't be honest to claim I feel what you mean."

"Reckon you don't," he said. "Between them, immortality and star travel changed everything. Not necessarily for the worse. I pass no judgments on anybody." He pondered. "Could be," he said, "if I'd stayed on Earth, Mary and I would've grown apart too. Could be. But this wanderin' keeps me, well, fresh. Then I come home and tell her everything that happened."

He picked up his omnisonor again, strummed a few bars, and murmured those lyrics I had heard when first we met.

> "I'll sing me a song about Mary O'Meara, with stars like
>   a crown in her hair.
> Sing of her memory rangin' before me whatever the ways
>   that I fare.
> My joy is to know she is there."

Well, I thought with startling originality, it takes all kinds.

# V

WE WERE ready to jump.

Every system was tuned, every observation and computation finished, every man at his post. I went to the bridge, strapped myself into recoil harness, and watched the clock. Exact timing isn't too important, as far as a ship is concerned; the position error caused by a few minutes' leeway is small compared to the usual error in your figures. But for psychological reasons you'd better stay on schedule. Pushing that button is the loneliest thing a man can do.

I had no premonitions. But it grew almighty quiet in my helmet as I waited. The very act of suiting up reminds you that something could go wrong; that something did go wrong for others you once knew; that our immortality isn't absolute, because sooner or later some chance combination of circumstances is bound to kill you.

What a spaceship captain fears most, as he watches the clock by himself on the bridge, is arriving in the same place as a solid body. Then atoms jam together and the ship goes out in a nuclear explosion. But that's a stupid fear, really. You set your dials for emergence at a goodly distance from the target sun, well off the ecliptic plane. The probability of a rock being just there, just then, is vanishingly small. In point of fact, I told myself, this trip we'd be in an ideal spot. We wouldn't even get the slight radiation dosage that's normal: scarcely any hydrogen for our atoms to interact with, between the galaxies.

Nevertheless, we were going two hundred and thirty thousand light-years away.

And I do not understand the principle of the space jump. Oh, I've studied the math. I can recite the popular version as glibly as the next man: "Astronomers showed that gravitational forces, being weak and propagating at light velocity, were insufficient to account for the cohesion of the universe. A new theory then postulated that space has an intrinsic unity, that every point is equivalent to every other point. One location is distinguished from another only by the n-dimensional coordinates of the mass which is present there. These coordinates describe a configuration of the matter-energy field which can be altered artificially. When this is done, the mass, in effect, makes an instantaneous transition to the corresponding other point in space. Energy being conserved, the mass retains the momentum—with respect to the general background of the galaxies—that it had prior to this transition, plus or minus an amount corresponding to the difference in gravitational potential."

It still sounds like number magic to me.

But a lot of things seem magical. There are primitives who believe that by eating somebody they can acquire that person's virtue. Well, you can train an animal, kill it, extract the RNA from its brain, put this into another animal, and the second beast will exhibit behavior characteristic of that same training.

The clock showed Minute One. I cut the drive. We ran free, weight departed, silence clamped down on me like a hand.

I stared out at the chaotic beauty which flamed to starboard. *So long, galaxy,* I thought. *I'll be seeing you again, in your entirety; only what I'll see is you as you were a quarter of a million years ago.*

The time reeled toward Minute Two. I unfastened the safety lock and laid my gloved finger on the red button.

Nothing came over the comsystem into my earplugs. We were each without words.

Time.

The shock was too horrible. I couldn't react.

No blackness, with the great spiral for background and a wan red star glowing before us. A planet filled the screen.

I saw the vision grow, kilometers per second, hurtling upon us or we upon it. Half was dark, half was mottled with landscape, agleam with waters, under a blood-colored day. No chance to reset the jump unit and escape, no chance to do anything but gape into the face of Death. A roaring filled my helmet. It was my own voice.

Then Hugh Valland's tone cut through, sword-like with what I should have cried. "Pilots! For God's sake, reverse us and *blast!*"

That jarred me loose from my stupor. I looked at the degree scale etched in the screen and the numbers on the radar meters, I made an estimate of vectors and ripped out my commands. The engine boomed. The planet swept around my head. Acceleration stuffed me down into my harness and sat on my chest. Unconsciousness passed in rags before my eyes.

We had too much velocity to kill in what time remained. But we got rid of some of it, in those few minutes before we struck atmosphere; and we didn't flash directly down, we entered at a low angle.

With such speed, we skipped, as a stone is skipped across a river. Shock after shock slammed into us. Metal shrieked. The viewscreens filled with incandescence. This ungainly hulk of a vessel was never meant to land. She was supposed to lie in orbit while our two ferries served her. But now she had to come down!

Somehow, Bren and Galmer operated the pilot board. Somehow they kept the drive going, resisting our plunge, bringing us groundward in a fury that only sufficed to boil away our outer plates. When the main drive was ruined and quit, they used the steering units. When those went out, one by one, they used what was left. Finally nothing remained and we fell. But then we were so low, our speed so checked, that a man had some chance.

I heard the bellowings, the protest and the breaking of steel. I felt the furnace heat from the inner bulkheads, through and through my spacesuit until lips cracked open and nasal passages were tubes of anguish. I saw the water below, and braced myself, and remembered I must not. Relax, float free, let harness and suit and flesh absorb the shock.

We hit.

I crawled back to awareness. My mouth was full of blood, which had smeared my faceplate so that it was hard to see out. One eye being swollen shut didn't help. Hammers beat on every cell of me, and my left arm wouldn't respond. I thought in a dull, vague way, *My skull can't really be split open . . . .*

*The men!*

Nothing sounded except my own rattling breath. But surely, I cried, this was because the comsystem had been knocked out. *Got to go see. Got to unstrap and find my men.*

I didn't set my teeth against the pain of movement. That would have taken more control than I had, in my present state. I whimpered through the many minutes of fumbling. At last I slid free, onto the canted, buckled deck. I lay there a while before being able to get up and feel my way aft.

The ship was dead. No screens functioned, no ventilators whispered, no lights glowed except the evershine panels spotted along the corridors. By their dim greenishness I stumbled and slipped, calling out names.

After some part of eternity a human shape met me in the passage. Not quite human, a two-legged bulk with a grotesque glassy head; but the radio voice was Hugh Valland's. "That you, skipper?" I clung to him and sobbed.

"We're lucky," he told me. "I've been lookin' us over. If we'd crashed in a sea we'd be done. The whole after section's flooded. We've sunk. But the nose seems to be pokin' out into air."

"How are the others?" I dared ask.

"Can't find anyone in the engine compartment," he said grimly. "I took a flash and went into the water, but no trace, just a big half-melted hole in the side. They must've been carried out with the main reactor. So there's two gone." (Let me record their names here: Morn Krisnan and Roli Blax, good men.) Valland sighed. "Don't seem like young Smeth'll last long either."

*Seven men*, I thought, *in poor shape, wrecked on a planet that every probability says is lethal for them.*

"I came through fairly well, myself," Valland went on. "Suppose you join the rest. They're in the saloon. I want to gander out of a lock. I'll report to you."

The room where we met was a cave. One evershine, knocked out of its frame, had been brought in for light. It threw huge misshapen shadows across crumpled walls. Snags of girders protruded like stalactites. The men slumped in their armor. I called the roll: Bren, Galmer, Urduga, Rorn. And Smeth, of course. He hadn't left us yet.

He was even conscious, more or less. They had laid him out on a bench as well as might be. I peered into his helmet. The skin looked green in what light we had, and the blood that bubbled from his mouth was black. But the eyeballs showed very white. I tuned up his radio for him and heard the harsh liquidity of his breathing.

Rorn joined me. "He's done," he said without tone. "His harness ripped loose from the stanchions when they gave way, where he was, and he got tossed against a bulkhead. So his ribs are stove through his lungs and the spine's broken."

"How do you know?" I challenged. "His suit's intact, isn't it?"

Teeth gleamed in the murk that was Rorn's face. "Captain," he said, "I helped carry the boy here. We got him to describe how he felt, when he woke, and try to move his arms and legs. Look at him."

"Mother, mother," said the gurgle in my earplugs.

Valland came back. "The ferryboats are smashed too," he said. "Their housin's took the main impact. We won't be leavin' this planet soon."

"What's outside?" I asked.

"We're in a lake. Can't see the oppsite edge. But the waters fairly shallow where we are, and there's a shore about two kilometers off. We can raft to land."

"For what?" Rorn flared.

"Well," Valland said, "I saw some aquatic animals jump. So there's life. Presumably our kind of life, proteins in water solution, though of course I don't expect we could eat it."

He stood a while, brooding in gloom, before he continued: "I think I can guess what happened. You remember the Yonderfolk said their system included a planet in the liquid-water thermal zone. The innermost one, with a mass and density such that surface gravity ought to be two-thirds Earth standard. Which feels about right, eh?"

Only then did I notice. Every motion had hurt so much that nothing except pain had registered. But, yes, I was lighter than before. Maybe that was the reason I could keep my feet.

"The Yonderfolk gave us information on each planet of this star," Valland went on. "I don't know exactly who made the big mistake. There was that language problem; and the the factor on Zara was in a hurry to boot. So my guess is, the Yonderfolk misunderstood him. They thought we wanted to land here first, it bein' more comfortable for us; they even thought we had the means to land directly. So they supplied figures and formulas for doin' just that. And we assumed they were tellin' us how to find a nice, safe, convenient point way off from the sun, and cranked the wrong stuff into our computer."

He spread his hands. "I could be wrong," he said. "Maybe the factor's to blame. Maybe some curdbrain in the home office is. Fact remains, though, doesn't it, that you don't blindly jump toward a point in space—because you have to allow for your target star movin'. You use a formula. We got the wrong one."

"What do we do about it?"  Rorn snapped.

"We survive," Valland said.

"Oh? When we don't even know if the air is breathable? We could light a fire, sure, and test for oxygen. But how about other gases? Or spores or— Argh!" Rorn turned his back.

"There is that," Valland admitted.

He swung about and stared down at Smeth. "We have to unsuit him anyway, to see if we've got a chance to help him," he said finally. "And we haven't got time—he hasn't—for riggin' an Earth-atmosphere compartment. So—"

He bent onto one knee, his faceplate close to the boy's. "Enver," he said gently. "You hear me?"

"Yes . . . yes . . . oh, it hurts—" I could scarcely endure listening.

Valland took Smeth's hand. "Can I remove your suit?" he asked.

"I've only had thirty years," Smeth shrieked. "Thirty miserable years! You've had three thousand!"

"Shut up." Valland's tone stayed soft, but I've heard less crack in a bullwhip. "You're a man, aren't you?"

Smeth gasped for seconds before he replied, "Go ahead, Hugh."

Valland got Urduga to help. They took the broken body out of its suit, with as much care as its mother would have given. They fetched cloths and sponged off the blood and bandaged the holes. Smeth did not die till three hours later.

At home, anywhere in civilization—perhaps aboard this ship, if the ship had not been a ruin—we might have saved him. We didn't have a tissue regenerator, but we did have surgical and chemical apparatus. With what we could find in the wreckage, we tried. The memory of our trying is one that I plan to wipe out.

Finally Smeth asked Valland to sing to him. By then we were all unsuited. The air was thin, hot and damp, full of strange odors, and you could hear the lake chuckle in the submerged compartments. Valland got his omnisonor, which had come through unscathed while our biogenic stimulator shattered. "What would you like to hear?" he asked.

"I like . . . that tune . . . about your girl at home."

Valland hesitated barely long enough for me to notice. Then: "Sure," he said. "Such as it is."

I crouched in the crazily tilted and twisted chamber, in shadows, and listened.

*"The song shall ride home on the surf of the starlight and leap to the shores of the sky,*
*Take wing on the wind and the odor of lilies and Mary O'Meara-ward fly.*
*And whisper your name where you lie."*

He got no further than that stanza before Smeth's eyes rolled back and went blind.

We sank the body and prepared to leave. During the past hours, men who were not otherwise occupied had taken inventory and busied themselves. We still had many tools, some weapons, clothes, medicines, abundant freeze-dried rations, a knockdown shelter, any number of useful oddments. Most important, our food unit was intact. That was no coincidence. Not expecting to use it at once on Yonder, nor at all if our stay wasn't prolonged, we had stowed it in the recoil-mounted midsection. With the help of torches run off the capacitors, as long as they lasted, the work gang assembled a pontoon raft. We could ferry our things ashore.

"We'll live," Hugh Valland said.

I gazed out of the lock, across the waters. The sun was low but rising, a huge red ember, one degree and nineteen minutes across, so dull that you could look straight into it. The sky was deep purple. The land lay in eternal twilight, barely visible to human eyes at this distance, an upward-humping blackness against the crimson sheen on the lake. A flight of creatures with leathery wings croaked hoarsely as they passed above us. The air was dank and tropical. Now that my broken arm was stadered, I could use it, but those nerves throbbed.

"I'm not sure I want to," I muttered.

Valland spoke a brisk obscenity. "What's a few years? Shouldn't taken us any longer to find some way off this hellball."

I goggled at him. "Do you seriously believe we can?"

He lifted his tawny head with so much arrogance that he wasn't even aware of it, and answered: "Sure. Got to. Mary O'Meara's waitin' for me."

# VI

THE SUN crept down almost too slowly to notice. We had days of daylight. But because the night would be similarly long and very dark, we exhausted ourselves getting camp established.

Our site was a small headland, jutting a few meters above the shore and thus fairly dry. Inland the country ran toward a range of low hills. They were covered with trees whose broad leaves were an autumnal riot of bronzes and yellows, as far as we could identify color in this sullen illlumination. The same hues prevailed in those tussocky growths which seemed to correspond to grass, on the open stretch between woods and water, and in the reedy plants along the mud beach. But this was not due to any fall season; the planet had little axial tilt. Photosynthesis under a red dwarf star can't use chlorophyll.

We saw a good deal of wild life; and though the thin air deadened sound, we heard much more, off in the swamps to the north. But having only the chemical apparatus left to make a few primitive tests—which did show certain amino acids, vitamins and so forth missing, as you'd expect—we never ventured to eat local stuff. Instead we lived off packaged supplies until our food plant was producing.

To get that far was our most heartbreaking job. In theory it's quite simple. You fit together your wide, flat tanks, with their pumps and irradiator coils; you sterilize them, fill them with distilled water, add the necessary organics and minerals; you put in your cultures, filter the air intake, seal off the

36

whole thing against environmental contamination, and sit back. Both phyto- and zooplankton multiply explosively till equilibrium is reached. They are gene-tailored to contain, between them, every essential of human nutrition. As needed, you pump out several kilos at a time, return the water, cook, flavor, and eat. (Or you can dispense with flavors if you must; the natural taste is rather like shrimp.) You pass your own wastes back through a processor into the tank so that more plankton can grow. The cycle isn't one hundred percent efficient, of course, but comes surprisingly close. A good construction only needs a few kilos of supplementary material per year, and we had salvaged enough for a century, blessing the Guild law that every spaceship must be equipped fail-safe.

Simple. Sure. When there are machines to do the heavy work, and machines to control quality, and it isn't raining half the time, and you're acclimated to air and temperature, and your nerves aren't stretched wire-thin with looking for the menaces that instinct says must lurk all around, and you don't keep wondering what's the use of the whole dismal struggle. We had to assemble a small nuclear generator to supply current, and level a site for the tanks with hand shovels, and put up our shelter and a stockade, and learn about the planet faster than it could find new ways to kill us, simultaneously.

About hazards: No carnivores attacked. A few times we glimpsed web-arctoid giants. They kept their distance; doubtless we smelled inedible to them and doubtless we were. But a horned thing, thrice the mass of a human, charged from the brush at Rorn and Galmer as they went surveying. They gave it the full blast of two heavy torchguns, and it didn't die and didn't die, it kept on coming till it collapsed a meter away, and then as they left it crawled after them for a long while . . . . Bren almost drowned in a mudhole. The ground was full of them, concealed by plants growing on their surface . . . . Urduga came near a sort of vine, which

37

grabbed him. The sucker mouths couldn't break his skin, but he couldn't get loose either. I had to chop free; naturally we never left camp alone . . . . Though we had portable radios and gyrocompasses, we dreaded losing our way in these featureless marshlands . . . . From time to time we noticed bipedal forms skulk in the distant brush. They disappeared before we could bring optical aids to bear, but Galmer insisted he had glimpsed a spear carried by one of them. And without the main reactor, the ship's heavy weapons were inert. We had a few sidearms, nothing else.

Microbes we simply had to risk. We should be immune to all viruses, and odds were that no native bacteria or protozoa could make headway in our systems either. But you never knew for certain, and sometimes you lay awake wondering if the ache in your body was only weariness. Until we got our hut assembled, endless dim day and frequent rains made sleep hard to come by.

In spite of strain, or perhaps because of it, no quarrels flapped up at first—except once, when I told Bren and Galmer to make measurements. I wanted precise values for gravity, air pressure, humidity, magnetism, ionization, horizon distance, rotation period, solar spectrum lines, whatever could be found with a battery of instruments from the ship.

"Why now?" Rorn demanded. He was no more gaunt and dirty than the rest of us, as we sat in our shelter while another storm drummed on the roof. "We've hardly begun the heavy work like building a stockade."

"Information-gathering is just as urgent," I answered. "The sooner we know what kind of place we're in, the sooner we can lay plans that make sense."

"Why those two men, though?" Rorn's mouth twisted uncontrollably. We hadn't yet installed lights, and the single flash hanging overhead cast his eyes into thick shadow, as if already a skull looked at me. "We can take turns. Easy to sit and twiddle with a pendulum and clock."

"Well," Bren said mildly, "that sounds fair."

"Veto," I said. "You boys are trained in navigation and planetography. You can do the job quicker and better than anyone else."

"Besides," Valland pointed out, "they won't sit continuously. Between sun shots, for instance, we'll put 'em to somethin' real hard." He grinned. "Like maybe findin' some way to make the bloody plankton imitate steak."

"Don't remind me!" Rorn grated. "Aren't we miserable enough?"

"What do you propose to do about our troubles?" I asked sharply. A gust of wind made the thin metal walls shake around us.

"What do *you?* How do we get off of here?"

"The most obvious way," Urduga said, "is to fix a radio transmitter that can beam to Yonder."

"If they use radio," Rorn countered. "We don't any more, except for special things like spacesuits. Why shouldn't they space-jump electron patterns, the same as us? Then they'll never detect our signal—if you actually can build an interplanetary 'caster with your bare hands!"

"Oh, we got tools and parts," Valland said. "Or maybe we can fix one of the ferries. Got to take a close look into that possibility. Simmer down, Yo. Once I get a home brewery rigged, we'll all feel better."

"If you don't want to work with us, Rorn," Urduga added, "you have the freedom of this planet."

"None of that!" I exclaimed. "Once we turn on each other, we're done. How about a song, Hugh?"

"Well, if you can stand it." Valland got his omnisonor and launched into another ballad he had translated from old times on Earth. No doubt it should have been something decorous about home and mother, or something heroically defiant. But

39

our ragged, hungry, sweaty crew got more out of *The Bastard King of England*. Rorn alone didn't laugh and join in the choruses; however, he kept his despair quiet.

Over a period of standard days, Bren and Galmer accumulated quite a bit of information. Though the red sun was still aloft, their photoscreen 'scope could pick out other galaxies for astronomical reference points. Their laser-beam transit and oscilloscope could accurately measure that sun's creep down the sky. In calm weather they had a flat western horizon, out where the lake ran beyond vision. The short year enabled them to take a good sample of our orbit. And so on and so on. When added to what little the Yonderfolk had reported (they'd visited this world in the past, but were really no more interested in it than Earthmen in Sol I), and to general scientific principles, these data enabled us to make a fairly good sketch.

We were in the middle northern latitudes of a planet which had a diameter three percent greater than Earth's. The size was no cause for astonishment. Dim stars haven't enough radiation pressure to inhibit such masses from condensing close to them out of the original dust cloud. Nor were we surprised that weight was only 0.655 standard. The very old systems, formed in early generations, have little in the way of heavy elements like iron. This planet lacked a metallic core, must in fact be sima clear to the center. Hence the low mean specific gravity and the absence of a magnetic field.

Nor did it own any satellites. Solar gravitation had served to prevent that. This force had also, over billions of years, slowed rotation until one hemisphere faced inward. Then tides in water and atmosphere continued to act, until now the globe had a slow retrograde rotation. Combined with a sidereal year of ninety-four and a half Earth-days, this spin gave us a diurnal period of forty-four Earth-days on the surface: three weeks of lights, three weeks of dark.

Coreless, the planet had no vertical tectonic and orogenic

40

forces worth mentioning. Once the mountains formed by surface distortion had eroded away, no new ones got built. Nor were there great ocean basins. We were lucky to have come down by this wet land; we wouldn't likely find anything much better anywhere, and most of the world must be submerged.

Though the total irradiation received was only slightly less than what Earth gets, it lay heavily in the red and infrared. The sun's wavelength of maximum emission was, in fact, about 6600 ångströms, near the end of the human-visible spectrum. This accounted for the steamy heat we lived with. Scarcely any ultraviolet light was given off, and none of that penetrated to us; we needed artificial irradiation as much as our plankton did. Nor does a red dwarf spit out many energetic charged particles. Accordingly, while the planet was ancient indeed—fifteen billion years at a conservative guess— it still had plenty of water, and an atmosphere corresponding at sea level to a medium-high terrestrial mountaintop.

Given air, a hydrosphere, and an infrared oven in the sky, you don't have to have actinic radiation (what we would call actinic, I mean) for nature's primeval chemicals to become life. It simply takes longer. As we had noted, since we could breathe, there were photosynthetic plants. They probably utilized one of the low-level enzyme-chain processes which have been observed in similar cases within the galaxies. Likewise the animals. In spite of having less energetic biochemistries than we did, they seemed to be just about as active. Shooting and dissecting some, we found elaborate multiple hearts and huge, convoluted lungs, as well as organs whose purposes we couldn't guess. Evolution eventually produces all possible capabilities.

Including intelligence. The sun was touching the lake's rim when Urduga shouted us to him. From camp nobody could make out our ship very well, except through goggles. Those were uncomfortable to wear in this climate. Besides, the cells that powered their infrared conversion and photon

41

multiplication wouldn't last forever. So we left them off as much as possible. Now we slapped them on and stared out at the upward-thrusting nose of the *Meteor*.

There, in a fiery shimmer across the water, were four canoes. Long lean shapes with high prows, they were manned by a good dozen creatures apiece. We could barely see, against that sun-dazzle, that the crews were a little under human size, bipeds, powerfully legged and tailed. We launched our raft and paddled toward them, but they hastened off. Before long they had vanished into dusk.

I, who have met thousands of different races, still feel that each new one is a new epoch. Stars, planets, biological systems fall into categories; minds do not, and you never know what strangeness will confront you. Though this first glimpse of the Herd had so little result, I hate to tell of it casually.

But you can imagine what talking we did afterward in camp.

# VII

THIS EVENING the galaxy rose directly after sunset. In spite of its angular diameter, twenty-two degrees along the major axis, our unaided eyes saw it ghostly pale across seventy thousand parsecs. By day it would be invisible. Except for what supergiants we could see as tiny sparks within it, we had no stars at night, and little of that permanent aurora which gives the planets of more active suns a sky-glow. There was some zodiacal light, but that was scant help. We must depend on fluorescents, flashes, fire and goggles to carry on our work.

But then that work reached a crisis point. The generator was operating, the plankton tanks breeding food, the camp snugged down within a stockade of sharpened logs. We'd continued indefinitely manufacturing small comforts and conveniences for ourselves. But the question could no longer be shoved aside: what were we going to do to break free?

Would we? I knew the result if we didn't. When our teeth wore down to the gums, and no biogenic apparatus was on hand to stimulate regrowth, we could make dental plates. When monotony got unendurable, we could build or explore or otherwise occupy ourselves. But when at length there were too many unedited memory bits, we would gradually lose our reason.

Sleep evaded me. The shelter was hot and stank of man. The other cots crowded in on mine. Bren snored. My arm was healing with the speed of immortal flesh and bone, but on occasion still pained me. Finally I rose and walked outside.

The yard lights were off. No use inviting attention during a rest period. Between hut and stockade lay a well of blackness, relieved only by a bluish watery glow where irradiator coils energized our plankton. A wind boomed softly, warm and dank, full of swamp musks; the generator whirred in its shell; distantly came a beast's hoot; lake water lapped among those rustling plants we called reeds.

And I heard another sound: Valland's omnisonor. He was on watch. Tonight he didn't sing, he stroked forth lilting notes that spoke of peace. I groped my way to the crude skeleton tower on which he sat, light switches and a gun ready to hand.

He sensed me. "Who's there?" he called.

"Me. Mind if I come join you for a little?"

"No. Glad of company. Sentry-squat gets a mite lonesome."

I climbed up and sat on the platform's bench beside him. Since I hadn't taken my goggles, he was no more than another big shadow. The sky was clear, except for a few thin clouds reflecting the galaxy's glow. It sheened on the lake, too; but shoreward, night drank down its light and I was blind.

Vast and beautiful, it had barely cleared the horizon, which made it seem yet more huge. I could just trace out the arms, curling from a lambent nucleus . . . yes, there was the coil whence man had come, though if I could see man by these photons he would still be a naked half-ape running the forests of Earth . . . . Otherwise I was only able to see three glitters which we now knew were planets.

"What was that tune you were playing?" I asked.

"Somethin' by Carl Nielsen. Doubt if you've heard of him. He was a composer on Earth, before my time but popular yet when I was young."

"After three millennia, you still remember such details?" I wondered.

"Well, I keep goin' back there, you know, on account of

44

Mary," Valland said. "And Earth doesn't change much any more. So I get reminded. My later memories are the ones I can dispense with."

I realized that this must the reason he, with his abilities, was not commanding a ship. That would have had him star-hopping at somebody else's orders. I didn't know when I'd see Lute and Wenli again, for instance, if I got back into space. The company rotated personnel among home stations, so fifty years was an entirely possible gap. Valland must return home a good deal oftener.

"She seems to be quite a girl, yours," I said.

"Oh, yes," he whispered into the wind.

"You're married?"

"No official contract." Valland laughed. "Plain to see, skipper, you're post-exodus. Mary'd follow the old custom and take my name if—" He broke off.

"You know," I said, for I wanted to speak of such things in this foreign night, "you've never shown us her picture. And everybody else practically carries an album of his women around with him."

"I don't need any stereo animation," he said curtly. "Got a better one in my head." Relaxing, he laughed once more. "Besides, she said once—this was when breeks had hip pockets—she said it didn't seem like a very sentimental gesture, carryin' her picture next to my"—he paused—"heart."

"You've got me curious, though. Dog my hatch for me if I'm prying, but what does she look like?"

"Shucks, I'm only too glad to talk about her. Trouble is, words're such feeble little quacks. That's why I made me a song. Adapted from an old Swedish one, to be honest."

"Swedish? I don't recall any planet named Swede."

"No, no, Sweden, Sverige, a country, back when Earth had countries. Nice people there, if a bit broody. I'm part Swede myself."

45

Valland fell silent. The galaxy glimmered so coldly above the lake that I had to say something. "What about Mary?"

"Oh." He started. "Yes. Well, she's tall, and has a sort of rangy walk, and laughs a lot, and her hair catches the sunlight so— No, sorry, words just won't fit her."

"Well, I'd like to meet the lady," I said, "if we reach Earth."

"We will," Valland answered. "Somehow." His arm rose, pointing, a massive bar across the clouds. "That planet there, orange color. Must be Yonder. We don't need to go any further than that."

"Two hundred and thirty thousand light-years in no time," I said bitterly, "and a few million kilometers are too much for us."

"Well, it's a big universe," he said. "We don't shrink it any by crossin' it."

After a moment he added: "We can make Yonder, though. The more I think and look at what's available to us, the more I'm convinced that between two wrecked ferries and parts of a wrecked ship, we can put together one sound vessel. No use wishin' we could do anything with the space jump apparatus. That's so much scrap, and we'd never fix it even if we knew how. So we won't be sendin' the Yonderfolk any signals that way."

"Frankly, I'm skeptical about our chances of simply building an interplanetary maser," I confessed.

"Oh, we'll do that, kind of incidentally," Valland said. "Same as we'll make conspicuous marks in the territory around here, in case somebody comes flyin' by. But Yo was right, a while back. They aren't likely to have the right kind of radio receivers on Yonder. And as for a rescue party, well, at best it'll be an almighty long time before anybody figures out what could've happened to us, and I'll make book that nobody does. Not with so scanty and confused a record to go on.

"So . . . I figure our sole decent chance is to flit to Yonder in person. We needn't build a very fancy spaceboat, you realize. A one-man job for a one-way trip, with no special radiation screenin' required. I've checked. Been an engineer myself, several kinds of engineer, now and then, so I know. One powerplant is almost intact. Repairman's data in the microfiles aboard ship amount to a complete set of plans, which we can modify for our particular purposes. What machine tools we don't now have, we can repair, or build from scratch.

"Sure, sure, a long, tough job. The precision aspects, like assemblin' control panels or adjustin' drive units, they'll be worse than any sheer labor. But we can do it, given patience."

"Hold on," I objected. "The brute force problem alone is too much for us. Six men can't juggle tons of metal around with their muscles. We'll need cranes and—and make your own list. We'll have to start this project down near the bottom of shipyard technology.

"Hugh, we haven't got enough man-years. If we don't go memory-crazy first, we'll still be making bedplates when the supplementary chemicals for the food tanks give out. And I refuse to believe we can do anything about *that*."

"Probably not," Valland admitted. "I never claimed we could start a whole biomolecular industry. But you're overlookin' somethin', skipper. True, half a dozen men make too small a labor force to build a spaceship, even by cannibalizin', in the time we have. However— Hey!"

He sprang to his feet.

"What is it?" I cried.

"Shhh. Somethin' out there. Approaching' real slow and careful. But two-legged, and carryin' things. Let's not scare 'em off. Valland stepped to the ladder and handed me his goggles. "Here, you stay put. Cover me as well as you can, but don't switch on any lights. Our kind of light may well

47

hurt their eyes. I'll kindle a torch to see by. They must know fire."

I stared and stared into murk. Shadow shapes in shadow land . . . . "Looks as if they're armed," I muttered.

" 'Course they are. Wouldn't you be? But I doubt they'll slip a pigsticker into me on no provocation." Valland laughed, most softly but like a boy. "You know," he said, "I was just speakin' of the devil, and what came by? A bigger pair of horns than Othello thought he had!"

I didn't follow his mythological references, but his meaning was plain. My own heart jumped inside me.

There is an old game in which you show a picture of a nonhuman to your friends and ask them to describe the being. No xenological coordinates allowed; they must use words alone. The inexperienced player always falls back on analogy. Like Valland, simply to be jocular, remarking that the Azkashi resembled web-footed kangaroos, a bit shorter than men, with hands and hairless gray skins, bulldog muzzles, mule ears, and eyes as big as the Round Tower. Which means nothing to that ninety-nine percent of the human race who have never been on Earth and have never heard of animals many of which are extinct anyway.

Myself, I think the game is silly. I'd be satisfied to speak of bipeds adapted to a world mostly swamp and water. I would mention the great yellow eyes, which saw only a short way into those frequencies we call red and otherwise had to focus infrared waves—largely because they could also see fairly well at night. I might say the beings didn't have nostrils, but closable slits beneath the ears, since this gave their voices an odd snarling quality. The barrel chests were also significant, betokening a metabolism that required more oxygen per breath than we who are blessed with iron-based hemoglobin. It is certainly worth recording that the species was bisexual, viviparous, and homeothermic, though not technically mammalian.

In general, though, I don't care what image you develop. What matters about a people is technology, thought, art, the whole pattern of life.

As for technics, the score of hunters who entered our compound were high-level paleolithic. Their weapons were spears, tomahawks, daggers, and blowguns. Stone, bone and wood were beautifully worked and tastefully ornamented. They went nude except for a sort of leather harness, which supported a pouch as well as tools and armament. But an older one who seemed to be their leader had a representation of the galaxy tattooed on his head.

We were relieved to find no obviously alien semantics. These people would be much easier to understand than the Yonderfolk—or so we thought. For example, they had individual names, and their gestures were the kind humans would make in attempting sign language. When we fetched gifts—a steel knife for ya-Kela the boss and some bits of plastic and other junk for his followers—they yelped and danced with delight. They had brought presents of their own, local handicrafts, which we accepted with due dignity. There came an embarrassing moment, several hours later, when three Azkashi who had slipped out into the woods returned with a big game animal for us. We were doubtless expected to eat it, and had no idea if it would poison us. But Valland carried the situation off by soaking the body in camp fuel and setting it alight on a heap of wood. Our visitors got the idea at once: this was how the strangers who indicated they had come from the galaxy accepted an offering.

"In fact," Valland remarked to me, "they're smart fellows. They must've watched us from the woods for a long time before decidin' to send a delegation. My guess is they waited for the galaxy to rise; it's a god or whatnot to them, and then they felt safer against our *mana*. But now that they're here

49

and know we don't mean any harm, they're tryin' hard for communication."

Ya-Kela was, at least, and so was Valland. Most of the other hunters left after a while, to take word back home. Man and nonman squatted in the compound, by firelight, drew pictures and exchanged gestures. Rorn complained about the darkness outside our hut. I overruled him. "We've seen them cover their eyes against our normal illumination," I said. "We don't want them to go away. They may be our labor force."

"Indeed?" Rorn said. "How'll you pay them?"

"With metal. I don't know how many thousands of knives and saws and planes we can make out of scrap from the ship, and you must have noticed how ya-Kela appreciates the blade we gave him. I saw him holding it up once and singing to it."

"Nice theory. Only . . . captain, I've dealt with primitives too. Generally they don't make proper helpers for a civilized man. They don't have the drive, persistence, orderliness, not even the capability of learning."

"Rather like your caveman ancestors, huh, Yo?" Urduga gibed.

Rorn flushed. "All right, call it a culture pattern if you want. It's still real."

"Maybe it isn't in this case," I said. "We'll find out."

With a good bit more hope in me, I started organizing us for work. First we had to jury-rig a better lighting system aboard the *Meteor*, so we could operate effectively. Next, with spacesuits doubling as diving rigs, we must patch most of the holes in the hull, seal off the remaining compartments, pump out the water and float her ashore. Then there'd be the construction of a drydock, or whatever we decided was best. Then we must take a complete inventory, so we'd know exactly what was possible for us to build; and lay concrete plans; and— The list looked infinite. But we had to begin somewhere. By burning torch and electric flare, we rafted out to the wreck.

Valland stayed behind, dealing with ya-Kela. That didn't look very strenuous, and again Rorn protested. "I don't give a belch if it's fair or not," I threw back at him. "Somebody has to spend full time learning the language, and Hugh's got more talent for that sort of thing than any two of you clump-feet put together."

Which was true. With the help of his omnisonor for noises that the human throat would not form, he could soon produce every Azkashi phoneme; and then it was not so much linguistics as a sense of poetry that was needed to fit them into meaningful phrases.

I was not too surprised when, after several Earth-days, he told me that ya-Kela and the others wanted to go home—taking him along. He was eager to make a visit. What could I do but agree?

# VIII

WITH A woodsranger's wariness, ya-Kela reserved judgment. Perhaps he had misunderstood those few words and gestures the stranger called ya-Valland could make. Perhaps ya-Valland did not really claim to be the emissary of God.

For surely he had curious weaknesses. He was as night blind as any downdevil once he took off his fish-resembling mask. Without tail or footwebs, he stumbled awkward through the marshes; and whenever the party swam across a body of water, he was still more clumsy and soon grew tired. Besides, he must push those things he carried on his back a-head of him, lashed to a log. One could accept that he did not speak the speech of the Pack—God must use a tongue more noble—but he was ignorant of the simplest matters, must actually be restrained from walking into a dart bush. There might be some magical reason for his not touching ordinary food and, instead, opening little packets of powder and mixing them with water to swell the bulk before he cooked himself a meal. But why must he send the water itself steaming through a thing of bottles joined by a tube, rather than lap up a drink on his way?

Ya-Eltokh, one of the four who had remained to accompany them back, growled, "He is weirder than any of the Herd. And that great thing he came in, sitting out in Lake Silence! How sure are you that he is not some downdevil animal sent to trap us?"

"If so, the Herd has been clever," ya-Kela said, "for our watchers told how their canoes fled when the strangers tried

52

to come near. And you know well that prisoners we tortured were made to confess that the downdevils did not appear to have anything to do with that which, generations ago, came from the sky. Why, then, should the enemy have brought this new manifestation about?" He signed the air. "I am the One of the Pack. The thought was mine that we should seek the strangers out, for they might be from God. If I was wrong, it is my souls that will suffer; but with this hand I will plunge the first spear into ya-Valland."

He hoped that would not come to pass. The big ugly creature was so likable in his fashion, and the music he made was somehow more important than the sharp blade he had given. He explained, after much fumbling on both sides, that the tune he made most often was a song to his she. But when he heard those notes, little ghosts ran up and down the skin of ya-Kela. There was strong magic in that song.

They continued to seek understanding whenever they camped. Ya-Valland guided the lessons with marvelous skill. By the time they reached the lairs, he could do a little real talking.

It was good to be back in hill country. The Herd fighters seldom ventured into this land of long ridges and darkling valleys, noisy rivers and silent woods. Ya-Kela snuffed a wind that bore the odor of ninla nests, heard the remote scream of a kurakh on the prowl, saw God swirl radiant above Cragdale, and bayed to call his folk. They slipped from dells and thickets until the trail was a stream of lithe, padding hunters, and went together to the caves where the Pack dwelt.

Ya-Kela took ya-Valland into his own place. His aunt, su-Kulka, made the guest welcome and prepared a bed. His she and youngs were frightened and kept in the background, but that was as it should be anyhow. Now ya-Kela settled down to toil with the newcomer as he might have settled down to chasing a onehorn till it dropped. And as God mounted yet higher in heaven, serious talk became possible. It went haltingly, with many misunderstandings; but it went.

The great question was hardest to pose and get answered. Ya-Valland seemed to make an honest effort, but his words contradicted each other. Yes, he was from God. No, he was not of God . . . . Finally he swung to asking questions himself. Ya-Kela replied, in the hope of making himself clear when his turn came again.

"God is the Begetter, the One of the World. All others are less than Him. We pray to God alone, as He has commanded," ya-Kela said, pointing and acting. He returned from the cave mouth and squatted against his tail once more. The fire was big, throwing the painted walls into lurid smoky relief. But it didn't appear to make much light for ya-Valland.

"The downdevils are the enemies of God. They deny Him, as does the Herd which serves them. But we know we are right to course for God: because He does not rule our lives. He asks only worship and upright conduct of us. Furthermore, He lights the night for us, on those times when He is risen after sunset. And then the downdevils can see but poorly." Mutter: "Almost as poorly as you, my friend-?-enemy." Aloud: "Such of the Herd as we have captured when they came raiding say the downdevils made the world and rule it. And true, they have powerful things to give. But the price is freedom."

"The Herd people are like you, then?" ya-Valland asked.

"Yes and no. Many of them resemble us, and we have learned over generations that certain Azkashi whom Herd raiders take prisoner are used for breeding stock. But others look most unlike any member of this Pack or any other Pack, and none of them think like us. They are afraid of God, even when the sun is in the sky at the same time to hide Him; and they worship the downdevils."

That much conversation took the entire while between two sleeps. Then ya-Kela must judge disputes among his folk;

for he was the One. Meanwhile ya-Valland studied language with su-Kulka, su-Iss, and other wise old shes.

Thus he was better able to explain himself at the following talk: "We fell from the sky, where our own Pack hunts. We cannot return until we have fixed our boat. That will be the work of many years, and cannot be done without many hands. For this we will pay in goods, blades such as we gave you, tools that will lighten your labor, perhaps also teaching of arts you do not know yourselves."

"But how shall the Pack be fed meanwhile?" ya-Kela asked.

"Given the use of certain weapons we own, fewer hunters can bring in ample game. Besides, they will soon drive off those enemies who trouble you."

*Now this I may doubt,* ya-Kela thought. *You showed us your thunderous arms back at your camp. But are they really more potent than the downdevils'? I do not know. Perhaps you do not either.*

He said merely, "That is good; yet such is not the ancient way. When you go, and leave a large number of our youngs who have not had time to learn the skills we live by, what then?"

*"You're one hell of a bright boy, you know?"* said ya-Valland in his own speech. He replied, "We must consider that also. If we plan well, there need be no hungry years; for the tools and weapons you earn will keep you fed until the old ways are learned afresh. Or it is even possible—though this I cannot promise—that my people will wish to come and trade with yours."

He leaned forward, his eyes brilliant in the firelight, the musicmaker in his lap talking sweetly as God Himself. "We must begin in a small way in any case, ya-Kela. Find me only a few clever young hes that are willing to come back with me and work for knives like yours. Then, in the course of a year or so, we will find out if this is good for our two sides."

"Gr-r-um." Ya-Kela rubbed his muzzle thoughtfully. "You utter no ill word there. But let me think on the matter before I say anything to the Pack at large."

That period, shortly before sleep, ya-Valland spoke into a little box he carried. It answered him, as had often happened before. But this time ya-Kela saw him grow tense, and his voice was chipped sharp and his smell became acrid.

"What is wrong?" asked the One, with hand on knife.

Ya-Valland bit his lip. "I may as well tell you," he said. "I know you still keep watchers, who will send word here as soon as they can reach the drums. Vessels have landed by the camp of my people, and some from the crews have entered the stockade to talk."

"The Herd does not use the laguage of the Pack," ya-Kela said. Dampness sprang forth on his skin. "Some have learned it, true. But none of your folk save you have mastered any but a few shards of Azkashi. How can there be talk?"

Ya-Valland was silent for a long while. The waning fire spat a few flames. That light picked out the shes and youngs, crouched frightened in the inner cave.

"I do not know," ya-Valland said. "But best I return at once. Will you give me a guide?"

Ya-Kela sprang to the cave mouth and bayed after help. "You lie!" he snarled. "I can tell that you hold something back. So you shall not leave before we have the entire truth from your downdevil mouth."

Ya-Valland could not have followed every word. But he rose himself, huge and strange, and clasped the weapon that hung at his belt.

WE ALWAYS left one man on the guard tower while the rest were at the ship. What Valland had radioed—good thing our gear included some portables!—suggested that attack by certain rivals of the Azkashi was not unthinkable. He hadn't learned much about them yet, except that they belonged to quite a different culture and must have sent those canoes we'd spied at sunset.

No doubt the Azkashi were prejudiced. They were . . . well, you couldn't call them simple hunters and gatherers. A Pack was only vaguely equivalent to a human-type tribe; Valland suspected that rather subtler concepts were involved. He was still unsure about so elementary a matter as what "Azkashi" meant. It referred collectively to the different Packs, which shared out the inland hunting grounds and lakeside fishing rights, spoke a common tongue and maintained a common way of life. But should the name be translated "hill people" as he thought at first, or "free people," or "people of the galaxy god," or what? Maybe it meant all those things, and more.

But at any rate, the Shkil, as ya-Kela called them, sometimes preyed on the Azkashi; and in the past, they had driven the Packs out of lands on the far side of Lake Silence. This, and certain other details which Valland got during his struggle for comprehension, suggested a more advanced society, agricultural, spreading at the expense of the savages. Which in turn made me wonder if the Shkil might not be potentially more useful to us. On the other hand, they might be hostile, for any of a multitude of reasons. We took no chances. A man in the tower, with gun and searchlights, could hold off an assault and cover the landing of his friends.

By chance, I was the sentry when the Shkil arrived. The galaxy was hidden in a slow, hot rain; my optical equipment could show me nothing beyond the vapors that steamed under our walls. So I had to huddle cursing beneath an inadequate roof while they maddened me with snatches of radioed information from the spaceship. Finally, though, the data were clear. A large band of autochthones had appeared in several outsize canoes and a double-hulled galley. They wanted to confer. And . . . at least one of them spoke the Yonderfolk language!

I dared not let myself believe that the Yonderfolk still maintained an outpost on this planet, so useless and lethal to them. But I felt almost dizzy as I agreed that two or three of the newcomers might enter our compound along with the returning work party. And when they came, destruction take thoughts of treachery, we left no one on the tower. We settled for barring the gate before we led our guests into the hut.

Then I stood, soaked, hearing the rain rumble on our roof, crowded with my men between these narrow walls, and looked upon wonder.

Our visitors were three. One resembled the Azkashi we had already met, though he wore a white robe of vegetable fiber and a tall white hat, carried a crookheaded staff like some ancient bishop, and need but breathe a syllable for the others to jump at his command. One was a giant, a good 240 centimeters in height. His legs and arms were disproportionately long and powerful, his head small. He wore a corselet of scaly leather and carried a rawhide shield; but at our insistence he had left his weapons behind. The third, by way of contrast, was a dwarf, also robed, but in gray. He kept his eyes shut and I took a while to realize that he was blind.

58

The one with the staff waved his free hand around quite coolly, as if extraplanetary maroons were an everyday affair. "*Niao*," he said. I gathered this was his people's name for themselves. He pointed to his own breast. "Gianyi."

"Felip Argens," I said, not to be outdone. I introduced my comrades and summed them up: "Men."

"We've told him that much," Urduga murmured in my ear. "He stood in the prow of that galley and talked for—you know how long. But you're better at the Yonder lingo than any of us, captain."

I ought to be. I'd studied, as well as electro-crammed, what little had been learned on Zara. Not that we could be sure the language was what the Yonderfolk used among themselves. It might well be an artificial code, like many others I had met, designed for establishing quick communication with anyone whose mind wasn't hopelessly alien. No matter. Gianyi of the Niao had also mastered it.

"Sit down, everybody," I babbled. "What can we offer them? Better not anything to eat or drink. Presents. Find some good presents, somebody. And for mercy's sake, whisky!"

We had a little guzzling alcohol left. It steadied me. I forgot the rain and the heat and the darkness outside, bending myself to talk with Gianyi.

That wasn't any light job. Neither of us had a large vocabulary in that language of gestures as well as sounds. What we had in common was still less. Furthermore, his people's acquaintance with it antedated mine by many generations, and had not been reinforced by subsequent contact. You might say he had another dialect. Finally, a language originated by beings unlike his race or mine was now filtered through two different body types and cultural patterns—indeed, through different instincts; I had yet to discover how very different.

So I can no more set down coherent discourse for Gianyi

59

and me than I could for ya-Kela and Valland. I can merely
pretend:

"We came from the sky," I said. "We are friendly, but we
have been wrecked and need help before we can leave. You
have met others, not akin to us but also from the sky, not
so?"

"They tell me such beings came," Gianyi said. "It was before my time, and far away."

That made sense. In an early stage of space travel, the
Yonderfolk would have visited their neighbor planets. Finding intelligent life here, they would have instituted a base
from which to conduct scientific studies—before they discovered the space jump and abandoned this world for ones
more interesting and hospitable to them. And it would have
been an unlikely coincidence if that base happened to have
been anywhere near here.

How, though, had the mutual language been preserved
through Earth centuries after they left? And how had it
traveled across hundreds or thousands of kilometers to us? I
asked Gianyi and got no good answer through the linguistic
haze. The Ai Chun could do such things, he tried to explain.
The Ai Chun had sent his party to us, making him the commander since he was among those Niao who were traditionally
instructed in sky-talk. He bowed his head whenever he spoke
that name. So did the blind dwarf. The giant remained mo-
tionless, poised; only his eyes never rested.

"A ruling class," Bren suggested to me. "Theocrats?"

"Maybe," I said. "I have an impression they're something
more, though." To Gianyi: "We will be glad to meet the Ai
Chun and make gifts to them as well as to the rest of your
people."

He got unreasonably excited. I must not lump Niao and
Ai Chun together. That was wrong. That was bad medicine.
I apologized for my ignorance.

Gianyi calmed down. "You will meet the Ai Chun," he said. "You will come with us to them."

"Well, one or two of us will," I agreed. We had to take some risks.

"No, no. Every one of you. They have so ordered."

Not being sure whether that last term indicated a fiat or simply a request, I tried to explain that we could not abandon our camp. Gianyi barked at the giant, who growled and took a stiff-legged step forward. I heard guns leave their holsters at my back.

"Easy! Easy!" I sprang to my feet. "You want to start a war?" Gianyi rose also and waved his bully boy back. We faced each other, he and I, while the rain came down louder. The dwarf had never stirred.

I cleared my throat. "You must know that those from the sky have great powers," I said. "Or if you do not, the Ai Chun should. We have no wish to fight. We will, however, if you insist we do what is impossible. Have all the Niao come here? Certainly not. Likewise, all of us cannot go away with you. But we will be glad to send one or two, in friendship."

When I had made this clear, which took time, Gianyi turned to the dwarf and spoke a while in his own high-pitched language. Something like pain went across the blind countenance. The answer was almost too low to hear. Gianyi folded his hands and bent nearly to the floor before he straightened and addressed me again.

"So be it," he told me. "We will take a pair of you. We will leave two canoes here to keep watch. The crews can catch fish to live. You are not to molest them."

"What the bloody blazes is going on?" Urduga whispered behind me.

I looked at the dwarf, who was now shivering, and made no replay. That poor little thing couldn't be the real chief of the party. Well, I've met different kinds of telepathic sensitives among the million known civilizations; none like him, but—

"Think it's a good idea to go, captain?" Galmer asked.

"I don't think we have much choice," I told him, trying hard to keep my voice steady. Inside, I was afraid. "We'll be here a long time. We've got to know what we're up against."

"They may mean well in spite of their manners," Bren said.

"Sure," I said. "They may." The rain gurgled as it fell onto soaked earth.

While Gianyi and his escort waited impassively, we discussed procedure. Our representatives were to be taken to the opposite shore, where the Niao had a frontier settlement. From Valland's questioning of ya-Kela, we knew the lake was broad, an inland sea. Still, we should get across in a couple of standard days, given those swift-looking boats. We might or might not be able to maintain radio contact. Valland could, but he hadn't traveled so far. Under the tenuous ionosphere of this planet, we needed a hypersensitive receiver to read him.

I must go, having the best command of Yonder. An extra man was desirable, both as a backup for me—the situation looked trickier than Valland's—and as evidence of good faith on our part. Everyone volunteered (who could do otherwise, with the rest of us watching him?) and I picked Yo Rorn. He wasn't my ideal of a traveling companion, but his special skills could be duplicated by Valland and Bren working in concert, whereas nobody but Urduga could fix a drive unit and Galmer was alone in knowing the ins and outs of a control system.

We started to pack our gear, more or less what Valland himself had taken along. Bedrolls; plastic tent; cooking and distilling utensils; lyophilized food from stores; medical kit; torchguns and charges; radio, extra capacitors, hand-cranked minigenerator for reviving them; flashes, goggles, photoplates, space garments— The receiver buzzed. I thrust across the crowded hut and sat down. "Hello?" I shouted.

"Me here," Valland's voice said, tiny out of the speaker. "Just reportin'. Things look pretty hopeful at this end. How's with you?"

I told him.

He whistled. "Looks like the Herd's found you out."

"The what?"

"The Shkil. You remember. I've about decided it translates best as 'Herd.' What'd you say they call themselves?"

"The Niao. With somebody else in charge that they name as Ai Chun."

"Um. The downdevils, I suppose. My own translation again, of an Azkashi word that means somethin' like 'the evil ones in the depths.' Only I thought the downdevils were a set of pagan gods, as contrasted with the local religion where the galaxy's the one solitary original God, beware of imitations."

Valland's lightness was not matched by his tone. I realized with a jolt that this was putting him in a bad fix. What with the strain of the past hours, trying to unravel Gianyi's intent, we'd forgotten that our shipmate was among people who hated and feared those I was to depart with.

And . . . surely the Pack had watchers by the edge of wilderness.

"We can hardly avoid going," I said, "but we'll stall till you can return here."

"Well, I'll try. Hang on a bit."

There followed some ugly noises.

"Hugh!" I cried. "Hugh, are you there?"

The rain had stopped, and silence grew thick in the hut. Gianyi muttered through the dwarf to his unknown masters. I sat and cursed.

Finally, breathlessly, Valland said:

"Matters peaked in an awful hurry. Ya-Kela figured treachery. He called in his goons and wanted to put me to the question, as I believe the polite term is. I pointed out that I could shoot my way clear. He said I'd have to sleep eventually and then he'd get me. I said no, I'd start right back to camp if need be, might not make it but I'd sure give him a run for his money. Only look, old pal, I said, let's be reasonable. My people don't know anything about the downdevils. Maybe they've been tricked. If so, I'll want your help to rescue them, and between us we can strike a hefty blow. Or suppose the worst, suppose my people decide to collaborate with the enemy because they offer a better deal. Then I'll be worth more to you as a hostage than a corpse. I got him calmed down. Now he wants to lecture me at length about how bad the downdevils are."

"Try to explain the idea of neutrality," I said. "Uh, Hugh, are you sure you'll be all right?"

"No," he said. "Are you sure for yourself?"

I tried to answer, but my throat tightened up on me.

"We're both in a bad spot," Valland said, "and I wouldn't be surprised but what yours is worse. Ya-Kela swore by his God he won't hurt me as long as I keep my nose clean. I won't be a prisoner, exactly; more like a guest who isn't permitted to leave. I think he'll stand by that. I've already handed him my gun, and still he's lettin' me finish before he sequestrates the radio. So I ought to be safe for the time bein'. You go ahead and sound out the whosits—Ai Chun. You've got to. Once you're back, we'll parley."

I tried to imagine what it had been like, standing in a cave full of wolves and surrendering one's only weapon on the strength of a promise. I couldn't.

# X

THE GALLEY walked fast over the water. Except for creak
and splash of oars, soft thutter of a coxswain's drum, an occasional low-voiced command, it was too silent for my liking.
Torches lit the deck built across the twin hulls. But when
Rorn and I stood at the rail, we looked into murk. Even with
goggles, we saw only the galaxy and its wave-splintered
glade; the accompanying canoes were too far out.

Rorn's gaunt features were shadow and flicker beside me.
"We're facing something more powerful than you maybe
realize," he said.

I rested my hand on my gun butt. Its knurls comforted me.
"How so?" I asked.

"Those boats which first came, and ran away. They must
have been from the place we're headed for now. What's its
name again?"

"Prasiyo, I think."

"Well, obviously they simply chanced on us, in the course
of fishing or whatever. The crews were ordinary unspecialized
Niao, we saw that. But they didn't take the responsibility
of meeting us. No, they reported straight back to Prasiyo.
Now normally, you know, given a generally human-type instinct pattern, a technological-geographical situation like this
one makes for individualism."

I nodded. Tyranny gets unstable when a cheap boat can
pace a warship and there's a wilderness for dissatisfied people
to vanish into. The Niao had not fled us because of timidity.
Their harrying of the Azkashi proved otherwise. So the Niao
must *like* being subservient.

"Nevertheless," Rorn continued, "it took some while before this delegation arrived. That means it had to be organized. Authorized. Which means word had to get back to a distant front office."

"Now that needn't take long, given telepathy."

"My exact point. The masters therefore debated the matter at length and took their time preparing to contact us. There's also the business of the Yonder language having been preserved so long and carried so far. What these clues point to is: we're on the marches of a very big and very old empire."

I was surprised. Rorn hadn't seemed capable of reasoning so clearly. "Makes a good working hypothesis, anyhow," I said. "Well, if we can get them to help us, fine. They'll have more resources, more skills of the kind we need, than the Pack does. Of course, first we have to get Hugh back into camp with us."

Rorn spat.

"You don't like him, do you?" I asked.

"No. A loudmouthed oaf."

"He's your crewfellow," I reminded him.

"Yes, yes. I know. But if matters should come to a pass—if we can only save ourselves, the whole remaining lot of us, by abandoning him—it won't weigh on my conscience."

"How would you like to be on the receiving end of that philosophy?" I snapped. "We orbit or crash together!"

Rorn was taken aback. "I didn't mean—Captain, please don't think I—"

Ghostlike in his robes and hat, Gianyi glided to me. "I have thought you might be shown the ship," he offered.

We were both relieved at the interruption, as well as interested in a tour, and followed him around the deck. The cabin assigned us was pretty bare. The others, for Gianyi and three more Niao of similar rank, were a curious blend of austere furnishing with ornate painted and carved decoration. I noticed that two symbols recurred. One was a complicated knot, the other a sort of double swastika with a circle super-imposed. I asked about them.

Gianyi bowed deep. "The knot is the emblem of the Ai Chun," he said.

"And this?"

He traced a sign on his breast. "The *miaicho* bound fast by the power of the solar disc."

A few minutes later, I observed that helmsmen and look-outs wore broad hats with that second insigne on them. I asked why. Gianyi said it was protection against the miaicho.

Rorn was quick to understand. He pointed at the immense spiral in heaven. "That?"

"Yes," Gianyi said. "Its banefulness is great when there is no sun at the same time. We would not have crossed the water tonight had the Ai Chun not commanded."

So, I thought, the God of the Azkashi was some kind of demon to the Niao. Just as the Niao's venerated Ai Chun were the downdevils of the Pack. . . .

Gianyi made haste to take us below. The hull, like every-thing else, was well built. No metal anywhere, of course; ribs and planks were glued, then clinched with wooden pegs. Con-struction must have been a major job. Gianyi admitted there was just this one ship on the lake; otherwise only canoes were needed, to fish and to keep the savages in their place. But whole fleets plied the oceans, he said. I was prepared to be-lieve him after he showed me some very fine objects, cera-mic and plastic as well as polished stone.

The crew intrigued me most. The rowers worked in sev-eral shifts on a well ventilated, lantern-lit deck. They were all of a kind, with short legs, grotesquely big arms and shoulders, mere stumps of tail. Some fighters were on board too, like the colossus I had already seen. To our questions, Gianyi replied that other types of Niao existed, such as divers and paddy workers. He himself belonged to the intel-lectual stock.

"You may only breed within your own sort?" I asked.

"There is no law needed," Gianyi said. "Who would wish to mate with one so different, or keep alive a young which was not a good specimen? Unless, of course, the Ai Chun command it. They sometimes desire hybrids. But that is for the good of all the Niao."

When I had unraveled that this was what he had actually said, and explained to Rorn, my companion reflected in our own tongue: "The system appears to operate smoothly. But that has to be because hundreds, thousands of generations of selective breeding lie behind it. Who enforced that, in the early days?" I saw him shudder. "And how?"

I had no reply. There are races with so much instinct of communality that eugenics is ancient in their cultures. But it's never worked long enough at a time for others, like the human race, to be significant. You get too much individual rebellion; eventually some of the rebels get power to modify the setup, or wreck it.

So perhaps the autochthones of this planet did not have human-type minds after all?

No—because then how did you account for the Azkashi?

In spite of the temperature, we felt cold. And belowdecks was a cavern, full of glooms, lit by no more than a rare flickering lamp. We excused ourselves and returned to our little room. It had only one sconce, but we stuck spare candles in their wax around us.

Rorn sat down on his bedroll, knees hugged to chin, and stared at me where I stood. "I don't like this," he said.

"The situation's peculiar," I agreed, "but not necessarily sinister. Remember, the Yonderfolk suggested we might base ourselves here."

"They supposed we'd arrive with full equipment. Instead, we're helpless."

I regarded him closely. He was shivering. And he had been so competent hitherto. "Don't panic," I warned him. "Remember, the worst thing that can happen to us is no more than death."

"I'm not sure. I've been thinking and—well, consider. The Ai Chun, whoever they are, haven't much physical technology, for lack of metal. But they've gone far in biology and mentalistics. Consider their routine use of telepathy, which to this day is too unreliable for humans. Consider how they could regulate the Niao, generation after generation, until submissiveness was built into the chromosomes. Could they do the same to us?"

"A foul notion." I wet my lips. "But we have to take our chances."

"Harder for me than you."

"How so?"

He looked up. His features were drawn tight. "I'll tell you. I don't want to, but you've got to understand I'm not a coward. It's only that I know how terrible interference with the mind can be, and you don't."

I sat down beside him and waited. He drew a breath and said, fast and flat, eyes directly to the front:

"Faulty memory editing. That's not supposed to be possible, but it was in my case. I was out in the Frontier Beta region. A new planet, with a new med center. They didn't yet know that the pollen there has certain psychodrug properties. I went under the machine, started concentrating as usual, and . . . and I lost control. The technicians didn't see at once that something was wrong. By the time they did, and stopped the process— Well, I hadn't lost everything. But what I had left was unrelated fragments insufficient for a real personality. Worse, in a way, than total amnesia. Yet I couldn't bring myself to wipe the slate clean. That would be like suicide."

"How long ago was this?" I asked when he stopped to gulp for air.

"Forty-odd years. I've managed to . . . to restructure myself. But the universe has never felt quite right. A great many

69

very ordinary things still have a nightmare quality to them, and—" He beat the deck with his fist. "Can you imagine going through something like that again?"

"I'm terribly sorry," I said.

He straightened. His aloofness came back to him. "I doubt that, captain. People have to be far closer than we are to feel anything but a mild regret at each other's troubles. Or so I've observed. I spend a lot of time observing. Now I don't want to talk further about this, and if you tell anyone else I'll kill you. But take my advice and watch your mind!"

## XI

WE CAME to Prasiyo in darkness, and left in darkness, so to me it was only torches, shadows, sad strange noise of a horn blown somewhere out in the night. Afterward I saw it by day, and others like it; and as I became able to ask more intelligent questions, the Niao I met could give me better answers. Thus I learned a great deal, and never in my traveling have I met a society more outlandish.

But that's for the xenological files. Here I'll just say that Prasiyo wasn't a town, in the sense of a community where beings lived in some kind of mutual-interest relationship, with some feeling of common tradition. Prasiyo was only a name for that lakefront area where the docks happened to be. This made it convenient to locate certain workshops nearby. So the igloo-shaped huts of the Niao clustered a bit thereabouts—unlike in the wide, wet agricultural region that stretched behind Lake Silence, on and on to the ocean. Yes, and still further, because there were Niao who had been bred for pelagiculture too.

The Pack maintained a true community, in those lairs where Valland was now a prisoner. Later we found that there were other savages, in other wild parts of the world, who did likewise. Some of them had progressed to building little villages. But the Niao, who appeared to be civilized, had nothing of the kind anywhere. For they were the Herd, and herds don't create nations.

Neither do gods.

Our galley didn't go to the wharf. Instead, we moored

71

alongside a structure built some distance offshore: a square, massive stone pile that loomed over us in the night like a thundercloud. Lanterns picked out soldier Niao guarding the ramparts. Helmeted and corseleted, armed with knives, pikes, bows, catapults, they stood as if they were also stone. Gianyi and three fellow scribes conducted us off ship, in a stillness so deep that the gangplank seemed to drum beneath our feet. The blind dwarf scuttled after us. They all bent low in reverence to the gate.

"What is this?" I asked.

"The house that is kept for the Ai Chun, when they choose to visit us here," Gianyi said mutedly. "You are honored. No less than two of them have come to see you."

I had a last glimpse of the galaxy before we entered. The sight had always appeared unhuman to me before—lovely, but big and remote and indifferent. Now it was the one comfort I had.

Lamps burned dim down the wet, echoing length of a hall. There was no ornament, no furniture, only the great gray blocks. We passed through an archway into a room. It was too broad and feebly lit for me to see the end, although I had my goggles on. Most of the floor was occupied by a pool. I conjectured rightly that this place must connect with the lake by submarine passages.

The downdevils lay in the water.

A physical description would sound like any amphibious race. They were pinnipeds of a sort, about twice the length and several times the bulk of men. The sleek heads were notable chiefly for the eyes: not so large as those of the bipeds, a very beautiful luminous chalcedony in color. Evolution had modified the spine so that they could sit up when on land. And I suppose the front limbs had developed digits from internal bones: because what I saw was a flipper with four clumsy fingers.

The sea doesn't often bring forth intelligence. But under

special circumstances it can happen. The dolphins of Earth were a famous example. If they had gained the ability to go ashore, to travel cross country in however awkward a fashion, who knows what they might have become? I think the environmental challenge that brought forth the Ai Chun occurred billions of years ago. As the planet lost hydrosphere—which happened slowly indeed, under so chill a sun; but remember how old this world was—more and more dry land emerged. With so many ages behind it, the life that then, step by step, took possession, was not modified fish as on Earth. It was life already air-breathing, with high metabolism and well-developed nervous system. New conditions stimulated further development—you don't need hard radiation for mutation to occur; thermal quantum processes will do the same less rapidly. At last the Ai Chun came into being.

I think too that there was once a satellite, large and close, which lit the nights until finally the sun's field, intense at this short remove, perturbed it away. Or maybe the Ai Chun evolved when the planet had a permanent dayside. For their eyes weren't well adapted to the long nights they now faced. They had substituted firelight for the optic evolution that had taken place in younger species. Perhaps this is the reason they hated and feared the galaxy. In the day sky it was invisible to them, but on alternate nights it ruled the darkness.

All that is for the paleontologists to decide. And it happened so long ago that the evidence may have vanished.

What mattered to Yo Rorn and me, confronting those two beings, was their words. They did not deign to speak directly. They would have had trouble using the Yonder language anyway. The dwarf opened his mouth, moved his arms, and said:

"Through this creature we address you, as we have already observed you from afar. You are kin to those which dwelt here for a space, numerous years ago, claiming to be from above, correct?"

"There is no blood relationship," I said. My heartbeat knocked in my ears. "But you and we and they, like the Niao and the hill people, are thinking animals. I believe this is more important than our bodily shapes."

Gianyi made an appalled hiss. "Have you forgotten whom you speak to?" he cried.

"No offense intended," I said, wondering what local custom I'd violated. "Since you have followed our discussions with your . . . your servants, you know we are ignorant and need help. In exchange we offer friendship as well as material rewards."

"Say further," commanded the Ai Chun.

They drew me out with some extremely shrewd questions. They had forgotten little of what the Yonderfolk had evidently told them. I explained our background, I spoke of the galaxy, its size and distance, the millions of worlds and the powerful races which inhabited them— Why did the scribes, the will-less dwarf himself, cringe?

Sweat glistened on Rorn's skin. "You're telling them the wrong things," he said.

"I know," I answered. "But what's the right thing?" I dropped hand to gun—started to, but my arm wouldn't obey. It was as if the muscles had gone to sleep. With a curse, I focused myself on the task. My hand moved, jerkily, to clasp the butt.

Rallying nerve, I said: "Are you trying to control me? That is no friendly act. And you can't, you see. Our minds are too unlike."

A part of me thought they must also have tried this on the Yonderfolk, and failed so completely against brains based on hydrogen and ammonia that the attempt wasn't noticed. Otherwise we'd have been warned. Then the Ai Chun dissembled, hid their real nature like the hidden part of an iceberg, gave the impression of being harmless primitives. A telpathic folk with a unified, planet-wide culture could do that.

In our case, they didn't bother. They knew far too well that no one would avenge us. The dwarf's monotone said:

"We dismissed the former visitors, and we shall not let you run free in the world. Have no fear. Your potential usefulness is admitted. While you obey, you shall not be harmed. And when you grow old you will be cared for like any aged, faithful Niao."

Rorn and I moved until we stood back to back. The scribes edged off into a dark corner. One downdevil raised himself higher, so that the lamplight gleamed on him. The dwarf spoke:

"We have pondered what reason we might have had in the beginning to bring forth creatures like you and those others. Where we do not supervise it, life on shore often develops in curious ways. Perhaps you do not yourselves know your ancestral history. However, you are ordered at least to desist from telling falsehoods. For we believe now that your existence is not accidental but intended."

Rorn whimpered. "They're in my mind. I can feel them, they're in my mind."

"Shut up and keep ready to shoot," I told him.

I felt it myself, if "felt" is the right word. Unbidden images, impulses, bursts of terror and anger and bliss and lust, a stiffness in my body, my clothes drenched and stinking with perspiration. But the impressions were not intense—about like a mild drunkenness, as far as their power to handicap me went. I told myself, over and over: *These beasts are projecting energies of a type that've been known to our scientists for hundreds of years. They want to stimulate corresponding patterns in my brain. But I belong to another species. My neurones don't work like theirs. I won't give them a chance to find out how I do work. And remember always, in spite of the horror stories, nobody can be "taken over" who keeps his wits about him. It's physically impossible. You're closer to your own nervous system, and better integrated with it, than anyone else can be.*

I clamped my teeth for a moment, then started asking questions.

Abruptly the disturbances in my head stopped. Maybe simply because of the contrast, I felt more in possession of myself than ever before in my life. So for hours I stood talking. All the while, Rorn was silent at my back.

The downdevils responded to me with cold candor. No use trying to reproduce our discussion as such. I don't remember the details. And naturally our conference was often interrupted by explanations of some new term, by arguments, by cogitation until a meaning became clear. They didn't press me, these two in the pool. They weren't in the habit of hurrying. Besides, I slowly saw, they were quite fascinated. They didn't hate us any more than we would hate a pair of wild beasts we had captured for study and possible taming.

At least, there was no conscious hatred. Down underneath, I don't know. We threatened their whole existence.

You see, they were gods.

It was not just that their Niao worshiped them. I doubt the Niao did, anyway, in the human-like sense in which you could say the Azkashi worshiped the galaxy. The Niao were devoted to the Ai Chun as a dog is to a man; they'd been bred for that trait; but aside from a few gestures of respect, they didn't conduct ceremonies. For that matter, the Ai Chun had no religion, if you mean by that a belief in a superior power.

No, they simply thought this was the only world, the whole universe, and they had created it.

The idea was not crazy. Their planet showed few phenomena to inspire awe, like stars or volcanoes or seasons. The Ai Chun had existed in their present form for over a billion years, I imagine. Their natural enemies were exterminated before their recorded history began. In spite of much empirical knowledge, they had never developed a true science. They did not quarrel with each other, they parceled out the world and refrained from overbreeding. One generation lived exactly like the next. Their culture was sufficiently complex that intelligence didn't atrophy; but change was so slow that there remained vast land areas they had not so much as explored. Only lately had their minions been pushing into the Lake Silence region—and not in any pioneer rush, but by calculated degrees. Theirs was a static world.

Individual Ai Chun suffered accidents, grew old, died. That didn't matter. They believed in reincarnation. So it was reasonable to imagine that at some time in the past, in earlier lives, they themselves had made the universe. It was an obvious analogy to the building and stockbreeding they now practiced. Likewise, they knew they made occasional mistakes in their present lives—which accounted for unruly elements in the cosmos.

Besides, had they not, within historical times, added a thinking race to the world?

They had. I saw no reason to doubt their claim. Being poorly adapted to dry land, they domesticated a promising bipedal animal and spent half a million or so Earth-years breeding it for intelligence and dexterity. That was the last great advance their frozen society had made. Now the Niao did for them what they were not able to do for themselves.

Of course, intelligence is a tricky thing. And without techniques of molecular biology, you can never get every wild gene out of a stock. Certain Niao, here and there on the planet, for one reason or another, had gone masterless into new territories. There the demands of an independent life had quickly winnowed out submissiveness. An instinct of devotion remained, making for religion and mutual loyalty. The end result was the Azkashi and other cultures—feral.

The Ai Chun were not alarmed. They thought in million-year terms. They didn't let their Niao expand fast: that could have introduced upsetting factors. Bit by bit, as agricultural acreage increased, the savages would be whittled away. Meanwhile they posed no real threat.

The Yonderfolk, and now we, did. Not that we desired this wretched planet for ouselves. But our very attitude was an insult. Our claim to be from other worlds in an unimaginably big and complicated universe ran into the teeth of a mythology that was old while the dinosaurs still lived. Our machines, our weapons, something as simple as a steel knife, had not been dreamed of here and could not even be copied. By existing, we doomed this whole culture.

The Yonderfolk hadn't stayed long enough to do more than shake the Ai Chun. What they had taught was preserved and brooded on. Now we were here, still another race. But this time the intruders were few and vulnerable. If we could be subjugated, that would prove we were inferior. Then the Ai Chun could assure themselves that outsiders like us had also been created by them in the distant past, for the purpose of inventing things which we would now offer to our gods.

I argued. I tried to show them the pathetic, ridiculous futility of their scheme. I said we couldn't possibly give them more iron than there was in our ship; and if we built them plants to extract light metals, they could still make only the most limited use of the stuff; and if our people should decide to base on this planet, there wouldn't be one damned thing the Ai Chun could do about it; and if they cooperated with us we could offer them infinitely greater rewards— Useless. Such concepts didn't lie within their horizon.

Yet they were neither stupid nor mad. Only different from us.

"The seed we planted long ago is bearing its fruit," said the voice of the dwarf. "We will occupy your camp and put you to work."

"Like fury you will!" I drew my gun. Their minds didn't try to stop me.

78

I fired a beam into the air. The Niao wailed and covered their eyes. The Ai Chun dived. "You see?" I shouted. "We can kill you and every one of your folk. We can seize a boat and sail back. Our friends will not open their gates to you, and their own weapons will burn you at a distance. We do not want to fight, but if we must, then it is you who will be dead!"

A hand closed on my wrist. An arm locked around mine. The gun clattered free. I stumbled from a push. Whirling, I saw Yo Rorn.

His own gun was out, aimed straight at me. "Hold still," he said.

"What the chaos!" I lurched toward him.

"Stop. I'd hate to burn you down." He spoke quietly. Haloed by darkness, his face was altogether serene. "You've lost," he said.

## XII

THE GALAXY was high in heaven when we started back, and first glimmers of dawn paled it. I still needed my goggles to see; they showed me Lake Silence ice-gray and ruffled by a light wind. Rain clouds grew in the north. The air had turned cold. I stood on the galley deck, looking across to the score of canoes which escorted us, and again felt horror at how quietly the Niao worked.

Down below decks, the two Ai Chun rested in a tank of water. They were going to make a personal inspection after our camp was occupied. Through their sensitives they were in touch with their fellows around the globe. Not only this little fleet was moving against my crew; a planet was.

"No," Rorn said, "they didn't get inside me and pull any strings. I'm doing what I want to do."

I couldn't look straight into the nirvana of his eyes. The downdevils were clever, I thought. Sensing his weakness, they had left me alone, holding my attention with talk, while through hours they studied him. Not that they had battered down any defenses he had. He would have known, then, and appealed for my armed help. But they had watched his reactions as one subtle impulse after another was tried. In the end, they had understood him so well that they had been able to—to what?

I asked him.

"It was a stroke of luck for them that you took me with you instead of someone else," Rorn said impersonally. "They couldn't have operated on a well-developed personality. They've admitted to me it's not possible to tame even a captured savage through mentalistics; he has to be broken first by physical means. And we humans are less kin to them than any Azkashi. But in my case, I didn't have much ego strength. I was a bundle of uncoordinated impulses and poorly understood memories. Galactic civilization had little to offer me."

"What did they give you?"

"Wholeness. I can belong here."

"As a nice, safe slave?"

"You don't get any closer to the truth with swear words. I was shown something great, calm, beautiful, at peace with itself. Then they took it away. I got the idea: they'd give it back to me if I joined them."

"So you stopped being human," I said.

"No doubt. What was the use of staying human? Oh, in a hundred years or so I'd have crystallized into your pattern again. But it's a poor one at best, compared to what I have *now*."

I didn't believe he had acted quite freely. Once the Ai Chun got past his feeble resistance, they could explore the neuronic flows until they learned how to stimulate his pleasure center directly. (I wouldn't have allowed them that far in; no normal man would, at least not before techniques like sensory deprivation had made us disintegrate.) But there was no point in telling Rorn that.

Defeat tasted sour in my mouth. "Why do you bother explaining to me?" I asked.

"They told me I should. They want your cooperation, you see."

I made a last attempt. "Try to think," I said. "Your reasoning ability can't be too much impaired yet."

"On the contrary," he smiled, "you wouldn't believe what a difference it makes, not to be insecure and obsessed any longer."

"So think, blast you! I won't remind you of what the rest of us want to get back to, everything from friends and families to a decent yellow sunlight. You've dropped those hopes. But you'll live here for centuries, piling up data that can't be removed, till you go mindless."

"No. They can help me better than any machine."

"They're not supernatural! They can't do everything—can't do a fraction of what we can—why, we've personally outlived a dozen of them, end to end."

"So I've told them. They say it makes us still more valuable. They're not jealous, being reborn themselves."

"You don't believe that guff. Do you?"

"A symbolic truth doesn't have to be a scientific truth. As a race, at least, they're more ancient than we dayflies can imagine."

"But . . . but even in psychology, mentalistics—they're primitive. They don't speak directly to you, mind to mind, do they?" He shook his head. "I thought not," I went on. "There are human adepts back home who could. If that's what you need, you can get it better from them."

"I tried them once. No good. Not the same as here."

"No," I said bleakly, "at home you weren't offered any return to a womb. You weren't presented with any self-appointed gods. You weren't tinkered with. Human therapists only tried to help you be your own man."

His blandness was not moved. "Evidently I didn't want that, down inside," he answered. "Please understand. I don't bear you ill will. In fact, I love you. I love everything in the universe. I could never do that before." He broke off for a moment, then finished in a flat voice: "This is being explained to you so that you'll see you're beaten and won't do anything foolish that might get you hurt. We humans have an important role to play in this world."

He turned and walked off.

My radio had been confiscated, of course. Rorn used his own set to call ahead. His message was exactly what our men hoped for. The Niao were a civilized people who would be glad to supply us with workers in exchange for what we could teach. The brief stay of the Yonderfolk had wakened an appetite for progress in them. I was remaining behind for the time being to arrange details, and treated like an emperor. The Azkashi could easily be persuaded to release Valland. Rorn was bringing the first work gang—a large one, for the initial heavy labor of salvage.

When the wild edge of Lake Silence hove in view, I was taken below. Tied to an upright, I heard snatches of what went on in the following hours. The first exuberant hails, back and forth; the landing; the opened gates; the peaceful behavior, until all possible suspicions were lulled; the signal, and the seizure of each man by three or four Niao who had quietly moved within grabbing distance of him. I heard the Ai Chun wallow past my prison, bound ashore. I sat in darkness and heard the rain begin.

At last a soldier came to unfasten me. I shouldered my pack and went ahead of him, down a Jacob's ladder to a canoe, through a lashing blindness of rain and wind to the beach. Day had now come, tinting the driven spears of water as if with blood. My goggles were blinkered with storm; I shoved them onto my forehead and squinted through red murk. I couldn't see our spaceship. The headland where our compound stood was a dim bulk on my left. No one was visible except my giant guard and the half dozen canoe paddlers. We started off. My boots squelched in mud.

Well, I thought, hope wasn't absolutely dead. After a while, getting no report from us, our company would send another expedition. Presumably that crew would take less for granted than we had, and avoid shipwreck. In time, a human base might be founded on this planet. They might eventually learn about us, or deduce the truth after seeing things we'd been forced to make for the Ai Chun.

Only the downdevils, with Rorn to advise them, would

have provided against that somehow. And would probably, after we had gotten their projects organized for them, take time off to give us a good brainwashing and shape us all into Rorns.

I stumbled. The guard nudged me with a hard thumb.

Rage exploded. I wheeled about, yanked his knife from the sheath, and slashed. The flint blade was keen as any steel. It laid open the burly arm that grabbed at me. Yellow blood spouted under a yellow flare of lightning.

The guard roared. I broke into a run. He came after me. His webbed feet did not sink in the mud like mine and his strides were monstrous. He overhauled me and made a snatch. I dodged. His tail swung and knocked me off my feet.

Rain slapped me in the eyes. He towered above me, impossibly huge. I saw him bend to yank me up again. He kept on bending. His legs buckled. He went down on his belly beside me, trying to staunch the arterial flow with his good hand. His hearts, necessarily pumping more strongly than mine which had hemoglobin to help, drained him in a few seconds.

The boat crew milled closer. They could have taken me. But they had been bred into peacefulness. I reeled erect and stabbed the air with the knife I still held. They flinched away. I ran from them.

A glance behind revealed that one dashed off to report. The rest trailed me at a distance. I made inland. Thunder bawled in my ears. Rain hissed before the wind. My pack dragged me and the breath began to hurt my throat.

The Niao would not leave me. They kept yelping so that when the soldiers had been alerted they could find us. I was no woodsman, least of all on a strange planet. I belonged out among the clean stars that I'd never see again. There was not one chance of my shaking pursuit, not even in the thickest part of the woods that now loomed before me.

I glanced down at my stone knife. There was a release. I stuck it in my belt and kept going.

The forest closed about me. My cosmos was leaves, trunks, withes that slapped my face, vines that caught at my ankles, as I plowed through muck. My eyes were nearly useless here. Swamp rottenness choked my nostrils. I heard some wild animal scream.

It was following me. No . . . those were Niao voices . . . they wailed. A lupine baying resounded in answer. I stopped to pant. In a moment's astounded clarity I knew that of course the Pack had kept a suspicious watch on us. Beneath every fury and fear, I must have remembered and hoped—

When the Azkashi surrounded me I could just see them, four who looked saurian in the gloom. Their weapons were free and the rain hadn't yet washed off every trace of the butchery they had done.

I summoned my few words of their language and gasped, "We go. Shkil come. Go . . . ya-Valland."

"Yes," said one of them. "Swiftly."

Their pace was unmerciful. I've only the haziest recollection of that trip into the hills. Memory ends with a red sun in a purple sky, well over the crags and treetops that surround the lairs. Hugh Valland meets me. He's kept himself and his outfit clean, but hasn't depilated in some while. His beard is thick, Sol golden, and he stands taller than a god. "Welcome, skipper!" his call rings to me. "Come on, let's get you washed and give you a doss and some chow. Lord, you look like Satan with a hangover." I fall into his arms.

I woke on a bed of boughs and skins, within a painted cave. A native female brought me a bowl of soup made from my rations. She howled out the entrance, and presently Valland came in.

"How're you doin'?" he asked.

"Alive," I grunted.

"Yeah," he said, "I can imagine. Stiff, sore, and starved. But you aren't in serious shape, far's I can see, and we've got a lot of talkin' to do." He propped me in a sitting position and gave me a stimulo from his medikit. Some strength flowed into me, with an odd, detached clearness of thought.

I looked past Valland's cross-legged form, through the cave obscurity to the mouth. There was considerable stir outside. Armed males kept trotting back and forth; the smoke of campfires drifted in to me; I heard the barks and growls of a multitude.

"S'pose you tell me exactly what happened," Valland said.

After I finished, he uttered one low whistle of surprise. "Didn't think the downdevils had *that* much goin' for them." He extracted his pipe, stuffed and kindled it, while he scowled.

"We haven't got much time," he said. "I'm damn near out of tobacco."

"I'm more concerned about food," I said. "I remember what you took along and what I was carrying. Between us, we might last till sundown."

"Uh-huh. I was tryin' to put the idea in a more genteel way." He puffed for a bit. "The drums sent word ahead to us here, about the Herd enterin' our camp and then about you bein' on your way to us. That last was the best thing you could possibly have done, skipper. Ya-Kela couldn't have protected me for long if the Pack figured my people had sold out. As was, I got Rorn on the radio. He was pretty frank about havin' taken over on behalf of the downdevils, once he knew I knew you'd run off. He said I should try to escape from here, and he'd send a troop to meet me. I told him where he could billet his troop, and we haven't talked since. My guess was he'd turned coat out of sheer funk. I didn't realize what'd actually happened to him. The poor fool."

Hopelessness welled beneath the drug in me. "What can we do except die?" I asked.

"Hadn't you any notions when you cut out?"

"Nothing special. To die like a free man, maybe."

Valland snorted. "Don't be romantic. You haven't got the face for it. The object of the game is to stay alive, and get back our people and our stuff. Mary O'Meara's waitin' on Earth."

That last sentence was the soft one, but something about it yanked me upright in my bed. *God of Creation,* I thought, *can a woman have that much power to give a man?*

"Relax," Valland said. "We can't do anything right now."

"I gather . . . you've been busy, though," I said.

"Sure have. I stopped bein' a prisoner the minute ya-Kela got across to the Pack that my folk were now also down-devil victims. He'd been ready to trust me anyhow, for some while."

Afterward, when I knew more Azkashi, I was told that Valland had been along on a hunt in which a twyhorn charged past a line of spearmen and knocked down the One. Before the animal could gore him, Valland had bulldogged it. Coming from a higher gravity was helpful, of course, but I doubt that many men could have done the same.

"The problem's been to convince 'em we aren't helpless," Valland said. "They still have trouble believin' that. Throughout their past, they've won some skirmishes with the Herd, but lost the wars. I had an ace to play, however. The Herd's crossed the lake, I said. They'll build an outpost around our ship. Then, to support that outpost, they'll call in their loggers and farmers. If you don't wipe 'em out now, I said, you'll lose these huntin' grounds too." He blew a dragon puff of smoke. "We got the other Packs to agree in principle that everybody should get together and attack this thing while it's small."

"Stone Age savages against energy guns?" I protested.

"Well, not all that bad. I've done soldierin' now and then, here and there, so I can predict a few things. Rorn can't put guns in any other human hands. He'll demonstrate their use to the Herd soldiers. But you know what lousy shots they'll be, with so little practice. Cortez had good modern weapons too, for his time, and men a lot better disciplined than the Aztecs; but when they got riled enough, they threw him out of Mexico." Thoughtfully: "He made a comeback later, with the whole Spanish power behind him. We have to prevent that."

"What do you propose to do?"

"Right now," Valland said, "I'm still tryin' to hammer into the local heads some notion of unified command and action under doctrine. Fightin' looks easy by comparison."

"But—Hugh, listen, the Packs may outnumber the Herd detachment, but they'll have to charge across open ground. I don't care how poorly laid an energy barrage is, they can't survive. Not to mention arrows. Those Herd archers are good."

"So who says we'll charge?" Valland countered. "For our main operation, anyhow. I've got a plan. It should take the downdevils by surprise. Everything you've told me fits in with what ya-Kela knows, and it all goes to show they can't read minds. If they could, they wouldn't need to transmit words through those midget sensitives. The downdevils read Rorn's emotional pattern, all right, and shifted it for him. But that was done on a basic, almost glandular level. They couldn't've known what he was thinkin', nor what we think."

"Our men are hostages," I reminded him. "Not to speak of our food tanks and the other equipment we need for survival."

"I haven't forgotten." His tone was mild and implacable. "We'll have to take chances, for the men as well as ourselves. Because what have they really got to lose? If we get in fast—"

A shadow darkened the cave mouth. As he joined us, I recognized ya-Kela. He hailed me with the courtesy that most savages throughout the universe seem to use, before he turned to Valland. I couldn't follow his report, but he sounded worried.

Valland nodded. " 'Scuse me," he said. "Business."

"What?" I asked.

"Oh, one of those silly things that're always comin' up. Some Pack chiefs decided they don't like my ideas. If cut-and-run guerrilla fightin' by little independent gangs was good enough for granddaddy, it's good enough for them, and to hell with this foreign nonsense about unity and assigned missions. Ya-Kela can't talk sense into them. I'll have to. If we let anyone go home, pretty soon everybody will."

"Do you think you can stop them?" I fretted, for I knew something about pride and politics myself.

"I been doin' it, since we started this project. Now get some rest. You'll need your strength soon." Valland left with ya-Kela. He had to stoop to get out.

I lay there, cursing my weakness that would not let me go too. Noises came to me, shouts, yelps, snarls. There was the sound of a scuffle; Valland told me later that he had had to underline a logical point with his fist. But presently I heard notes like bugle and drum. I heard a human voice lifted in song, and I remembered some of those songs, ancient as they were, *Starbuck* and *La Marseillaise* and *The March of the Thousand,* forged by a race more warlike than any on this world; then he set his instrument to bagpipe skirls and the hair stood up on my spine. The Packs howled. They didn't comprehend the language, they hardly grasped the idea of an army, but they recognized strong magic and they would follow as long as the magician lived.

## XIII

WE CAME DOWN to the shore well south of our objective. By then time was short for Valland and me: little remained of our powdered food. And what had gone on with our people these Earth-days of their captivity? Nevertheless we had to wait on the weather.

That didn't take long, though, on this planet. Rain was succeeded by fog. The Packs divided themselves. A very small contingent went with Valland, a larger one with me; the bulk of them trailed through the woods, ya-Kela at their head.

I was in charge of the waterborne operation, ya-Kela my lieutenant. He was also my interpreter, being among the few who could understand my pidgin Azkashi; for I had no omnisonor to help. And as far as the crews were concerned, he was the commander; I didn't have Valland's prestige either. But this was the key to our whole strategy. The Packs kept dugouts by the lake. They had never used them for anything but fishing. How could it be expected that they would assault what amounted to a navy?

We glided through clouds that were chill and damp, red-gray like campfire smoke. Nearly blind, I could only crouch in the bow of my hollow log while six paddles drove me forward. The Azkashi saw better, well enough to maintain direction and formation. But even they were enclosed in a few meters of sight. And so were our enemies.

I am no warrior. I hate bloodletting, and my guts knot at the thought that soon they may be pierced. Yet in that hour of passage I wasn't much afraid. Better to die in combat than starve to death. I dwelt on the people and places I loved. Time went slowly, but at the end it was as if no time had passed at all.

"We are there," ya-Eltokh breathed in my ear. "I see the thing ahead."

"Back water, then," I ordered unnecessarily; for my watch said we were in advance of the chosen moment. The waiting that followed was hard. We couldn't be sure that some boatload of impulsive hunters would not jump the gun and give us away. With a fortress to take, we depended on synchrony as well as on surprise. When the minute came, I screamed my command.

We shot forward. The spaceship appeared before me, vast and wetly shimmering in the mist. Two canoes lay at the ladder we had built to the above-water airlock. Their paddlers shrieked and fled as we emerged.

I grabbed a rung. Ya-Eltokh pushed ahead of me, up to the open entrance. A Herd soldier thrust down with a spear. Blowguns sighed at my back. The giant yelled, toppled, and splashed into the lake. Ya-Eltokh bounded inside. His tomahawk thudded.

My mates boiled after him, forcing the doorway. I came last. Our crew had to be first, for only I could guide our party through the ship. But my knowledge made me too precious to spend in grabbing a toehold.

I got into battle aplenty, though. Three of the Pack were down, ripped by soldiers who had come pounding at the alarm. Ya-Eltokh dodged, slashing with his ax at two huge shapes. One of them spied me and charged. Valland had had something new made for me, a crossbow. I had already cocked it. I pulled the trigger and the bolt slammed home. The corridor boomed with his fall.

Then more of our people were aboard. They formed a living wall around me. I cocked and fired as fast as I was able. It wasn't much help, but I did down a couple of worker Niao who had joined the fray. Ax, knife and spear raged around us. Howling echoed from metal.

We needed only hold fast for some minutes, till an overwhelming force of hunters had boarded. There weren't any guards on the ship; no one had looked for this maneuver of ours. When the last of them fell, the workers threw down the tools they had been using for weapons. I tried to stop my people from massacring them, but too much ancient grudge had to be paid off.

Ya-Eltokh came to me, his feet painted with blood. "I see the big boat now," he rasped.

"Don't let it near, but don't let our boats attack it either," I ordered. With fifty or so Azkashi to help, and a single doorway to defend, he shouldn't have a problem. I led a small troop to the lower decks, where we had commenced salvage operations before the Niao arrived.

That job was not any further along. The Ai Chun had no interest in a spaceship as such. Their gangs had been stripping away metal for more prosaic uses.

But Urduga was there, hastily bound when the fight started. I cut him loose and he wept for joy.

"How've you been?" I asked.

"Bad," he told me. "They haven't mistreated us yet, in a physical sense, I mean. We're still being . . . explored, so they'll know exactly what they want to do with us. But I'd gotten to the point where I begged them to send me out here as a supervisor." He looked around with haunted eyes. "So far I've managed to keep them from damaging anything essential."

"We've got to be quick," I said. "The plan is that we draw most of their strength out on the lake. Then our shore force hits them. But Hugh's boys have to take the compound before the enemy thinks to wreck our survival equipment. What can we improvise here against a warship?"

Urduga threw back his head and bayed like one of the Pack. "I'll handle that!"

I left him in the laboratory while I went back topside to see how the fight was going. The galley stood off, barely visible in the fog, deck crowded with soldiers. Those of our crews that had not boarded with us had prudently withdrawn from the neighborhood. Thus far our scheme had worked. Rorn must feel sure that Valland and I had organized the attack. But he'd figure, we hoped, that we knew better than to attempt storming the compound against energy weapons. Instead, we must expect to use the *Meteor* for a bargaining counter; and he in his turn must expect to besiege us here.

Valland couldn't long delay his own move. And if then that shipload of giants returned to meet him—

An arrow whistled past me. I ducked back into the lock chamber. "What next?" ya-Eltokh growled. The hunters around him hefted their weapons and twitched their tails. They could keep the galley at arm's length, but it had them bottled up. Enclosed in these hard walls, they grew nervous.

"Wait," I said.

"Like beasts in a trap?"

"Wait! Do you follow ya-Valland or not?"

That quieted them a little for the necessary horrible minutes. But I was close to crying myself when Urduga joined us. Several of the Pack, whom I'd detailed, accompanied him with a load of bottles.

He peered into the swirling grayness. "We'll have to lure them closer," he said.

I explained the need to ya-Eltokh. He turned to his folk. "Out!" he cried.

He led them himself, down the ladder into a sleet of arrows. They entered the water and swam toward their scattered boats. A horn blew on the galley. Its oars chunked. It slipped alongside us. Now that the Pack had gotten so desperate as to attempt a battle on the lake, the warriors could recapture the spaceship and then deal with our flotilla at leisure.

Urduga struck fire to fuses. I helped him pitch out the bottles. Mostly they contained liquid hydrocarbon, but he'd found some thermite as well.

Fire ran across the deck. Soldiers ululated when they burned, sprang overboard and were slain from our dugouts. A few got onto the ladder. Such blowgunners as we had kept dealt with them.

An armored colossus, brave and cool-headed, shouted his command. The oars moved again. The galley started for shore. But flames roared red throughout the hull. Dugouts and swimmers kept pace. If any of the Herd reached land, they would not be hard to kill.

Wolf howls resounded from afar. Ya-Kela had seen, and led his charge out of the woods. Energy beams flashed like lightning in the fog. They took their toll. But ya-Kela's mission was simply to distract the defenders—

—while Hugh Valland and a small, picked cadre went unnoticed on their bellies, up to the stockade.

We'd built well. A battering ram could not have gotten the palisade down before the crew was shot from above. But he expended his own pistol charges. Wood did not burn when those bolts hit. Cellular water turned to steam and the logs exploded. He was through in a minute.

He sped for the food tanks. Soldiers and workers alike tried to bar his way. His gun was exhausted, but he swung an ax, and his hunters were with him. They gained their position, formed a circle, and stood fast.

They would soon have died, for the diminished garrison still outnumbered them, and had those other firearms to boot. But they had purchased ya-Kela's opportunity. In one tide, he and his men reached the now ill-defended wall and poured through the gap.

Yes—his *men*.

Combat did not last long after that. At such close quarters the Herd was slaughtered. Never mind the details. What followed was all that mattered. I have to piece it together. But this was when we lost everything we thought we had gained.

Valland broke through the remnants of the fight and led a few Azkashi toward our shack. The door was locked. His fist made the walls tremble. "Open up in there!"

Rorn's voice reached him faintly: "Be careful. I have Bren and Galmer here, and my own gun. I can kill them."

Valland stood for a space. His followers growled and hefted their weapons. Unease was coming upon them like the fog that roiled past their eyes.

"Let's talk," Valland said at length. "I don't want to hurt you, Yo."

"Nor I you. If I let you in, can we hold an honest parley?"

"Sure."

"Wait a minute, then." Standing in red wet murk that was still cloven by the yells and thuds of combat, Valland heard some sounds of the Yonder language. A treble fluting responded.

His Azkashi heard too. A kind of moan went among them, they shuffled backward and ya-Kela exclaimed shakenly: "That is one of the dwarfs. I know how they talk. Our scouts did not see that any of *them* had landed here." He gripped Valland's arm with bruising force. "Did you know, and not tell us?"

*As a matter of fact*, the human must have thought, *yes*. He had not his omnisonor with him, to aid in shaping tones, but he managed to convey scorn. "Do you fear the down-devils even when they are beaten?"

"They are not like the Shkil. They do not die."

95

"We may find otherwise." Somehow Valland made them stay put until the colloquy inside ended and the door creaked open.

The blind telepath stood there. Blackness gaped behind him. Rorn's order rasped from within: "You come by yourself, Valland." As the gunner trod through, the dwarf closed the door again.

Rorn activated the lights enough for him to see. Bren and Galmer lay on two bunks, tied hand and foot. A pair of soldier Niao flanked a great wooden tub filled with water. They crouched tense, spears poised, lips drawn back from teeth. Rorn stood before the tank. His energy pistol was aimed at Valland's midriff. His features were also drawn tight; but—maybe just because he had put on a little weight —serenity remained beneath.

Valland glanced at his comrades. "How're you doin', boys?" he asked softly.

"All right," Galmer said.

Bren spat. "Hugh, don't let this cockroach use us against you. It'd be worth getting shot by him, as long as we know you'll squash him later."

Rorn smiled, without noticeable malice, and reminded: "You'll never build your escape vessel if you lose their skills, Hugh. And there's no other way off this planet. The Yonderfolk left nothing behind except a few items the Ai Chun took apart centuries ago. What I've learned while we were here convinces me the Yonderfolk really don't use radio for communication, nor are they likely to notice a laser flash, nor— Never mind. You've got to have these men."

"For their own sakes, if nothin' else," Valland agreed. He leaned his ax against the table and folded his arms. "I can't believe you'd murder your fellow human bein's, Yo."

"Not willingly. Only if I absolutely must, and then in love and service. But they are hostages. They'll leave with us."

"Now you know I can't allow that. We'd never get 'em

96

back." Valland sought the gaze of the prisoners. "Hate to sound theatrical, but stayin' laconic is hard work. Which'd you rather be, dead or slaves?"

Sweat glistened on their skins. Galmer jerked out, "You needn't ask," and Bren nodded.

"You see," Valland told Rorn, "you can buy your own escape with their lives and freedom, but that's all."

Rorn looked uncertain. A splashing resounded from the tank, and the two great sleek heads broke surface. Through the scant illumination, chalcedony eyes probed at Valland. He gave them stare for stare.

The Ai Chun spoke via their dwarf. In the Earth-days since he renounced his species, Rorn had improved his command of Yonder until he could readily use it; so much does the removal of inward conflict do for the mind, and you may decide for yourself whether it's worth the price. "Do you follow them, Hugh?" he asked. "Not so well, eh? They say—" He stopped. "Do you know just what they are?"

"The skipper told me about them," Valland said shortly.

"He's prejudiced. They are . . . good, wise— No, those words are too nearly meaningless. . . . They are as far beyond us as we are beyond the apes."

"I'm not sure how far that is." Valland shrugged. "Go on, what do they want?"

"You've . . . we've caused them a heavy loss. This latest episode goes further to prove that they can't tolerate us running loose, any more than we could tolerate pathogenic bacteria. But they don't strike out, blindly destructive, as men would. They'll take us in. They offer us more than we could ever hope to gain, or know, or feel, by ourselves."

"Like your case?" Valland said. "Sorry, but I am bein' sarcastic. The answer is no. You and they can go in return for our friends. Then, if you all leave us be, we'll do the same for you."

Rorn translated. The Ai Chun were slow to reply, as they were slow to most things. In the end:

"Negative," Rorn said. "They don't fear death. They're reborn, immortal in a way we'll never achieve."

"Have you swallowed that crock yourself?"

"Makes no difference. I'm not afraid either, not of anything any longer. But think. It doesn't matter whether their belief is correct or not. What does matter is that they hold it. By taking these men away from you, whether by death or captivity, they'll ruin you. For the sake of that, they don't much mind cutting short a pair of incarnations."

"They'd better not mind," Valland grinned bleakly, "with their chums listenin' in."

"Don't you understand what that means?" Rorn breathed. "You aren't just confronting two individuals. An entire world! You can't win on your own terms. But let go your pride. It's no more than a monkey screaming from the treetops how important he is. Let go, use your reason, take their guidance, and you'll have our true victory."

"Spare me the sermon, Yo. I got a girl waitin' on Earth. The rest of us have our loves too, whatever they may be, as strong as yours. We'd sooner die than give them up. I've lived a fair spell, and it's been my observation that hate doesn't make for conflicts which can never be settled. People who hate each other can still strike bargains. But conflictin' loves are somethin' else."

Valland stood a while, stroking his beard and sunk in thought. Outside, the battle had ended. In the silence that now filled the hut, one grew aware of breathing, the faint lap of waves in the tank as the Ai Chun stirred, the thump of a spear butt on the floor, the heat and stenches and inward-crowding shadows.

Finally Valland gusted a sigh. He raised his head and spoke, low but resonant. "How about me?"

"What?" Rorn gaped at him.

98

"I organized this attack, you know. Modest as I am, I doubt if my gang is any military threat without me. If you must keep a hostage, suppose you take me instead of those fellows."

"No, Hugh!" Galmer cried.

"We can't afford heroics," Valland said to him. "You can spare my technical knowledge, at least. And maybe I can talk these people into makin' peace. Think you could?"

Bren thrust his face up, so that light could touch the lines and hollows lately carved therein. "*You* don't know what they're like," he said.

Valland ignored him. "Well?" he asked Rorn.

"I . . . I don't know." A conference followed. "They must consider this."

"All right," Valland said. "I'll leave you alone to talk the proposition over."

He started for the door. "Halt!" Rorn yelled. A soldier sprang in pursuit.

Valland obeyed, turned about and said evenly, "I've got to tell them outside in any event, and prove this is my personal idea. Otherwise you could get attacked soon's you cross the threshold. I'll come back in two, three hours and see what you've decided. Agreed?"

They stood dumb and let him depart.

## XIV

VICTORY was dead meat in ya-Kela's mouth. Word had run through the Packs: There are actual downdevils here, now when God is withdrawn from heaven. Ya-Valland himself could not prevail against them, he left the house they have taken without those he went in to save, and however strange his kind may be to us, we can see, we can even ˌsmell the horror that clutches him and his mates. Day glares upon us. Best we slink off under the forest roof.

Many had already done so. And more and more of them followed, picking up their gear and vanishing into the mists. They spoke little, but that little made a mumbling across the land like the first wind-sough before a storm.

He himself was fain to leave. But because ya-Valland asked it, he used his last shreds of authority to hold some in place. A hundred or less, they squatted well away from the compound in a ring about such prisoners as had been taken. They dared not tend the dead of either side. Corpses littered the tussocky ground, rocked among the reeds, sprawled beneath the walls; and the carrion wings wheeled impatiently overhead.

Ya-Valland, ya-Argens, and ya-Urduga stood disputing in their own tongue, which no longer seemed likely to be God's. Ya-Kela waited, slumped down on heels and tail, feeling his age and his weariness. He had been given to understand that ya-Valland would go away with the downdevils as the price of liberty for his other two mates. But without him, what were the rest? They seemed to feel likewise, for the talk waxed fierce until ya-Valland cut it off and would listen to no more.

Then he addressed the One. He had fetched his music-maker. The Azkashi sounds limped forth: "Be not disheartened, my friend. We did not succeed as well as we hoped, but the hunt is far from ended."

"We have run ourselves breathless," ya-Kela said, "and the quarry swings about to gore us. Who may prevail against the downdevils save God, Who has forsaken the world?"

"I do not plan to stay with the enemy for long," ya-Valland said.

"They have taken captives often and often. None ever returned. Old stories tell of a few whom the Packs recaptured in skirmishes. They were so changed that naught could be done but kill them as gently as might be."

"I shall not suffer such a fate if you will stand by me."

"I owed you a blood debt," ya-Kela said, "but it has been paid with folk who were dear to me."

"You have not yet paid your debt to your people," ya-Valland said sharply.

Ya-Kela started, glanced up at him, and rose to bring their eyes more nearly level. "What do you mean by this newest riddle?"

"Something that you—all the Azkashi—must come to understand. Without it, you are doomed. With it, you have hope; more than hope, for when free folk know what freedom costs and how to meet that cost, they are hard indeed to overcome."

A faint tingle ran along ya-Kela's skin. "Have you a new magic for us?"

"Better than a magic. An idea." Ya-Valland sought words. "Listen to a story.

"In the sky-place whence I come were two countries. One was called Europe, where dwelt a people like myself. The other was called America, and a different folk possessed it

101

whom we named Indians. The people of Europe crossed the waters between and started to take land in America. Most of the Indians were hunters. At best, they could not match the powers of the Europeans, who were not only farmkeepers like the Niao but also had new weapons. Thus, in time, the Europeans took all America away from the Indians."

Ya-Kela stepped back. His ax lifted. "Are you telling me that you are akin to the Herd?" he shouted.

Ya-Velland's mates clapped hands to those fiery weapons they had repossessed. He waved them back, spread his own empty hands, and said:

"In some ways, yes. In other ways, no. For example, the Indians held a faith in beings not unlike the downdevils, whereas the Europeans worshiped one God. I am trying to teach you a lesson. Are you brave enough to hear me out?"

Ya-Kela could say nothing but, "Yes." Lowering his ax was harder work than his charge into arrows and flame.

"For, you see," ya-Valland said, "the Indians need not have lost. In the early days, at least, they outnumbered the European settlers. They were masters of the wilderness. They were not slow to get for themselves weapons like those of the invaders. In truth, at times they had better ones, and inflicted numerous bloody defeats on their foe."

"Why, then, did they lose?"

"The reasons were several. But a great one was this. They were satisfied to win a battle. To them, any piece of land was as good as any other, provided both had game. They fought for honor and glory alone. If once a territory had been occupied, and farms had covered it, they did no more than raid its outskirts. And seldom did they stand and die like Europeans, to hold a place that was holy because their fathers were buried there.

"Furthermore, ya-Kela, they did not fight as one. If a Pack of them was overwhelmed, that was of small concern to other Packs elsewhere. Some even helped the Europeans against

102

their own kinfolk. None thought of bringing the whole American land together, under a single council. None planned generations ahead, sacrificing lives and goods that their great-grandchildren might be free. All these things the Europeans did. And thus the Europeans conquered.

"Can you see what may be learned from this?"

Ya-Kela bowed his head. "The lesson is hard."

"I do not expect the Azkashi to learn it soon," ya-Valland said. "If you yourself do so in your lifetime, and teach a few others, that may suffice." He was still for a moment. "And perhaps then I will have paid a part of the blood debt my ancestors left me."

Ya-Kela cried in anguish, "What has this to do with your going away?"

"Only that, whatever becomes of me, you must think ahead and hold fast to common purpose. You must not be content with a single victory like ours today, nor lose your will because of a later defeat such as we have also met. I am the one who hazards the gelding of his souls, and I have not yet despaired. Be you likewise. God has not left you."

"Look in the sky and tell me so again," ya-Kela said.

"Why, I shall. Come here."

Ya-Valland led him into the compound, though he cringed from the silent, locked house. A lean-to behind held the enigmatic tools he had observed on his earlier visit. "We are lucky that we did not wish to be crowded by those in our living quarters," ya-Valland said. He took one, a box and tube mounted on three legs, and carried it back to free ground.

"This," he said, "we call a *photoscreen 'scope*. Suppose you have a very hot fire. Cast a small ember into the coals, and you will not be able to see it, for the coals flood it with their brilliance. Yet if the place were otherwise dark, the ember would seem bright enough. True?"

"True," ya-Kela said. Wonder began to take hold of him. The mere sight of magics like this gave spirit.

"The 'scope has the power to pluck faint lights out of greater," ya-Valland said. He consulted with his mates and a set of leaves covered with curious markings, and pointed the tube heavenward. "I will show you the sky—yonder part— as if n'ght had fallen. See."

He touched a projection. A smooth flat plate on the box grew dark. One point of light burned near the middle.

"Is that not where the planet Oroksh should be?" ya-Valland asked. Ya-Kela assented mutely. As the One, he had long been intimate with the heavens. "Well, find me another." Ya-Kela gestured at unseen Ilyakan—if it really was there, his thought shuddered. Ya-Valland aimed in the same direction. "Hm, not quite right. Here." As he moved the tube, another steady spark drifted across the plate. "Do you see?"

"I see," ya-Kela said humbly.

"Now let us try low in the east."

Ya-Kela gasped, sprang back, fell to all fours and howled the first lines of the Welcome. God shone upon him. Ya-Valland twisted a knob, and God blazed brighter than mortal eyes had ever before seen Him.

"He is still aloft," ya-Valland said. "This you could well have known for yourselves, save that you would not agree that the sun could hide Him. Think, though. It does not mean He is less than the sun. A bonfire a great distance off may be veiled by a torch close to hand. Fear not the downdevils; God is with you yet."

Ya-Kela crouched on the wet earth and sobbed.

Ya-Valland raised him up and said, "I ask only courage of you, which you have already shown. We have little time before I must go back into the house. Let us make plans. Later you shall bring those hes whom you think will take this sight as you did. Then we shall be ready for whatever may befall."

He looked at his comrades. His teeth showed, in that gesture which seemed to betoken mirth among his breed, and he said in their language: *First time this gadget was used for*

104

*religious purposes, I'll bet. Wonder if the manufacturer will be interested in buyin' an endorsement?"*

"Hugh," said ya-Argens, *"I don't know whether to call you a hero or a devil."*

Ya-Valland lifted his shoulders and let them fall. *"Neither,"* he said. *"Just a fanatic, for reasons you know."*

## XV

THE BEST BARGAIN we could make was harder than awaited. We must release every Niao prisoner. And I too must become a hostage.

In exchange we got Bren and Galmer back, and kept the guns we had recaptured. Rorn was obviously satisfied. ("He's the real negotiator," Valland remarked. "The Ai Chun can't know beans about war or politics. So they kid themselves that they made him for the purpose.") We were the leaders. Without us, the Azkashi alliance must soon fall apart, after which the last three men could be picked off at leisure. Naturally, Rorn maintained the fiction that once in Prasiyo we would negotiate; and naturally we pretended to be taken in by it, less from logic than from wishful thinking.

Disarmed, burdened with our survival gear and a fresh food supply, we walked from the hut in the middle of a soldier cordon who held knives to our ribs. The weather had cleared for a while, though fresh thunderheads were piling up in the north, blue-black masses where lightning winked. The Ai Chun went before us. On land they were gross, clumsy, and still somehow terrible. A forlorn party stood to watch us off: Urduga, Bren, Galmer, an Azkashi handful. They scarcely stirred. Our compound seemed very small in that vast dark landscape.

Several canoes had been drawn ashore, along with the Pack dugouts. Rorn gave them a hard look. "Are these all you have?" he demanded.

"Yes," I said. "No doubt a number are drifting free, and probably others went home in panic."

"We'll be pretty crowded." Rorn spoke with his masters. Voiceless messages flew across the water. "A detachmant from Prasiyo will meet us, and we can transfer some of our party. But that can't be for many hours."

"Or we might come on one or two abandoned boats," Valland suggested. "I hope so. Don't fancy sittin' cheek by jowl, myself, when the jowls are so hairy." He took a long breath. "Ah-h-h! Even this Turkish bath air is good, after all that time in the cabin arguin' with you."

"You needn't have dragged matters out as you did," Rorn told him.

"Can't blame a fellow for tryin', can you?"

The canoes were long, with more than a meter of freeboard and great stability even after we filled them from stem to stern. To be sure, overloading much reduced their speed. The Ai Chun, who took ample room for themselves, could easily have run away from their escort. But we stayed together. Coxswains chanted low beneath the breeze, waves, distant muttering thunder; paddles bit; we started forth across the lake. My last clear glimpse of land showed me the men we had liberated, wading out among the reeds to stare and stare after us.

We three humans were in the same canoe. I hadn't expected that. But Rorn wanted to talk. We squatted as best we could near the bow, so that the other passengers only squeezed us from one side. They were mute, hardly moving save to nurse a wound or change a shift at the paddles. Their gods had come through for them, but they were still exhausted and shaken by what had gone before. As we passed the wreck of the *Meteor*, many signed themselves.

"Why didn't you bring your omnisonor, Hugh?" Rorn asked.

"I'm not exactly in a mood to sing," Valland grunted.

107

"But it'd be useful for communication."

"We got Yonder."

"Nevertheless—"

"Damnation!" Valland exploded. "That instrument made my song to Mary O'Meara. You think I'll use it for talkin' with your filthy owners?"

"Spare the emotion," Rorn said. "The Ai Chun have as much right to preserve their culture as anyone else does. You've done them harm enough."

*Well*, I thought, *I guess I am sorry that old Gianyi got killed. He was a decent sort, in his fashion.*

"We didn't set out to hurt anybody," Valland said. "If they'd left us alone, none of this would've happened."

"Oh? What about your effect on the savages? You planned to organize them, give them new techniques, whole new concepts. And they are the enemy. They'd have become a good deal more dangerous to the Niao. Furthermore, whatever your personal intentions, could you guarantee to keep men off this world indefinitely?"

"No," Valland said, "and I wouldn't care to anyhow. Your right of cultural self-preservation is a lot of belly rumble. Anybody's got a right to defend himself against attack, sure—which is what we were doin'. But his right to wall off new ideas comes from nothin' but his ability to do so. If he can make the policy stick, fine. That proves he's got something which works better than the so-called progressive notions. But if he can't, tough luck for him."

"In other words," Rorn jabbed, "might makes right."

"I didn't say that. Of course there are good or bad ways to compete. And if somebody doesn't want to play the game, he should be free to pot out. Only then he can't expect to be subsidized by those who do want to keep on playin'." Valland began to remove his boots and tunic. "Judas, it's hot! I could use some of that thundershower over there."

"The Ai Chun were ancient when we hadn't yet become

108

mammals," Rorn said. "Do you dare call yourself wiser than them?"

"Garden of Eden theory of history," Valland murmured.

"What?"

"Used to hear it often on Earth, a long time ago when things were still fermentin' there. People would look around at everything that was goin' wrong and blame it on the fact that men had left the good old tried-and-true ways of their grandfathers. I always thought, though—if those ways had been so fine, why were they discarded in the first place?"

"You mean," I ventured, "if the downdevils really are superior, they should have nothing to fear from us?"

"Right," Valland said. "Besides, speakin' of self-determination and so forth, how much has the Herd got?"

A trace of irritation crossed Rorn's features. Remembering how he had once snapped at us all, I felt a hideous kind of pity. This was like seeing a ghost.

"You may rationalize as much as you will," he said. "The fact is, the Ai Chun are proving their superiority at this moment."

"They've grabbed a temporary tactical advantage," Valland said. "We'll see how things work out in the long run. Just what do you propose to do?"

"Prevent the establishment of a base on this planet," Rorn said candidly. "Not by force, I think. There are better ways. We'll convince any future visitors that the planet is useless to them. I have some ideas along those lines."

"They'll need you, for certain, the downdevils," I agreed. "But how do they intend to keep you alive? You took along a supply of portable rations. But what about when those give out?"

"The food tanks are intact, back in camp," Rorn said. "Your friends won't refuse to feed you, even if it means feeding me too."

*Until such time as you kill them and seize the units for yourself,* I thought sickly.

"Why don't you peel down also, before you melt, skipper?" Valland asked.

The reminder was a shock. Heat weighed me down like thick wet wool. A strengthening breeze from the north gave small relief. In fact, if it blew us off our straight-line course, or those rising clouds covered the sun by which we were presumably navigating— I fumbled at my garments. My muscles felt stiff. *Won't do to be cramped,* I thought amidst a beating in chest and temples. *No room here for a real stretch, but a few isometrics ought to help.*

"Makes me remember the High Sierra," Valland mused.

"The what?" I asked. Anything was welcome that would make me forget for a while that I was here, and would quite likely soon be dead. But I don't know if he was really talking to me. He looked across the waters, into the murk of day and the livid storm, and almost he sang.

"Mountain section on Earth. Parts were kept as wilderness. Mary and I backpacked in there once. That was just before the antithanatic came along. But of course everybody knew it'd soon be in production. Nobody who was alive would have to grow old. Those were strange weeks. Thinkin' back, I have trouble makin' them seem real. The world had grown so quiet. Wasn't so much that people got extra cautious, knowin' what they stood to lose. It was an air. For a bit, while the human race waited, it felt kind of like wakin' after a fever had broken. All mankind, since first it began to think, had gone around with that sickness, the fear of old age. You'd look at a little girl, like yours, say, and you'd think of your grandmother, and know that in less'n a century this packet of happiness would be blind and in pain and hungry for death. Then suddenly we didn't have to take that any more. People needed a while to get used to the idea.

"Mary and I, though, we were young. We couldn't sit

110

still. We had to do somethin' to . . . to show ourselves we were alive enough to rate immortality. What'd be the use of it, if we only spent our centuries bein' careful? Eventually most people felt likewise, of course, and went to the stars. But we did from the first. Or, rather, Mary did—that kind of girl—and made me see it too.

"So we flitted to the Seirra, and loaded up, and started hikin'. Day after day; sun overhead, wind through the pines, till we got above timberline and looked down those tremendous blue slopes, crossed a pass and stopped for a snowball fight; and one night we camped by a lake where the moon and Jupiter rose together and threw two perfect glades, and Mary's the only sight I've seen that was more beautiful.

"Though, you know, we weren't simply havin' fun. To her, anyhow, and to me on her account, it was a sort of pilgrimage. Others had loved this place. But death got them and they'd never come back here. We wanted to do this for them. We swore to each other we'd always remember our dead." A small sad smile crossed Valland's lips. "Oh, Lord, but we were young!"

Rorn half opened his mouth. I bristled. How much more preaching could a man be expected to take? Precisely in time, a voice hailed from the leading canoe.

"Ya-o-o-o-a aie! Aie!"

The Niao shifted their packed bodies down the length of our boat and peered across the heads of their fellows. The soldiers among them laid hands on weapons. The paddlers stopped work. I heard the wind, still stiffening, pipe in my ears; little whitecaps slapped our hull and rocked it. Sliding my goggles off my brow and activating them, I also stared.

The gloom was made lighter for me and I saw another Herd canoe a few kilometers to the west. It wallowed alone without visible sign of life. But the dwarf shrilled on the vessel of the Ai Chun and his word was bayed thence by the giants.

"What're they sayin'?" Valland asked.

"People of ours in that craft," Rorn said. "Frightened . . . in pain, I believe . . . I haven't many words of Niao yet. The Ai Chun sense their minds."

And could not actually read the thoughts, leaped through my own brain. However, by now they must have studied humans enough that they can identify our basic emotional patterns too. If they should tune in on me, what would they observe?

I struggled to suppress the fear-hope-fury that churned in me. I might as well have told the approaching storm to go home.

"Survivors of the battle, evidently," Valland said. "Must've been wounded, escaped, haven't the strength to maintain headway." At a shouted command, our group veered and started moving anew. "Well, an extra boat should relieve the jam somewhat for us."

Could the Ai Chun tell Herd from Pack purely by mentalistics? I believed not. There was no real species difference. Ai Chun telepathy must be short-range and imprecise; otherwise they wouldn't have had to operate through the dwarfs. When you develop a tool, you don't evolve the tool's capability in yourself. Nor does it have yours. The dwarfs were specialized; they didn't keep watch or give warning unless told to. For millions upon changing millions of years, no one on this world had needed any equivalent of radar—nor, in the downdevils' omnipotence, the cruel tricks of war.

Such reasoning had been the basis of Valland's strategy, which had worked until he'd encountered Rorn. We must hope it remained sound.

Certainly the Ai Chun would notice rage and terror aboard that canoe. They should dismiss it as a natural after-math of battle. Valland's and my flare of emotion, though— why should *we* get excited?

"Shut your hatch, you dog!" I yelled at Rorn.

"What in the universe?" He blinked at me.

"Talking about 'our people.' They aren't ours. Nor yours. You sold yours out!"

I made an awkward lunge at him. He fended me off. A soldier behind him prodded me back with his spear. Valland took my arm. "Easy, skipper," he said. To Rorn: "Not that I don't agree!" He added some obscenities.

"Be quiet," Rorn said. He smoothed his lank, wind-tossed hair. "I'll talk to you after you're fit to think."

A question was flung at him from his masters. He replied in Yonder. I could follow the exchange, more or less. "Nothing serious. The hostages got unreasonable."

Valland and I swapped a glance. We must not let ourselves feel relief. That might also be noticed.

"How do you expect us to do anything but hate your guts?" he growled.

"I said be quiet," Rorn answered. "I'll have you punished if you aren't."

We nurtured revengefulness like a cherished flower. The canoes crawled forward. Presently a Niao stood up in the distant one—how distant!—and waved. He was unmistakable, a soldier type, and hideously hurt. I didn't like to think of the means by which his cooperation had been gotten. *Not my idea or Hugh's,* I told myself, wishing that could justify me. *A flourish of ya-Kela's, I suppose. What do you expect, after the way his people have suffered?*

If time had seemed unbearably long before, it now became infinite. The gap between vessels narrowed as if we were on a hyperbola seeking its asymptote. I must have been half crazy when Valland's roar pierced the clamor in me:

"Look out!"

An order bawled through the wind at the same instant. Paddles stopped. Someone had observed something suspicious.

"Let's go!"

I sprang to my feet. We were not so close that I could look into the drifting boat. I knew that the several bodies huddled in the hull should not look different from ordinary Niao. But perhaps— The wounded soldier had collapsed.

Rorn snatched at me. My injured arm batted his hands aside, my good fist struck his face. The impact rammed back into my bones. A spear thrust at Valland. He sidestepped and dived overboard. I followed.

The water was warm and murky-red. I held my breath and pumped arms and legs until it was no longer possible. When my head must go up into air, Rorn's craft was still nearly on top of me.

Arrows smote the waves. I went below again and swam blind.

Now the Azkashi in the canoe revealed themselves, seized paddles and drove frantically to meet us. This had been Valland's idea: precarious indeed, but any chance was worth taking to escape what had been done to Rorn.

While the enemy was kept in the hut, bargaining, most of the captured Niao boats were taken off and hidden. A few were left, a number not so small as to be unlikely but small enough that they would be overburdened and slow. One went ahead, over the horizon, lightly manned with ya-Kela for captain.

Our men ashore took a compass bearing on the Ai Chun course. Hastily instructed, ya-Kela likewise had such an instrument, and a radio. Bren, Galmer, and Urduga could get a fix on him and tell him where to go lie in wait. And . . . his folk took along a couple of torchguns.

Their bolts flashed against a curtain of lightning as I reemerged. Water puffed in steam; those were inexperienced hands on the triggers. Nonetheless, the Ai Chun group backed off.

Yet the enemy had not quit. Four huge forms sprang out

114

and started swimming. Adapted to a watery planet, those soldiers could overhaul us well before ya-Kela arrived. They could drag us back—at the least, kill us. My strength was already going. I am not much of a swimmer.

Valland was, by human standards. But when he saw the shapes churning after, he came about. His powerful crawl brought him to me in a couple of minutes. "Tread water," he panted. "Conserve your energy. You'll need it."

"We're done," I choked.

"Maybe. Maybe not. Better this way, anyhow."

The nearest soldier darted ahead. Valland got between me and him. They clinched and went under.

A hand closed on me. I looked into the open muzzle, tried weakly to break loose, and was submerged myself. It roared in my head. I thought confusedly, *Breathe water, you fool. Drown and die free.* But reflex was too strong, I gasped, spluttered, and whirled toward night.

My face was back in the air. I was being towed. Valland came alongside. He had broken his opponent's neck, down in the depths. He used his thumbnail, twice. The soldier ululated and let me go.

Valland must support me. The remaining pair closed in, through the stained waves. He used his legs to move away from them. They swam around to his head. I saw a dagger lifted.

Then the water was full of bodies and weapons.

Ya-Kela's were also good swimmers. Half a dozen of them had plunged the moment they'd seen our plight. Outpacing any canoe in their sprint, they got to us. Their comrades were not so far behind; and while the gunners dared not shoot near us, they could prevent any reinforcements from coming.

I did not see the fight. Darkness took me once more.

—Afterward I lay in the canoe, vomited, coughed, and wept. It wasn't merely reaction. I was altogether sickened. Galaxy God—any God—must we kill through all time, until time ends when the disgusted universe collapses inward on us?

Worse followed. I am glad I was only hazily aware. With yells of joy, the Azkashi gave chase to the Ai Chun. We were soon so close that a marksman like Valland could pick them off. One reached the water and went below, but he waited until the creature rose to breathe and shot him.

The storm rolled upon us. Clouds drove black across the sun, lightning blazed, thunder crashed, the first rain whipped my bare skin. I looked across the gunwale to Yo Rorn's boat, which we were now pursuing to reclaim our gear. My goggles still worked. I saw him stand up, screaming, such agony in him that it was almost good when a soldier's ax broke open his skull.

Valland hunkered beside me. Water ran over his cheeks, into his beard, like tears. "I never intended that," he said dully. "They must've gone insane, seein' me kill their gods. They had to strike back, and he was the handiest." He watched the boats scatter and flee. The one we were after was abandoned by those left in it. "Thanks for that. No more slaughter needed. . . . You were one of us too, always, Yo."

"But why did you kill the Ai Chun?" I blubbered. "We were safe by then. Why?"

"We're not safe," he answered. "Won't be for a mighty long time. I reckoned it'd make a good lesson for everybody concerned, to see they can be struck down like anyone else. We'll need everything we can get workin' for us."

He shook himself. "No use in regrets," he said. "We've got to be ruthless, or surrender right now. I suppose there are limits to what we can decently do, but I don't think we've reached 'em yet. Come, skipper, you'll feel more cheery after a good long sleep. Let's get on home."

116

# XVI

Day stood at afternoon. We had rested, repaired damage, started to organize ourselves afresh, and slept some more. Nonetheless, when we stepped out of our compound and saw the lake glow red in that purple twilight, we had a sunset feeling. A great hush lay on the land. Further down the shore twinkled the fires of ya-Kela's people. Most Pack members had gone home after a skyhooting victory celebration for which many returned from the woods; but he stayed with some. We were to join them and lay plans.

For a while, just beyond the gate, we paused. Valland, Bren, Galmer, Urduga, and me—we seemed terribly few.

Galmer voiced what we thought. "Do you really believe we have a chance?"

"Why sure," Valland said. His gaiety was strange to hear in so big and dark a place. "We've got our camp back. Nothin' was ruined that we can't get along without. We have allies. Son, if we don't get home again, we won't deserve to!"

"But the enemy, Hugh. The Ai Chun. They won't take this like sportsmen. They'll come against us. We can't stand off a planet."

"We'll have our problems, all right," Valland admitted. "But think. We've shown the Packs you can beat the down-devils. So they'll go with us through a supernova, if only we handle them right, and I reckon I know how." His gaze went across the broad waters. "Distance makes a good defense. Any attackers' line of communications will get stretched thin. Woodsrangers like ours can cut it in two. Though I don't aim

117

to sit and wait. I'm takin' the offensive soon's may be. We'll burn Prasiyo, lay the countryside waste everywhere around, chase the Herd clear to the sea. The downdevils aren't used to actin' fast, I gather. So they'll need some time to recover from that shock and mount a counterattack. By then we'll be ready."

"Still," I said, "a war— When can we do our work?"

"Not our war," Valland said. "Mainly the Packs are concerned. We'll give them leadership, new kinds of weapons, sound tactics, a concept of strategy. I think that'll suffice. Remember, there can't be an awful lot of Herd soldiers. The downdevils never needed many, and won't have time to breed a horde—which they couldn't supply anyhow. No, for the most part we should be free to work, we and the ones we're goin' to train as helpers."

After a moment, reflectively, he added: "Won't be a war of extermination anyhow. Our side'll be content to hold this territory, maybe get back some of what was stolen before; but the Packs aren't about to try conquerin' the world. If the downdevils aren't hopelessly stupid, they'll make terms, once we've rubbed their noses a bit. Then we five can really buckle down to business."

Bren sighed. The weight of his captivity was still heavy on him. "That's assuming we're not killed in some fracas," he said. "More, it's assuming we can stay with our purpose. I wonder if we won't get so tired at last that we'll simply quit."

Valland squared his shoulders. The light turned his shock head to copper. Huge against the sky, he said, "No, we won't. We'll keep ourselves reminded of what this is all about—what we're goin' back to."

He started toward the campfires, and striding, he keyed the omnisonor he bore to help him talk with the Pack, and his song arose.

"So softly you hear it now, Mary O'Meara, but soon it

*comes joyful and clear.*
*And soon in the shadow and dew of your hilltop a*
*star-guided footfall rings near.*
*My only beloved, I'm here."*

We followed him. And we built our spaceboat and won to the help of the Yonderfolk. The job took four decades.

# XVII

(Thus far the account published by Guild Captain Felip Argens in his autobiography. An additional tape was found among his effects by the redactor of the posthumous edition.)

EARTH IS A QUIET WORLD.

Oh, yes, wind soughs in the great forests that have come back, now that so few people live there; birds sing, cataracts brawl, the oceans rush on the moon's trail around the globe. You can find ample enjoyment in the starport towns, and the educational centers are bright with youth from every part of the galaxy. Nor is this a museum planet by any means. The arts flourish. Science and scholarship are live enterprises.

But there is too much of the past. One does not build new things there, one preserves the old. That isn't bad. We need traditions. From a strictly practical standpoint, it's good to know you can leave your Earthside property in charge of some robots, return in five hundred years, and find not only it but its surroundings unchanged. Nevertheless, when the adventurers come from the stars on a visit, they walk quietly.

Hugh Valland and I parted in Niyork. Bren, Galmer, and Urduga had gone their separate ways. I had to report, however, and he had his girl, so we traveled together on the *Luna Queen*. Though he'd avoided discussing his plans in detail, I assumed he'd be met when the ferry set us down.

"No," he said. "That's not her way. How about one hell of a good so-long dinner tonight? I know a restaurant where the escargots consider themselves privileged to be cooked."

He was right. We put away a lot of wine too. Over brandy and cigars, in a fine comradely warmth, I asked if he meant to take as lengthy a vacation as I did.

"Mmm—probably not," he said. "We were stuck on that single planet for such a confounded chunk of time. I've got a universeful of places to go see again. And then new places, where nobody's been yet."

"D'you mean to sign on for exploration?" I raised my eyebrows. "I hoped you'd ship with me."

His massive face crinkled in a smile. "Skipper," he said, "you're a fine chap, but don't you think we need to split up for a century or two?"

"Maybe." I was disappointed. True, we'd lived in each other's breath long enough to drive anyone who wasn't immortal, who couldn't set the years in perspective, to murder. But we'd fought and worked together, and laughed and sung and hoped: and he was the one who had kept us doing so. Having a war on our hands had been a help—broke the monotony, Valland used to say—but we wouldn't have won it without his leadership. I didn't want to lose touch.

"You'll be around for a while, anyway, won't you?" I asked.

"Sure," he said. "What'd you think was drivin' me?"

"Mary O'Meara," I nodded. "What a girl she must be. When do I get an introduction?"

"Well, now . . . ." For the first time I saw him evasive. "Uh, that won't . . . won't be so easy. I mean, I'd like to, but—well, she's not keen on guests. Sorry. How about another cognac?"

I didn't press him. We had learned, out beyond the galaxy, not to intrude on a man's final privacies. I speculated, of course. Every immortal develops at least one quirk. His was that fantastic monogamy which had saved us. What was hers?— Then Valland's grin broke loose again and he related a couple of jokes he'd heard, bumming around in the rim-planet town where we waited for passage to Earth. We said goodnight in a hilarious mood.

After that, for several days, I was busy at the universarium. The scientists wanted to know everything about the planet of our shipwreck. They'd be sending a mission there, to operate out of the commercial base our company would establish. Before the unique Ai Chun culture died—before that race adapted to reality and became just another race—they meant to study it.

When I finished, I must return to Niyork on business. The Guild had suddenly decided our employers owed us a bonus for our troubles. A rather disgruntled chief accountant told me the sum, which explained his disgruntlement, and put me through various formalities.

"Payments are required to be made directly to the men," he said. With so many people on so many planets, the Guild no longer trusts the mails. "I've arranged about the others, but when I called Master Valland, he wasn't at the address he had given. It was a hotel here in town, and he'd moved out with no forwarding code."

"Gone to see his girl, of course," I said. "Hm. We plan to get together once more, but not for some while."

"Can't you find him before then? Frankly, I'm tired of having your association ride me about this matter."

"And Hugh'd no doubt find good ways to spend the money. Won't be so useful to him on the eve of shipping out." I pondered. From time to time he had said things about Mary O'Meara, though now that I added them together they came to surprisingly little. "Well, I'm at loose ends for the moment. I'll see if I can track him down."

That was for my own sake as well as his. To the company I wasn't a hero, I was a captain who had lost his ship. I wanted to get back into favor, or they'd put me on some dreary shuttle run for the next fifty years.

I walked into the street. Little traffic moved—an occasional groundcar, a few pedestrians. The tall towers that walled me in were mostly empty, ivy and lichen growing on their facades. Though the sun was glorious, the sun of Manhome, light seemed only to drown in that stillness.

*Let's marshal the facts,* I told myself. *She lives on, what's the name, yes, the coast of Maine. A historic but microscopic residential community. He never did say which one, but can't be many these days that fit. I'll check with data service, then run up and inquire. Do me good to get out in the countryside anyway.*

As things developed, the search robot gave me just one possibility. I rented a flitter and headed north. The woods have swallowed this part of the continent, I flew above green kilometer after kilometer. Dusk fell before I reached my goal.

That village was built when men first fared across the ocean which rolled at its feet. For a while it was a town, alive with lumberjacks and whalers. Then men moved west, and afterward they moved to the stars, and now a bare two hundred dwelt here: those curious, clannish folk who—even more than on places like Landomar—are not interested in worlds out yonder, who use their immortality to sink deeper roots into Earth.

I parked on an otherwise deserted carfield and walked downhill into town. Behind me lifted a birch forest; white trunks gleamed in twilight, and the air was fragrant with their leaves. Before me lay the few houses, peak-roofed, shingle-walled, their windows shining yellow. And beyond them reached the sea, and the first stars of evening.

A passerby directed me to the civil monitor's house. His name, Tom Saltonstall, suggested how old he must be. I found him seated on the porch in a rocking chair, smoking a pipe, while his one wife prepared dinner. He greeted me with polite reserve. There was something about him— After a minute I recognized it. He looked as youthful as I did; but he

123

had the manner of beings I have met who cannot be immortalized and have grown gray.

"You want Hugh Valland?" he said. "Yes, sure, we know him." He squinted at me through the dimness before adding, with each word chosen beforehand: "A very decent fellow."

"I ought to realize that!" I exclaimed. "I was his captain this last trip. Hasn't he told you what happened?"

"Yes. A little." Saltonstall looked relieved. "Then you understand about— Sure. I'm sorry I didn't identify your name, Captain Argens. I'm overdue for mnemonic treatment. He's spoken fine of you, sir. An honor to meet you." He made the archaic handclasp with me. "Would you pleasure us by staying to eat?"

"Well, thanks, but I ought to find Hugh. Where is he?"

"He owns a house, next street down, third from the left corner. You won't find him there, though. He'll not be back till late, on a night like this."

Ah-ha! I grinned to myself; for the full moon was casting her foreglow into the eastern sky.

I wish I had stayed, and talked with the monitor and his wife. But I only expected the gossip of the Earthbound, which was tedious to me. Pleading weariness, I returned to my flitter. It had bunk, bath, and food facilities. I'd call on Valland tomorrow.

But after dinner I got restless. The multisense programs that I tuned in were not for a spaceman. The moon was up, throwing a broken bridge across the waters and turning the birches to silver. Crickets chirred, almost the only sound beneath those few stars that weren't hidden by moon-haze. This was Manhome. No matter how far we range, the salt and the rhythm of her tides will always be in our blood. I decided to go for a walk.

A graveled road wound further uphill, and scrunched softly under my feet. As I neared the forest, the live green smell strengthened. Dew glittered on long grass. Beyond the village, now dark, the sea murmured.

And then another tone lifted. For a moment, blindingly, I was back in a sinister red-lit crepuscule where nothing but those chords and that voice gave me the will to fight on. "Hugh!" I cried, and broke into a run.

He didn't hear me. I rounded a copse and saw where I was bound, just as he finished. The last stanza he had never sung to us.

*"Sleep well once again if you woke in your darkness, sleep knowin' you are my delight*
*As long as the stars wheel the years down the heavens, as long as the lilies bloom white.*
*My darlin', I kiss you goodnight."*

I huddled into the thicket and cursed myself. He walked past me, down to his house, as proudly as on that day when our new-built boat first went skyward.

After a while I continued my walk. Ahead of me stood a small building with a steeple, white under the moon. White, too, were the flowerbeds and the stones among them. I searched till I found the one I was after. It must often have been renewed, in the course of eroding centuries. But the inscription was unchanged, even to letter style and dating. Not that there was much. Only

MARY O'MEARA
2018 - 2037

I believe I managed to confront him the next day as if nothing had happened.

## Just $1.50 each

Is Anyone There?

Jupiter

Of Matters Great and Small

**Only a Trillion**

Science, Numbers, and I

The Stars in Their Courses

Twentieth Century Discovery .

*Available wherever paperbacks are sold or use this coupon.*

**ace books,** (Dept. MM) Box 576, Times Square Station
New York. N.Y. 10036

Please send me titles checked above.

I enclose $. . . . . . . . . . . . . . . Add 35c handling fee per copy.

Name . . . . . . . . . . . . . . . . . . . . . . . . . . . . . . . . . . . . . . . . . . . . .

Address . . . . . . . . . . . . . . . . . . . . . . . . . . . . . . . . . . . . . . . . . . . .

City. . . . . . . . . . . . . . . . . . . . . State. . . . . . . . . . . . . . Zip. . . . . . . .

66 A

# A.E. VAN VOGT

## Just $1.25 each

- Children of Tomorrow
- The Worlds of A.E. van Vogt
- Quest for the Future
- The Silkie
- The Universe Maker
- The Weapon Shops of Isher

*Available wherever paperbacks are sold or use this coupon.*

ace books, (Dept. MM) Box 576, Times Square Station
New York, N.Y. 10036

Please send me titles checked above.

I enclose $.................. Add 35c handling fee per copy.

Name ...........................................................

Address ........................................................

City..................... State.............. Zip........

36 F

# Mack Reynolds

## Just $1.25 each

Ability Quotient

Amazon Planet

Day After Tomorrow

Depression or Bust/Dawnman Planet

Five Way Secret Agent/
Mercenary from Tomorrow

Looking Backward From the Year 2000

Planetary Agent X and The Rival Rigelians

Section G: United Planets

Satellite City

Tomorrow Might Be Different

*Available wherever paperbacks are sold or use this coupon.*

ace books, (Dept. MM) Box 576, Times Square Station
New York. N.Y. 10036

Please send me titles checked above.

I enclose $............... Add 35c handling fee per copy.

Name ...............................................

Address ..............................................

City...................... State.............. Zip........
                                                    35J